W9-CQZ-315

PRAISE FOR ELAINE FOX!

THE IMPOSTOR

"Ms. Fox has written a time-travel romance with a twist. . . . Needless to say, there is much hilarity and embarrassment along the way . . . 4 stars!"

—*Romantic Times*

UNTAMED ANGEL

"In this innovative take on the Pygmalion plot, Elaine Fox demonstrates a virtuoso understanding of American class divisions and attitudes. This one's a carefully created romance every bit as entertaining as 'My Fair Lady.'"

—*Romantic Times*

TRAVELER

"A delightful heroine, a dream of a hero and a timeless love combine for a charming debut! Elaine Fox's *Traveler* is a winner!"

—Nora Roberts

"Hurray! There's a vibrant new voice in romance, and her name is Elaine Fox. Time-travel romance at its absolute best—a stunning debut from an exciting new talent!"

—Patricia Gaffney

"Author Elaine Fox hits on a winning combination with this moving tale of passion overcoming time itself."

—*Romantic Times*

A WALTZ TO REMEMBER

"Shall we dance?" he asked. He took her waist and turned her into his arms to dance in the garden. "This is how one begins if one is to waltz. Would you like to learn to waltz?"

A protest rose to her throat and died there, unuttered. He began to move slowly, his face so close to hers that she could feel his breath on her hair. She was acutely aware of the nearness of his body, his chest filling and emptying of air, his strong, steady heartbeat. She looked up at him to find his gaze upon her. Their eyes met, and stayed.

Catra wasn't sure when, but they both stopped moving. His eyes were dark and unreadable, and his back blocked the light. Slowly, he pulled her closer, his chest hard against hers, his arm tight around her waist. She felt like a butterfly clasped against him, gently but firmly pinned, unable to move. Her lips parted as her breathing became shallow.

"You're out of place here, Catra," he said in a voice low and compelling. Her eyes could not leave his. "And Ferris is the wrong man for you."

"Is he?" She felt paralyzed, unable even to be angry at this presumption. Instead she simply watched the scene, as if waiting to see what might happen next.

Ryan's eyelids descended a fraction as he looked at her . . . the cat eyeing the canary. "He is."

Catra's skin went simultaneously hot and cold, and she watched in suspended disbelief as his lips descended toward hers.

Compulsion

Elaine Fox

LEISURE BOOKS   NEW YORK CITY

For Greg Cunliffe.
Thanks for the Scrabble, the exotic beers, the many, many
dinners, and most of all, for your friendship.
Here, for you, The Carriage Shook.

A LEISURE BOOK®

December 1999

Published by

Dorchester Publishing Co., Inc.
276 Fifth Avenue
New York, NY 10001

ISBN 0-8439-4648-2

Compulsion

Chapter One

Good God, she was bored. The ball had only begun an hour earlier and already most of the guests looked as wilted as the melting candles.

Catra Meredyth fanned herself and watched her friend, Mayliza Thayer, pick her way through the crowd toward her. At one point, a gentleman stepped onto the back of her gown, and Mayliza, in a fit of pique, yanked it so unceremoniously from under his foot that he stumbled. She rolled her eyes heavenward and continued her journey without even a glance at the bewildered gentleman.

"Lord in heaven, what a crowd," Mayliza breathed. Her strawberry curls bounced as she plopped into the chair next to Catra. "How in the world do you stay looking so fresh in this ungodly heat?"

Catra turned her head toward the dancing. "I avoid *that* as much as I am able. If I have to hold one more sweaty palm or have one more hot paw pressed against my back, I shall pretend to faint. I swear it."

"And have one of those sweaty men pick you up?" Mayliza smiled. "I should rather die."

Catra laughed and with one hand tucked away a loose curl that had fallen against her neck. "Do you think we have attended too many balls in our short lives? Could we be jaded already, do you think?"

"If we're not yet, we will be after this evening. Have you ever seen a more tiresome group? I mean, honestly, I have danced with every single one of these men twice a month for years. Oh! That reminds me. Did you see your handsome fiancé dancing with Mary Carter Randolph?" She gave Catra a sly look.

"No." Catra sat up, astonished, and turned on her friend. "Mary Carter Randolph?" She collapsed into peals of laughter. "You watch; he'll be limping the next time you see him. Is he dancing with her now? He's doing it just to goad me. I should go hint to Phillip Hale that I'm sick to death of being a wallflower. Wouldn't that give Ferris a laugh! Phillip and me clumping along beside him and Mary Carter." She laughed again, clutching her fan to her chest.

"What's this?" Mayliza sat forward in her chair to look through the crowd. "I thought I just saw . . ."

Catra sat up and craned her neck to look in the same direction. "What?"

"Who is that?" Mayliza discreetly pointed her fan toward a knot of people near the door.

Catra saw the back of Ferris's blond head and could tell by the movement of his shoulders that he was shaking the hand of the dark-haired gentleman across from him. Her view was blocked by Ferris, but she could just make out the other man's presence as he stood taller than the rest of the group.

"I can't really see him," Catra answered. "I'm not sure who he is."

Mayliza sighed and sat back. "Somebody new would be nice. Somebody who could actually dance. Perhaps a waltz—wouldn't that be fun?"

"And how would you dance a waltz?" Catra asked.

Mayliza giggled. "Well, he'd have to be a good lead."

Catra squinted in an effort to more clearly make out the man's face. "He doesn't look like someone who would already know how to waltz. He'd have had to come from Europe. I don't think he's European."

"How can you tell?" Mayliza's nearsighted brown eyes had already given up the struggle to identify the stranger.

"He's dressed like a Yankee."

"A Yankee! How does a Yankee dress?" Mayliza tried with renewed interest to focus on the stranger.

"In black," Catra replied, leaning back in her chair. "At any rate, if he's someone Ferris knows, we'll be introduced to him soon enough. I don't think any Yankees know how to dance—not properly."

She grasped the fan that dangled on a cord from her wrist and began to cool herself once again.

"Punch, miss?" A servant bowed with his tray.

"Thank you." Catra took one of the silver cups and ran her finger along its damp exterior. "Good and cold." She brushed the wet finger along her temples and closed her eyes.

"Oh, my goodness, here he comes." Mayliza bolted upright in her chair and toyed with her perfectly coifed hair.

Catra opened her eyes to see Ferris and the stranger approaching them. She, too, straightened in her chair and smoothed the silk skirt of her dress.

As the two men neared, Catra could not help but compare them. Ferris, with his light hair and eyes, medium build and boyish gait, and the stranger, whose dark hair shone rich in the candlelight and whose long strides threatened to leave Ferris behind.

As they neared the spot where Catra and Mayliza sat, they were distracted by Dahlia Chester, Ferris's cousin and a spinster of nearly five and twenty, who bolted out of the crowd and attached herself to the stranger's arm.

"Mr. St. James, you *made* it! Oh, I'm so happy, *truly*, to see you. This party was looking to be so *dull* without you!" Dahlia was one of those women who felt the need to punctuate her sentences with emphatically drawn-out words. Catra and Mayliza often amused themselves by mimicking both Dahlia's speech and her odd habit of re-arranging her dress by pulling at different parts of it. Catra noticed that she was even now tugging at the waist of the yellow satin gown.

"What a pretty picture you both make, sitting here together," Ferris said to Catra and Mayliza as they rose. He caught Catra's hands in his own and bestowed a kiss on them. "Cat in her lavender and Mayliza in her rose. Makes me wish I could paint."

"Goodness, why?" Catra laughed. "Would you alter us?"

Ferris pursed his lips and eyed her for a moment. "Yes. I would have you both in mustaches and long, stringy beards." He smiled. "Though in truth you should both be captured, as you are now, on canvas for all time."

"What a pretty speech, Ferris. Is it for the benefit of your guest?" she teased. "For I vow I never hear such adulation except in the company of strangers. It's as if that's the only time you feel you need to ensure my good feelings." She turned her eyes to the dark-haired man caught in Dahlia's clutches.

"Sharpest tongue in the county," Ferris said. "Cat, let

me introduce you to my friend. Excuse me, Dahlia.'' Ferris interrupted Dahlia's chatter and she shot him a scathing glance. "My fiancée, Catherine Meredyth, this is Mr. Ryan St. James. Ryan, of course, is Uncle's business partner from Boston. You may recall my mentioning his impending visit.''

Mr. St. James gently extricated his arm from Dahlia's hold and took Catra's extended hand. "My pleasure, Miss Meredyth,'' he said in a clipped northern accent. Catra congratulated herself—a Yankee born and bred, of course. "I had heard tell of your beauty from Ferris's uncle, Mr. Chester,'' he continued. "Now that I've gotten to meet you, I'm happy to note he wasn't exaggerating.'' The man smiled easily and bowed over her hand.

Catra inclined her head in return and allowed her gaze to linger on what struck her as the most remarkable gray eyes she'd ever seen. Pale, pale gray, and so direct as to make her breath catch in her throat.

It was not just the obviously intelligent eyes that made him so arresting, however. He was a symphony of intriguing features. High cheekbones, strong jaw, broad shoulders and fluid movement accompanied that uncompromising gaze and finely shaped mouth. All of which was unfortunate, because he seemed quite aware of his attributes and the power they could exert on women who were merely mortal.

His mouth quirked into a smile as he noted her hesitation. "Ah, yes. Well.'' She mentally shook herself. "It is certainly wonderful to meet you, at long last, Mr. St. James. I've heard of you for years as well—and now—suddenly here you are. Welcome.'' She cursed her own awkwardness and curtsied, glancing at Mayliza as she rose. Her friend looked at her quizzically.

"At long last,'' Mr. St. James returned, looking amused.

"And Miss Mayliza Thayer," Ferris continued. "Close friend and neighbor. Mayliza, may I present Mr. St. James."

"Miss Thayer." Mr. St. James took her hand and bowed over it as well. "It's nice to enter a room and be brought immediately to the two prettiest women in it."

"How kind of you to say so." Mayliza curtsied in return. Just before rising, she lifted her large, velvet brown eyes to his and smiled a coquettish smile. "You don't happen to know the waltz, do you, Mr. St. James?"

"*Heavens,* Mayliza, are you asking Mr. St. James to *dance?*" Dahlia squawked. "I've never *heard* of such a thing." She tugged briefly at the neck of her dress.

Mayliza rose, an earnest look directed at Mr. St. James. "Please don't think me rude. It's only that no one around here seems to know the first thing about any of the new dances, and I only thought that perhaps you could, if you knew it, show us sometime. I was not trying to be so bold as to coerce you into a dance. Forgive me."

"On the contrary, Miss Thayer, I'm intrigued by women who ask for what they want. And yes, I do know how to waltz. I would be more than happy to instruct you."

"I hope you're a strong lead," Catra murmured, shooting a glance at her friend.

He turned his attention back to Catra. "I am when I need to be." He paused, then said, "Is it Catherine or Catra, as I have heard you called, Miss Meredyth?"

"Both, actually. My father calls me Catherine, but almost everyone else calls me Catra. It's been a nickname since I was very young, and it was the closest my younger brother could come to pronouncing Catherine."

"Unusual," he said.

"Yes. I like it for that very reason. I am never confused with anyone else."

"I doubt that would be a problem in any case." He let his gaze linger on her, causing the color to rise to her cheeks.

What *was* it about him? Catra thought, impatient with herself. It wasn't like her to be thrown so by a pretty face. And Mayliza didn't seem to be feeling any of the same distraction.

"You know," Ferris chimed in, "we've discussed this waltz thing with the local musicians and I don't believe they even know how to play one. We were anxious to have it at Mayliza's birthday ball next month."

"Yes, so anxious." Mayliza pouted prettily. "I thought it would be quite grand to introduce something new on my eighteenth birthday. But it seems we're to have to content ourselves with the same old reels and minuets."

"Mayliza's mother has put her in charge of the whole evening," Catra explained, "in honor of her new maturity."

"And it's going to be the best evening yet. Honestly, I don't know why some women go on so about getting older. I'm simply thrilled to be treated as an adult the older I get. All it seems to take is eighteen birthdays or so."

"You would think there would be some better measure of a woman's maturity, wouldn't you, Mr. St. James?" Catra turned a questioning gaze on him. She refused to let a handsome stranger with a sardonic expression intimidate *her*.

"I believe there is, Miss Meredyth." He paused.

She waited. Then, "And what way might that be?"

The stranger's lips curved and his eyes trailed from her face to her bared shoulders and the plunging bodice of her dress. Catra felt her blush deepen to an angry red and she mentally kicked herself for allowing him such an opening.

"Intelligence." His eyes met hers. "An ability to handle

15

the unexpected. I've always found that the way a woman deals with, say, an uncomfortable situation, is indicative of her maturity. A quick mind is invariably associated with it.''

''Many children have quick minds,'' she replied sharply. Where the devil was Ferris? she wondered, then spotted him in muffled conversation with Dahlia. Smoothing ruffled feathers, no doubt.

''But they have yet to be able to use them effectively.''

''I wonder what makes you so qualified a judge, Mr. St. James?'' She brought up her fan and fluttered it angrily. ''I've always believed that to recognize true intelligence one must possess it oneself. It's quite easy to fool a fake.''

His mouth widened to a genuine smile. Beside her, Catra felt Mayliza's stare.

''I couldn't agree more.'' He beamed. ''And so I shall leave you to be my judge for the remainder of the evening. If you find me speaking with an unsuitable young lady, please deter me, for I shall have no other means of determining either her maturity or her intelligence.''

''It would be my pleasure,'' Catra replied, ''for there are many here who might fool you.''

With unconcealed amusement, Mayliza interrupted their sparring. ''Ferris said you're from Boston, isn't that right, Mr. St. James?'' He inclined his head. ''What brings you out to our fair countryside?''

''The Westbrook wedding. I am,'' he said with a slow smile, ''an old friend of Mrs. Westbrook's.'' He bent slightly toward her as he spoke in a chivalrous way. No doubt giving her the benefit of those incredible, intimidating eyes, Catra thought sourly.

She studied the side of his face and thought about how despite having a pretty daughter of sixteen, Mrs. Westbrook was the one renowned for her beauty.

"He's also looking to let a house in Richmond, and Uncle suggested that before he returns to Boston he visit a while with us," added Ferris, who'd turned back to them.

"Yes. Mr. Chester has been so touting the benefits of country living to me in every missive I receive that I thought I should come to see what he meant."

"And have you?" Catra queried. "Discovered the benefits of the country, I mean."

He looked at her steadily. "I certainly have." This seemingly innocuous answer sent another blush creeping up her neck and over her face. The situation was becoming absurd.

"Ferris." Catra turned to him in exasperation. "Have you shown Mr. St. James all that he needs to see of country living? I do hope you're presenting a good case for us. If it were left to your uncle, all he would see was a pipe and the inside of his library."

"Regrettably, we haven't had much time to explore beyond the library yet," Mr. St. James said, "fine as it is. But I am hoping before I leave to do some riding. I'd like to see the plantation operation, and the river is quite scenic, I understand. I've also heard you're an accomplished rider, Miss Meredyth. Perhaps you would honor us with your presence?"

"Mr. St. James," Dahlia interrupted and curled her arm through his, "this is *our* dance, is it not? I did promise you *this* very one, *didn't* I?" She looked up at him through her lashes, then jerked around to look at the rapidly filling dance floor, brushing her brown curls against his shoulder. "I *declare*, if we don't hurry there won't be any more *room!*"

Dahlia's boldness was more than Catra could witness without laughing. Dahlia fixed her with a narrow, hateful stare.

"Is something *funny*, Catra?" Her tone was so catty that

even Mr. St. James raised his eyebrows at her.

"I'm sorry, Dahlia," Catra replied, delighted at this opportunity. She fingered the dance card that hung from a string on her wrist. "But Mr. St. James had asked me for this dance. I was laughing at his forgetfulness." She smiled sweetly at the man and ignored Dahlia's outrage.

"Miss Meredyth, please accept my humblest apologies," Mr. St. James said, picking up the lie perhaps too smoothly. He wrestled his arm from Dahlia yet again. "To slight my hostess in such a way—you understand, do you not, Miss Chester?"

Before Dahlia could answer, Catra continued magnanimously, "Don't be silly, Mr. St. James. I forgive you and I'm sure I can manage to wait for another dance. Do be more careful, though; if it were to happen again, someone's heart might be broken." She smiled wickedly at Dahlia. "Perhaps I could persuade Ferris here to assuage my slighted feelings and substitute for you."

At the mention of his name, Ferris turned from Mayliza and said, "I'm sorry, Catra. Did you say you wanted to dance?"

"There, you see? No harm done." Catra noticed the unflappable St. James struggling with facial composure as he led Dahlia, bright red with fury, into the dancing.

"If your cousin throws herself any more obviously at Mr. St. James, your uncle may not be able to conclude his business with him," Catra said, laying her hand on Ferris's proffered arm. "Men have an uncanny knack for sensing marriage-hungry women and avoiding them."

"Now, what would you know about that?" Ferris teased.

"I know what I see."

Ferris led her toward the dancing. "You've let Dahlia get your goat again, Cat. Why can't you just ignore her?"

She was on the verge of telling him that it was not Dahlia

who had gotten her goat, when she thought better of the idea.

They began the dance, and Catra made a supreme effort to forget about Dahlia and Mr. St. James, staring distractedly in the opposite direction to watch the women in their brightly colored gowns spin and swirl, their skirts swinging over wide petticoats like so many church bells.

"What do you think of Ryan?" Ferris asked, redirecting her thoughts. "I must say I quite like him. And Uncle thinks the world of him."

She hesitated. "He seems charming . . . if a little brazen."

Ferris chuckled. "Ryan's not brazen. He's just very . . . *worldly*. It's an attractive quality, don't you think? He's been presented at court, you know. We're hoping, Uncle and I, for a stronger alliance with him and his family. Uncle has proposed . . . that is, he confided to me that perhaps a marriage between Ryan and Dahlia would be the thing."

Catra was consumed with a distaste she could not explain—at least not to Ferris, as it had a lot to do with her complete dislike for his cousin.

"Uncle says she seems to like him," he continued, "and I can't deny it would be a coup to have a St. James in the family. He's quite well known in shipping. He's a Boston St. James, you know. Benjamin St. James is his father. What I'm hoping is that we can persuade him to make Virginia his permanent residence, which would be marvelous. I would be able to meet with him at any time it might be necessary, once I take over the business from Uncle. Of course, Uncle's right; it would be a splendid match for Dahlia. Couldn't do better."

Catra stole a glance at the objects of Ferris's plan, at Dahlia, who held her yellow skirt in one hand, too tightly, obviously longing to pull at the seam; and at Ryan St.

Elaine Fox

James, who squired her about the floor, smiling in that charming way, oblivious, it seemed, to Dahlia's clumsiness.

So he knew how to treat a woman, Catra thought, as if she were the only one in the room. With those eyes it was not a difficult feat. But for anyone with perception it was obvious that he lacked sincerity, she decided. For her it was that which detracted from any real appeal he might have had.

"No, she couldn't do better," Catra agreed. "But she doesn't quite seem his type. Nor he hers. Though whose type *she* is could be destined to remain a mystery."

"What do you mean?" Ferris asked, looking intently into her eyes. "What type do you suppose he is?"

Catra thought about this, struggling to find the words to describe St. James diplomatically, since Ferris so obviously held the man in such high esteem.

"Uncle thinks marriage would be the perfect solution," Ferris continued, upon her silence. "And a capital way for us to ensure the future of our business alliance. She wouldn't exactly be a burden to him; her dowry is substantial. The association would benefit him as much as it would us. And if you'll excuse me for saying so, the Chester name is nothing to sneeze at—"

"That's not what I meant." Catra sighed. "Lord, Ferris, why do you think she's twenty-five and unmarried? You're ignoring the fact that her personality is completely disagreeable to all who meet her. And I doubt Mr. St. James is at a loss for female companionship. In fact, I have the feeling he quite immerses himself in it." Though she wondered, really, how any woman in her right mind could fall for his calculated charm.

"I think that's extreme," Ferris replied, a wounded tone in his voice. "I don't think Ryan is one to be obsessed with *female companionship*. He has as good a head for business as anyone I know. And Dahlia may have a difficult personality, but 'to all who meet her' is going a bit far.''

"Ferris, she irritates *you*.'' Catra smiled.

He cleared his throat. "In any case, it's not as if he has to fall in *love* with her. Marriages these days are business ventures, and St. James is nothing if not a businessman. He would see the wisdom in it, I'm sure. He's extremely intelligent.''

Catra didn't reply to this bit of marital skepticism, as she was of a similar mind on the subject, though it pained her in this case to think of it.

After a minute Ferris continued. "But he's a hard man to pin, St. James is. Hasn't seemed inclined toward marriage, which I find most interesting. I heard the Fairchilds in Richmond were angling for an alliance, but it fizzled. Not really sure why. Perhaps the Fairchilds were not a distinguished enough family.'' He paused thoughtfully, then said, as if to close the subject, "So Dahlia might be perfect for him, with her name and her southern planter connection.''

The dance came to an end and Ferris bowed to her, still apparently preoccupied with the Dahlia problem. Catra curtsied low and looked discreetly around for Ryan. He arrived at her elbow as she rose. Had he sprinted away from Dahlia? she wondered briefly, or just scraped her off on a pillar as he passed?

"Miss Meredyth, I would never forget a dance with you *twice* in one evening,'' he said, impudently interpreting her wandering eyes. "May I?'' he asked Ferris.

"Of course.'' Ferris gave Ryan a gentlemanly bow, clapping him on the shoulder with one hand as he rose. "But seek me out when you're finished. There are some more people you should meet.''

Catra turned to Ryan, about to accuse him of assuming her card was not full, when he said, "You've gotten me into trouble with the indefatigable Miss Chester.''

She couldn't help but smile at the thought when he took her hand in his.

"I fear the damage may be irreparable," he continued. "How do you plead, Miss Meredyth?"

His eyes looked friendly now, not taunting, and full of a surprising warmth. "I plead guilty, Mr. St. James. Of trying to do you a favor, which you will no doubt undo. You see, one kind word from you will unquestionably renew her injured heart."

He laughed. "Shall I try to return the favor in kind, Miss Meredyth?"

"Oh, no. There is no need. Dahlia and I have long since established our boundaries."

"I wasn't speaking of Dahlia," he said, still smiling. But the look in his eyes was astute—too much so.

"I don't know what you mean." She looked at him politely.

"Shall I tell you?" The intimate tone of his voice surprised her.

She looked away, bothered. Who did he think he was, acting so familiar with her? It was completely unsuitable. He seemed to think he could break any rule he chose.

"I think not." She said it firmly and let the silence between them hang just long enough to make her point. Then, so as not to appear uncivil, she continued, "You are quite the best dancer here tonight, Mr. St. James. Might I ask how you came to be so accomplished?" She met his eyes with a cool look.

His gaze assessed her. "You might," he returned finally, in a tone as formal as her own. "The Continent, of course. All *respectable* gentlemen learn their deportment on the Continent, do they not?"

She smiled reluctantly. "Such insolence."

Really, she felt as if she was being drawn into some joke she was not sure she understood. As if he wanted an accomplice . . .

"There," he said, again in that intimate voice, "we won't have that smile disappearing again."

She glanced up at him, but before she could reply he whirled her around with such renewed enthusiasm that she was relieved of the obligation to speak again.

As confusing as the man was, however, Catra was sorry when the dance ended, when his confident, securing arm was removed from her waist, when his large hand released hers and he bowed with perfect formality. "Thank you, Miss Meredyth. It was delightful."

She curtsied and was all too quickly claimed by another partner. But as the music began and the young man took her hand nervously in his, she looked cautiously back at Mr. St. James, only to meet his eyes, watching her.

Chapter Two

"That's as unhappy as I've ever seen you, dancing with a handsome man," Mayliza stated when Catra found her way back to her seat. "What were you and Mr. St. James talking about?"

"That man is about as insolent as any I've ever met." Catra flounced into a chair with a frown. "He's an arrogant, cocky know-it-all and he enjoys making people uncomfortable."

Mayliza tried to hide a smile with her punch cup and sipped. "Pity he's so disgustingly good-looking. And witty. Didn't he know he was to have any existing wit removed before coming to a ball in this part of the country? And to challenge you, of all people. To actually attempt to engage you in a conversation that you hadn't practiced countless times before with every other man in the room . . . *well*. What effrontery!"

Catra watched her with narrowed eyes. "Are you finished?"

Mayliza laughed. "Goodness, Cat! He's the most interesting thing to walk into this room in years. Why does he offend you so? He's just what we said we were looking for earlier this very evening." She looked about the room for him, unable to see him from where she sat.

"Oh, I don't know," Catra admitted with a sigh. "He's just so—overconfident. He seems to try to—to *best* me with every conversation. It's one thing to be witty, quite another to be so constantly challenging. He disturbs me."

Mayliza sighed too. "Yes, he is somewhat intense. Not light and funny like your Ferris. I guess that proves Ferris is right for you. I can see where it would be . . . oh, I don't know, fatiguing somehow to keep up with someone like Mr. St. James all the time. I know he's too much for me."

Catra frowned at the assessment. Had she gotten lazy after all these years with the same old friends? Was she not as quick as she thought, but merely indulged by former conquests? She began to fan herself again. The room was quite stuffy still, though she had to admit she was no longer bored. Now she was edgy and dissatisfied. She almost felt as if she wanted another chance with him, another opportunity to keep up—or even best *him*.

"I'm going to get some air," she said, rising. "Would you like to join me?"

"I'd love to. But this dance is nearly finished and I've the next one with Horace Van Camp. Perhaps I'll meet you afterwards, if you're still out there. It is dreadfully hot in here."

Catra nodded and strode toward the open French doors, glad for the solitude. The evening was warm for October, and through the doors music followed her onto the patio.

Several couples sat on benches set on the flagstone porch, and a single white-coated servant hovered nearby with champagne on a silver platter.

She breathed deeply of the soft-scented air and, without making any decision to do so, wound down the first path she came to, toward the summer house. She stopped in a secluded spot by the old elm tree and sat on the wrought-iron bench beneath it.

The garden smelled of boxwoods and freshly mown grass. She lifted the rolled curls off her neck to the cooling breeze and leaned back on the bench, her eyes closed. Her left hand fingered the emerald betrothal ring she wore as she pictured a pair of warm, smiling gray eyes. Yes, they had been warm. *We won't have that smile disappearing again.* She smiled at the memory. Perhaps he could be kind.

Challenging, Mayliza had said. Indeed. She had felt tongue-tied and slow next to his exacting wit. *Perhaps that proves Ferris is right for you.* But it had always bothered her that Ferris was so easy. He had no challenging thoughts, but took hers for right and adjusted his own to meet them. Was she lazy? Did a little competitive conversation send her running to the security of Ferris's adoration? The idea bothered her.

Mr. St. James was not only challenging, however, she reminded herself, but openly impertinent. She tried to recall something rude that he'd said but was only able to remember his eyes and the assurance of his lead as they danced. And the confidence of his dancing . . . the energy of his touch, how she'd felt the imprint of his hand on the small of her back long after their dance had finished . . . *that* she'd never experienced. She felt again his hand enclosing hers—

The snap of a twig interrupted her reverie. Catra's eyes

flew open to see Ryan St. James standing not five feet away, as if her thoughts had conjured him.

"Excuse me, Miss Meredyth," he said promptly, looking nearly as surprised as she felt. "I came out for some air and thought this path might provide me with a moment of privacy. I'll leave you with yours." She stared up at him in stunned disbelief. "I'm sorry if I startled you." He turned to leave.

"No, no." She collected herself quickly, struggling to regain her presence of mind. "Please—are our girls driving you to escape? You know, we are awfully starved for new faces out here in the country, and single men for dancing are scarce." She was speaking too fast so she stopped. She moved over on the bench and placed her hand upon it, determined to overcome the agitation she felt around the man. "Please sit down. I'm glad for the company. I was drowning in my own thoughts."

Ryan walked to the bench and, flipping his coat tails out in a practiced motion, folded his long frame onto it. They sat for a moment in silence, neither looking at the other, until Catra found her voice and mentioned something about the lovely night.

He agreed and the quiet descended again. Catra racked her brain for some topic of conversation but rejected most that came to mind as too trivial or overused. She hated admitting to herself that what Mayliza had said about her conversations, though it stung, could well be true.

Mr. St. James, in the meantime, did not seem disconcerted by the silence at all, she decided as she looked discreetly at him. How typically Yankee. Then it occurred to her that perhaps this silence was yet another facet of his game of intimidation, and anger bubbled beneath her breastbone again. Had he come here specifically to torment her? She studied the side of his face as he leaned his elbows on his knees, his strong, well-formed hands dangling in front of him.

It was a hard face, with high, prominent cheekbones and a long, straight nose. She noticed a faint scar on his left temple and was tempted to reach out and touch it, but of course she did not.

"That's an interesting scar, Mr. St. James. Do you mind if I ask how you came by it?" she inquired, braving the impropriety of such a personal question in order to shock him just a little.

"Gladly, if you'll tell me where you got yours," he answered without a trace of laughter.

Startled, she raised a hand halfway to her face, then lowered it. "What do you mean?"

He looked at her for a moment, his face shrouded in darkness because of the light behind him, then said, "Nothing." He smiled. "Just being—insolent. Why did you provoke Dahlia that way?"

She studied him for a moment, sure he was toying with her, but controlled her irritation. "I was mostly trying to provoke you. Dahlia is no longer a challenge."

"Me?" he exclaimed with mock horror. "What could I have done to deserve that?"

She didn't hesitate. "I mistrusted your manners. I wanted to see how you'd handle a rock in your path."

He shifted, and his eyes sparkled in the thin light from the ballroom. "And how did I do?"

She shrugged. "Excellently. High marks for a star pupil. Perhaps I may now ask why you perform those manners with such disdain?"

Mr. St. James's laugh was sudden and complete. "Bravo, Miss Meredyth! Bravo! Well spoken, and well discerned. However, I must insist that 'disdain' is perhaps too strong a word. 'Amusement' might be better, if you're willing to give me the benefit of the doubt. If not, then perhaps 'cynicism' would do. And I have no excuse for my conduct, except for the poor one of thinking most proprietary gestures silly, nothing more.''

Catra was impressed. His candor drained away a good portion of her hard-earned annoyance. She thought for a moment. ''What did you mean, asking me where I got my scar? What scar?''

He studied his hands. ''Perhaps I was speaking out of turn. No, I was *definitely* speaking out of turn. I do not know you nearly well enough to hope to understand you.''

Despite herself, she was intrigued that someone would even try to understand her. ''What did you think you understood?''

''I only meant a feeling I had while watching you with various people. Miss Chester, of course, and Ferris particularly.'' He paused. ''It's as if you're humoring them. You're holding something back from them.''

''You presume to understand a great deal in a short amount of time.'' Catra immediately wished she hadn't asked him to continue. He obviously thought her rude and she was unintentionally proving him right every time she opened her mouth.

''It was just a feeling. I could well be wrong. Please accept my apology.''

She took a deep breath. ''No. *I'm* sorry. I asked you to continue.'' They sat in silence for several minutes more. ''You know, of course, that Ferris and I are engaged to be married.'' It was an inane comment, for she knew he was aware of it. She was not sure what prompted her to say it.

She felt his eyes upon her for a long moment before he answered. ''Yes. I know.''

She twisted her ring around and around her finger until she realized what she did and stopped. ''We grew up together, Ferris and I. He's been more of a son to my father than my own brother, Jimmy, who Ferris might have told you was born with a limited mental capacity. In fact Ferris probably knows me better than anyone. I can't imagine what would make you think I was 'holding back' from him.'' She looked up at him, but his face was turned from her. Her eyes concentrated on his broad shoulders beneath the fine black broadcloth.

Who was this stranger? This unfamiliar man? Why was she sitting here, trying to make some sort of connection with him? He was simply a business associate of Mr. Chester's. A Yankee, distant and untouchable. She wished impulsively that they were back on the dance floor, his arm around her waist, his laughing eyes upon her.

"Well, who have we here?" Mr. St. James broke the silence with the soft-spoken words.

Catra could hear the smile in his voice and looked up at him, then followed his gaze to the edge of the garden. Edging fearfully around a shrub, clutching his stuffed dog with a small, white-knuckled fist, was Jimmy. In the dim evening light, with his pale skin, shock of blond hair, and slight build, he looked more like a child of six or seven than a boy of ten.

Catra rose and bustled toward him. "Jimmy! What are you doing out of bed?"

Jimmy shrank back, smiling shyly, then swayed back and forth once.

Catra smiled, as she frequently did at Jimmy's inventive communication. He almost never spoke and when he did it was only a word or two, but he was always able to get his point across. At least to Catra he was. Her father usually let her deal with him and Ferris never took the time to try to understand him.

"You like the music, don't you?" Mr. St. James said, rising and moving toward them.

Catra turned her head sharply, surprised that he'd grasped Jimmy's meaning so quickly. Mr. St. James's hands were in his pockets and he moved in a slow, unintimidating manner, but she felt Jimmy grab her skirt and hold on. She placed a comforting hand between his shoulder blades, the feel of his small bony back bringing out her protective instincts.

"My brother is quite shy, Mr. St. James," she began, intending to explain Jimmy's unresponsiveness when she felt him nod against her side. She glanced down in time to see him smile up at the Northerner.

"I'm shy too, sometimes." The man smiled and when he glanced at Catra, she could see a teasing glint in his eyes. "But I wouldn't be, if I had what you have."

Jimmy looked down at his stuffed dog, pulling it up to his chin as if the man might snatch it away, before letting his eyes trail back up to the stranger's face.

Mr. St. James shook his head. "Not that, though it's a fine looking hound." Ever so gently he reached a hand toward Jimmy's face. He paused a second when Jimmy shrank back, then moved forward again and pulled a marble from behind the boy's ear. "This," he said with a smile. "If I'm not mistaken, it's a good luck piece."

Jimmy gaped at the blue glass ball. Mr. St. James extended it toward him.

Time stood momentarily still. Catra was amazed that Jimmy didn't run back into the house the way he'd come. He'd done as much once when Ferris had teased him about something, and he'd known Ferris his whole life.

"Take it," Mr. St. James said. "It's yours. It was behind your ear."

Jimmy looked doubtful but Catra could see the longing in his eyes.

"Go on," she urged softly.

"How about if I give it to your sister? She'll keep it for you. Can you trust her, do you think?"

Jimmy slanted a skeptical look up at her, and Mr. St. James laughed. Catra glanced at Jimmy and nearly laughed herself when she saw the sly smile cross his face. Nobody ever understood Jimmy's jokes but her. And now, she thought with growing interest, this man as well.

"If you can't trust me, Jimmy, you'd best take the marble yourself." She pulled her skirt gently from the grip of one of his hands. "Unless you'd rather let Mr. St. James keep it."

With a short look at her, Jimmy gazed back at Mr. St. James and held out his hand.

Mr. St. James placed the marble in the middle of the boy's palm. "There you go," he said with a nod of camaraderie. "Maybe someday we can shoot a game. I used to be pretty good, you know. Think we could do that?"

Catra watched Jimmy nod. Then he made a motion she recognized, he scooped his left arm around as if gathering up all the marbles and pointed to his chest. He smiled, eyes glittering.

"He means—" she began.

"I know what he means," St. James said, folding his arms across his chest. "He means he'd have no trouble beating me out of my best marbles. Well, we'll just have to see about that, won't we?"

At that, Jimmy laughed. Actually laughed out loud. Catra was so stunned she was sure that her mouth dropped open. Not that Jimmy had never laughed before. He laughed all the time. But only *with her*. She had never seen him so much as chuckle in front of a stranger.

"Jimmy! Where'd you get to, boy?" The whispered call was clearly audible from the other side of the bushes. "Come here, now. You got to take your bath and I won't take no for a answer."

"He's here, Bethia," Catra called.

Jimmy slid around Catra's back and to her further surprise clung to Mr. St. James's leg.

She was still staring at her brother in shock when the old nanny came around the bushes and stopped, her hands on her hips. "My lord, but you nearly wore me out. I'm sorry Miss Catra, but he slipped away from me when I was getting his bath. Lucky he's wearing clothes is all I can say."

Mr. St. James laughed again and Bethia looked up at him in surprise. Despite Jimmy's position, Bethia had obviously not noticed to whose leg the boy clung.

"It's all right, Bethia," Catra said. "Mr. St. James was just showing Jimmy a little magic before we went back in to the ball."

Bethia's amazed look slid from the tall handsome stranger to Catra. "He was?" she said, clearly more surprised by Jimmy's acceptance of the man than of their situation alone in the garden.

Catra nodded. "Yes. I believe he's found a new friend. Jimmy, show Bethia what Mr. St. James found behind your ear."

Slowly, Jimmy's grip on Mr. St. James's pants loosened and he held out the marble.

"Well, I'll be," Bethia said, shaking her head. "That sure is a pretty one. Whyn't you bring that with you and we'll get you just as clean, hmm? You can take it with you in the tub then you'll both be shiny as new."

Jimmy moved toward Bethia's outstretched hand and, clutching his dog and his marble, allowed her to lead him from the clearing. Just as the two rounded the bushes to-

33

ward the house, Jimmy turned to look back at St. James, offering one last shy smile before disappearing.

Once they were gone, Catra stood silently for a long moment before turning to her guest.

"You were quite good with him." It was an understatement of massive proportions.

He shrugged. "I like children."

She continued to stare at him, perplexed. "Yes, but he's . . . you understood him. Most people don't understand—his sort of communication."

He cocked his head, his eyes suddenly seeming nothing but kind to her, and said, "Don't they?"

She shook her head. "No."

He had done everything perfectly. He hadn't patronized, he hadn't squatted down to Jimmy's level—something that inexplicably frightened the boy—and he had amused him with a simple, well-executed trick.

The man was an enigma.

"Whatever were you doing with a marble in your pocket?" she asked, the oddness of the circumstance just occurring to her.

Mr. St. James laughed and glanced at the ground. "I had the feeling you would ask that." He looked back up at her and shrugged. "It was just something I found a while ago that for some reason I ended up carrying around. I'm not sure why. But it's nothing I can't do without."

Catra thought about this, about his noticing a marble and being interested enough to pick it up. For him to carry it around after that must have meant it was something of a good luck charm of his own. Aside from him not seeming the type to even have such a thing, to give it away so easily to a child said much about the man.

In the silence that ensued strains of music from the open

patio doors threaded their way through the night to them. She mentally shook herself.

"I should return to the ball," she said. "Please, feel free to stay and enjoy your privacy. I've enjoyed talking with you."

"I'm afraid my privacy would feel quite lonely now," he said. "Must you go?"

She smiled. It was tempting to stay. Far too tempting. "This song is one of my favorites," she explained, and gestured toward the doors from whence the music came. "I never miss dancing to it when it's played."

"In that case, would you do me the honor of dancing with me?" He watched her.

She inclined her head. "I would like that." She started to return to the ballroom, but was stayed by his touch on her sleeve.

"No," he said gently. Instead, he took her wrist in his hand and turned her into his arms to dance in the garden. "This is how one begins if one is to waltz. This might be the perfect opportunity to start those lessons."

A protest rose to her throat and died there, unuttered. He began to move slowly, his face so close to hers, she could feel his breath on her hair. She was acutely aware of the nearness of his body, his chest filling and emptying of air, his strong, steady heartbeat. She looked up at him to find his gaze upon her. Their eyes met, and stayed.

Catra wasn't sure when, but they both stopped moving. His eyes were dark and unreadable and his back blocked the light. Slowly, he pulled her closer, his chest hard against hers, his arm tight around her waist. She felt like a butterfly clasped against him, gently but firmly pinned, unable to move. Her lips parted as her breathing became shallow.

"You're out of place here, Catra," he said in a voice

low and compelling. Her eyes could not leave his. "And Ferris is the wrong man for you."

"Is he?" She felt paralyzed, unable even to be angry at this new presumption. Instead she simply watched the scene, as if waiting to see what might happen next.

Ryan's eyelids descended a fraction as he looked at her . . . the cat eyeing the canary. "He is."

Catra's skin went simultaneously hot and cold, and she watched in suspended disbelief as his face descended toward hers. Though she expected it, a swift, delicious shock swept through her as his lips touched hers. A shiver of excitement straightened her spine. His kiss was light at first, requiring just the slightest response from her. Then it grew more insistent. When it did, Catra's soul floated upward in her body and her feet lost the feel of the ground. Her eyes closed and her hand gripped his.

This was not just another kiss in the garden with one of the local boys, provoked and controlled for her own amusement. Catra was consumed in a way she had never before experienced and did not analyze. He pulled her against him as his tongue pushed past her lips to entwine with her own, and Catra felt her body react in ways she did not recognize. A hot flush began in her thighs and swept upward, releasing with it any desire she might have harbored to stop him, or herself. A longing she did not recognize pushed her to move against him, closer than their two already sealed bodies were, to pull him into herself.

She raised her hand to grasp his lapel, then slid her arm around his neck. His hair was soft and thick between her fingers and his coat smelled faintly of tobacco, his skin of soap. She could feel the studs on his shirt pressed against her chest.

All these impressions whirled in her brain, intoxicating her, drowning out all the voices in her head screaming to *pull away, stop this insanity,* and *remember Ferris.* No, the feeling was too delicious, and Catra, never one to deprive herself of something she truly wanted, thought she could stand in that spot, be enraptured by that kiss, forever.

"Catherine Meredyth!" The voice behind them cracked like a whip in the silence. Ryan turned so sharply that Catra would have fallen but for his arm around her waist. Catra's shock turned to terror as she looked into the white, livid face before her.

"Father." The word was a whisper as her throat seemed to swell and block all air.

"Mr. Meredyth." Ryan's voice was careful.

"Don't say a word, you *libertine,*" Thurber Meredyth growled. His large body was tensed with rage. His face, suffused with red, contrasted sharply with his white hair.

Catra was stunned at her father's insult—even despite the circumstances—and hastened to make him aware of who he was addressing. "Father, this is Mr. Chester's *partner—*"

"I know who the devil he is," her father snarled. "And for Bernard Chester's sake I will not throw you off this property immediately, *Mr. St. James.* You will go back to the party and leave when your hosts do. But you will never set foot in this house again, do you understand? I should never have let you set foot in it to begin with." Her father's body was positioned rigidly with his arms out from his sides, as if ready for a fight.

Ryan stood for a moment looking at him with an unreadable, but unintimidated, expression, his arm still about Catra's waist. She moved a step sideways, away from him, and hoped she would not wilt without the support.

After what seemed an eternity, Ryan turned to Catra and fixed her with a last look, almost as if expecting her to say something, then turned to her father and bowed. He walked calmly from the clearing.

Catra nearly collapsed at his exit, which left her face-to-face with her father, alone. He was completely, overwhelmingly angry. Angrier than she'd ever seen him.

"Your *fiancé* is looking for you." He looked with contempt at her left hand, the huge ring unmistakable. "Come with me."

It was then that Catra found her voice and shocked even herself with her next statement. "Father," she squeaked. He swung around and glared at her. "Father, I don't love Ferris." She was amazed at the admission, and for a moment felt a great weight lifted at the expressing of it.

"Catherine, I don't give a goddamn if you hate the man," her father said. "You will follow me into that ballroom and you will go to your betrothed. St. James isn't worth the dirt on my shoes and I'll see him dead before he touches you again. Don't think I won't."

"*Father,*" she breathed. She'd never heard him speak so. Of all the strange things that had happened during the evening, this was the most unnerving.

"You know nothing of the sort of man he is," her father continued, that same bloodless tone in his voice. "You know nothing of what is good for you. While there's breath left in my body you'll not throw yourself away on a blackguard such as Ryan St. James."

While Catra was shocked at his tone, to say nothing of his words, she was even more stunned as he caught her upper arm in his hand and nearly flung her ahead of him up the path. She stumbled, her mind reeling, and walked unsteadily toward the house.

They arrived in the ballroom, and Catra's eyes involuntarily scanned the crowd for Ryan. She hoped to God he'd left the house. She didn't know what her father was capable of at this moment and she didn't want to find out.

Mayliza, a worried frown on her face, hurried over.

"Ferris is over there," her father said and motioned to the front of the room, near the orchestra. "Go to him."

Mayliza followed her as Catra made her way toward Ferris, her body so numb she could barely feel the floor beneath her feet.

"What has happened?" Mayliza whispered as they walked.

Catra walked on, trying to steady her breathing, sure she was incapable of explaining what had just occurred. She thought she might be in danger of hyperventilating.

"Mr. St. James stormed in here a moment before you did and looked as black as a thundercloud," Mayliza whispered again. "Has something happened with him? Are you all right, Catra?"

At that point the crowd seemed suddenly to part, and there across the room, well within view, stood Ryan St. James. The intensity of his look made her knees tremble and the breath leave her body.

Someone shoved a glass of champagne in her hand.

She felt the hot air in the room like a blanket wrapped around her, and for a moment she thought she could actually hear it as it squeezed between the multitude of bodies, pressing in against her, closer and closer. Suddenly the light began to dim and all sound to fade as her eyes slid from Ryan's face to Dahlia's, next to him. She just noticed the angry sneer and narrowed eyes stretched across Dahlia's face before she fainted.

Chapter Three

Catra awoke the next morning with the uncomfortable feeling of having forgotten something important. Several minutes passed before she could clear her head, and it wasn't until she lifted her arms to stretch that she stopped, remembering in a rush the events of the previous evening. A hot blush bloomed inside her when she recalled Ryan St. James's kiss. But even though she pushed that memory from her head, the next one, her father's angry visage, was just as unsettling.

She bolted upright in bed just as Bethia entered with Catra's maid, Lucy, each of them carrying a tray with her breakfast. Bethia was Catra's old nursemaid, a woman who, despite Catra's age, insisted on treating her just as she had when Catra was a child.

"Well, Miz Sleepybones finally decided to rouse herself," Bethia chided as she positioned the tray over Catra's knees. Lucy put her tray, bearing a teapot and a milk pitcher, down on the small table near the window and poured the tea into a china teacup. She set it on the tray in front of Catra.

"Bethia, what happened last night?" Catra asked, afraid to explore her own memory further, but worried that she could remember nothing past entering the ballroom after the incident with Mr. St. James.

She sipped the hot tea while trying to tally how many glasses of champagne she'd had before her memory lapse. Too many, apparently.

"You fainted, Miz Catra," Lucy interjected. "You fell plum over, right in the middle a the room—just about ruined your pretty dress with champagne. It's all over the skirt . . ."

"Hush, child," Bethia scolded. "The doctor say it's just from the heat. It was so hot in there last night, and what with all the dancing and excitement—Oh, let me see that pretty ring again. I just can't get enough a that ring, ever since he gave it to you." Bethia finished plumping Catra's pillows and leaned over her hand. "Mm-mm," she hummed, "that man sure put a brand on you with that ring. Ain't nobody for five miles won't be able to see that."

Catra, who knew her well, thought she sounded just a little too chipper.

"I fainted?" she asked skeptically. "But I've never fainted. It certainly wasn't that hot . . ." She trailed off, remembering the dizzy feeling, the hot, swimming air, the nasty look on Dahlia's face across the room.

"Must have been the excitement then," Bethia said, bending over the foot of the bed to retrieve the blanket. "And I swear I've never seen so many young men anxious to carry you to your room." As if surprised at her own words Bethia straightened abruptly, glanced at Catra, then exclaimed with nervous energy, "Lucy, don't put the flowers over there, put 'em on the bedside table where Miz Catra can look at 'em.'' Lucy placed the vase full of white hothouse orchids on the table beside Catra's bed, making something of a production out of straightening them. "They're from Mr. Ferris." Bethia beamed, nodding.

Catra ignored the flowers. "Who did carry me to bed?"

"Why, Mr. Ferris did, as was only proper, your daddy with his troublesome back an' all." Bethia busied herself in Catra's armoire.

"Only after pulling you like a rag doll from the arms of that tall, evil-looking friend of his." Lucy skirted artfully out of Bethia's reach as the older woman turned on her.

"What evil-looking friend?" But Catra was beginning to understand.

"That Mr. St. James," Bethia said angrily. "Almost created a scandal, he did. He had the look of the devil on his face when everybody crowded 'round. Demanding everyone get back and give you some air. Anybody'd thought *he* was your betrothed. Picked you right up like a feather, shouting to know where he could take you. Had Mr. Ferris pointing up the stairs, before your daddy stood up for what's proper." Bethia chuckled, seemingly against her will. "By golly, honey, you steal hearts almost quicker'n they can get through the door. But your daddy, he had to threaten to throw that bad man out before he gave you up." Bethia turned back to the armoire, shaking her head.

"He's not a bad man," Catra murmured.

Bethia turned on her. "What do you know about that man, missy? *Nothing*, that's what. Don't you go flirting with that one, now that you're engaged to be married. That one's a dangerous one, he is. I can tell."

Catra sank down a little in her bed and nibbled on a corner of toast. "Jimmy trusted him," she said. "But you're right. I don't know anything about him." *And I am not likely to learn anything either,* she thought morosely. This was ridiculous. She had been caught kissing a man she barely knew and was engaged to a man she didn't love. Branded, as Bethia had aptly put it.

Of course, she'd known she didn't love Ferris when she agreed to marry him. He knew it too. They'd made a deal, she and Ferris. They'd give everyone—his family and hers—what they wanted and adjoin the two properties, but they would each be free to do as they pleased. To Catra, marriage to her best friend was a small price to pay for the independence she could never have as an unmarried woman.

Besides, she had to marry to keep the property out of her cousin's hands. If she didn't, it would go to her father's only male relative—other than Jimmy, who while sweet would never be much brighter than a six-year-old the doctors said—and her father wouldn't be dead a week before Baker Mansfield would turn her and Jimmy out of the house, she was sure. She was also sure it wouldn't take much more than another week before he'd gamble it away at cards or some other such wicked activity.

Ryan, she murmured the name silently to herself. Unfortunately, she thought, she needed to see him again. She needed to prove to herself that what happened last night between them was just a fluke, a passing passion, the sort that only comes with forbidden behavior. But the way he'd made her feel—no one, not one of the many men who had courted her, flattered her, even kissed her, had made her feel that way. She could still feel a tingling along the back of her neck as she thought of it.

But of course she would see him again. He was a guest of the Chesters, and he was going to Shelly Westbrook's wedding. She would *have* to see him again. The thought touched off a lovely feeling of anticipation. How would she act? As if it were nothing, of course. He was quite worldly, she knew, and a kiss like that in the garden was probably nothing compared to what happened at, say, Parisian balls. Though she did have to believe she'd affected Mr. St. James at least a little, for he certainly gave no sign of stopping until her father's interruption.

Her *father*. She'd almost forgotten. He'd ordered him off the property. Well, he was angry. He would probably relent when Mr. St. James came to apologize. After all, it was only a kiss. It wasn't as if she were ruined or anything.

She looked down at the ring and twirled it on her finger as Bethia and Lucy filled the large bathtub in the dressing room for her. But why *had* he kissed her? Was he interested in courting her? Impossible; he knew she was betrothed. So why would this extremely handsome and eligible bachelor waste his time on a woman he knew to be engaged? And why would he risk a lucrative business partnership? For if Ferris or Bernard Chester had found them instead of her father . . .

Catra moved the half-eaten breakfast from her lap and swung her legs over the side of the tall four-poster bed. She could just hear Bethia's voice scolding Lucy for something or other in the next room. She looked once again at the ring, then removed it from her finger and set it on the bedside table.

Later that morning, while Catra and Jimmy were in the parlor playing checkers, Ferris stopped by. Long used to entering the Meredyth house at will, he arrived unannounced. Still, despite her resolution to think nothing of him, she found herself looking expectantly behind Ferris for Ryan.

Would he come, even though he'd been ordered to stay away? What would he say to Ferris about her father's angry decree? How would he apologize if he didn't come to the house?

But Ferris was alone.

Catra blushed as he entered and she busied herself with the checkerboard, kinging several of Jimmy's pieces. Though she was certain Ryan would have said nothing about the kiss, the memory of it sprang up afresh when she looked at Ferris's boyish face. What would he say, if he knew, she wondered. It wasn't that she felt as if she'd cheated on him—despite their engagement their relationship was still purely platonic—it was more that his presence highlighted the difference between himself and Ryan. As well as the difference between her friendship with Ferris and the powerful feelings generated by Ryan's kiss.

"No, Jimmy," she said. "You only jump my black ones. Not your red ones, remember?"

Jimmy continued jumping his piece around the board regardless of the colors and Catra smiled. He frequently got carried away midway through the game.

"You're just in time," she said to Ferris. "Jimmy's beaten me three times in a row. Perhaps you'd like to take a turn."

Ferris glanced at Jimmy and shook his head. "You know me. I've got no patience for things like that."

For a second Catra imagined that Ryan would have sat right down and begun playing. Then she drew herself up. That was unfair. Just because Ryan had been good with Jimmy one night did not mean Ferris was not. Ferris just approached the boy differently.

Ferris settled himself catty-corner to her in the sofa and lay his arm along the back. "So, how are you feeling today?"

"I'm *fine*," she said firmly, waving a hand. "Last night

was nothing. Just too hot, I suppose, and too much champagne.''

"That's what I thought. Good thing Ryan was there, eh?''

Catra's eyes shot to his face. "What do you mean?''

"I mean in the panic after your faint nobody knew quite what to do. I'm ashamed to say I didn't either. Good thing he was there to straighten us all out.'' He laughed. "The place sounded like a henhouse with everyone squawking opinions until he took over.''

Catra's brow furrowed. "Really, Ferris, I would've thought it would occur to *you* to carry me somewhere. You know Father's got a bad back and you didn't expect to leave me on the floor, did you?''

"No, of course not.'' Ferris shrugged. "But who knew whether it would be better to let you cool off first? Or come around on your own before we moved you? I confess, I was at a loss until Ryan came through.''

From the corner of her eye Catra could see Jimmy mimicking Ferris's posture and movements. Even his mouth moved with Ferris's words. She tried to suppress a smile as he leaned back in his chair and crossed his short legs in the slow, precise way Ferris crossed his long ones, laying one arm along the back of his chair.

Catra faced Ferris so as not to encourage him. "I'm certainly glad you didn't let it go so far as to let Mr. St. James carry me upstairs, in any case. You know Bethia would've had a fit. She did anyway, in fact.''

"He wouldn't have done any harm,'' Ferris said with an indulgent smile. "He's a perfect gentleman. And he seems to have taken quite a shine to you, Cat.''

Catra's face flamed. "Jimmy, stop that,'' she said sternly.

Ferris glanced at Jimmy, noticed nothing, and continued

talking. "Yes, indeed. He talked quite a bit about how smart you were. How witty. He said he envied me. Can you imagine that? *He* envied *me*."

"Did he?" she murmured, gathering the checkers to set them up for a new game.

"Yes. He said he'd never get married, but if he was ever to be tempted it would be by someone like you. So I guess I've impressed him in a way too, having been the one to capture you and all."

Catra laughed and gave him an exaggerated look. "Ferris, you know perfectly well you haven't captured me, just as I haven't captured you. We have a deal, right? Now stop being so big-headed and play checkers with Jimmy. I'm through losing for today."

Ferris rose and shook his head. "I can't. Sorry, Jim." He shrugged a shoulder in Jimmy's direction.

Jimmy mimicked it perfectly when Ferris's glance reverted to Catra.

"Ryan and I are off to Fredericksburg today. He wants to buy a new gun and I have selflessly volunteered to accompany him." Ferris moved in the direction of the door.

Catra smirked. "Yes, I'm sure that will be a hardship for you. Be sure to tell the boys at the Rising Sun Tavern I said hello."

"Don't be silly, we won't be drinking. Not more than one or two, at any rate." He grinned. "Oh, and by the way, Ryan asked me to send his apologies for not joining me this morning. Said he had some letters to write before posting them in town, but that he'll look forward to speaking with you at the next opportunity."

"Will he?" She couldn't help raising a brow. Obviously Ferris knew nothing of her father's angry dictate last night. How interesting.

"I'm sure he will. Glad to see you up and about, Cat. I

wanted to make sure you were all right, and now I see that you are.''

''Yes, quite,'' she murmured as he strode toward the door.

''Until tomorrow,'' he said with a quick bow, and he was gone.

Catra sat looking at the door for a long moment. Sometimes it struck her as a very odd thing that Ferris was her betrothed.

Jimmy got up and strode to the door with Ferris's slightly bouncing stride. He turned with a flourish, gave a fleeting bow, and they both started laughing.

The following morning was cool. The damp ground sucked gently at her horse's hooves as Catra traveled the western edge of the Meredyth property. A light, early morning mist curled up from the grass like smoke. The world was silent but for the warm blasts of breath from her stone-gray mare, Jupiter.

Catra spurred Jupiter to a canter, up the crest of a hill and over it, then galloped with reckless abandon down the grassy slope. She reveled in the powerful motion of the Thoroughbred, in the thick muscles that carried her over the fast-moving earth. The wind tugged at her hair, loosened it from its braid, sent the long skirt of her riding habit flapping over the horse's haunch. The exertion of staying one with the beast tested her endurance and tore at her breath, but it strengthened her heart as nothing else could.

The more she'd thought about it after Ferris's visit, the more disappointed she was that Mr. St. James had not come to apologize yesterday. The fact that he saw no need to come and set things right with her father—not to mention herself—irked her, and not just because she was denied the opportunity to assess the feelings he'd aroused in her the night of the ball. The omission showed a lack of respect. And since he hadn't come she'd had little to do but stew over all the reasons he might have kissed her, and all the motivations he might have for not apologizing.

Hence, her desire to run her horse into a lather and spend some much-needed time alone on the calming banks of the Rappahannock.

Gradually she slowed and came to a halt at a point just before the river. Nothing showed before her but a thick line of trees, but Catra knew that just beyond it, at the end of a thin private path, lay the water. Like a jewel encased in dark soil banks, the river at this point came from the north and bent eastward to create a sandy point that was, due to the thick forest around it, quite secluded.

As she paused and breathed deeply of the fresh, damp air, she heard the muted patter of a horse's hooves behind her. She turned in the saddle. Not a quarter of a mile away, a lone figure on horseback approached. She was unsure who it was but hoped against reason it was not Ferris. She did not want to talk with him today, not with all the tumultuous thoughts she'd been having about Mr. St. James since the ball.

The figure neared and her heart again took up its frantic beat as she recognized the broad shoulders and dark hair of Ryan St. James.

He rode a large roan, as fine as Ferris's best, that cantered with admirable grace down the slope to the point where she was stopped. With an easy smile and dancing gray eyes, Ryan reined in the horse before her. Both horse and rider emanated warmth and companionship into the crisp isolation of the day.

"Miss Meredyth, what a wonderful surprise." He inclined his head with that preciseness that seemed almost sarcastic. His expression gave no sign of remembering their last parting, though he looked sincerely happy to see her.

"Mr. St. James." She greeted him coolly and hoped her face was not flushed.

"What brings you out so early this morning?"

"Exercise," she answered curtly and turned her horse to walk along the trees toward the path. Ryan turned his as well and they walked side by side.

"Catra . . ." he began in a different tone, as if acknowledging that their meeting was not as accidental as it seemed. At the familiar use of her name Catra stiffened and gave him a cold look. "Miss Meredyth," he amended with a grin, "I would like to speak with you about the events of the other evening."

Catra sniffed and raised her chin. "Oh, that. I'd nearly forgotten. So, since we've conveniently met up, you thought you'd justify your actions?"

Ryan sighed. "If you will recall, I was forbidden to return to your house."

"You might have written to explain yourself. I understand you found the time to pen some letters yesterday."

Ryan smiled and then laughed aloud. "It sounds like you've been thinking about this. Good."

Catra turned a stony look on him. "Mr. St. James, regardless of what your own immoral mind may believe, I am not the type of woman who passes out her favors indiscriminately at family balls. If I have been thinking about this, you have not your conceit to thank." She stopped. So much for acting as if nothing had happened. This was not how she had envisioned their next interview. He should have been humbler; she, more forgiving. Instead, he sat calmly on his horse and regarded her throughout the tirade with what could only be described as curiosity.

"Well, since you have, already, discriminately passed out your favors, which is to me a matter of great import and not conceit, what type of woman you *normally* are is irrelevant.''

She reined in her horse with a jerk and whipped around to face him. She wished she could slap the smug expression off his face and for a moment seriously considered doing just that.

''Why did you join me, Mr. St. James?'' she demanded finally. ''To taunt me?''

His lips curved, but his eyes looked serious. ''No, Miss Meredyth. I would like to discuss the night of the ball, if you will let down your guard long enough to allow it.''

She glared at him for a moment more, then jerked her eyes to her hands, clasped on the horse's mane. Her fingers twined and untwined in the coarse hair, squeezing the leather reins so hard that her knuckles were white. ''I— would like to hear what you have to say,'' she said finally. ''This matter has been the cause of some concern.''

''I'm sure it has.''

She looked at him quickly but found no sarcasm in his face. ''We can talk privately down here.'' She motioned to a barely discernible break in the tree line several yards in front of them.

Ryan swung his leg over the back of his horse and dismounted. Then he grabbed Jupiter's reins to hold the horse while Catra dismounted. She gathered the excess skirt of her riding habit in her left arm and smoothed her wind-blown hair with her right hand. She felt his eyes upon her and quickly made her way into the forest.

''You may bring the horses,'' she called to him. ''There is a clearing farther along in which you may tie them.''

The forest was dark, and once past the opening the path narrowed so it was just barely passable to the two horses. Catra ignored any struggle he might have been having as she picked her way confidently through the trees, ducking under low branches and deftly pulling her skirt from the clutches of prickly vines.

At last they arrived in a small clearing, covered with grass and buttercups, where Ryan tied the horses. Without a word Catra continued through the trees until they reached a broad, sandy beach. A weeping willow stood at the end to their left, its long, leafy branches trailed in the current like fingers testing the water's temperature. There were small rocks at the water line along which the current tripped and tumbled with a peaceful sound.

She looked at him discreetly as they stepped from the darkness of the forest and noted the way his eyes drank in the scene with unconcealed appreciation. When the sun broke through the morning fog to sparkle on the water, Ryan filled his lungs with the fresh smell of the water and glanced up at the sky, where a vee of geese flew by.

Catra stepped over a log to stand by the water. Both were silent for a minute before she said, "You can talk here; no one will hear you."

He stepped toward her. "Does that mean no one is listening?"

She could hear the humor in his voice. "I'm listening. You know what I meant."

"Catra," he said, "look at me." She turned slowly, sand crunching beneath her boots. "I am unable to justify my actions of the other night. I cannot excuse them by pleading ignorance of your situation. I knew before I arrived that you were betrothed to Ferris."

She gazed at him, unsure of what to say. "Is that it? Is that all you have to say?"

He frowned, then shrugged. "I should apologize, I suppose. But I regret nothing."

She stood rigid, glaring at him, outrage pouring through her veins. "You regret nothing. Could you perhaps explain then why you made such an advance? You knew of my obligation to Ferris. And what of *your* obligation to him?''

He shifted his weight to one hip and put his hands in his pockets, watching her placidly. ''I can ask you the same things, Miss Meredyth. Why did you allow it? You, also, knew of your obligation to Ferris and yet you responded, ardently, I might say, to my advance.''

She straightened her back and clenched her jaw. ''You are a beast. You are the lowest, most despicable sort of gentleman—''

''Catra,'' he interrupted, ''trust me, this sort of name-calling becomes tedious in a hurry.''

''Why . . . you . . .'' The words came out as gusts of air.

His brow furrowed and he crossed his arms over his chest. ''Two nights ago you were a saucy, flirtatious woman. Now, today, you're playing the outraged school-girl. Tell me, which is the real Catherine Meredyth, hmm?''

She had no idea what to say. Part of her knew he was right. She hadn't fought him the other night. In fact, she'd enjoyed his kiss—just as she'd planned to enjoy the apology and the flirtation afterward. But he hadn't played that part of the game right. He'd switched all the rules and now she wasn't sure which way to be.

''Well?'' he asked conversationally.

She squared her shoulders and raised one eyebrow, much the way she'd seen him do earlier. ''Maybe they're *both* the real Catherine Meredyth, did you think of that while you were plotting how to torment me next? So from now on you're just going to have to take your chances on which one you're meeting.''

For a second he stood motionless, looking at her through narrowed eyes, as if recalculating who she was. Then he chuckled and turned toward the water, bending his head back and running a hand through his hair. After a minute he turned back to her. "You are something, Catra, I'll give you that."

"I'm sorry, but that's not what I was looking for." She was going to win this game, dammit. *She* was the one making the rules here. She allowed a small smile.

"What were you looking for?"

Her gaze didn't waver. "I think you know."

Ryan shook his head. "You know, when I met you . . . no, before I met you, I had heard Ferris speak of you, and I fully intended to go to that ball and meet you and—leave. Nothing else. I had no designs on Ferris's fiancée. I was simply curious." He smiled slyly at her. "I'd heard so much about you and your beauty, I have to admit I was skeptical." He took a moment to stand smiling at her, studying her face again. She worked not to alter her expression. "But when I met you . . . ." He crossed his arms over his chest again and pressed his lips together.

"I've been to thousands of balls in dozens of cities," he started again with more vigor, "had countless matrons offering me untold daughters, been flirted with, flaunted at, even threatened by women with an eye on my bachelorhood."

He took a step forward and stopped before her. Then he reached out a hand and lightly touched her forearm. Her breath stopped and she kept her eyes on his.

"But I have never met anyone like you." He brushed a strand of hair from her cheek. "Your frankness and passion, your intelligence and wit are so rare. And it's simply *wasted* out here. I haven't been able to stop thinking about you. I thought about writing to you, but what would I say? I couldn't apologize; I'm not sorry it happened. I couldn't explain. Hell, I still can't explain." He brushed his hand through his hair again. "All I know is, it's wrong, this marriage of yours. And I feel the need to speak out. When

Ferris talks about you, about your wedding—'' He stopped, shook his head. ''I've said too much.''

''Mr. St. James . . .'' she began, wanting to sound flippant but too confused to pull it off. His sudden sincerity threw her. ''This is sounding something like the prelude to a proposal.'' Her tone was far more questioning than she'd intended, and as soon as the statement was out of her mouth she wished she could suck the words back in. He look so shocked, so completely taken aback, that Catra felt mortified to her core.

He'd had no intention of proposing, though what he'd said had sounded like countless other offers she'd received. No, he was saying something else entirely. But what? He was telling her not to marry Ferris and offering nothing himself. He was, she realized suddenly, trying to flatter her into a compromising situation.

Did he expect his flowery talk to convince her to continue or, God forbid, increase their inappropriate behavior? Why else would he tell her all this? Anger expanded inside her. He was deeply mistaken if he thought the mere fact of an impending passionless marriage would make her jump into bed with the first cavalier to come along. She was speechless with fury.

Ryan took a deep breath. ''Catra, I'm concerned for you,'' he continued, oblivious to her burgeoning rage. ''You and I both know the circumstances here. I just want to stop you from making a mistake. I know you're betrothed, but I've seen you with Ferris—can you possibly be in love with him?''

She just barely controlled her breathing, though she knew her face must be burning red. ''Love? What in the world has love got to do with marriage?'' she asked, as if he were an idiot. ''Ferris has been my friend since childhood, but if he'd dropped out of the sky yesterday and my father wanted me to marry him, I would. That is just the way it's done. Love is something for novels and fairy tales. My situation is neither. I'm surprised I need to clarify this for such a man as you—such a *worldly* man." She drew the word out in a throaty voice that dripped with venom. "You must think me the biggest simpleton the South ever produced if you think that talking me out of a respectable marriage would induce me to take up an illicit affair with you."

Ryan's eyes widened, then showed wry comprehension. He laughed once, utterly without humor. "So you're not so different after all from the proper misses I've encountered up to now. For some reason I thought cloistering yourself in a nice, safe marriage like all the others would be beneath you, Catra. Apparently, in trying to save what I thought was one exceptional woman from a life of mediocrity, I've uncovered an experienced tease who knows exactly what she wants." He laughed again. "No, I hardly think you're a simpleton, sweet; but if what you wanted was not an illicit affair, just what were you doing with me in the garden that night?"

Catra finally found her voice. "I was being *accosted*. And if you ever try such a thing again, I will make sure Ferris and everyone else concerned knows about it. I was— and *am*—a betrothed woman, a fact you'd best remember."

"Just as you did the other night." His attempt at indifference was belied by an obvious anger. He seemed to realize it and gave in to it. "What has so changed today, Catra? Hmm? Two days ago you were the picture of a woman in control. You didn't simper with the others of your sex, espousing insipid banalities to try to bury your flirtations in the hearts of shallow men. You were all talons and fire, with a disregard for conformity that I respected more than anything I'd ever seen in a woman. And here you are today, a different person. I've never heard so much platitudinous morality imposed from such an unexpected source. Based on your actions last Thursday, I don't believe you have any grounds to condemn my confusion. You got just what you wanted that night, and you know it. If now it suits your purpose to deny it, you can bloody well know that you're fooling no one here. However"—he paused and took a breath—"if it's an apology you want, here you are: I apologize for my conduct, Miss Meredyth." He executed a short, condescending bow. "Consider it a case of mistaken identity."

His anger was swift and complete, and confused even Ryan himself with its intensity. He was disappointed in her, he told himself. Perhaps he hadn't expected an easy liaison with her, but he hadn't expected her to turn into a prim southern maiden either. The dalliance of a flirtation would have been enough for him, but this creature who had seemed so intriguing a few days ago had suddenly turned into exactly what he'd spent the last ten years avoiding.

Disgusted, he turned to leave when she grabbed his arm and turned him back with unexpected strength. A thrill shot up to his shoulder at her touch, and the picture that greeted him was one he would not soon forget. The trim blonde stood just in front of him with scalding eyes and fiery cheeks, one finger directed into his chest.

"Now *you* will listen to *me*," she hissed with a brazen poke of her finger. "Whatever it was you expected when you followed me down here was entirely a fantasy of your own making. And if what constitutes an original and intelligent female in your estimation is one who will tumble willingly into your arms without regard to her own status or prospects, then you are destined for a future of cotton-headed floozies. I will not have you leaving here believing me to be one more female you can manipulate to your will with your cocky ways and your underhanded smiles. You have just tangled with probably the only woman of intellect who will give you the time of day, and that only because you caught her in a weak moment. I'm truly sorry I have let down my gender so disgustingly. It's a lesson I shall never forget. I should thank you for that.'' She stopped for a moment and looked at him, as if at last seeing him for the scoundrel he was. ''Now you may leave. I am *finished* with you.''

She took one step back and glared at him with such energetic dislike, her jaw lifted and her features composed—no trembling maiden here—that he suddenly thought he'd never seen so beautiful a creature.

She was right, he realized. She was absolutely right. It was his own expectations that had failed him, not her. He had expected an experienced woman of the world and had uncovered innocent intelligence. Then he'd cast her as a manipulative nymphet and had been brought up short there too. Something in the embarrassment of her indignation and the completeness of her anger convinced him that she had not tried to beguile him, though she almost surely could have, he mused. And he marveled at how, for the second time in less than an hour, he'd misjudged her. He, who'd believed he had such an eye for character.

He smiled then; a wide, genuine smile, he believed, not an underhanded one. ''You're right,'' he admitted to her hostile glare and held his hands out to his sides with a shrug. ''I'm sorry. Truly.''

She wavered. Her eyes darted away and then back, and her shoulders relaxed slightly. ''So,'' she said uncertainly, ''we understand one another.''

''We're beginning to.'' He nodded slowly. ''Though I think you've got me pegged a little better than I have you.''

His smile turned lazy. "I'm a cad. I'll admit it. I guess I was hoping you wouldn't notice."

A reluctant laugh escaped her, but she stopped it immediately. Still, a smile tugged at her lips, he could tell.

"Please go now," she said sincerely. "I don't want to like you."

This drew a burst of appreciative laughter from him, and she smiled with him.

Ryan put his hands in his pockets. "But I want you to. In fact, I find myself suddenly desperate for your good opinion."

She swiped at the loose strands of hair that blew across her face with the breeze. "I don't for a moment believe you are desperate for anything, Mr. St. James."

"Don't underestimate me, Miss Meredyth," he said. "I have been known to get desperate. It helps me to get what I want. But I know I must leave. Thank you for this— lesson. I'm glad we've cleared the air."

She smiled and nodded her head once, then began to make her way to the path.

"Catra," he added impulsively, "will you meet me here tomorrow?"

Her eyes widened and she laughed incredulously. "What on earth for?"

He chuckled at her response. "Never fear, fair maiden. I've no designs on your virtue, now that we've established the complete miscalculation I've made about you." He regarded her slowly, head cocked to one side. "I guess I would just like to know what it's like to have a lady of your stature give me the time of day . . . in a *strong* moment."

She looked at the ground, then flicked her eyes upward, looking at him through her lashes. "I'm afraid I don't have many of those when I'm with you, Mr. St. James," she admitted. "Good-bye." She turned and left without looking back.

Catra awoke the following morning to the dim early light of dawn. Still wrapped in sleep, her mind played eerily over the dream she'd just had. She was married to Ferris and they lived in a one-room hovel. She wasn't particularly unhappy, she didn't think, but she sat on the dirt floor of the home with a ball of string and a knife. Then she was at the door; a fine mist fell down around her from the overcast sky and she was trying to will a black cat into the house from the edge of a nearby forest. The cat prowled back and forth along the trees, ignoring her. She wanted to throw something, but the knife would kill it, and she could not get the tangled string off her fingers. She scratched and yanked at it so hard that it sliced the skin of her hand. Then, just as the cat turned to saunter toward her, she heard Ferris move into the room behind her. She tried to hurry the cat, to get him into the house before Ferris noticed, but it was too late. Ferris shoved her from the door and screamed in an eerily high-pitched wail to drive the cat away, but the animal stood quietly by the forest, its back to the cottage. Catra ran to the window and tried to smear away the fog, working furiously, for the glass steamed as quickly as she could wipe it. Just as she'd opened an area large enough to see the cat, it turned, flashed ice-gray, *human* eyes at her and disappeared into the trees.

That was when she'd awakened. She felt a shiver of apprehension and snuggled deeper into the warmth of the down comforter. She wished the sun would rise faster to dispel the pall the dawn light held over the room.

Jane Atherton came to call on Catra two days later. Jane was a town girl from a working family whose mother used to be a maid at the Meredyth estate, Braithwood. Jane had probably been Catra's closest friend when they were youngsters, but the friendship had faded as their lives took different paths.

Catra had not noticed the friendship waning until one day several years earlier, when they were together after an extended absence and she discovered she had nothing at all to say to her friend. All of the people she would talk about, Jane would not know; all of her hopes and dreams for the future would be goals that Jane herself could never realize. Catra began to feel uncomfortable about her wealth and station compared to Jane's modest life.

So although it was with surprise that Catra greeted Jane, the happiness she felt upon seeing her was unfeigned. "Jane! I'm so glad to see you. And how well you look." It was true. Jane had always been a pretty child, but womanhood had blossomed her into a beauty. Her thick auburn hair was pulled back in a chignon that made her angelic face serenely beautiful. Her brown eyes were fringed with long dark lashes that were, Catra could swear, lined lightly with kohl. The effect was stunning, though, and coupled with her wide, sensual mouth, Catra thought her the most beautiful woman she knew.

"How nice of you to say so, Cat." She smiled back. "But no one could hold a candle to you. And look at your glorious gown."

Catra felt her face warm at the compliment, for Jane wore a plain woolen gown of gray with black trim and still managed to look beautiful, while Catra had on a dark green grosgrain gown with a gold mantelette and a large hoop. She would never admit it to another living soul, but she had dressed every morning for the last two days as if Ryan St. James might come to call—for a reason she could not fathom even in her most creative fantasies.

61

"Oh—this." Catra waved at her dress and wondered if she would look half as beautiful as Jane did in plain wool. "I suppose I was trying to cheer up a dull day with a nice gown. But come, sit down and tell me all about you. Would you like some tea?"

"Actually, I thought we might take a ride together," Jane suggested with a bright smile after a brief glance around the opulent room. "Like we used to."

Catra understood Jane's discomfort in these surroundings and immediately acquiesced. She ran up the stairs to change into a riding habit and hoped she had one that would look plain. After digging through her closet, she emerged with the plainest one she could find; but in spite of its subdued color and lack of trim, it still looked rich, with a dark blue velvet jacket and gold buttons. The gray skirt was extremely long to cover the horse's flank, but at least it was not the red one with gold braid, or the stunning purple, which would have stood out far more next to Jane's gray.

They cantered down toward the river, which had always been their favorite ride, and Catra was so caught up in their conversation that for the first time in days she did not think about Ryan St. James.

"I hear you're to be married soon," Jane said. "I'm so happy for you. I remember so many times when you and Ferris and I would ride out looking for adventure. I should have known you two would end up together."

"Good heavens, I don't know why. I had no idea. Or I had an idea, but I guess I was hoping it wouldn't actually come to pass." She laughed lightly, then realized what she'd said.

"You mean you don't want to marry him?" Jane exclaimed. "Why, I thought the match perfect. You two were always such good friends. I have to admit I was a little jealous when I heard about it. Your life always seems so perfect.''

''Well, it's not,'' Catra said with more distaste than she'd intended. ''But it's done now, and at least the pressure of a decision is gone. Goodness, how I hated having to come up with kindly rejections. And I know you've had the same problem, Jane. In fact, it seems to me the last time we talked you were trying to foist off one man on your sister and another on your friend Kate. Whatever happened?''

''Oh, them!'' She laughed at the memory. ''My sister did marry that boy, Thomas, and they're doing very well. She's about to give birth to their second child. The first was a girl.''

''Their second! Isn't your sister younger than we are?''

''She was fifteen when they married. She's seventeen now.''

''And what about you? Aren't your parents anxious to get you married off?'' Catra teased. But the blush on her friend's face made her aware of the truth of the statement. Her parents probably did want exactly that. They couldn't afford to feed children so far into their adulthood.

''That's one reason I wanted to see you, Cat. I'm betrothed,'' she announced weakly. ''To an Englishman named Frederick Pinchon.''

''An Englishman? Wherever did you meet one of those?''

Jane steered her horse in the direction of the Chester properties. ''He's apprenticing with Father. I suppose he's a good man.''

''You're not in love with him.'' Catra recognized the resignation on her face.

''No. But it's not that which bothers me,'' Jane said. ''It's that he'll never be any different from my father. My life will never be any different. He wants to stay and take over the business from Father, and of course Mother thinks that a marvelous idea. But sometimes I see my life stretching before me as one long bolt of the same material. No changes. Nothing new. No hope.''

Catra reached over and took Jane's gloved hand in hers. Their horses' shoulders bumped gently. "I know what you mean, Jane. I know exactly what you mean."

Jane looked into Catra's eyes. "I think you do," Jane whispered.

At that moment a gunshot close by startled both them and their mounts. The horses jumped and pranced nervously after the sound. Catra looked about to determine where it had come from, when another off to their right sounded again. Then again.

"Sounds as if someone's practicing," Jane decided.

"Shall we take a look to see who?" Catra asked.

Jane answered by spurring her horse in the direction of the sound, and they cantered through a copse of trees down to a grassy field where two men stood together.

Catra recognized them at once. One blond head, the other dark: Ferris and Ryan. They appeared to be taking shots at a lone tree, blackened and grizzled from a lightning strike several years earlier.

At the sound of approaching horses the two turned toward them. Smiles lit both their faces, Ferris's full of open delight, Ryan's with an interested glance at Jane.

"Miss Jane Atherton!" Ferris exclaimed. "Where have you been hiding?"

"You should come to town more often. I'm working in the milliner's now. Perhaps now that you'll have a wife to buy gifts for, I'll see more of you."

"Miss Meredyth," Ryan greeted Catra with a significant look, then turned to Jane.

"Mr. St. James, I would like to present you to one of

my dearest friends, Miss Jane Atherton.'' Catra felt a pinch of jealousy as he reached up and took Jane's hand in his. ''Jane, this is Mr. St. James.''

''A pleasure,'' he said. ''May I help you down, or are you two just passing through?''

Catra noticed the becoming blush on Jane's cheeks as Ryan held her hand just a moment too long, and her anger flared. Did St. James think he had a chance at Jane now that she had rejected him? Jane looked appealingly at her friend, and Catra knew that Jane wanted to stay. Of course.

Catra had to admit that Ryan looked devastatingly handsome in an open-necked white shirt and snug, fawn-colored pants.

''I suppose we could stay for a moment,'' Jane said with a shy smile.

She was rewarded with Ryan's warm eyes and dazzling grin. He reached his hands up to her waist and lifted her effortlessly down.

Ferris scurried over to Catra's side and began to reach for her, but Catra was too incensed to notice and sprang down from her mount without him. He stepped back so as not to be landed upon but, undaunted, took her arm in his.

''Ryan and I were just practicing,'' he explained needlessly. ''Quite an amazing shot, Ryan is. I can't even come close, though I'm not such a slouch myself. Shall we show you?''

''Oh, do,'' Jane exclaimed, her hand still on Ryan's arm as he led her to the spot from which they'd been shooting.

''I'm sure Mr. St. James has had ample opportunity to practice his aim, what with his lifestyle and all,'' Catra said pointedly, sure that he'd been engaged in numerous duels over debauched young maidens. No one seemed to understand exactly what she meant, however, other than Ryan himself, who shot her an unreadable look. She gathered her prodigious skirt in one hand and followed them to the spot.

"Are you from the West?" Jane asked him, trying to discern Catra's meaning.

"No." Ryan finally released Jane's hand to load the pistol. "I think Miss Meredyth must have meant that I export a great many firearms, particularly rifles, through trade to England."

"Actually, that's not what I meant," Catra remarked.

Ryan smiled at her, his eyes knowing, then raised his eyebrows at Jane in an eloquent expression of ignorance.

"Here, watch this," Ferris said, oblivious to the exchange.

Jane, however, missed none of it and gazed with inquisitive eyes at Catra.

"See that branch there," Ferris continued, "the lowest on the right-hand side? Now see how it branches out there, and the twig rising up at the tip?"

Catra and Jane turned their attention to the tree. "Yes," they answered almost in unison.

"Go ahead, Ryan," Ferris said.

Ryan raised the pistol, and Catra saw him wink at Jane. Then he shot the twig neatly off the branch. Ferris laughed and clapped him on the back. "Isn't it something?" he cried and smiled into Catra's face.

"It's something," Catra murmured. She wished they could leave now.

"Goodness," Jane breathed and turned soft eyes to Ryan's face.

"Well, I've succeeded in impressing half of them." Ryan shrugged at Ferris. "What would it take to impress the sophisticated Miss Meredyth? To shoot the tail off a dragonfly? The eyelash off a gnat?" He turned teasing eyes on her that slowly widened with mock insanity. "Or perhaps one hair off her own head?'' He walked toward her slowly.

She backed off a step and gave him a disgusted look. He reached her and smiled into her eyes, a companionable smile, one that said they shared a secret. ''Trust me?'' he asked softly and reached up to deftly pluck one hair from her head. ''Now, if you'll take this''—he held the hair to his side between one raised and one lowered hand—''and hold it out just so, tautly. I shall split it from between your fingers.'' His eyes glittered with amusement.

Ferris laughed uncomfortably and came to stand next to Ryan. ''Oh, come now, you can't be serious. She'd fall away in a dead faint when the bullet whizzed by. And besides, suppose you were to hit her?''

''What? My staunchest ally losing faith? Surely you have more belief in me than that, Ferris.''

''Well, of course I do,'' Ferris blustered. ''I've no doubt you'd miss her, but why scare her to death? Besides, she'd never agree to it. I couldn't—that is, I don't think I should let her.'' At that Ryan's eyes shot to Catra.

Catra glared at Ferris. ''Just what do you mean, you couldn't *let* me?''

''Catra, surely you can't be considering this,'' Jane pleaded. ''Come now; we should be off. I must be home soon.''

''I just mean we're to be married. You're to be my wife. I can't have you getting shot up and all,'' Ferris defended under Catra's angry visage.

''Oh, good heavens, you said yourself he'd miss me! Where shall I stand, Mr. St. James?''

Ryan led her in silence to a spot and turned her toward him. ''Don't move, understand? And hold it out here, to the side, away from your body.'' He stopped and looked into her widened eyes, then chucked her under the chin.

"Good sport," he said seriously. "Let's hope you don't get killed for it."

Catra gaped at him, but he only gave her a ghost of a smile and turned away. As he sauntered back to Ferris and Jane, Catra suddenly wondered if she'd lost her mind. This man was about to shoot at her from *yards and yards* away. Was she *mad?* She barely even knew him. And what she did know was less than favorable. It was one thing to shoot a twig off a tree, but quite another to shoot a hair from between two violently shaking human hands.

"Are you ready?" he called, and she saw him motion from what seemed like an enormous distance for her to hold out her hands. "Ready?" he called again.

Catra could see Ferris saying something to Ryan and imagined him pleading for her, explaining her terror to the cold-hearted brigand. Determined not to be mollycoddled, she held out shaking arms, the thin blond hair stretched between them. Her heart beat wildly in her chest, and she thought she could see her hands shake in time with it. A bird twittered nearby, and she could just hear over her own shallow breathing a soft breeze in the trees. She felt her palms go damp and gripped the hair more tightly.

She looked back at the small group so far away and saw Jane with her hands to her face. Ryan loaded the pistol and Ferris faced him, gesturing in a half-awkward way. Catra was sure he was trying to reason Ryan into quitting.

At last Ryan patted Ferris on the shoulder and turned to her. He raised the pistol in what looked like an almost nonchalant manner, and Catra held her breath. The report of the pistol cracked the still air. Suddenly the taut hair between her fingers gave way. Her hands fell abruptly apart. She expelled a hard breath and brought her still-clenched fingers in front of her to see that the hair was gone.

The relief was so tangible, she couldn't help herself; she

began to laugh. By the time the group reached her, she was red-faced from laughter and embarrassment and could only turn smiling eyes upon her tormenter.

"Mr. St. James," she said, wiping her eyes, "you are truly an amazing individual."

"Ah," he said with satisfaction. "You noticed."

She smiled at him. "I couldn't help it."

"Great God in heaven, St. James! That was the most stunning thing I've ever witnessed," Ferris bubbled. "Absolutely the *most* stunning thing."

"Catra, how brave of you to stand there so still," Jane exclaimed. "I would have fainted dead away. Are you all right?"

"I'm fine, really." Catra glanced again at Ryan. Eventually the anxious solicitations subsided and they all turned to move back to the horses. Ferris and Jane walked ahead, still marveling over Ryan's skill and Catra's bravery, but Ryan hung back. Catra turned questioning eyes to him.

"Are you coming?" she asked.

He concentrated a moment on cleaning the barrel of his pistol as Ferris and Jane got farther away, then slowly raised his eyes to her. "You see?" he said with a small half-smile. "You do trust me. You don't want to, but you do." And with that he strode casually by her.

Chapter Four

Catra lay wide-eyed that night, thinking about the day. She relived again and again the way Ryan had raised the pistol so casually and without a moment's hesitation shot the hair she held a foot and a half from her body. He'd had no doubt he would miss her. He'd had no doubt he would hit the hair. She had to admire his confidence.

She remembered his eyes, laughing, as he'd led her to the spot where she was to stand; and the way the column of his throat had looked tan against his white shirt collar. She watched again in her mind's eye as he walked back to Ferris and Jane, narrow hips below the billowing white shirt, the sleeves rolled up against strong forearms. She remembered seeing a lock of his dark hair blow in the breeze that arose just before the shot, and that same lock afterwards falling against his forehead as he approached her.

"You see?" she heard again, remembering the flash of white teeth. "You do trust me . . ."

No, she thought, *I do not trust you. But I want to, and that is far more dangerous.*

She didn't bother to argue with herself about the decision she made that night; she just rose in the morning and dressed with care. She did her own hair, in a simple braid down her back, and left the house just after breakfast, before Bethia could corner her and sense her intentions.

She ran Jupiter hard, galloping across the familiar terrain in the crisp autumn air toward the path to the river.

When she came to the small clearing before the shore she saw his horse and smiled. He was here, just as she knew he would be, waiting for her. She trod softly through the brush, keeping to the path but moving silently in order to catch a glimpse of him before he saw her.

The water shot sunlight through the trees and onto the undersides of the leaves as she neared and peered through the foliage. He had his back to her and stood gazing out over the river, his hair reflecting blue-black highlights in the cool sun. He was like a finely groomed stallion, unaware of his own beauty and strength.

Ryan turned from the river to walk several yards downstream. She slipped back into the shadows a fraction, not ready to abandon her unabashed perusal of him.

His hands were in his pockets and he faced into the breeze, his eyes squinted against the glare off the water. Yes, it was a dashing figure he cut, she thought. Broad shouldered and sleek. His cheekbones high, his jaw cleanly shaven but still brushed with evidence of his beard. She remembered with a blush the feel of that beard against her cheek when he'd kissed her.

"It's nicer out here," he announced then, unexpectedly. His voice was loud and Catra jumped, glancing swiftly about the shore for whoever was with him. She was thankful that she had not simply walked out to him without considering whether or not he'd brought a companion. Her face felt positively scalded when she realized he might even have brought Ferris.

But she saw no one and heard no answer. Slowly he turned and faced the forest. "Or perhaps I should come in there? If it's as nice as all that." With a flash of that infuriating grin, he advanced in the direction of her position, and she realized with mortification that he was talking to her.

Blushing to the roots of her hair, she straightened and stepped out of the trees onto the shore. "I merely stopped to lace my boot." She kicked one heel up to show him, but managed only to coat the boot with sand. She stepped quickly forward. "And when I heard you speaking, I thought perhaps you had company, so I paused."

"What a straight-faced liar you are." But his eyes danced and the warmth of his smile thrilled her. "I'm glad you came," he added simply.

Catra's heart accelerated, but she forced herself to keep from smiling too broadly in return. "I felt I should compliment you on your extraordinary shooting yesterday afternoon, not to mention your eyesight." She spoke lightly, moving toward the water, but thought she could have done without the extraordinary eyesight today.

"I believe you already did so yesterday. In fact, I could not have been more gratified by your reaction. You were so relieved to be alive that the trust you had to have put in me must have been considerable, though what I've done to deserve it I may never know."

"You did nothing to deserve it," she replied pulling at her glove. He didn't need to do anything, she thought. That was the confounding part. "You may thank Ferris for my participation. I dislike being told what I should and shouldn't do."

"So you did it to spite him. I thought as much."

She turned toward him, ready to debate his choice of words, but he continued as if she hadn't moved.

"And since we're being so honest, I will confess that my eyesight, and I suppose therefore my aim, is not quite as superlative as you may think. I couldn't see the hair at all." He smiled at what must have been a surprised look on her face. "What I could see, my brave friend, were your hands, and the point in between was what I aimed for."

She exhaled, relieved that her status among the living was not owing to a mere stroke of luck.

"Why, how perfectly clever of you!" she exclaimed. She smiled at him as she removed her other glove. "To think we were all so dazzled by your ability to *see* the hair at such a great distance, when what you really sought to impress us with was the simple task of not shooting off all my fingers."

The look Ryan gave her was so disbelieving, so hurt, that she could not help but let loose a peal of laughter. "My goodness! Was it so important to you that we were impressed? You, with your disdain for public opinion?"

He turned partly away from her. "No, not particularly. And you're right, of course," he said, folding his hands behind his back and inclining his head toward her. "I don't generally care what people think. But I must confess I was hoping to impress *you*."

His answer—his unconcealed disappointment—produced within her an immediate stab of affection for him.

"Me?" She strolled to the water's edge, lightly slapping her gloves from one hand into the other. Trying to quell the butterflies in her stomach, she turned a teasing look on him. Parrying men's flattery was something with which she was quite familiar. "If that is the case, then I'm afraid you'll have to work harder than that. I would be more impressed if you were to excel at something that came perhaps less naturally to you.''

''Such as?''

She tilted her head, studying him. ''I'm not sure. Name something you do poorly.''

A grin started. ''That would be difficult. I am good,'' he said deliberately, ''at everything.''

The memory of his kiss popped onto her head, and she managed to just conceal the thrill that shot through her. She looked at the ground thoughtfully. ''I see. Then let me help you. You could start with modesty. Overcoming such over-whelming self-esteem would be most impressive.''

The grin did not disappear, but it did turn rueful. ''I shall endeavor to work at it, Miss Meredyth.''

She curbed an indulgent smile, delighted by his response. ''And perhaps at the same time you could improve your regard for women. If you were to accomplish both of those things I should be sincerely awed.''

He crossed his arms over his chest. ''Ah, but this I must protest. I have nothing but the highest regard for women. In fact I seek them out whenever possible, preferring their company to that of most men of my acquaintance.''

She raised a brow. ''I don't doubt you do. However, seeking female companionship is different from seeing us as intelligent persons rather than objects of salacious solic-itation.''

''Salacious solicitation,'' he repeated and laughed. ''A very pretty turn of phrase for one whose assets are purely physical.''

She felt, inexplicably, provoked and flattered at the same time. ''That, sir, is precisely the type of comment I mean. Such surprise—even such delighted surprise—over a ra-tional comment from a female is insulting.'' Catra moved toward him and touched the gloves lightly to his arm. ''You don't converse with me as an equal. You toy with me."

His eyes lowered. "Let me offer my sincerest apologies, then, Catra. If it's any consolation, I toy with everyone."

For a second, she felt deflated. Had she really expected him to feel the same exhilaration conversing with her that she did with him?

"But," he added, "I enjoy toying with you more than any other."

A smile rose to her lips and her heart skipped a beat. "If you think I shall take that as a compliment, you're mistaken," she lied, turning away. "I dislike being treated as a plaything. I would rather be considered ugly than slow, ill-favored than stupid."

"Fancy speech for one without either of those options."

Catra laughed and turned back to him, her arms crossed over her chest. "There; you see? You belittle me again. It is a dreadful habit of yours. Here is what you don't understand, Mr. St. James. Most women care not what you think of their face or their form, it is their mind they should like appreciated."

He chuckled. "Most women? I doubt that. Most of the women of my acquaintance would rather be considered pretty than anything else."

"That says much about the kind of company you keep, Mr. St. James, but little about women as a whole. You see, you've no idea what it is like to be judged solely on the basis of your sex." She hesitated. "Or perhaps you do, from the opposite point of view. You are a male and as such are naturally considered intelligent, productive and worthy of even the most complex of conversations. Do you tire of these perhaps groundless assumptions? Maybe you're bored with being expected to have knowledge you do not possess. Or even interest in such things as farming, say, or politics."

Ryan inclined his head, amusement on his face. "Point taken."

"I, on the other hand," she continued, warming to the subject, "as a female, am subjected to some of the most inane chatter ever produced. Imagine how you would feel if every stimulating conversation ground to a halt upon your arrival, only to be replaced by mindless chatter that serves no other purpose than to amuse. You wouldn't believe how fatiguing it is to be so constantly amused. I should love, just once, to be allowed to be beguiled by someone's mind, rather than tickled by their witticisms."

Ryan laughed, the look in his eyes admiring. "You have my leave, Miss Meredyth, to be beguiled by my mind at any time," he said with a bow. "But on behalf of my fellow clods, I must point out that perhaps those gentlemen to whom you refer were not altering their conversations to accommodate your inferior mind, but to spare you the tedium of their discussions."

"That," she said dryly, "is hardly likely."

He shook his head. "You are difficult to please, Miss Meredyth. I only wish someone would go to such lengths to amuse me."

"Oh, but we do, Mr. St. James," she breathed with a hard, exaggerated smile, fluttering an imaginary fan before her. "Why, we just do our poor little best to keep you gentlemen callers amused. Particularly our northern visitors. Lord knows, we go to great lengths to determine just *what* would please a Yankee."

Ryan held up his hands, wincing. "Please don't ever resort to such measures, Catra, or I shall give up all hope for intelligent females. You are the most remarkable creature I've ever met. Truly, I'd almost despaired of finding a woman like you."

Catra smiled, flushed with delight. She couldn't remember the last time she'd so enjoyed a conversation.

"Now, now, Mr. St. James," she said, shaking her head. "That kind of flattery is a form of amusement, and I believe I've made myself quite clear on that subject."

"Compliments are inadmissible?"

"On pain of death."

Ryan's gaze rested on her face, his eyes glittering with the smile on his lips. "I'm sorry to be so amused, but I'm afraid it must come naturally to you. Do try to be more dull or I shall have to resort to witticisms in return."

Catra gave him a sly look. "You've done tolerably well without them so far."

Ryan laughed so thoroughly that against her will Catra felt laughter bubble up within her too. And a strange thing happened when she let it out. She discovered that laughing with this man made her feel more of an equal than she ever had before in her life.

And the feeling was dangerous.

With a deep breath Catra noted the angle of the sun and informed Ryan that she had merely intended to ride for a short while. She had tarried far too late with him. Lord knew, she couldn't afford to stay and enjoy him any longer lest she throw caution and sanity completely to the wind and take him up on his earlier offer.

"I'm sorry to have kept you so long," Ryan said. "I would hate to have you hesitate to come back on the morrow."

Her heart jumped in her chest. "Hesitate? Whatever made you think I would come at all?"

Ryan shrugged, bent down and picked up a stone from the sandy beach. "I'll promise to be intelligent. I'll work up some topics tonight." He looked down at the rock he had retrieved and turned it in his fingers. "It's pretty, isn't it?" he mused, extending it to her.

Catra looked at the offering, resisting the temptation to take it. She did not want to risk even their fingers brushing or she might find herself doing something she would later regret. "Keep it for yourself," she said. "You need it, do you not? You gave your old good luck charm to Jimmy."

"Very well." He pocketed the stone. "I shall see how much luck this stone brings. If you come tomorrow I'll vow never to part with it."

"I'm sorry," she said gently, "but, as much as I've enjoyed our conversation, it would not be proper for me to continue to meet you. Someone might misconstrue our intentions."

Ryan came toward her and took her hands in his. Catra's heart leapt at the contact and she debated pulling away, but her hands felt too good in his.

"I know you won't believe me, but I have a great deal of respect for you." His gaze made her face hot, but she could not look away. "And if you don't come tomorrow, or even ever again, I want you to know that there is at least one person—one man—on earth who bows to your superiority." His hands pressed hers lightly. "I only wish I could alter every man's mind to see you as I do. But to be completely free of our amusements, I'm afraid you would have to become a man; and that would be a crime too great for even me to wish to see."

Catra, concentrating with great fortitude upon his speech and not the touch of his fingers, was left breathless by his words. She hardly knew what to say in response and was acutely sorry when he took his hands from hers. He dropped his gaze and stepped back.

"I wish you would come tomorrow," he said. "If I could visit you in the proper manner I would. I would come make pretty speeches to you and talk to your father of— farming and politics." He smiled gently. "I would bring flowers and say all the right things. But I'm forbidden to come—and rightly so. So I am robbed of your presence except for what I can beg from you now. I won't compromise you, Catra. I'll even behave with the utmost propriety; more than you may suspect I am capable of. But I would like see you.''

Catra swallowed hard, wondering if this was how he'd managed to get such a reputation with women. He was too charming. Too virile. Too attractive for his own good.

''But you see you are not capable of complete propriety. Even now you call me by my given name and hold my hands.'' She wrestled for a moment with her next words. ''However, you should understand that it is not only because of you that I refuse. I confess I—I do not dare trust myself to return.'' The spark of excitement she saw plainly in his eyes unnerved her and, fearful of the fire onto which she had thrown such kindling, she added quickly, ''And I dare not risk what others might think. If people were to misunderstand our—our desire to converse innocently, I could lose a great deal.''

''What, Catra?'' he asked gently. ''Do you think you would lose Ferris? To be honest, I doubt you would. But, even if you did, you don't love him. I can see it in your eyes when you speak to him. What else might you lose? Not your family. Not your wealth. Reputation, perhaps. But without that, you might be treated less delicately, less as an object to be pampered and protected, and more as a person who makes her own choices—''

''That isn't so, and you know it,'' she protested, her heart hammering in sudden fear. Of what, she was not sure. Herself, perhaps.

''Do I? You said yourself you wished to be rid of the posturing, the falseness—what better way than to do as you please and the devil take the consequences?''

She laughed helplessly, incredulous. "But I do not wish to be *shunned*, as you very well know would happen. Do not pretend my fears are groundless when you know they're not." Catra turned from his outrageous suggestion, her body shaking with the uncomfortable feelings he aroused in her. His words hit a nerve. Something inside her longed to show the world that she could make her own decisions, be her own woman, free of the constrictions of society. The idea of throwing social values to the wind at once intrigued and terrified her. All her life she'd been governed by "what people would think." And something inside told her that if she were to decide right now to ignore society's dictates, she could live free of them for the rest of her life.

But of course she couldn't. It was not just society's promise she would lose, not just her friends, her family, her home and station in life. No, she would lose Braithwood to her cousin, and even if she could consider life outside the only home she'd ever known, she could never forget Jimmy. For she would be solely responsible for him once her father passed on, and she loved him far too much to jeopardize his future.

She watched the toe of her boot dislodge some of the rocks near the shore, then glanced across the river.

Behind her, Ryan said softly. "I wish you could be just a little bit bolder, though I know it's not the correct way for a young lady to behave. Perhaps then you might be persuaded to do something foolish with me."

Catra turned and looked at him, at the charming half-smile, the intensely sensual eyes, the rakish posture, and she knew that if she were to give in to his invitation she would risk everything. Still, it tempted her more than she liked to admit.

"Something foolish?" she asked him. "Or something stupendously unwise? I know my choices, Mr. St. James."

"Yes, we all know our choices," he said. He pulled the stone from his pocket again and studied it for a moment.

She took a deep breath. "Good-bye, Mr. St. James," she said decidedly, turning from the water. "I've enjoyed talking with you. Perhaps we shall meet again someday, in a proper location."

He watched her walk toward the path. "Perhaps."

She looked at him for a long moment. "I'm sure of it. Someone will give a ball somewhere and there you shall be, ready to blind me with your intelligence, and I shall promise to be amused by it."

He gazed at her and slowly tossed the stone back onto the beach. Catra fought the urge to pick it up, suddenly curious about what he'd found pretty.

"Just remember one thing," he said.

"What is that?" She was unable to tear her eyes from his.

"You like me," he said with the shadow of a smile.

With a slow nod she said, "Yes. I do."

Three days later, after Catra's father had left for Richmond and Bethia had gone to town, a visitor was announced. Bard opened the door of the drawing room, where Catra was reading in a slant of late afternoon sunshine, and ushered in none other than Ryan St. James.

He looked even more handsome than she remembered him—and she remembered him often. When she got up, when she got dressed, when she went out, when she went to sleep.

He wore a dark brown frock coat and buff-colored pants, and as he leaned against the doorframe she wondered how he could look so remarkable in such everyday garb. Ordinarily it took something like fancy evening attire to create a man so striking.

"What are you doing here?" she whispered urgently after Bard had departed, leaving the door quite properly open. "If Bethia returns and finds you—" She broke off at his amused expression, realizing he wasn't the least bit concerned about Bethia's whereabouts.

"She's only just left," Ryan responded. "Besides, it's been several days since we last parted and you decided once again never to see me. I wanted to see if you could do it three times in a row."

Catra fought to conceal the excitement in her heart but gave up when she could not contain her smile. "You know," she said, "if I didn't happen to be bored with this book, I would consider you an insufferably conceited rake."

"As it is, I appear interesting?"

Catra laughed. "Precisely."

He smiled, too, and the look they shared was so intimate it bespoke their growing understanding of one another. They were very similar, she realized. He was, she thought, just the way she would like to be if she were a man.

"You may as well come in," she said, "since the damage is already done and my father will discover that you've come. I don't suppose it occurred to you that I might be the one to suffer the consequences of this visit, and not you."

"Actually, it did occur to me." He strolled into the room. "But I decided to come anyway. However, in keeping with my newfound desire to behave in a chivalrous and gentlemanly fashion, I shall await your father's return and fend for both you and myself."

"Heavens, what a cavalier attitude. I'll pretend to believe that you didn't know he was out of town. But even if he weren't, I would talk you out of it. He would only order you off the property again, and then we should never be able to talk even if we happened to meet somewhere. I should be obliged to snub you at every opportunity.''

"And that would disturb you, would it?''

"Immensely. Just think of the inconvenience.'' She gave him a teasing smile. "You and my betrothed are friends. We would meet, occasionally, in a social context.''

Ryan crossed one leg over the other, his ankle resting on one knee. "Tell me something,'' he said, leaning forward. "What is the real reason you're marrying Ferris?''

Catra paused. "You say that as if I might have some ulterior motive.''

He shrugged lightly.

"That question does you no credit, Mr. St. James. I'm disappointed in you.''

"Which makes me think you had some high expectation of me. How gratifying. But it was merely a question. I meant no disrespect.''

"Ferris is your host,'' Catra insisted. "And my betrothed,'' she added with less enthusiasm. Speaking of Ferris with Ryan brought out uncomfortable comparisons between the two. Comparisons that did little to reconcile her to her choice of a fiancé. "Surely you owe him the decency of not asking such things behind his back.''

"All right. If it bothers you, forget I asked.'' He leaned back once again. "It seems I've already fallen off my gentlemanly perch, so to speak. It doesn't appear I'm cut out for . . . for courting.''

Catra nearly choked on the word. "*Courting?* Who on earth are you courting?''

She could not be sure, but she thought he blushed.

"Why, you, of course.'' He smiled, but his hands were clasped tightly in front of him. "And please don't tell me you don't like it or I shall be disheartened. I am, after all, a beginner.''

Catra laughed and felt her face flame, consumed with feelings, none of which she could name. Surely he was joking, and yet his expression had an element of self-consciousness that had her heart soaring in her chest.

In lieu of any other response, she fell back on the obvious. "You can't court *me*. I am betrothed. I should not even be speaking with you."

"Is that how it works?" He rose from his chair and rubbed his palms absently on his pants. "I had thought one was not truly off limits until one had spoken some sort of vow." He moved toward the settee where she sat, his eyes averted.

"Of course the ceremony is yet to come, but one would hardly ever break one's betrothal agreement," she stammered as he approached. Craning her neck to look up at him, she continued, "Particularly not for one whose idea of courtship is—is—"

"Is what?" He sat close beside her on the love seat.

"Is—is surreptitious meetings, innuendo, and continual—verbal—sparring." She just got the last word out as he bent his head to hers and caught her lips in a simple yet eloquent kiss.

"You shouldn't have done that," she whispered, staring at the lips that had just left hers.

He inhaled deeply. "I know. I just wanted to be sure," he said softly, his face still near, his hand resting softly along the nape of her neck, "that you tasted as sweet as I remembered." He kissed her again, slowly, his tongue touching her lips, urging them to open to him. When they did, the kiss deepened and his other arm found her waist, pulling her to him.

Catra's thoughts whirled in her head, none of them alighting long enough to provoke any action. Her body was awash in unfamiliar longings and swift fingers of excitement trilled up her spine. Her hands seemed to rise of their own volition, moving up to his jacket to pull him closer.

Ryan pulled back, and Catra reluctantly let him go. Neither said a word as they looked into the other's eyes. Ryan's expression was intense and his breath came fast and furious, like hers. Catra stared at him, trying to figure out why she didn't order him out of the house immediately. But she couldn't. All she wanted to do was kiss him again.

There was no trace of humor in his face, no ironic twist to his lips or amused chuckling at his triumph over her. What she thought she saw on his face was a confusion similar to her own.

"What are you doing to me?" she whispered.

Ryan's eyes did not leave hers.

"I don't know," he murmured, his expression as overwhelmed and disconcerted as she felt. "My feelings . . . I . . ." He shook his head, his gaze as vulnerable as she'd ever seen it. His hand found hers and gripped it. "I feel . . . God help me."

Catra's heart lifted and her fingers tightened around his. "God help us both."

Chapter Five

Catra's toe tapped a rapid rhythm on the front porch as her eyes bored into the wall around which the chaise would come. Where was that groom? She'd sent for the chaise fifteen minutes ago. She had to see Mayliza. Her mind was a tumult of emotions and until she could verbalize them to her friend she wouldn't know what to make of them.

At last the groom trotted around the corner with the chaise and a sprightly bay in tow. Catra lifted her skirts, hastened down the steps and met him on the drive. Without a word she jumped into the carriage and snapped the reins, sending the horse into sudden motion and the groom scrambling to get out of the way.

The day was crisp and sunny, and Catra felt an energy she hadn't known in weeks. True, she was exhilarated by the spectacular autumn weather, but the knowledge of Ryan St. James's feelings for her was the real cause of her mood.

Mayliza did not live far away. Down the drive to the

county road and then a couple of miles to the Richmond road. The Thayers were just this side of Fredericksburg, the closest town.

Mayliza greeted her curiously. Catra was welcome at any time, she always said, but Catra knew it was uncharacteristic of her to arrive before the morning meal. Mayliza invited Catra into the breakfast room, where the rest of the Thayers were dining.

Catra sat but could barely contain herself during the long, social meal. She had so much to tell Mayliza, so much to ask her, that the time it took little Will to butter his toast, and the tediousness of Mrs. Thayer's story about her bug-ridden peonies nearly drove her to distraction.

When at last they were alone in the parlor she could barely contain herself.

"Mayliza, I think I'm in terrible trouble," she announced the moment the door shut behind her friend. She whirled away after the words and plopped dramatically on the sofa.

"I thought something must have happened to get you up so early this morning. What is it?" Mayliza sat across from her on the divan, leaning forward with her hands clasped and her elbows on her knees.

Catra swallowed, all at once reluctant to simply blurt out the story. If she told her friend, she realized, spilling the news the way she had been dying to do since last night, she would be putting it on a level with all the other useless bits of gossip they shared. And for some reason she couldn't define, she was afraid that making her feelings for Ryan known would diminish or jinx them.

But there was Mayliza, so anxious, so expectant, waiting to hear this shocking thing that Catra had led up to.

"It's rather strange," she began, hoping if she weighed her words carefully, perhaps she could bring up the topic with the proper amount of discretion and import. "Some-

87

thing's happened I didn't count on. Something . . . strange."

"What is it?" Mayliza's eyes were round in her face. "You said you're in trouble? What sort of trouble? You've driven all this way—now *tell me.*"

"Well . . . it's a secret."

"A *secret.*" Mayliza sat back.

"I mean, it's something I haven't told anyone. And you can't possibly breathe a word . . ."

Curiosity turned to affront. "Of course I wouldn't, not under any circumstances. Why are you speaking this way? You've told me hundreds of secrets."

"This isn't like those secrets." Catra wrung her hands and watched her uncertainly. "This is not—oh, I don't know—This is so important to me. Really important." She fixed her friend with an imploring look. "Please understand."

Mayliza crossed her arms over her chest. "What's happened?" Abruptly the girlish excitement was gone and Mayliza became the true confidant Catra had known her to be when she'd raced over here at breakneck speed. It was easy to forget, she thought, in the frivolous life of parties and balls they'd been leading, that their friendship was built on something deep, a complete, secure confidence.

"I've fallen in love," Catra said quietly, sounding incredulous even to herself, "with Ryan St. James."

Time stood still for a moment, Catra felt, and she pictured even autumn leaves stopping midfall from the trees. Mayliza's expression froze and the only sound that marked the existence of either of them was the ticking of the mantel clock.

"And he has with me," she added after a moment.

Her words broke the spell and Mayliza expelled a breath.

"Ryan St. James. Catra, what are you saying? How has this happened?''

The relief Catra felt with the admission was palpable. ''I've met him since the party. At first it was in company, until one day I happened upon him in a secluded place. I was riding, early, and he was too. We met upon the south hill, near the path to the river. I have to admit I'd been thinking about him. But to suddenly see him there! It was quite shocking. Anyway, he wanted to apologize—'' She stopped, suddenly realizing she'd never told Mayliza about the incident in the garden.

''For?'' Mayliza prompted.

Catra made great work of pulling a handkerchief from her pocket. ''Yes, well, he had—some cause. . . . Do you remember at the party, just before I''—she paused, searching for another word but having to use the obvious—''well, just before I fainted.'' She reddened with the memory. ''You remember, when I came from the patio with Father?'' Mayliza nodded, comprehension dawning on her face. ''And Ryan had just stormed in, you said, looking angry.''

''Did he—did he—compromise you?'' Mayliza exhaled.

Catra flushed. ''Of course not. He merely kissed me.''

''He *kissed* you?'' Mayliza leaned forward again. ''Something tells me this was not a simple peck on the cheek. . . .''

Catra shook her head, studying the handkerchief in her hand.

''How *was* it?''

Catra glanced up at Mayliza and laughed. ''That part was wonderful.'' Her gaze drifted off to a corner of the room. ''Like nothing I've ever felt before. It was almost frightening, the way I did not ever want to stop, the feeling I had of fearing myself more than him.'' She straightened and directed her eyes at Mayliza. "But Father caught us."

"Oh, my."

"Yes, for a moment I thought the world would end. That's why he was so angry. And Ryan too, I suppose, though he said nothing at the time. Father ordered him off the property. Oh, it was dreadful. But in any case, that's what he was apologizing for."

Mayliza sat back. "That explains a lot."

"What do you mean?"

"Didn't you hear what happened after you fainted? I thought sure Lucy would have told you, with relish. Your Mr. St. James made an enormous fuss over you. I don't know why I didn't make more of it at the time, but I guess I thought he simply knew more what to do about unconscious women than the rest of us. He has such an air of competence about him." Mayliza stood and wandered a few steps to the window.

"Yes," Catra murmured. She had, of course, heard the story from Lucy, but she wanted to hear the whole thing again, from Mayliza's point of view.

"Then," she continued, "and this I do remember thinking was odd, after he'd picked you up, he looked directly at your father, in a very challenging way now that I think on it, and asked where your bedchamber was. Not 'Where can I take her?' or 'Is there a sofa?' but 'Where is her bedchamber?' Your father was noticeably taken aback. That's about the time he ordered Ferris to take you from Ryan."

"Ryan *challenged* Father? Lucy didn't tell me that. Good Lord, that's even worse than I knew. Why didn't you tell me this earlier? Oh, I *knew* I should have come before. I wanted to tell you about the kiss all along, but I had such unsettled feelings about it." The handkerchief was now a dense ball wadded into the palm of her hand.

"I planned to come to see you too, of course, but Miss Bellyaches upstairs . . ." Mayliza rolled her eyes toward the ceiling, indicating the room where her sickly aunt stayed. "She couldn't be without me, and Mother hasn't been home much, what with the Carters in town."

Catra stood and joined her friend at the window. "It seems so long ago now, that night."

"What did your father say? After it all happened, I mean."

"He never mentioned it again. But he left for Richmond just afterward and won't be back until tomorrow."

"Oh," she said, surprised. "I didn't know he was going away."

"Yes, that's part of the reason I wanted to talk to you today. These feelings I have for Ryan—I just know something could happen if we were allowed to see each other. You know, let the . . . friendship develop naturally. So I need to speak to Father about the engagement. I would like him to receive Ryan, but that would never happen while I'm engaged to Ferris. And I just don't know what I'll do if I can't see him. I can't stop thinking of him. So you see, I can't possibly marry Ferris, not with the way I feel about Ryan."

Mayliza put her hand gently on Catra's arm. "But—has Ryan offered for you?"

Catra looked down, then away. "Not—officially."

"Do you think he intends to?"

Catra threw her hands down and turned from the window. "I don't know. He's so confusing. He kisses me with such passion. And he compliments me, and talks to me like—like an equal. He told me he was afraid of his feelings for me."

Mayliza watched her deposit herself into a chair.

"But Father will never receive him." Catra sighed.

"Why should he? I've betrothed myself to Ferris, and betrothed women do not have gentleman callers."

Mayliza knelt by Catra's chair and gazed up at her. "Perhaps if you explained to your father—told him all you've told me—perhaps he would understand. After all, he was in love once, wasn't he? With your mother? He might remember and sympathize with your feelings."

"Do you think so? Do you think I can convince him to let me cancel the wedding?"

Mayliza thought for a moment, then stood up, sighing. "No."

Catra slumped back. "I don't either. Oh, it's all so confusing. What in the world does Ryan want? If I knew he wanted to marry me, it would be easier. But I can't simply tell my father that I want to postpone my wedding so another man can court me."

"You need to discover if what Ryan wants is marriage," Mayliza stated. "Surely he will understand that you cannot continue to see him if he is not ready to propose. You would be forsaking all your future prospects for nothing."

"He cares nothing for such things." Catra waved a hand, wondering how on earth she could explain to her friend that in some secret, forbidden way, she didn't care about propriety or future prospects either. At least some of the allure of Ryan St. James was the idea of running free with him, of being a worldly woman who did what she wanted without bowing to society. How could she tell Mayliza that part of what set her heart thundering in her chest was the feeling he gave her of independence? Of courage? Of real strength?

She couldn't. Because it was ludicrous, thinking she could, should or even *would* throw her future—and Jimmy's—to the winds. No amount of independence would make up for losing her home and being shunned by her friends and family.

"Oh, it's no use," Catra continued. "I don't blame him for not asking for my hand. We barely know each other. And he is not the type for marriage. No, I know what I must do. I suppose I've been deluding myself, thinking there might be some other answer. Just . . . dreaming. The only thing for me to do is stop this before it goes any further. I must have been crazy to think anything could come of it." She paused for a moment. "But it's funny . . . when I'm with him it all seems possible. Everything seems . . . so possible."

Mayliza patted Catra's arm. "It might be for the best to let him go, dearest. As daring and romantic as it all sounds, I can't see your father alienating the Chesters for what would most likely appear to him a whim. And it's natural for women about to get married to suddenly feel they've fallen for someone else. I believe I've heard a dozen stories like that."

Catra frowned. Disappointment hung like a flatiron in her chest. "You're probably right. Of course you're right." Her hands gripped the ends of the handkerchief in two tight fists. "But I don't know how I'll do it. I've told him I'll meet him again today and I'm not sure I have the strength to withstand him."

"Of course you have the strength. You're one of the strongest people I know, Catra," Mayliza chastened, then added cautiously, "but if you do have qualms, you might keep in mind what people are saying about him."

"Who? What are people saying?"

"Just that he's something of a lady's man. They say he's got a woman in every port and can't stand to stay in one place very long without—" Mayliza stopped, her expression horrified at what she was about to say. But she had clearly gone too far to stop. "Well, without a dalliance of some sort. Now, that's not to say that you are that dalliance. I don't know that he's ever admitted to having feelings for someone before. . . ."

Catra looked at her helplessly. "They're saying that? Who told you this?"

Mayliza gave a rueful shrug. "Well, some of it was Dahlia, so you needn't take the part about the dalliances so seriously. But the other came from Roberta Jenkins. She's apparently met him in Richmond before. In fact, now that I think about it, she said there was some sort of scandal involving him recently that she never did get the details of. She just heard his name bandied about some. And then she's seen him at several of the balls there with women all over him, much like they were here."

Catra stayed limp in the chair. "I think I'm a fool, May. I think I've set myself up for a terrible disappointment."

"That's not necessarily true. These are just stories, Cat. And stories always follow men as handsome as Ryan St. James. You need to speak to him and find out the truth." Mayliza sat on the sofa across from her. "Then, if all goes well, you need to speak with your father. He may well understand when you explain."

"He won't understand," Catra said hopelessly. "There will be nothing to understand. Ryan has no intention of offering marriage, I'm sure of it now. What a fool I am. I had him pegged the first time I met him, and yet I ignored it. He has already told me all I need to know. Now it's up to me to tell him the way things will be."

An hour later Ryan drilled her with those impossible eyes and took her by the shoulders to turn her fully toward him. "Have you suddenly developed a passion for Ferris to rival what you feel for me? Is that what has happened to make you shun me again? I should never have left you alone yesterday. What in the world have you been thinking?''

"The question is, what was I thinking yesterday while I was with you?'' she answered far more calmly than she felt. "I woke up this morning thinking about Ferris and my father. They're never going to let me out of my betrothal. Why should they? I agreed to it. And if there's one thing my father taught me, it's that we must abide by the choices we make. I'm surprised you haven't learned this lesson in your own life.''

Ryan studied her thoughtfully. "Yes, we make choices. And we have choices made for us. Which is yours, Catra? Did you truly want to marry Ferris, or did you do it to comply with the wishes of your father?''

"Whatever my motivations might have been won't matter to my father. The fact is, Ferris asked, I said yes and the promise was made. The choice *was* mine. How can I renege on it now?''

"The trick to choices is to tell the good ones from the bad ones before it's too late. And it's not too late for you, Catra. You're not married yet. You're young. You have feelings you haven't even recognized yet, feelings for me. Powerful feelings, Catra. I can see them when I look at you, feel them when I hold you. And they are matched,'' he said with a dark smile, "by mine for you. Take my word, Catra, this is not something that happens often. You don't know yet, but I do, passion like ours is hard to find. Are you willing to throw that all away for a life of mediocrity?''

This was a powerful tonic, a heady brew of words that left Catra with the dizzy sense of having left reality behind. She had grown up wanting something different—an exciting, eccentric, nonconformist life. When she was younger she'd wanted to go to Paris to study art. Then she'd wanted to go to India, the Orient, somewhere other than here, where she'd spent her whole life. No matter what she did, though, she did *not* want to be like every other girl she knew, repeating the same lives lived by their mothers and grandmothers, and *their* mothers and grandmothers.

But then she'd grown up. She'd realized she had to care for Jimmy, and she had to save Braithwood from the clutches of her cousin. More than anything else, though, she'd become afraid, so afraid, of what it took to be different.

"You don't have to sell yourself for your father," he added quietly. "Does your father even know how you feel?"

She tried to turn away, but his grip was too tight. "It doesn't matter. He would do nothing if he knew; he *could* do nothing. I've committed myself; I gave Ferris the answer to his question, no one else. And how could I hurt Ferris like that? He's been my friend my entire life. No, I can't back out now."

"Oh, but you can, Catra. You feel trapped, but you're not. You *can* change your mind. Do you think it's kinder to Ferris to marry him and not love him? Doesn't he deserve a wife who *wants* to be with him?"

Catra stopped, looking up at Ryan with a kind of desperation. This was something she had not considered before—that Ferris might be better off without her.

She tore her eyes from Ryan's and turned away, clutching her head with her hands. "Oh, I don't *know.* I don't know. I can't make all these decisions for everyone else. It's all so confusing."

"No, it isn't," he said quietly.

She turned with a frustrated growl. "Yes, it is. Oh, I'm so *tired* of your easy answers for everything. Suppose I do break my engagement. Then what? What possible reason could I give my father for changing my mind? What exactly are *you* offering, Ryan?''

"Freedom," he said then, urgently. "Love. A life of excitement and passion. You know that's what you want, Catra."

She forced herself to hold his gaze, forced the words out with a strength she did not feel. "But nothing so ordinary as marriage."

He dropped her shoulders and stepped back, looking at her as if she'd just proposed murder.

She laughed, breathlessly. "I see. Yes, I see now. There is nothing I can do."

"Catra," he said gently and pulled her into his arms, "there is never nothing you can do. You just need to decide what you want to do. And how badly you want it." His hand reached up to stroke her hair, softly, so softly. "I'll never marry, Catra. I can't. I swore to myself years ago I would never do it."

The pain within her chest was surely her heart breaking. She stood frozen in his embrace. "How convenient."

He pushed her away and looked at her until she raised her eyes. "It's not convenient, Catra. Not at all. But it is the way I am. I abhor the institution of marriage and I believe it would do you no good either."

She shook her head. "Whether or not it would do me good, it is my future."

"Why? *Why* is it your future? Can't you take another path? One not quite so well worn? You and I belong to-gether."

She threw her gaze skyward and laughed incredulously. "You don't even know what you're asking. You know nothing of my life."

He gave her a little shake, but his voice was gentle. "Then tell me. Maybe I can help you."

She looked at him, uncertain, yet tempted beyond reason, to tell him everything. About Jimmy, about her cousin. If nothing else, to prove to him that she was not so cowardly as he might think. But she didn't trust him, she realized, not really. She might be falling in love with him, but she didn't know him.

"What have you got against marriage?" she asked then. "You said you will never marry, but why? Surely there is a reason."

He straightened and his grip loosened on her arms. His hands slid down to grasp her fingers. He looked down at their joined hands. "I believe marriage ruins women," he said, looking back up at her. "Destroys their spirit, makes them into something their husbands don't want and they themselves can't stand."

"And the life of a harlot is a better one?"

He smiled slightly. "I'm not asking you to be a harlot. Just to live a more eccentric, more independent life."

"Independent?" She shook her head. "I doubt that. In fact a woman living outside the bounds of propriety probably finds herself more dependent on the mercy of society than the one living within it."

One corner of his mouth lifted in an ironic smile. "So you will attach yourself to Ferris Chester in marriage so that you are not at the mercy of society? You don't think once you've married him society will have new demands? They will be clamoring next for a child. And then another one. You will have to be the perfect hostess, the perfect mother, the perfect wife. Don't you think that before long you will become the same as every other matron in the country? Of course you would. What sort of independence is that?"

Catra's hands lay still in his, docile, but her heart hammered in her chest. "You ask a great deal of me to satisfy your own prejudice. All I can think is that your mother must have been a very unhappy woman.''

He laughed. ''Actually, no. She loves my father. And she rules the roost.''

''So this is purely your own invention, this aversion to marriage.''

''My *invention*, if you will,'' he said in a hard voice, ''is that I'll not let myself be pushed into a life I don't want. Just as you shouldn't. It does no one any good.''

''Fine,'' she snapped, yanking her hands out of his. ''Then I will not have *you* forcing me into a life either. I have my own concerns to consider. And it's not just that I want to be married and become the perfect hostess. I have responsibilities, something you don't seem to know much about.''

''You have a responsibility to yourself.'' He folded his arms over his chest. ''But if you prefer to let others make your decision, that's your right.''

''I have a responsibility to my brother.'' She glared at him, then turned away and took a step toward the river. She sighed slowly. ''You know how he is. His birth was a difficult one. Some complications arose, and he was delivered after my mother died. He was blue, they said, when he was born.'' She swallowed and turned back to him. ''Because of that he'll never truly develop; he will be a child his whole life. And my father's will, as dictated by *his* father, is that Braithwood be left to me *only* if I marry. If I do not, it must go to his closest male relative, who— because Jimmy is the way he is—would be my cousin. Unfortunately *he* would think nothing of his responsibility to me or to Jimmy. He rarely thinks of anyone other than himself. And so you see, we would be quite destitute, Jimmy and I, if we were to lose Braithwood.''

''So you must marry,'' Ryan murmured.

"That's right." She took a deep breath to calm herself, but she could not help glaring at him.

"But you don't have to marry Ferris. You could marry someone you loved, if you wanted."

Catra hesitated, looking out over the water. "I suppose that's true. But I have agreed to marry Ferris. And without . . ." She chose her words carefully, turning to look out over the water. "Without just cause, reneging on the betrothal would be impossible."

"You think Ferris would sue you for breach of promise?"

"I don't know." But she doubted it. She turned back to Ryan, determined. "In any case, we must forget this ever happened. You must promise me you will. We will undoubtedly meet again, on social terms, after I am married. And I do not want to feel this hanging in the air every time we are in the same room. Above all I do not want Ferris to know. Ever."

He expelled a deep breath and moved away. Turning to follow him with her eyes, she saw him brace his boot on one of the fallen trees that lay on the sand, his back to her. His hand raked back through his dark hair.

In a decisive motion, Catra picked up her skirts and started toward the path to leave.

At the sound of her petticoats, he turned swiftly and she stopped, caught by the look on his face. The lock of dark hair had loosened and lay on his forehead, above eyes that betrayed confusion. In those transparent gray depths she saw the torment of indecision, the struggle of wanting to say something but holding back. The intensity of the look made her nerves tremble and reminded her that with Ryan she was playing with fire.

"There is nothing else to do, Ryan," she said, still half hoping he would contradict her, offer her hope, love, *mar-*

riage. "For appearances' sake—for Ferris's sake—we must never let on what's passed between us. Please. We must appear to act normally when we meet again. Now I'd best be going. I've been gone too long."

Ryan looked at her enigmatically, then stepped closer and took her hand. "All right. I will mask my feelings," he said, a hint of hardness in his tone, "for appearances' sake. But you will know, every time you look at me, that I have not forgotten. I will never forget." He leaned over and touched her lips with his, lingering. She closed her eyes and fought the urge to touch him. She didn't look at him as he pulled back, but turned and walked back up the path to the horses.

Early the following morning a light tapping sounded at Catra's bedroom door. Through the fog of sleep, she was unsure she'd actually heard anything when it occurred again. She pushed back the covers and slid her feet to the chilly floor. The room was bathed in early morning sunlight and she could hear breakfast sounds from the kitchen through her open window. Pots clanged against one another, a door slammed and the creak of the pump sounded.

Catra moved silently and opened the door a crack. Seth, one of the stable boys, stood holding a folded piece of paper, his attention momentarily taken from the door as he gazed anxiously down the hall. His hand was still raised to knock again.

"What is it, Seth?" she whispered. The boy jumped at the sound of her voice and thrust the paper toward her.

"A man asked me to give this to you," he explained nervously. "I ain't supposed to be in the house."

"I know, Seth. That's all right." She took the paper from him. "Run along now. No one's up yet and I won't tell."

Without another word the boy sped off down the hall on coltish legs, quiet and quick.

Catra closed the door and examined the paper. It was thick writing paper that had been folded around a small object. She opened it carefully. There, amid fine black handwriting, was a smooth marbled stone such as was common on the shore of the river.

She cupped the stone in her hand and pressed its smooth surface into her palm. *Meet me, please. One last time,* the note read.

She read the line again and tried to quell the immediate pounding of her heart by analyzing each curl and slash of the masculine handwriting. She had no doubt who it was from—she'd known the moment she felt the stone—as he had probably intended. It was considerate; no one but herself would know who had written the note.

She would go, of course. As soon as she could get her trembling knees to move, she would go.

The day was cool but the sun, unhindered by clouds, warmed her back. She rode quickly but not at the reckless pace she wanted to ride. She made a point of keeping to a controlled canter. How undignified it would be to arrive all in a lather, overanxious and expecting—what? He wanted to see her. What had he to say? It was all she could do to keep herself from whipping Jupiter into a frenzy.

She distracted herself by picturing Ryan's face and reliving every word, every touch, from the previous day. She saw again his pale eyes, their troubled depths speaking emotions he would not put into words. She recalled the way his hand pulled through the waves of his hair, brushing the one unruly lock from his forehead, only to have it fall again in an arc just above the sweep of one of his lean, dark brows. She saw his firm mouth soften into a smile, then grow serious to kiss her. Kiss her good-bye.

Until the ball a week ago, she had never dreamed of the depths of emotion with which she now wrestled, would not have been able to fathom the irrational moods and feelings she now dealt with every time the thought of Ryan St. James entered her head.

At the bottom of the last hill she slowed the heaving horse to a walk. She stopped at the entrance of the path to the river and slid from the saddle. Willing herself to move slowly, she led Jupiter down the wooded path.

When she reached the clearing she found, tethered to a tree, the large bay that Ryan had been riding the day before.

Despite the knowledge that he would be there, her heart leapt to her throat. She tethered Jupiter next to the bay with trembling hands which then flew to her face, frantically wisping away stray hairs and pinching her cheeks for color.

Then, throwing self-control to the wind, she took off in a run down the path toward the beach. The branches whipped at her skirts and clawed at her hair, yet she ran on to emerge from the forest at the edge of the beach, her hair loosened and streaming around her face in long golden strands. Her eyes glittered with excitement and her breath came in rapid bursts as she quickly scanned the sandy cove.

Downstream, by the water's edge, he turned swiftly at the sound of her arrival. Their eyes fused, and Catra's face glowed with the sight of him, her chest heaving with the exertion of running.

She made no move and said nothing. She merely stood, letting her eyes lay helplessly upon him, every emotion laid bare in their blue depths, her longing exposed to his searching gaze.

He reached her in four swift strides, folding her roughly into his arms, holding her so tightly that the breath left her body in a gasp. Her arms wrapped around his waist and she pulled him to her, her lips seeking his and her mind whirling in an eddy of release with his kiss.

"I've been thinking," he said into her hair, holding her close, "there's only one thing for us to do."

She stopped her breath, her lungs knotted, unable to hold air.

"I must go to your father and explain the situation," he said. "I can't go on like this. I think about you incessantly. Christ, I even dream about you! I can't let you marry Ferris, Catra. I can't let you go." Catra felt happiness begin to explode behind her eyes. "I will come straight to the point and ask your father's permission for your hand, offering to cover any breach of promise compensation the Chesters might demand, and present my arguments for being the best husband he could choose for his daughter. I have means that are comparable to the Chesters; he could not possibly have a problem with that. If we can settle quietly, we may be able to avoid a large part of the scandal. Shall I do that, Catra? Is it me that you want to marry?"

Catra's relief was immediate and complete. "You want to *marry* me." Tears of joy slid down her cheeks.

"Yes, I want to marry you," he rejoined, pulling her closer, then looked down at her through laughing eyes. "Despite all my ideas to the contrary, I find I cannot, I *will not* live without you. It's been quick, and it's sure as hell been unorthodox, but if marry you must, marry we will."

She laughed. "What a romantic you are. Oh, Ryan, why don't we just run away, right now, and forget about everyone else?"

He held her close, smelling the fragrance of her hair, feeling the heat of her body. "Aside from the fact that I know you don't mean that, I think I'd like to do this right. Walk down the aisle like every other couple who ever lived,

104

and not run as if someone might catch us in the act.''

"Ryan," she said, pulling back from him, her eyes raised to his in concern, "there is still my father to consider.''

Ryan smiled wryly. "Oh, I haven't forgotten him. You can be sure of that."

"We must handle him just right. I think it would be best if I were to talk to him first. I can explain things in terms he might be more willing to understand. There are a few things—options you might say—he has with the Chesters without which he will never consent to our marriage. This is all very sordid and monetary, but for my father, it must be discussed."

"He can disinherit you for all I care," Ryan said. "I'm not after your money."

"But wouldn't the estrangement between you and Ferris affect your company? Surely it would not be good for your business to alienate the Chesters. The scandal involved in my broken betrothal may affect more than just our social lives."

"Sweetheart," he said, his eyes dancing, "it's a drop in the bucket. Now, when will you speak to your father?"

"Tomorrow, in the afternoon. He's usually in a good mood after returning from a trip. I'll talk to him then. But I must warn you, he can be quite stubborn. I'll let you know what is said, but if he's obstinate, we must think of another plan."

"Then I shall speak to him. I believe we established a sort of rapport at our last meeting," he said dryly. "And if that doesn't work, we'll consider the alternatives. If we must, we'll elope. It will be his own fault for driving us to it."

Chapter Six

When Catra heard her father arrive, her stomach lurched and she was consumed by a blinding sense of having forgotten every argument she'd worked out in support of her marriage to Ryan. All day she had waited with anxious anticipation for her father's return, at some moments feeling particularly strong and ready to face him, at others praying he would be just one more hour so she could again formulate the perfect speech, the precise combination of words that would make him see that she must marry Ryan.

He arrived close to supper time, after Catra had just passed through a strong stage to one of nearly complete mental exhaustion.

As she heard his footsteps cross the marble hall below, she ran to her bedroom door and waited, heart pounding in her ears, to catch her breath, which she'd unwittingly been holding since she heard the carriage arrive.

Should she go now and catch him before he had a chance

to sink back into the daily routine of the household? Or should she let him relax, have a drink, then corner him alone in the library? How long would it take him to relax? Could she stand to have him in the house and not speak with him? Could she actually face him now, outside of the imaginary realm of her head, with this plea that she knew would shock him?

She opened the door, deciding that what she needed now was action. Any more time alone to think would surely drive her mad. She crept to the top of the stairs and peered below at the curve of the staircase, the white marble floor, the silent door to the study.

Where had he gone? Not a soul seemed to stir in the main house. Perhaps he'd gone to the kitchen for something to eat. She moved down the stairs without feeling them under her feet, so intent was she on any movement or noise in the house. Her petticoats rustled softly under the soft grenadine of her gown and she stopped once again at the bottom to listen to the silence.

Then, with a clatter, the back doorway opened and she heard her father's purposeful step echo through the empty house, heedless of the silence he shattered.

Catra fluffed her skirt and turned from the stairway to stroll casually down the hall.

"Hello, Catherine!" her father boomed. She hoped he didn't notice her jump.

"Father, you're home," she said, smiling tremulously. "How was your trip?"

"Well, it could have gone better, could have gone worse," he said. He gave her a bear hug and a kiss on the forehead when he'd reached her. "How was your week, eh? Get all your shopping done? You should be preparing for your wedding, you know."

Catra flushed. "It was a good week, really. I'd like to tell you about it."

"And I'd like to hear it, princess. But right now I smell like the dickens, and nothing would suit me better than a hot bath and some supper. How about you? Did you wait to join your father for dinner?" He began to move back toward the stairs. Catra followed.

"Yes, I did. But I'd like to speak with you, if I could, before supper," she said as he rose the first couple of steps.

Her father turned back to her. "What's all this now, is something wrong? You're looking awfully serious."

"Nothing is wrong, Father." She didn't want him to look on it as bad news. "However it is rather serious. But it can wait until you've had your bath. It's not so pressing as that." She smiled and saw him relax. "I'll just wait for you in the library. I'll pour you a brandy, how would that be?"

Her father chuckled. "So you want me clean and a wee bit drunk, is that it? All right. I'll meet you in the library. And a brandy sounds fine. You'd best make it a big one if your news matches your expression."

Catra laughed at the jest but knew that she'd best do just that. Her father could have no idea what lay in store for him, and she was sure his good humor would suffer under the news she had to impart.

Catra had the brandy poured and set on a table by the armchair with one of her father's favorite cigars. She paced by the windows, alternately watching one of the grooms brush down Calypso, the horse that had brought her father home, and staring alertly at the door.

At long last it opened. Her father, freshly shaved and with his white hair combed straight back, emerged with Jason, the overseer. Their voices were boisterous as they exchanged information about the past week, and Jason's clothes reeked of pipe smoke that Catra could smell the moment he entered the room.

Her father looked surprised upon first seeing Catra waiting there; then he tapped his finger at his temple for a moment before saying to Jason, "Why don't we continue this discussion after supper? I have a few things to attend to before we get started."

"Sure, anytime, Mr. Meredyth. I'll be right there in my cabin. You just give me a holler." Jason tipped his hat in Catra's direction as he exited.

"Your poor father's getting old," her father said ruefully. "I'd forgotten you wanted to speak to me."

"That's all right," she said. At least he hadn't been dreading whatever she had to say. He began to sit at his desk when he noticed the brandy and cigar by the armchair. But Catra, wanting him to be comfortable wherever he was, quickly scooped the two up and brought them to him at his desk.

Her father took his time pinching the end of the cigar, then lit it and puffed gently. His eyes narrowed either in contentment or to mask his thoughts, Catra could not tell which. He cupped the brandy snifter in his left hand and swirled it so the amber liquid made two arcs along the inside of the glass. He gestured for her to sit in the chair across from him.

"Now, what's troubling you, Cat?" he asked finally. "You've got a guilty look on your face that worries me."

Catra straightened and changed her expression to consternation, bothered that he could read her so easily. "I've nothing to feel guilty about, Father," she began, then decided that was the wrong tack to take. "No, that's not completely true. I do feel somewhat guilty for the trouble I'm about to cause. But that does not mean I believe myself to be in the wrong." She paused. Her father merely puffed his cigar, awaiting her revelation. "The fact is, and I don't know how to say this other than to simply tell you straight out—so I will tell you—simply—that"—she inhaled—"that I must break my engagement to Ferris."

She waited, expecting some sort of large reaction from her father, but he continued to look at her with a contemplative expression.

"I know that these are plans you've had for a long while," she continued, unsettled by his lack of response, "and that it was Ferris's father's wish that we marry—"

"And yours as well," he added mildly.

"Yes, well, in a way." She cleared her throat, trying to sound like a reasonable adult rather than the desperate child she felt like inside. "You know, for a long time I never realized things could be any different. Ferris and I are friends—"

"Good friends," he interjected, again in a quiet voice. "For a long time. He's been very good to you."

Catra squirmed slightly in her chair. "Yes. And I hope I've been a good friend to him as well."

"Up to now."

"Actually, I think I would be acting the better friend, doing the better deed, by not marrying him," she exclaimed. "You see, I'm not in love with him. And so many marriages, built on nothing but tolerance and resignation, become so ugly. You must know what I mean."

She searched her memory for a good example of an awful marriage, but while she could find many in her head that were unsatisfactory to herself, she could see that from her father's point of view these very same would be seen as successful. Children had been born, land had been acquired and cultivated, families had been enriched. But the women all looked so sad and worn, and the men had no time for anything but work and each other, smoking and drinking and engaging in pointless competitions to amuse themselves.

"I don't want one of those marriages that degenerate into—into—" She couldn't even voice what was wrong with them. It was too comprehensive. Too prevalent. And too sad.

"I've expected this," her father said with a somber smile.

"You have?" Catra could barely contain the hopeful leap her heart took.

He placed his cigar in an ashtray and swirled the brandy again. "This is a natural reaction. You're still young, though plenty old enough to be married, mind." He chuckled. "But you're probably feeling some apprehension about the idea of marriage. You've been mighty popular with the boys, and you're probably wondering if all your fun will be over. Trust me, honey, it won't be. I wish your mother were here to explain this to you. She probably felt the same way. But we were happy, very happy."

Catra's hopes descended halfway back to earth. "I don't care about the boys, Father. And I'm not looking for any more fun," she insisted to her father's amused expression. "Was Mother in love with you? Did you love her?"

"I loved your mother more than anything on earth," he said with conviction. "The same way Ferris loves you, you can't deny that."

"But I don't love *him*. Don't you see how important that is? Oh, I wish Mother were here. Surely she would have understood. She must have felt the same way. She must have had to love you to marry you."

"I imagine she did," he said gently. "As you love Ferris. You've loved him all your life. You couldn't be any closer; I've watched that with much gratification over the years."

Catra's frustration at the turn in the conversation was extreme. She stood and circled her chair until she was behind it, her hands on its back, facing her father. "I don't love him the way I should. I don't love him as a *husband*. He's like a brother to me."

"That will come. You don't know him as a husband yet."

She gripped the leather back of the chair. "It won't come, Father. I know it won't. The fact is, I'm in love with someone else," she blurted. "I know what I'm supposed to feel, and I feel it, but not for *Ferris*."

She immediately regretted her words. A thundercloud of anger gathered on her father's brow.

He placed the brandy on the desk and leaned forward ominously. "I don't suppose," he said in a low, acerbic tone that made Catra's skin prickle, "this 'someone' would be the infamous Ryan St. James of the garden."

She nodded mutely, aware of the coming storm but powerless to stop it.

"Out of the question," he stated and slammed his palm down on the polished wood of the desk. The ink bottle rattled as if in fear on the solid surface. "Completely out of the question. The man is a rake and a libertine. One chance kiss in the garden is nothing to a rogue such as he."

"It was not just one chance kiss in the garden," Catra replied, suddenly aware of how childish she must seem. "I've seen him many times. We—we've gotten to know each other—"

Her father thundered to his feet. "What have you done together? What has he done to you?"

Catra was at once aware of his stature and the fact that both the desk and her chair were between them.

"We've fallen in love. We know each other, now. I

know others have wanted him and he was not interested. But he's asked *me* to marry him.''

With every word her father's face grew darker, and Catra searched frantically for something that would ease his mind about Ryan. He was not just the stranger who had stolen a kiss from her; he was real and kind and truly in love with her.

''He is even now anxiously awaiting word from me on your answer,'' she continued desperately.

''Why isn't he here himself? Because he's a coward, that's why. He knew what my answer would be,'' her father growled.

''He wanted to speak with you first, but I insisted. He's willing to do anything, match any compliance you have with the Chesters. Nothing will be lost in the bargain. I know we shall suffer some talk, some gossip, but we can weather it. We have discussed it all.''

''When? When did you discuss all of this? While I was away? Did you see him at the Chesters? By God, if he set foot in this house, I'll have him killed. Does Ferris know any of this?'' he boomed.

Catra was shaken. She'd never seen her father so angry. In fact, the only other time she'd seen him even close to this was the night he'd discovered them in the kiss. ''Truth to tell, Father''—she fidgeted with the lace of her sleeve— ''we happened to meet one day—''

''*One* day?''

''Well, the first time it was an accident, but then we met intentionally—''

Her father's chair slammed back against the wall as he rounded the desk. He took her roughly by the shoulders and she felt her insides turn to jelly with fear. ''What has he done to you? *Tell me.* If he's laid one finger on you, I'll see him dead before daybreak. I swear it. Tell me he hasn't ruined you. Tell me!'' he insisted in a voice that did not seem his own.

Tears of shock welled in Catra's eyes and her face flamed hot. She could barely get the words out over the lump in her throat. ''He *hasn't* ruined me. I swear it, Father.''

Slowly she saw her father's enraged eyes clear and a calmer expression take hold. He loosened his grip on her shoulders and pulled her to him. She felt herself trembling in his embrace.

''I'm sorry to have frightened you, honey,'' he said quietly, his voice still quaking with emotion. ''But you've no idea what that man can, and has, done. He is not worthy of you.''

Catra could feel his body tensing again. ''But what has he done?'' she whispered. ''What has he done to make you hate him so?''

He stepped back and held her again by the shoulders, this time more gently. ''Sit down, honey. I have something to tell you, and you must believe me that I don't want to hurt you.'' He slowly returned to the chair behind the desk. ''Candace Fairchild is a wealthy young woman, much like yourself, who lives in Richmond. Perhaps you've met her.''

''I don't believe so,'' she murmured. She wished he would stop now, before it was somehow too late.

''Well, St. James knows her,'' he said dryly. ''He courted her, briefly, as I understand it.''

Catra remembered then Ferris saying something about Ryan and the Fairchilds. Something about an alliance that had fizzled.

''But the moment the rumors started flying about his marrying her, trouble began,'' he continued. ''Perhaps he felt the right to take certain—liberties. In any case, he ruined her.'' Catra's father did not even pause to gauge the effect this statement had on his daughter, so anxious was he to reveal his story. "He took her out to one of those all-night parties, not the type for proper ladies to attend, and then took advantage of her. When the family pressed for a proposal, as was only right, he refused. Didn't even bother to deny that he'd ruined her. What he said, in fact, was that it was her own fault. The girl is ruined. No one will touch her. She'll grow old a spinster, regardless of her wealth and her family's position. What do you think of your Mr. St. James now?"

Catra felt the lump in her throat grow to an unmanageable size. Ferris hadn't known the reason Ryan's courtship of Candace Fairchild had ended. He obviously hadn't heard this story. Couldn't Father be wrong? He *must* be wrong.

She shook her head to clear it. Good heavens, what was she thinking? Of *course* he was wrong. Surely, even if there was a misunderstanding with the Fairchilds, Ryan would have told her about it. He had been more than candid in all of their talks. Wouldn't he have warned her that her father might use this rumor against him? He must not have even known about it.

Thurber Meredyth watched his daughter digest the information, the look on his face dark but confident. He was sure she would believe him, she thought. But he was wrong.

"No, Father. He wouldn't do such a thing. You are completely wrong about him. And I *shall* marry him."

Thurber's ire rose immediately at the contradiction. "Oh, you shall, shall you?" he pronounced in disbelief. "You don't believe me and you've known him how long? Two weeks? One? You know him so thoroughly in that time that for *him* you are willing to discard years of plans? Years of connection with the Chester family? You forsake your own father for him?"

"Father, please don't put it like that. I am not forsaking you. I am doing what I know I must do. I cannot marry

115

Ferris when I love Ryan. And I do know him," she said. "I have got a good mind, you've said so yourself, and I would have known had he been false with me. But he is not. You must believe me. He would not be so heartless or imprudent. He would not do such a thing."

"He would not be imprudent?" Thurber repeated. "Does this impetuous gesture seem to you like the actions of a man with good sense? Stealing the fiancée of one of his business partners, jumping into marriage with a woman he barely knows? My dear, he has more to gain through Ferris than he does through trifling with you. I don't even believe he intends to go through with it."

At this point Catra's anger awakened. "You see his business connections as more important than your own daughter? Can you not see that someone might find me at least as important as that? Not all men are as governed by business as you are, Father. You could not possibly understand. He is in love with me and he can do without the Chesters. I have asked him as much myself."

"He would say anything and with ease," Thurber spat.

"What for? He's gotten *nothing* from me."

"I hardly believe he's gotten nothing," her father stated.

Catra felt her face redden. It was true, he had gotten more than nothing. He had gotten passion from her that she would not have thought possible. Kisses that were disastrously improper. She was all too aware of the illicit nature of her meetings with him, and all the while her father did not take his eyes from her face.

"Be that as it may," Catra said in a voice low and quaking, "with or without your permission, Ryan St. James and I will marry. And you and Ferris and everyone in Virginia can go to the devil if you don't like it."

The tension in the room thickened with her words. Her father rose and approached her around the desk. He stared down at his defiant daughter with unmasked anger. "You will never have my permission to marry that man. You have a responsibility to this family, and these plans will not be thrown out on the whim of a silly, gullible girl. Ryan St. James is a scalawag of the lowest sort. I will not have my name dragged through the papers in a scandal for him. You are betrothed to Ferris Chester and *you will marry him.*"

"I will *not,*" she rejoined, rising.

The two glared at each other, Catra's eyes every bit as flinty as her father's. "You will go to your room now," he commanded. "If I thought there was any danger of St. James actually going through with the marriage, I would lock you in there. But he won't. Mark my words. He'll not marry you," he finished scornfully.

Catra stared at him, her knees shaking and her hands trembling. It was all too easy to believe her father's confident, commanding words, but she refused to accept them. Ryan *would* marry her; he'd said he would. He had no reason to lie to her. He was even now awaiting word from her.

Realizing that further argument was pointless, she turned stiffly and, with all the dignity she could muster, crossed the threshold and closed the door firmly behind her.

She would write to him now. If Ryan were to come speak to her father on the heels of this discussion, they might well kill each other. No, there was no way they could marry here now, not without her father's permission and his help in extricating Catra from her engagement as gracefully as possible. They must resort to the most desperate of plans. They must elope.

In the hall, Bard was laboriously polishing the brass doorknobs, most likely because it was the best vantage point in which to hear the argument between Catra and her father. Living as they did so quietly and, for the most part, harmoniously, the household rarely saw an argument or acquired material for any sort of gossip. Catra was sure this would top anything they had heard before in the sedate house.

"Bard, send Seth to my room. I have a message I wish delivered immediately," she stated in a controlled voice.

At Bard's assent she turned and walked up the stairs, her head erect with the effort of containing her anger, her eyes straight ahead. She did not see her father open the door from the study to watch her go.

Catra's bedroom door closed and Thurber walked from the study. At the base of the stairs he stopped and turned to Bard. "Tell Seth to come to my study before he delivers that message."

Chapter Seven

The clock ticked loudly and Catra heard the steady drumming of the rain as it hit the flagstone patio beneath her window. It was a cold, raw breeze that came through the open window, but Catra did not feel it. It had been nearly twelve hours since she'd sent the message to Ryan to come for her. Twelve hours. Two of them past midnight.

Her sleepless eyes burned as her glance fell from their vigil at the window to the small, worn carpetbag at her feet. She had instructed Seth to return to her only if he had trouble delivering the message and she'd not seen him. But this could mean any manner of misfortune had befallen him. He could have fallen from his horse and broken a leg, he could have been beset by thieves, he could have been waylaid by another servant. But surely she would have heard something by now, even if it was only that the boy was missing.

Two hours ago she had toyed with the idea of riding to

Waverly herself, but the threat of being seen or intercepted by one of the Chesters was enough to squelch the thought. She wanted to send for Seth, but did not want to alert the house to her plans.

She would just have to wait until the morning, which was now only a few hours away, and interrogate the boy herself. The only thing she could think of was that Ryan did not get the message. Surely if he couldn't come for some reason, he would have sent her a reply. She clung to the possibility that many things could have hindered Seth.

At long last the night succumbed to the slight gray of early morning. The dawn was dim, as the rain had not let up but lingered over the morning countryside the way a bad dream lingers over the waking mind.

She crept down the stairs, still dressed in her pleated wool traveling gown, and out the back door toward the servants' quarters. She breathed easier when she'd crossed the patio and entered the gardens, which concealed her from both the house and the kitchen. As she passed the bench where she and Ryan had danced that first, breathless evening they'd met, she spied old Daniel the gardener pruning a hedge of azaleas. Calling him softly to her, she asked him to seek out Seth and send him to her.

Long minutes passed while the rain misted upon her hair and made watery beads upon the wool of her sleeves. She moved to the wrought-iron bench upon which she had sat that fateful evening and ran her fingers along its wet, glistening back. She imagined the scene all over again: Ryan's silver, glittering eyes, her own nervousness, the thrill of his touch and the starry moment his lips had first met hers.

She heard the bushes shake their wetness and whirled to face Seth. He wore a sheepish expression on his face and he would not meet her eyes.

"Daniel says you sent for me," he mumbled.

"Yes," she said urgently. She moved toward him and took one of his thin arms in her hand. "Did you deliver my message?"

"Yes'm, I did."

"To Mr. St. James?"

"Yes'm." The boy dug his other hand down into his pocket, as if to protect it from being seized as well.

Catra was momentarily stumped, unable to imagine what might have happened. "Well?" She shook his arm slightly. "Look at me, Seth. What did he say? Did he send a reply?"

"He didn't, Miss Catra." He watched as his own hand pulled a string from his pocket.

"What did he say? Did he say anything or just take the note?"

Seth fidgeted with the string for a moment until Catra snatched it from his hand. "I need to know, Seth. What happened? Where is his answer?"

"He just looked at it, then he laughed kinda to himself. I asked him if he wanted to send you something and he told me no. He said it kinda mad, like. Then sent me off. That's all, Miss Catra." He gnawed at his bottom lip.

Catra felt the blood drain from her head and she grabbed his other arm in an icy grip. "That's a *lie,*" she hissed. "I don't know why, but you're lying. Tell me, tell me the truth."

Seth pulled back instinctively. "Miss Catra, I'm not lying. It happened. It did. He tore it up, tore it right down the middle. Then he burned it. I didn't know what to do."

She looked at him for a long second, assessing his fear, imagining how frightened he must have been of Ryan's forbidding face and stature, then she loosened her grip and rubbed his arm softly. "Go on, then," she said. "You did the right thing, Seth. I'm sorry if I frightened you."

She walked heavily to the bench and slumped onto it

with such despair and desolation, such a remarkable lack of color in her face, that Seth watched for a moment. Then slowly, he edged away from the clearing.

Catra's mind was so absorbed with the hideousness of his words that she did not notice that he had left. His message echoed over and over in her head as she sat numbly, her mind locked in a vortex of emotions.

Her breath coursed over an ever-growing lump in her throat and she swallowed several times as the thoughts in her head whirled. None of them stopped long enough for her to consider with any logic as she sat stunned. It wasn't until her muscles began to ache and her eyes to burn that she moved from her seat.

She walked up the path to the house and from there to her bedroom, where she lay gingerly on the bed. Why would Seth lie? she thought, because that was the only possibility. Seth must have lied. But her mind rejected the thought even though her heart clung to it in desperation. Seth would not lie to her. She knew that. His terrified expression testified to his honesty. She had frightened him and he had blurted out the whole story.

At eight-thirty Lucy knocked on the door to help her dress for the day, but Catra sent her away. She lay in the gloomy light of her room while her brain churned relentlessly over the events of the last week.

He'd been using her, she thought, and she had walked right into it. What a fool she had been. After the kiss in the garden, both of them knowing full well that she was spoken for, he must have thought her easy prey for an amusing affair while he was visiting. One of the dalliances Mayliza had mentioned. She should have known that first night, when he hadn't even tried to defend her or himself to her father when he had confronted them. What was she thinking? She *had* known. She had resisted him for that very reason. But he was too clever. He had won anyway, she thought bitterly. He must be quite experienced at seducing young girls with his good looks and his promises.

Her disgust at her own stupidity drowned any feeling of self-pity she might have felt. Her emotional confessions to Ryan rang in her ears like scenes from a bad play; such naïveté, such blindness; how could she have been so duped? She pictured Ryan's face and experienced such an intense surge of desire and hatred that she choked. By God, if it was the last thing she ever did in her life, she would make him pay. She would make him sorry he had ever thought of toying with her.

She relived each day they'd met, hating both Ryan and herself for every kiss. With each memory, each detail, she found more and more proof of his insincerity. His skill at avoiding detection, his flirtatious way with Jane that day they had met, his cocksure attitude when she'd come to the river after the day of the shooting.

It made so much sense now, even down to the very first feelings of mistrust she had had about him. Ferris's comments about some deal with the Fairchilds that had not been sealed confirmed her father's story. And Mayliza's rumors of his having an affair in every port, and of leaving Richmond after a scandal—all of it built a case against him from which no lawyer could have extricated him.

Not to mention the fact that he himself had admitted to her that his intentions were not honorable in the first conversation they had after the kiss. He had told her he was not to be trusted, and yet she had fallen for his seduction anyway. When he had pretended to be really falling for her, that was when she had succumbed. He probably realized after that first argument they'd had that she was one who needed to be lied to rather than cajoled.

But the crowning blow was for her to have insisted that

she talk to her father about their affair rather than letting him profess himself. What a crescendo of idiocy that was. If she hadn't insisted, would he have actually gone to her father as he had offered? Of course not. He was probably laughing up his sleeve the whole time. He knew at that point that she was so far gone for him that no one who heard her outlandish tale would believe she had not let herself be ruined by him.

She would never be able to tell Ferris, so his business partnership was intact. He probably knew that her father would tell her about Candace Fairchild, and then maybe Catra would consider herself lucky to have escaped with only her pride destroyed. And he knew that both she and her father would then keep any whisper of the affair quiet for fear of ruining Catra's reputation.

It was at this point that the tears came. Great, gulping sobs of self-pity engulfed her, torturing her, twisting her, until she was left, hours later, exhausted, her emotions turned to water on her pillow. She lay curled up on the bed in her wrinkled gown, with nothing left inside her but a hard, cold fury.

At twelve o'clock, Bethia entered the room and stopped short when she found Catra.

"Goodness, Catra, what is the matter?" Bethia asked, turning Catra onto her back with a large, comforting hand.

Catra felt a lump rising again to her throat at Bethia's concern and turned her head away, two tears escaping the corners of her eyes.

"Oh, my baby," Bethia cooed, "you can tell me. What are you so sad about, honey?" She sat on the edge of the bed and brushed Catra's hair from her forehead, a worried frown on her face as she felt the feverish brow. At the kind touch, Catra sat up and hugged Bethia tightly to her.

"Oh, Bethia," she choked out, "you're the only one

who loves me. You're the only true friend I've got in the world." Her tears coursed freely down her cheeks, wetting the shoulder of Bethia's dress where she leaned.

"Hush, Catra, hush now. Of course I love you. We all love you, honey. Hush, now," Bethia crooned, rubbing Catra's back and smoothing her hair. When Catra's sobs finally subsided Bethia asked her gently, "Now, what is this all about?"

"I've got to get out of here. I've got to get away. I can't stay here." She began to cry again.

"Now, you just listen to me. Your daddy'll be worried sick to see you carryin' on like this."

"Oh, God, Bethia," Catra said. "I don't care. I just want to get away from this place."

"Honey, if you want to get away, then we will," Bethia said, a pillar of calm strength. "We can go see that Mrs. Thompkins in Richmond who wrote to you. She wanted you to stay with her a spell, didn't she? Your daddy'd be right pleased if we told him we gonna go to Richmond to get your wedding dress. Don't you worry now," Bethia soothed, "I'll fix everything. Don't you worry."

"Yes. We have to. I want to go to Richmond." Catra gripped her arm.

The old nurse gently pulled away and said, "You just leave it to me. But today, you've got to get some rest. Let's just take off this gown and you sleep some today."

"No—we have to leave now, today," Catra insisted.

"Honey, I have to pack today. You rest and I'll talk to your daddy. We'll leave tomorrow," Bethia said decisively and began to unbutton Catra's dress.

Catra fell back, all energy suddenly gone from her, and allowed Bethia to put her to bed. She had expended her last morsel of strength and fell immediately to sleep.

*   *   *

125

The trip to Richmond was long and uncomfortable, but Catra hardly noticed. She sat motionless in the carriage her father had allowed them to take, staring out the window.

Bethia and Catra were alone for the first segment of the trip, but in Sharpsville two gentlemen and a woman, friends of Catra's father, boarded for the remainder of the trip. The newcomers chattered and laughed companionably, pointing out interesting and unusual sights to each other and laughing over the younger man's silly jokes. Catra tried to ignore them, but the younger of the two gentlemen amiably persisted in trying to engage her in conversation. Catra responded politely to his questions about her reasons for traveling but refrained from talking any more than was absolutely necessary to keep from being rude.

From her father she knew that the older gentleman and the woman were a married couple, the Forsythes, and the younger man was brother to the older. They were traveling to Richmond after a short spell in the country with their sister. Catra's father had stayed there briefly on his last trip.

They rode on, the three Forsythes conversing easily among themselves after perceiving Catra's desire for solitude.

Their arrival in Richmond was not a moment too soon. They dropped the Forsythes at their home on Porter Street and continued on to Wendy and Malcolm Thompkins's house. Upon alighting from the coach, they were met by Jasper, the Thompkins's butler, who directed them to the house. Wendy waved excitedly from the open front door, beckoning them to join her inside in the warmth while Jasper retrieved their luggage from the carriage.

The day was cold and the wind whipped riotously around them, grabbing Catra's bonnet and flinging it from her head, only to flap along her back by its ribbons. Bending into the wind, Catra headed for Wendy, one hand clasping her ermine muff, the other her brown camel's hair traveling skirt, which bounded out behind her in the wind.

"Come in here, quickly!" Wendy beckoned. "Oh, how good it is to see you." She kissed Catra on the cheek as she entered. "I've just been dying to see a friendly face from home. It seems ages since my sister Felicity was here, and she's been the only one to come see me since my wedding. Thank goodness you've come. Tell me all the news." To Catra, in her drained state, Wendy's excitement was hardly contagious. She almost visibly shrank from it.

"I'm awfully tired," she said, almost instantly wishing she hadn't come. "Do you mind terribly if we wait until I'm settled before we chat?"

"Oh, of course, how stupid of me," Wendy retracted, her disappointment and shame evident. "Malcolm says he thinks I'll never grow up to be a lady, and I guess he's right. I'll always be just a girl and too impulsive to be mannered. Come with me and I'll show you to your room."

"Don't be silly, Wendy. I'm glad you're excited," Catra said. She followed as Wendy proceeded up the stairs and, ashamed of the way she'd cut Wendy off, asked politely, "How is Malcolm?"

"Oh, he's fine." Wendy waved her hand airily. "He never changes."

"Are you happy being married?"

"Oh, Catra, what a question! Everyone's got to be married!" Wendy laughed and turned down a long, staid hall covered with portraits. No home could have reflected its mistress less, Catra noted.

"I suppose," Catra murmured, remembering Wendy's giddy enthusiasm the day of her wedding. She had positively beamed as she had marched, with controlled stateliness, down the aisle, like a child being treated, and trying

127

to act, like a queen for a day. "But is it what you'd hoped it would be? Do you like it?"

Wendy's face clouded. "Well, it's not something you like, exactly. It's just something you do. Well, anyway, we can talk about that later. Marriage is such a—a big topic, it would take more time than we have now. Now you should take a nap so you'll be all fresh for dinner."

"Yes," Catra said. "There'll be plenty of time to talk later."

Ryan reined his horse to a halt in front of the imposing house and dismounted, tossing the reins to the stable boy. Having heard nothing from Catra, he'd decided to take the matter into his own hands and face Thurber Meredyth himself. Though he didn't know the reason he had not received word from Catra, he was able to imagine a myriad of obstacles that might have stood in the way either of her writing or of his receiving the awaited note.

After all, he'd met Catra's father, and he believed it most likely that fear kept her from writing. He knew, also, that she could be having second thoughts about trusting him, as she had known him for such a short time, and in the face of her father's anger and disapproval her resolve could easily have been shaken.

He did not blame her for this weakness. He had witnessed Thurber Meredyth in a rage and had no desire himself to knowingly provoke another one. But he had dealt with men who would not listen to reason before and was confident he could overcome the man's refusal.

He strode up the stairs, across the veranda to the door and rang. It was answered almost immediately by the butler. Ryan assumed, the road up to the house being long, that the servant had seen him coming.

He handed the butler his card and waited while the man

loped off to inform Mr. Meredyth. Not two minutes passed
before he returned and directed Ryan into the dark, paneled
study.

"Marse Thurber will be right with you, sir. Is there anything I can get you, while you wait?" he asked politely.

Ryan had anticipated a less than courteous reception
upon his arrival at Braithwood, considering that the last
time he had been to this house he had been told never to
return. He had even thought Mr. Meredyth might not receive him. But here he was, in Mr. Meredyth's study, being
treated as a respected guest. He declined the butler's offer
and watched him leave.

A moment later Thurber Meredyth himself appeared.

"Mr. St. James," he said, extending one of his large,
square hands in greeting. Ryan took it. "Allow me to apologize for our last parting," Thurber continued magnanimously. "I've had plenty of time to think about it and,
frankly, I'm somewhat ashamed of myself for overreacting.
Why, if I were in your shoes, I'd have done the same thing
at your age. My girl's a pretty one, all right, but fickle, like
all girls that age. Sit down." He motioned Ryan to one of
the deep armchairs by the fire and sat in the one opposite.
"Cigar?" He extended a polished wooden box toward
Ryan.

Ryan selected one and leaned into the match Thurber
held. "Thank you. Mr. Meredyth, you've no need to apologize to me—"

"Nonsense. I was rude and there's the end of it. But I
was feeling some pressure that night, such a large party and
all. Also, I was a little confused; one minute Catra was
begging me to move up the betrothal—smitten, she was,
when Ferris first came back from the Continent and asked
her to marry him—next minute şhe's kissing another man
in the garden. But then, it's not the first time that sort of

thing has happened, if you know what I mean. Though of course I'm telling you this in strictest confidence, you understand. So if it's apologies you'll be offering, I'll have none of them, young man.''

Ryan was speechless at this display from Thurber Meredyth. He had prepared himself for every reception but this one, and faced with it he was not quite sure which tack to take. It was obvious Mr. Meredyth was glossing over the episode in the garden for some reason, but Ryan was not sure why. Leaning back in his chair, he drew slowly on the cigar and studied Thurber Meredyth's calm face.

''Actually, sir,'' Ryan said, ''though I meant no disrespect at the ball, I did not come to apologize.''

''Is that right?'' Thurber asked, also leaning back in his chair. Two fingers held his cigar nonchalantly near his right cheek. His posture was relaxed and he looked at Ryan through eyes narrowed against the smoke.

Ryan decided to take the direct approach. ''The reason I've come is to ask for Catra's hand in marriage.''

Thurber's countenance showed no surprise and, in fact, a slow, sad smile touched his lips. He leaned forward, his elbows on his knees, and looked for a second at his own hands clasped between them, the cigar drifting smoke up next to his face.

''Son,'' he said, looking up, ''I know she's bewitching. And I know you're in earnest when you say—''

''Sir,'' Ryan interrupted, tiring of whatever game Thurber Meredyth was playing, ''Catra and I have already spoken about this. I understand your reservations and we don't want to have to do anything rash, but we intend to be married—with or without your consent. With your consent, I have every intention of taking responsibility for the break with the Chesters. I know of the disrepute this may throw on you and your family, but we can minimize it if we all cooperate."

Thurber drew himself up and adopted the same businesslike tone Ryan had employed. "I can't say that this has come as a surprise to me. In fact, Catra confessed the whole affair to me. She was penitent but truthful. And the truth of the matter is, the girl does not know what she wants. One minute it's Ferris; the next, you. The next, who knows who? This isn't the first time she's 'fallen in love,' you know, if your ego will permit you to believe that. My God, it's happened more times than I'd like to count. In that very seat"—he motioned toward the chair Ryan occupied— "countless young men have sat, pouring their hearts out to me. I'm always left holding the bag, by golly." He shook his head mournfully. "But, Mr. St. James, her betrothal to Ferris was the first time she'd ever accepted a proposal, of her own accord, though I'll admit it's something both the Chester family and I have wanted for a long, long time."

Ryan listened patiently, believing that Thurber had indeed had to refuse many young men Catra's hand, but he also knew that they probably meant nothing to her, either. Mr. Meredyth was treating him like any one of the other young puppies that had panted after Catra. He could not possibly have spoken to his daughter about the two of them.

"Mr. Meredyth, this is an interesting story, but there is an easy way to solve this mystery," Ryan said. "If we summon Catra, I'm sure she will tell you just where her heart stands."

Thurber hesitated only a moment, as if reluctant to continue. "If only it were that simple," he said, rising. "You see, she left yesterday for Richmond with her nanny. Another example of woman's fickle nature." He chuckled mirthlessly as he walked toward his desk.

Ryan's eyes narrowed. "Mr. Meredyth," he said, rising

also, "forgive me, but it seems awfully convenient that she has gone so suddenly. Perhaps it was under your influence that she left? Certainly it would ruin your plans if we were to speak now and resolve this misunderstanding, would it not? But avoiding the issue will serve no purpose. You could save us both a lot of time by allowing this marriage to happen and gracefully extricating Catra from her current obligation." He stood in front of the desk, his voice calm but his eyes, level with Thurber Meredyth's, unyielding.

"My boy," Thurber protested, an indignant look upon his face, "Catra left of her own accord and her own determination. I don't wish to insult you, but perhaps it was due to your influence that she fled. Has it occurred to you that her feelings for you might have been less than you believe? As I've said, she is a beautiful girl, and more hearts than I'd care to count have been broken over her. Those boys also came here believing their love to be reciprocated. But Catra was not wearing their ring, as she is Ferris's."

Ryan sighed. "I had hoped you would not make this so difficult. Shall I be obliged to go to Richmond and find Catra to clarify this mess?"

Thurber spread his hands wide. "By all means, go if you feel you must. But before you do . . ." He shuffled through some papers on his desk and came up with a note. "Could you deliver this note to Ferris? She wrote it to tell Ferris of her departure. I'm not asking you to read it, but if you deliver it when you return to your hosts, perhaps Ferris will enlighten you as to its contents. It will save one of my people the trip, as well. Now, I know you're unhappy with the situation, but there is honestly nothing I can do. I don't want to end this interview on the same unpleasant note as our last one, but I don't intend to take your insinuations. Now, please, accept what I've told you and take it like a man. Believe me, most of the others had to and did.''

Ryan stood for a moment looking at Mr. Meredyth, his expression carefully controlled. ''Am I to understand, then, that if Catra had professed to you her desire to marry me, your consent would have been given?''

''We would have had to talk about it,'' Thurber hedged. ''But I can't say for certain one way or the other. The situation has not arisen.'' He shrugged helplessly.

Ryan's jaw clenched. ''I'm sorry to have wasted your time, then, Mr. Meredyth.'' With that he turned abruptly on his heel and strode toward the door. ''No doubt we'll talk further once I've straightened everything out with Catra.''

''Mr. St. James?'' Thurber stopped him with the words, and Ryan turned to see the man's hand half-extended with Catra's note to Ferris. His eyebrows were raised questioningly, subtle condescension lurking on their flat blue surface.

Ryan hesitated for a moment, then returned for the note. His eyes held Thurber's as he took it. He nodded slightly, turned and walked to the door.

He crossed the front hall in a rage, his boots clicking decisively on the marble floor. Bard stood by the door and opened it efficiently. As Ryan emerged onto the veranda, the stable boy appeared with his horse. His exit was quickly made. Everyone had been ready for his departure as if on cue, just a half hour after his arrival.

A mile down the road to Waverly, Ryan's resolve left him. Slowing his horse to a walk, he removed the note Mr. Meredyth had given to him from his pocket. It was folded and unsealed, which made any further resistance on Ryan's part evaporate. He read:

October 25, Sunday
Braithwood
Dear Ferris,
I am sorry to have to inform you so abruptly of my
departure, but I have been invited to visit with Wendy
Thompkins in her new home in Richmond. I decided
on a whim to accept her invitation. I should be gone
for one or two weeks at the most, but will be back in
time for the wedding.
Yours,
Catra

Ryan read the lines a second time, then a third. The writing was cramped and sloppy, written in haste. Had she penned it? He could not be sure; he had never seen her writing.

His earlier theory—that she was afraid of her father and the repercussions involved with breaking her engagement—was losing credibility, but he refused to abandon it. Perhaps she was unsure of him, unsure of his love. After all, the risks involved in this were hers; he had nothing to lose. It would be no wonder if she was afraid of the situation. If she were to break her engagement and he were to change his mind, as she might fear, she could lose everything—her future prospects, her reputation, everything.

He resolved to speak to her before reacting. He knew women well and he could not believe that she could so convincingly profess her love to him only to change her mind at the last minute. He had seen how nervous she was about her father, even to the point of insisting that she first speak to him about their plans—

His blood froze. She had insisted that she speak to her father first. Had she planned all along to change her mind?

Did she prevent Ryan from speaking to him because she had no real desire to pursue the affair? He clenched his teeth in anger and through sheer strength of will banished the thought from his head. He would form no more opinions until he spoke with her himself. But his stomach knotted and a bitter bile rose to the back of his throat as he continued on to Waverly.

Chapter Eight

Catra had been in Richmond for nearly a week, during which her mood had not altered in the slightest. She'd performed the rigors of socializing with a lackluster energy. Her only grateful thought was that she had no public humiliation to suffer with her heartbreak. Thankfully, her affair with the infamous Ryan St. James had been a private one.

Since her arrival she had heard much of Candace Fairchild and her unfortunate story. But while most people pitied her, they also seemed to blame her for what they called her headstrong flight to ruin. St. James had certainly acted immorally, but he had not raped the girl. Had she only maintained her virtue, what she might have had now was a husband, not a scandalous reputation.

These opinions made Catra sick, not only with disgust for the one-sided nature of the fault awarded, but sick with self-loathing. She was nearly as guilty as the Fairchild girl, aside from the irrefutable physical proof of Candace's ruin. If people were to cast aspersions on Candace Fairchild, they should do so also to Catra, she thought. Every time the subject arose in conversation she suffered guilt anew for her shameful secret.

Entertainments were abundant in the bustling city, but the pall of her disgrace followed her everywhere. Though she tried to participate, she found herself unable to escape a constant nagging in her own mind that she should be sequestered along with Candace Fairchild to suffer her heartbreak alone and in silence. In a way she envied Candace that luxury of seclusion, while she, Catra, had to pretend all was normal, had to put on a smile when she felt like crying, and had to remain calm and sociable when she felt like screaming.

During their only shopping expedition, Catra and Wendy had picked two gowns for her trousseau at Madame Jeanville's, a dressmaker renowned for her gift for making even the plainest of subjects attractive and appealing. Due to this reputation she was constantly besieged by homely but rich young ladies demanding miraculous transformations.

On this occasion, however, the couturier had been delighted with her client and so excited about Catra's figure and coloring that she proclaimed she wished to do the whole of Catra's trousseau and most especially the wedding gown. Here, at last, was a showcase deserving of her talents, she declared. But Catra had been too tired to order any more than an initial two gowns and they had gone home, promising to return when Catra had more energy to devote to the task.

Wendy, on the other hand, was full of anxious energy to make a good impression on Catra. After writing to invite Catra for a visit, she had consulted some of her friends in town on appropriate entertainment for such a guest. They had all suggested a party, perhaps even a ball, in her honor.

The idea suited Wendy tremendously, as she had yet to throw her first ball, and she immediately ascertained all the information she believed she needed on the proper procedure. She forgot, however, to get confirmation of Catra's arrival before she had planned the production and sent the invitations, never realizing what providence it was for Catra to have come at all.

The evening after they'd gone to Madame Jeanville's, Wendy announced her plans, emphasizing, at Catra's hesitation, that Catra simply *had* to like the idea because she had done it all just for her.

"A ball?" Catra asked. "But Wendy, you didn't have to do that for me. Please, don't go to the trouble. I would be just as happy to stay home with you and talk." But at the crestfallen look on Wendy's face she smiled. "It is a lovely idea, though. A ball would be a wonderful opportunity to show off my new yellow Jeanville satin, don't you think?"

"Oh, yes!" Wendy breathed, brightening immediately. "The one with the illusion flounces? Why, you'll have all the men at your feet in that dress. It will be such fun, Catra, you'll see."

Catra smiled again and collapsed on her bed as soon as Wendy left. Why had she come to Richmond? All she wanted to do was lie in her bed and not move, not think, until the day of her wedding. If she could make it till then, she thought, she would be all right.

She did not consider what would happen after the wedding, or the marriage itself; she simply maintained that if she could make it until the ceremony, somehow all of her confusing, crippling emotions would be wiped away. She would no longer feel this numbness and fear once she was married to Ferris. Once he had held her, kissed her, made love to her, he would erase all memories of those other kisses and would cleanse her guilt-wracked mind with the propriety of marital consummation. All of her doubts about Ferris were eliminated in her desperation to forget Ryan St. James.

Ryan St. James. Even his name sent shivers up her spine and a churning nausea in her stomach. If only he were dead and she didn't have to fear ever having to look on his face again. How would she ever accept him into her house as one of Ferris's business associates?

What if Ferris invited him to the wedding? she thought with a jolt. She tried to remember Ferris's part of the guest list. Surely Ryan wouldn't come, would he? The idea sapped what little strength she had left and she took to her bed for the rest of the afternoon.

But Catra had always been active, and despite the gnawing unhappiness at the back of her mind, she quickly grew tired of staying in her room and feeling sorry for herself. Ryan St. James, she reasoned, was not the man she believed him to be if he were able to wreak such cruelty. What she was really mourning was not the loss of the man, but the loss of the dream she had created around him. And life, as she knew, was not made of dreams.

For the few days before the ball Catra made an admirable effort to socialize energetically and meet people, so that the dance would be more interesting. Her spirits were lifted somewhat by the activity, and she even survived the surprise last-minute appearance of Dahlia Chester, who, upon hearing there was to be a ball, scurried posthaste to Richmond to join the fun. Though there was not enough room at Wendy's to stay, she conveniently finagled an invitation to stay with the Lothrops, some old family friends.

She had arrived with the news, however, that Ryan and Ferris—after attending Shelly Westbrook's wedding—had left Waverly last week to go to Washington. Apparently something drastic had come up with regard to some business thing Dahlia could not understand or remember, and so feeling lonely and bored, she'd left for Richmond. It was a shame, Dahlia had gone on to lament, because before that Ryan had been intent on coming directly to Richmond himself. But Ferris had talked him out of it.

The day of the ball Wendy could not contain her excitement and flitted between Catra's room and her own like any debutante at her first dance. She watched Bethia brush Catra's hair and chattered aimlessly about various guests and town gossip.

"Oh, and Cyril Potter will be here. He's the man whose wife ran off with the gypsy show last year, but he's such a sweet man. I'll never know why she did it. Those gypsies were so greasy-looking. Now she'll never have anything more than the clothes on her back, and Mr. Potter is so wealthy. Malcolm says he's making a fortune with those warehouses of his. Anyway, everyone said Millie Potter was nothing but trash anyway, and he only married her because she was pretty and young and would marry him even though he was so old. Let's see, who else . . . Penny Worthington will be here. You've heard of her. Everyone says she is simply breathtaking, and there was even a rumor of a duel between Baker Mansfield and Henry Stevens over her. Baker Mansfield denies it, but Henry Stevens wasn't seen for two weeks after the rumor started, and then he was walking with a very pronounced limp." She nodded knowingly at Catra's reflection in the mirror.

Bethia chuckled softly as she twisted Catra's long hair into a low, smooth bun. "That sounds like Baker to me, doesn't it, Miss Catra?"

Catra grimaced into the mirror and Bethia chuckled again.

"Junior Beresford will be here too . . ." Wendy rambled on until her maid finally found her and told her that if she wanted her hair done in time, she had best get back to her room. As she left, she whispered conspiratorially to Catra, "You're looking so pale—if you want some paint, I've got some. I only got it because when I first got back from our wedding tour I was white as a ghost, and what with everybody visiting and having teas, I just couldn't bear to look that way. Anyway, don't tell Malcolm, but I've got it if you want to borrow it."

Catra assessed herself in the mirror, noting the pale translucence of her skin and the vague shadows under her eyes. In the last two weeks she had lost weight and her cheekbones stood out most unattractively. Even the gown Madame Jeanville had just made for her had to be laced tighter than it did at the fittings. Angry with herself for allowing Ryan to get the best of her she turned to Wendy and said, "Thank you, I think I will borrow it."

As she donned a gold and onyx necklace, she looked approvingly at her reflection in the glass. Not a bad presentation, she thought. She was able to disguise her wan complexion with the use of Wendy's rouge and, though thin, her figure was acceptable in the beautiful gown.

Her hair was curled in ringlets over her ears and was caught at the back of her head in a bun that was covered by a beaded net of gold thread set with onyx stones. Her dress was of yellow-gold satin and had silknet flounces over a very wide skirt. The bodice was fitted and cut low, the sleeves dropped and edged with black velvet, and she carried a plumed fan of black feathers.

Wendy was in raptures about the dress and swore vehemently that she would steal every heart that ventured near their ballroom that evening. Malcolm, though quiet and understated at the most buoyant of times, echoed his wife's

141

sentiment and insisted on escorting them both into the great hall himself.

Soon after entering the ballroom, Catra caught a glimpse of the younger Mr. Forsythe, whom she had met on the journey to Richmond. His eyes lit upon seeing her, but he did not approach until she smiled in recognition at him. She was sure she had put him off with her silence on the way to town.

"Miss Meredyth, how lovely to see you." He smiled. "How are you finding Richmond?"

"Lovely, though a bit cool. I'm afraid I was not feeling particularly well the last time I saw you, Mr. Forsythe. Please accept my apologies if I was less than cordial," she said.

"No, not at all. I'm terribly sorry to hear you were not well, however," he said sincerely. "Have you seen our good Dr. Westin?"

"Oh, no. It was nothing as serious as that." Catra smiled, feeling a little of her heaviness of heart lighten at his kind interest. "Are your brother and his wife here this evening?"

"Why, yes, they are," he said, obviously delighted at her memory of them. "Annabel loves to dance and drags Stuart out at every opportunity." He laughed indulgently, and Catra thought for a second how comforting it would be to have this kind, good-natured man as a brother. "And you, Miss Meredyth, would you like to dance?"

"Thank you, Mr. Forsythe, I would," she replied. As they joined the dancers, Catra felt her mood lightening even further. The blood rushed through her veins, invigorating her tired limbs, and she began to abhor how weak she had allowed herself to become. She barely resembled the Catherine Meredyth of earlier days. Always strong, rational and uncompromising, six months ago no man would have been able to trifle with her so lightly and get away with it.

There was no excuse for her weakness of heart, she determined, and her subsequent retreat in the face of betrayal; but since she had already allowed herself that luxury, there was nothing to do but realize that the time for it was gone. She had learned her lesson and it had made her wiser. Her heart was closed now, she decided; after learning how easily it had been duped, it would never be opened again. Life had shown her, in no uncertain way, that passion was nothing short of foolishness.

As she and Mr. Forsythe moved easily through the steps of the dance, Catra felt the secret pride of conquest at the look in his eyes. He was not a handsome man, but his joviality and ease of manner made her like him. She raised her eyes to his, her old ways of flattery and flirtation returning to her despite the cumbersome ring on her left hand.

"I'm so happy to have run into you again, Mr. Forsythe," she said and noted with satisfaction the way his eyes shone. "Nothing could make me happier than to be dancing with you here now. I was quite ashamed of the way I kept to myself in the carriage."

Perhaps she hadn't lost her power over men, she thought with the first vestiges of confidence she had felt in two weeks. Just her power over one man, a nagging voice in her head reminded her, and she felt her heart constrict.

But he would never know it, she thought, angered at the way the mere thought of him could sink her spirits. Ryan St. James would never see the heartbreak his betrayal had wrought. For too long she had wallowed in self-pity and she would succumb to it no more.

The dance ended and Mr. Forsythe bowed deeply, extending his arm to her. "Shall we get some punch?"

They walked to the punch table, and Catra delighted in Mr. Forsythe's kindness and sense of humor. She was just thinking that she could withstand any sort of heartache now, when they were joined by another man.

"Joseph, old friend," a silky voice greeted Mr. Forsythe. "And Catherine Meredyth," Baker Mansfield exclaimed as she turned. "What a delightful surprise to see you here, cousin."

Baker turned heavy-lidded dark eyes on her and smiled, bowing. He looked much older than she remembered him, but it had been a number of years. Even still, he looked more worn than his forty-five years should have allowed. No doubt due to his dissolute lifestyle, Catra thought as she curtsied in return.

His medium build was bulging at the middle and his thinning hair fell in long curls along his neck. Though his deportment and dress all indicated a man of high standing and gentlemanly manner, his eyes, as they swept up and down her figure in frank appraisal, contained the same lascivious glimmer she remembered from years ago.

Catra could feel more than see Mr. Forsythe stiffen. "Baker," he said, casually enough, "nice to see you. I didn't know you were in town. How are things in Baltimore?"

"Actually, I have not come from Baltimore," Baker said, taking Catra's hand, "I've just come from Braithwood, where I'm happy to say I found your father in good health." He bent to kiss her hand, his eyes following her onyx necklace down to the edge of her bodice.

"I am glad to hear it," Catra answered.

"While I was there, I discovered that you had betrothed yourself to young Ferris Chester. Is this true?" Baker restrained his roving eyes to look directly into hers.

"It is." She glanced toward Mr. Forsythe, hoping to make an escape from Mansfield's distasteful presence, but he had been snagged into another conversation.

"Such a shame," he said casually. "I'm afraid I missed my chance to make my own desires for your hand known. Last I remembered, you were but a young thing in pigtails. How dismaying to find you all grown up into a beauty, with me having neglected such a *ripe* opportunity." His heavy lidded eyes looked coolly into hers.

"Do not concern yourself overmuch," Catra said, deciding it was pointless to disguise her distaste. "I doubt you would have stood much of a chance in any case."

"Oh, I wouldn't be so sure about that. It's my understanding that there was some question as to whether the marriage would actually take place. It seems a fox may have entered the henhouse before the rooster had a chance to move in." The man smiled in greasy satisfaction at her flushed face and indignant eyes.

Catra was astounded that he would make such a statement. What effrontery. She had no choice but to pretend not to understand his comment, but she was left wondering not only how on earth he had discovered her affair, but how she would figure out who had told him. Surely her *father* wouldn't have said anything . . .

Then she remembered Wendy talking about Mansfield. Catra had barely been listening to Wendy's idle chatter but did remember something about Baker's involvement in a duel—something over a woman.

"I don't know what on earth you're talking about, as usual, Mr. Mansfield. Perhaps you have me mistaken for some other unfortunate young woman. Perhaps Henry Stevens's young friend? What was her name . . . I'm afraid I can't remember," she finished, wanting to wipe the superior look off the arrogant man's face. "But perhaps *she* is who you were thinking of."

Unexpectedly, Baker laughed, his thick lips pulling back

over small, pointed teeth. "Touché, Miss Meredyth. It seems my—reputation precedes me."

"Indeed it does," she said, raising her chin slightly. "And it does you no favors in the process."

"No, it never has," he said in mock discouragement. "But I must apologize for my error. I had thought my old friend Ryan St. James had been lately in your neck of the woods, and rumors do tend to swirl around him, do they not? I suppose it's only natural they should include you, a young, beautiful woman—just the type to turn St. James's head, however briefly."

"I say, Miss Meredyth, would you like to take some air?" Mr. Forsythe said then, returning from the other conversation to rescue her from Baker's repulsive presence.

"Yes, I would like that, thank you," Catra said and placed her hand on his arm. "You can be quite sure that you are mistaken, Mr. Mansfield," she said coldly. "I suggest you investigate your facts before telling such tales. Good evening." She inclined her head slightly.

"Cousin," he returned, a smirk on his lips and his lascivious eyes lowering as he bowed.

"What an *odious* man," Catra said vehemently, once they had moved out of earshot. "Every time I see him I am appalled anew that he has any relation to me and my family."

Genuinely distressed, Mr. Forsythe apologized. "I'm sorry to have abandoned you to him, Miss Meredyth, but I could not escape my conversation. Mansfield is indeed coarse, but no one who did not know of your relationship would ever guess it. Relatives are, unfortunately, one aspect of society we cannot choose."

"Is it true that he was involved in a duel?" Catra asked. Ordinarily she did not indulge in gossip with people she did not know well, but the whole conversation had unnerved her.

"I don't really know," Mr. Forsythe said, mildly surprised at the thought. "It seems there was some talk about him not too long ago, but I don't recall exactly what it was about." He thought for a moment. "It seems to me it had more to do with his behavior with a certain young lady, who has since been revealed to have very little character, but I don't remember a duel. They are illegal, of course, though still practiced in some quarters, I understand. Perhaps it was something the authorities didn't find out about."

Mr. Forsythe opened the door to the patio, where a tent had been set up to keep out the cold but still afford a place for the dancers to go for cooler air. "Did he mention the duel?" he asked as they entered the tent.

"Only in passing," she said vaguely, then smiled up at him. "In any case, thank you for coming to my aid." Mr. Forsythe bowed humbly. As they walked toward one of the benches, a voice beckoned to him, and they were drawn into conversation with the elder Mr. Forsythe and his wife.

Ryan St. James descended the stairs with Penelope Worthington on his arm. His journey to Richmond had been postponed because of that damned wedding he'd had to go to, and then Ferris had informed him that they must travel to Washington. They were to dine with a government official who had the power to lighten the tax load on certain Chester shipments, thereby making more of them possible with Ryan's company. The meeting was scheduled for that Friday, canceled due to bad traveling conditions and rescheduled for the following week. Ryan's impatience to follow Catra had to be held in check. Besides, he decided, giving Catra more time to think about what she really wanted might not be such a bad thing.

The deal made, Ryan left immediately for Richmond. He frequently stayed with his father's friends, the Worthingtons, on his extended visits to Richmond, but since he now had his own home in town he stayed there. Mrs. Worthington, however, convinced that a bachelor alone could not take care of himself, made it her business to ensure that he was not bored, and so he was invited by her to the Thompkins ball.

Ryan spotted Catra immediately as she entered the ballroom from the patio. Her yellow ball gown and blond hair set her apart from the dark evening clothes of the men around her, and even the women nearby paled in comparison.

His eyes swept her hungrily and he felt an almost overwhelming urge to go straight to her and take her into his arms. Just days ago he had believed it would be possible. He had been sure they would win their way with Thurber Meredyth. But her weakness had made everything more difficult, and now he was cautious. Though he had reserved judgment on her actions, his heart was wary. Having never before expressed any desire for marriage, he had never been so vulnerable.

She smiled dazzlingly into the face of the man escorting her, a gentleman who was obviously under her spell, and Ryan's doubt increased.

"Miss Worthington, would you excuse me a moment? I see someone I must greet." Ryan bowed.

"Of course, Mr. St. James, but do come back," Penny Worthington said with a squeeze of his arm. She smiled into his eyes. "You did promise me a dance."

He made his way through the crowd toward the patio door. As he neared where she had been standing, he did not see her. Off to his right he spotted the man with whom she had been speaking and approached him.

"How do you do?" he said as he reached the man and extended his hand. "Ryan St. James."

"Pleasure to meet you, Mr. St. James." The man smiled and took the proffered hand. "Joseph Forsythe."

"I was looking for Miss Meredyth and noticed you speaking with her a moment ago. Do you know where she's gone?" Ryan asked.

Mr. Forsythe looked at him with interest. "She's off with the ladies, but I expect she'll be right back. Are you her fiancé?"

"No," Ryan replied curtly. The knowledge that he aspired to be just that stung. At Mr. Forsythe's keen look, he added, "I'm a business partner of his and I've just come from his plantation. I have a message for his betrothed."

Mr. Forsythe nodded and looked toward the door through which Catra had exited. "Here she comes now." He motioned with his punch cup.

Ryan looked quickly and saw her sweep through the door, the long skirt of the yellow gown trailing behind her, her honey curls shimmering in the candles' glow. Her eyes sparkled as she smiled at a woman she knew, holding a plumed fan in one hand and reaching to squeeze the woman's hand with the other. Ryan felt his blood rush at the sight of her and held his breath until her eyes alighted on him.

At the sight of him, she stopped abruptly. Her hand flew to her throat and her face flushed. Ryan's heart twisted in anguish when he saw her eyes harden.

She turned her face away from him and walked slowly to Mr. Forsythe. "I'm sorry I was so long," she said breathlessly, ignoring Ryan's presence.

"Mr. St. James here says he knows you, Miss Meredyth,'' Mr. Forsythe said, obviously confused. "He mentioned something about a message from your betrothed, did you not, sir?'' He turned a perplexed expression on Ryan, who wished the man would simply disappear so he and Catra could speak plainly.

"Indeed. I have just come from Waverly,'' Ryan said as he searched her face for a sign. He received only an icy stare.

"Oh? And have you finished with your *games* in the country?'' Catra replied so acrimoniously that Mr. Forsythe turned his confused look on her.

Ryan's eyes narrowed. So she *had* changed her mind. Was she now embarrassed by his presence? Would she be unkind, just to be relieved of his company?

"Actually, the country lost its appeal to me after the first couple of weeks,'' he said, alluding to her departure. He could not yet accept that she had changed so completely.

Her lips tightened. "How trying for you. You should perhaps return to Boston.'' She turned once again to Mr. Forsythe. "Do let's get some more punch,'' she said. "I'm simply parched.''

"Certainly,'' Mr. Forsythe responded.

"Good-bye, Mr. St. James,'' Catra said. And she departed on the arm of Mr. Forsythe, her head high.

Ryan watched her leave, anger seething from every pore. So that's how she wanted it. Well, if she was embarrassed to have her indiscretions flaunted, she would regret having used Ryan St. James.

At that moment Dahlia appeared with a rustling of skirts behind him and playfully pinched him on the arm. She giggled profusely when he whirled to face her.

"Why, Mr. St. James!'' she exclaimed, and pulled at the waist of her dress. "What a dark cloud you wear on your brow. Whatever is the matter?'' She glanced pointedly after the fleeing figure of Catra.

''Miss Chester.'' Ryan tore his eyes from Catra's slim back and bowed slightly. ''I didn't realize you were to be in Richmond. When did you arrive?''

''Just today. Has my future cousin-in-law been pestering you?'' Dahlia asked. ''She can be so troublesome. Why, just ask her father what a trial she was growing up. Such a willful, impulsive thing. And then there was that whole incident with her groom. Well. I can tell you *that* was just about the end of her reputation. If it weren't for the kindness of my Uncle George, promising his only son to her, she would probably never have found a husband. Not a respectable one, in any case. You *know* how unforgiving society can be of these unpleasant little incidents.''

Ryan's attention was involuntarily drawn to Dahlia's prattle with the introduction of Catra's past, and though he wanted to ignore her idle gossip, he was in such a state of confusion about Catra, he could not help pursuing it. ''What do you mean 'the incident with her groom'?''

''Why, they ran off together!'' Dahlia said deliciously. ''I thought *everyone* knew about it. She was twelve when it happened, but that was only the beginning. She has always been an outrageous flirt, toying with men right and left. It's been *all* her father could do to protect her virtue for a marriage bed. That's why he's so insistent about this marriage to Ferris, you know. Marry her off, save her from herself. Now I *hate* to talk like this about Catra—we've known each other for so long, you know—but since it's something everyone knows anyway . . . well, you're so close to the family, I felt I could tell you.''

''Yes,'' Ryan murmured. ''Yes, I'm glad you told me.''

* * *

Catra took a deep breath as they walked away from Ryan. Don't think, her mind screamed, don't think, don't turn back, and do not cry. She concentrated on taking deep, even breaths.

"I'm sorry to have had to subject you to that, Mr. Forsythe," she said, reining her composure. "No doubt you think me exceptionally rude."

"I'm sure you have just reasons for your actions," Mr. Forsythe said. "It is certainly not my place to judge."

"Thank you," Catra said, taking a glass of champagne from the table. "The man is indeed an acquaintance of my fiancé's. I have found him extremely disagreeable, however, and his own actions have left me no choice but to treat him as I do."

"Shall I ask that he be removed?" Mr. Forsythe asked, concerned.

Catra looked up at him in alarm. "No, no," she said hastily. "Our differences are personal ones. I don't believe he is dangerous." If Mr. Forsythe were to have him kicked out, the ruckus that Ryan could incite, the things he could tell—Certainly she could pass them off as unfounded lies, but the scandal . . . it was unthinkable. She fanned herself rapidly with the plumes.

"Please, calm yourself," Mr. Forsythe said. "Sit down. I'll get you some water."

"Yes, do. Thank you," she murmured. He rushed solicitously off.

Catra was just thinking she should leave the ball entirely when Baker Mansfield approached her.

"Cousin, you're looking a bit lonely; shall I come to your rescue?" He grinned what was no doubt intended to be a charming smile, but to Catra it looked evil and sinister. She didn't answer. "I would appreciate an opportunity to redeem what reputation I might from the jaws of malicious gossip and apologize again for offending you with my questions. No doubt you are right and I have mistaken you for some other pitiable young woman. Perhaps you would prove your forgiveness to me with a dance?''

Catra was about to tersely decline when from the corner of her eye she noticed Ryan. He was standing with Penelope Worthington, his eyes on Catra. She nearly shuddered at the cold look he gave her. But her pride held her in check and she raised her chin, meeting his look squarely.

''Yes, Mr. Mansfield. I will dance with you,'' she replied evenly, rising.

Mr. Mansfield clasped her hand in his and led her into the waltz. His clothes were exceptionally well-tailored, she noticed idly, trying not to think of Ryan, and briefly noted that he still clung, as some older gentlemen did, to the long, old-fashioned, ruffled shirt cuffs. Somehow they made him look piratical, she thought with distaste.

As they moved through the steps of the dance, Catra caught sight of Ryan dancing with Penelope Worthington. He laughed as his partner said something, and Catra's heart ached. Miss Worthington's hand rested comfortably in Ryan's as she smiled up at him. Catra could not help feeling that hand as if it were her own clasped in the warm, strong fingers. It was a striking contrast to the meaty paw she held now.

''I can't help noticing your ring,'' Mr. Mansfield said to draw her attention back to him. ''I suppose it is an engagement ring from the charming Mr. Chester?''

''Yes,'' Catra answered. Her eyes continued to follow Ryan, noting his easy movement, the broad shoulders erect beneath the fine cloth of his jacket, the neatly groomed waves of his dark hair. His arm was close against the girl's trim waist, and Catra remembered that same strong arm about her waist, pinning her body to his own.

"Ferris Chester," Baker said, "was always a most amiable young man. And when is the auspicious occasion, might I ask?"

"November the seventh," Catra said. She wished he would keep quiet. The pain of watching Ryan with such a pretty partner was almost more than she could bear.

"So soon. Ah, well. What a catch he is, eh? Your father must be quite happy. What a coup for him. The Chesters and the Meredyths, my goodness," he crooned.

Catra snapped her head around to face him. "He is to be *my* husband, Mr. Mansfield, not my father's. It was my decision."

"Obviously." Baker smirked and looked pointedly toward Ryan and Miss Worthington.

Catra flushed and clenched her teeth. "Mr. Mansfield, if I am looking in that direction, it is with you in mind," she said. "What with Miss Worthington being of such particular interest to you."

"Whatever do you mean, my dear?" he asked airily.

She looked at him coldly. "Is Mr. Stevens here this evening? Or doesn't he dance anymore?"

Baker's laugh was loud enough to draw many looks. Catra was mortified. To appear as though she were flirting with this greasy man would be even more humiliating.

"You have nothing to fear, Miss Meredyth," he said conspiratorially near her ear. "She is perfectly brainless."

"I would have nothing to fear if she weren't," Catra snapped.

How dare he presume so. It was nothing to her if Ryan decided to ply his tricks on yet another. But it would serve him right to end up in a duel because of it.

"You, however, should have reason to be concerned," she continued. "Mr. St. James appears to be succeeding where you did not. And I believe his marksmanship leaves little to be desired. But perhaps you feel Miss Worthington's 'brainlessness' is a sufficient excuse for not finding out.''

Baker laughed again, turning just a head or two this time. ''You won't have me killing off your unwanted suitors for you. No, no. I only come to the rescue if properly persuaded. Miss Worthington's powers of persuasion are quite remarkable, which is what angered poor Mr. Stevens. Look for yourself and see.'' He indicated the couple with his eyes.

Miss Worthington was reaching up to touch Ryan's face just next to his eye, where Catra knew a faint scar existed. She felt her breath constrict as she saw Ryan smile gently and say something. Miss Worthington looked surprised, then smiled back.

''Is it that you are afraid of being replaced?'' Baker hissed and bored into her with those insolent eyes.

Catra turned back to him angrily. ''Not I, sir, you,'' she said. ''It looks as though you've lost this time, Mr. Mansfield. And without firing a shot.'' She stopped abruptly and left the dance floor, offering him the most poignant slight at her disposal, that of walking off mid-dance.

Catra searched frantically for Wendy. Near the patio door she spotted her and moved briskly toward her through the crowd. The dance had ended just after she left Baker. At the door, she asked the others in Wendy's group if she could speak privately with Mrs. Thompkins, and at once she made her excuse.

''Wendy, I'm so sorry, but I'm afraid I can't keep up with all of this activity. It was a lovely ball, but I've got such a headache, I really must get to bed,'' she said.

Wendy sympathized, insisting she go up if she was not feeling well. The ball had been a success and Wendy was obviously no longer desperate for her guest to be present.

Catra waved away her offer to escort her up. Bethia would undoubtedly be there, she told her, and Wendy should not abandon her other guests.

Just as Catra reached the door to exit, she felt a firm grip on her elbow from behind. If that odious man had followed her from the room she would kick him, she vowed as she yanked her arm from the offending hand and whirled. She was met by the hard silver eyes and determined brow of Ryan. She caught her breath in surprise.

"I've got to talk to you," he growled. His steely gaze bored into hers.

"What could we possibly have to discuss?" Catra hissed, barely able to catch her breath.

"You may hope that I have forgotten my recent holiday, but I assure you, I have not," he said. He took her upper arm in his hand, a hard, bruising grip. "You have placed me in an interesting position. Shall I remind you of just how precarious the ground is you are walking?"

Catra stared up at him in anger and disbelief. Could he possibly mean what she thought? Did he hope to ruin her future now that he had broken her heart? Maybe she had been foolish and vulnerable in trusting him the first time, but he was mistaken if he thought she was defenseless now.

Her blue eyes flashed fire. "If you've a thought to blackmail, you have less sense than I believed possible," she said incredulously, fear and pain welling up inside her with the force of water behind a dam. "There is nothing that will prevent my marriage," she choked out, "least of all your dubious accusations."

"Accusations, perhaps," Ryan said as he moved closer to her than propriety allowed. She felt the door against her back as she retreated from him. "But dubious, my dear, you cannot argue. Each word true and damning to that artful facade you call a reputation." He was very close to her.

She could smell the warm scent of his body, and every nerve reached out to him while every muscle she had fought it.

"If I were you, I would not throw stones at *my* reputation. Not with Candace Fairchild's skeleton hanging in your closet, Mr. St. James." Catra drew herself up to look at him with what she hoped was contempt. "Even if Ferris were to believe you, which he would not, do you think he would continue to do business with you if you admitted to trying to steal his fiancée? Come now, Mr. St. James, watch your step. For if you threaten me, I have my own ammunition. If Ferris's beloved wife was to express displeasure with you, I doubt your partnership would survive it. There are plenty of other shipping companies."

Ryan's eyes hardened as he grabbed her wrist with the swiftness of a cat. His broad-shouldered form blocked Catra's view of the ballroom and his fingers held her arm like a vise, burning hotly into her skin. But she did not feel the pain, only the searing fire of his touch.

"Beware whom you threaten, sweet," he said in a low voice, his other hand raised to clasp her chin. "Enemies are easier to come by than they are to be rid of." He chucked her gently, derisively, under the chin, and dropped her throbbing arm. He stepped back a pace and bowed deeply. "Good night, Miss Meredyth."

She turned and fled the room.

Chapter Nine

Catra arrived home from Richmond in the early darkness of a November evening. Her wedding was barely a week away and preparations were yet to be made at home. Her trousseau was bought—Madame Jeanville worked furiously to have the gowns ready on time—and what remained now to do was the planning and catering of the post-wedding party.

Mayliza's mother, Sophie Thayer, and Ferris's aunt, Joan Chester, were helping plan the nuptial gathering in lieu of Catra's own mother, but it was still with surprise that Catra greeted Mayliza at her own house upon her return.

Mayliza's curly strawberry-blond hair was pulled back in a controlled knot at the back of her head and she wore a gown of somber gray wool. When Catra alighted from the carriage, Mayliza emerged from the front door to stand in the dim light from the hall on the verandah.

"Mayliza," Catra greeted with a wan smile. "Don't tell

me you and your mother are here 'til this hour working on the party. I'll feel terribly guilty.''

"Hello, Catra," Mayliza answered. "No, Mother is not here. It's only me."

"Is something wrong?" Catra queried. Mayliza's expression was so serious.

"I'm here at your father's request," she answered, tucking her arm in Catra's as they moved toward the door. "Something has happened—"

"Is Father all right?" Catra asked, stopping in her tracks with her heart in her throat.

Mayliza looked surprised. "Good heavens, yes. He's fine. Oh, Cat, I'm sorry to have scared you. It's nothing to do with him. But we thought it best that I tell you the news."

"What's happened?"

"It's Jane, dear. Jane Atherton. They've found her dead. Drowned in the river." Mayliza's brown eyes held concern.

Catra felt as if she'd been punched in the stomach. She had only just seen Jane. How could this be?

"I know you used to be close," Mayliza continued. "And I didn't want you to hear it from a casual source. I was a little afraid you'd hear it on the road. The circumstances were—unusual."

Catra's breath came back to her slowly. She felt as if she had to inhale with great strength to get the thick air into her lungs. Jane Atherton, dead. She conjured a vision of Jane on the last day she'd visited, so beautiful in her simple gown of dove gray. Her eyes so serene and clear.

"What were the circumstances?" she heard herself ask, as Mayliza guided their steps into the brightly lit front hall.

"They found her fully clothed, down near the rapids, there where it gets so rough. We all know there's no reason to go to that area unless you're fishing or something, so no

159

one could figure out how she'd gotten there or what she was doing. There was no sign of a struggle, no bruises upon her person, and the doctor thinks she didn't even float very far.'' Mayliza walked them into the parlor. ''Why don't you get us some tea, Bella?'' she asked the parlor maid. ''And perhaps something to eat for Miss Catra.''

Catra pictured Jane being thrown into the river. The picture of such beauty dying in the churning rocks and mud was horrible.

''Who would do such a thing?'' she murmured. Then more audibly, she turned to Mayliza. ''Do they know who did it?''

Mayliza looked at her steadily. ''They think the most likely possibility is that she did it herself. They think she took her own life.''

Catra's jaw dropped and she felt the pit of her stomach heave up as if she would retch. She covered her face with her hands as the feeling passed and she saw again Jane's image.

''They found a locket she always wore on a rock by the shore. It was placed most carefully, as if it were intended to be found. They say it was the only piece of jewelry she owned and it was given to her by her grandmother. Perhaps she'd meant for one of her sisters to have it.'' Mayliza put her arm around her friend's shoulders.

Catra pictured Jane unclasping the locket with slim, graceful fingers and bending to place it carefully on a rock before stepping cautiously into the water. She would have moved steadily, without indecision, farther and farther into the swiftly flowing river. First her shoes would be sucked into the mire at the bottom of the riverbed, then her skirts would be grabbed by the strength of the heavy current. Perhaps her hands would have trailed along the water's surface as she progressed deeper into the cold, murky water, and maybe she would have stumbled . . .

It would not have taken long in that turbulently surging part of the river, and the loud tumult of the water against the rocks would have drowned out the sound of any last-minute change of heart she might have had.

Catra opened her eyes and shook her head to erase the image. "Why?" she whispered. She took a handkerchief from her pocket and wiped tears from her eyes. "Why would she do it? Was there no explanation?"

Mayliza patted Catra's back. "No. They're not positive it was a suicide. But it seems most likely."

Catra again thought back to that last day they'd been riding. Jane had told her of her engagement, to the Englishman. What had she said about him? She could remember none of the specifics. But she did remember the basis of their conversation because she was surprised at how similarly they were both viewing their situations. Jane had put to words the exact emotion Catra had been feeling about her impending marriage, but she had said it about her own. What was it Jane had said?

"She told me her life was stretched before her like one long bolt of the same material," Catra said aloud, remembering. "She and I felt the same way. I thought we felt the same way." Tears sprang to her eyes again and coursed down her cheeks. "She was unhappy. Maybe that's why she came to see me."

Catra recalled Jane's eyes pleading with her to acquiesce when Ryan had asked if they were planning to stay and watch them shoot. Ryan had flirted with Jane and Jane had blossomed under it. Catra had been jealous at the time—Jane had been radiant at the attention from such a beguiling man. Then later, she'd been worried by his game with Catra.

Bella returned with the tea and placed the tray with a

slight clatter on the table in front of them. Mayliza thanked her in a hushed voice as Catra rose to stand by the window, dabbing at her eyes with her handkerchief. It was very dark outside the window. A cloudy night, no moon. Bard entered with some wood and stoked up the fire in the hearth. Catra hadn't noticed before, but now she noted that the room was chilly.

She turned back to Mayliza and watched her friend pour the tea. May's small, pale hands efficiently took up one cup, then the other, to pour the steaming amber brew.

"She did kill herself," Catra said and watched Mayliza's hands slow as she turned. "I feel sure she did."

Mayliza nodded. "It's a tragedy. She was beautiful. And so sweet. I saw her at the milliner's one Saturday."

"She didn't want to be like everyone else, I think," Catra said, feeling stronger. She moved back to the couch and sat. Mayliza handed her the tea. "And she didn't have any choice. I think maybe that's what happens when we start to feel we don't have any choice. We give up."

Mayliza stirred her tea thoughtfully. She stared into the teacup's shallow depth, at the swirl of cream, the errant tea leaf. "How are you?" she asked then. "You look thin."

Catra laughed shortly, without humor. "I suppose I'm one of the healthy ones. I just got depressed and cried. But I'm all right."

"Your father"—Mayliza paused—"he mentioned to me that you'd left so quickly because you were upset."

"Did he tell you why?"

"Only that you'd begun to get nervous about your marriage. I surmised the rest from our conversation. You told him about Ryan, didn't you?" It was not really a question.

At the sound of his name Catra saw his face and her stomach coiled again. She willed the feeling away. How long before she could expect to think of him without that painful stab of betrayal?

"I did. But it was pointless. He denied it and Ryan—" She was reluctant to voice the words. "Well, Ryan seems to have decided it was not worth the effort anyway." She felt the lump in her throat return and deliberately drank some tea to squelch it. "He was . . . an aberration in my life's history. I'll not think of him again."

"Oh, Catra," Mayliza said mournfully. "I was afraid it was something like that. We won't speak of it again. He'll disappear from your mind, sooner than you think. Don't worry."

Catra smiled wanly. "Yes, well . . ."

"If you're feeling better, your father said to tell you they're fixing your favorite dinner tonight. Ham and raisin sauce, sweet potato pancakes, the whole thing. He was so worried about you, you know. And then when Jane . . ." She trailed off. "Well, he just wanted to make sure you found out the easiest possible way. He loves you very much. He was afraid he'd made you very angry."

Catra felt a pang of guilt. She'd angered her father so thoroughly, worried and upset him over a stupid and dangerously naive affair with a worthless rake. To Ryan she had been nothing. And her father, the person she loved most in the world, felt badly for making her angry.

"I was angry, but he was right. I was just too stupid to see. I hope he didn't worry too much about it." She finished her tea and placed it on the tray, a thought coming to her. "It sounds like you two had quite a conversation," she said quizzically.

To Catra's surprise Mayliza flushed. "Not really. I was surprised when he sent for me this morning, but I understood why as soon as he explained. You know, about Jane. But as for the rest, he didn't tell me so much as I knew.

And I knew about your situation from you.''

"Yes. I must have left you quite curious about the outcome of that,'' Catra said.

"I was, yes,'' Mayliza admitted. "But I knew you'd make the right decision.''

Catra was on the verge of telling her that it was no decision of hers. All the decisions she had made had been bad ones. But she did not want to have to relive the whole story, did not want to have to even remember the whole story, so she let the matter drop.

Preparations for the wedding progressed rapidly now that the event was almost upon them. Orchids that were available from local hothouses were ordered, and silk and muslin arrangements were made by the women of the household. Catra's dress arrived without incident and she was coerced into trying it on for Mayliza, Mrs. Thayer and Joan Chester, Ferris's aunt.

Upon seeing her, the women exclaimed in their most emphatic tones that Catra would positively be the most radiant bride they'd ever seen. The gown was of satin in a soft shade of silver-gray with white Brussels point lace. The color set off Catra's blue eyes in startling contrast to her warm complexion.

Catra tried to muster some enthusiasm. The dress was indeed beautiful, and for any other occasion she would have been at least as energetic in her excitement as the other women at the prospect of wearing it, especially for a situation in which she would be the center of attention.

But all she felt now was a dull dread. She would not be excited to meet Ferris at the altar, to see his eyes light appreciatively upon her in this gown. Nor would she be anxious to remove the gown at the end of the evening. At that thought, Catra hastily made an excuse about being afraid of ruining the dress and hung it in the back corner of her dressing room.

Later that afternoon, Mrs. Chester invited her to join her in going to town. She had to pick up a few odds and ends for the party and thought Catra might be interested in getting out of the house. Catra jumped at the chance. She'd been cooped up inside with lists and plans and maps and diagrams until she thought she would go insane.

At one o'clock the carriage was brought round and the two women, along with Bethia, descended the wide steps of the house to the drive. Catra smiled at her traveling companion, but her thoughts were troubled. She tried telling herself yet again that everything would be fine once the ceremony was over. If she could just get through the planning and get past the knowing anticipation on everyone's faces, everything would be fine.

The day was sunny but cold, and the ground crackled as the carriage wheels broke through the half-frozen mud. Bethia sat on the narrow front seat, her dark eyes open but unseeing in that calm half-trance Catra knew she retreated to whenever she was traveling. Catra and Mrs. Chester sat on either side of the rear seat, each looking out her respective window.

The trees had lost their leaves in the wind and rains of the past two weeks and the countryside was suddenly wintry and bare, though the sun shone strongly overhead. Catra watched a flock of geese, flying in a perfect vee, pass over the trees. Oh, to be soaring up in the boundless skies, Catra thought. To fly in unison side by side in a life as flawless as the blue of the sky today.

Off in the distance a shot shattered the silence of the hills, and a second later another splintered through the trees. Catra watched in horror as two of the geese dropped, one after the other, in stark succession. The remainder continued across the sky in unbalanced synchronicity. A cold feeling of dread crept into her stomach at the sight and the ensuing quiet. She tore her eyes from the window.

The moment they entered the milliner's, Mrs. Chester was immediately captivated by a gown of midnight blue velvet that was on display, and as if by magic any tenseness she had exhibited on the ride from Braithwood seemed to drop away. Catra wished that her troubles could be forgotten as easily. She stood in front of a table covered with buttons, feigning interest, but in her mind she maintained the steady drumbeat of her chant: everything would turn out fine, as soon as this was over, everything would be fine.

As she systematically picked up and discarded cards of buttons, an unfamiliar voice from behind her slowly penetrated her preoccupation.

"Well, Mirabelle said she just ten minutes ago saw their carriage pull up to Pears' Inn," an old woman's voice said conspiratorially. Catra stood still, listening.

"I wonder what it is they're buying. You can bet the cost would feed our household for a month," a younger woman's crabby voice answered her.

"I'll bet it's things for a wedding tour they're shopping for. What I wouldn't give to be at that wedding," the first woman said with a sigh.

The younger stated with a snort, "Not *me*. Just the sight of all those prideful riches and waste would turn my stomach. Why, Sally just the other day said that the gown she wore for her engagement cost nearly five hundred dollars. Said it was twenty-five yards of pure silk with solid gold beads and pearls sewn into the skirt."

The older woman must have moved; her voice was farther away. "I'll bet she looked fine in that. What a lovely thing she is, living just like a princess too. Why, it's all just like a dream. Imagine being so rich and handsome. I'd pay money just to look in the window at their reception.'' She paused. "That's a nice piece there, Cynthia, why don't you buy that?"

"Isn't it? Well, I'll tell you, you'd do better to forge invitations and sell them. You can bet everyone in the county's going to want to go to that wedding. But not me, I tell you. I wouldn't go if they invited me personally. No sir, those people are snobs, nothing but rich, boastful snobs," the younger woman huffed.

The older woman cackled heartily. "You'd go in a second, Cynthia, and you know it. And if someone gave you half a chance, you'd step right into her shoes and marry Ferris Chester, you would."

"Well, he's different," the younger woman said. Catra could hear them moving toward the door. "Every time I see him he tips his hat nice as can be, with the most charming smile—but that Catherine Meredyth holds her nose so high in the air . . ."

"I still think you should buy that blue . . ." Catra heard the older woman say as they faded out of earshot.

Catra looked down at the buttons she was holding, a small, haphazard collection. She knew enough not to be offended by anything the women said; she had been the object of so much gossip in her life that it didn't seem strange anymore. But the conversation brought her mind back to Ferris. He didn't deserve the scandal she'd nearly created. He had been nothing but caring and gentlemanly all through their lives. If there was one thing in this whole mess to be thankful for, it was that she didn't need to embarrass him. But it was small consolation, considering how desperately she dreaded their marriage.

At that point Mrs. Chester called to her, a bolt of fabric in her arms, and Catra reluctantly abandoned her solitude to join her. She spent the rest of the afternoon absently perusing the shops and watching Mrs. Chester exult over one item after another that Catra could not have cared less about.

To Catra's profound relief, they finally started home after consulting the dressmaker and arranging for her to create two traveling gowns for Catra. It seemed to Catra they had entered every shop in town and bought something in half of them.

They arrived at Waverly, where Catra was to drop off Mrs. Chester, at tea time. Mrs. Chester had invited her for tea and Catra had politely declined; but when the coach pulled up in front of the house Ferris met them and insisted she come in.

"I've just had a letter," he said with excitement as he took her arm, "that I must share with you."

He lead her up the steps and into the house, with Mrs. Chester and Bethia trailing behind. As they entered the parlor Bethia continued down the hall to the back kitchen.

Tea was already prepared and arranged for them on a table which no doubt had to be cleared before placing it there. Everything in the Chester household was covered with knickknacks. They were a passion of Mrs. Chester's, and it seemed to Catra that every flat surface within reach contained trinkets, figurines, pieces of china or some other small article that Mrs. Chester had discovered and decided she could not live without. Catra frequently felt sorry for the house servants, having to dust so many little useless items.

Ferris waited for the ladies to sit before drawing an envelope from his breast pocket. Catra caught only a glimpse of the black, spidery handwriting, but it was enough to send her stomach flying into her rib cage. She had only seen his writing once before, but she was without a doubt that the letter Ferris held in his hand was from Ryan St. James. Had

Ferris's face held anything other than happy excitement she would have been terrified that the letter contained the blackmail with which Ryan had threatened her in Richmond.

"It's from Ryan," Ferris explained needlessly. "I'd written to him to ask a kindness and he has replied most favorably. Let me read it to you." He cleared his throat. " 'Dear Ferris, I've received your request and answer you quickly as you are due to leave so imminently. You are, of course, welcome in the St. James home at any time with the hope that we can receive and entertain you as warmly as you did me. As far as our home being a stop on your nuptial journey, I can unfortunately think of nothing particularly romantic or enticing about our humble city for a couple so newly wed. I could suggest many . . .' " Ferris trailed off, reading. "Here he goes into some suggestions for other places we might like as well, but . . . oh, here it is: 'However, if you are set on coming, the doors shall be open to you and, of course, your bride.' " Ferris folded the letter and beamed into Catra's horrified face. "What do you think of going to Boston?"

Catra could barely believe she was hearing correctly. "You—you want to visit *him* on our wedding tour?" she croaked.

"Yes! Why not? Why visit a bunch of places where we don't know anyone? The St. Jameses are wonderful people. You'll love them. Ryan's got a sister just a year or two older than we are."

She was so stunned by this proposal that she could barely do more than stare into Ferris's open, expectant face. He thought she would be delighted, she could see him waiting for it.

"I think it's a grand idea," Mrs. Chester piped up. "He's such a nice young man. And you're right, Ferris, it's so much better to visit friends rather than just places." She nodded her small, mousy head in agreement with herself.

"I thought we were going to New York," Catra managed.

"We still will," he coaxed, and took her hand in his. "We'll stop there first. We'll need to stop along the way anyway. But we'll have such fun in Boston. This way we'll know which parties to go to, where the best theater is. It'll be fun, you'll see." He patted her hand as if she were a child.

"Ferris," she began firmly, "I know you mean this to be for our enjoyment, but to be perfectly honest I did not particularly like your friend. I'm not at all sure I want to spend my wedding tour with him."

Ferris's face clouded. "Not like Ryan? Whatever do you mean? Come now, remember the fun we had that day we were shooting? You two were laughing together, we all were. Even poor Jane," he added reflectively.

Catra's gaze fell to her lap and a pain lanced through her chest, both for the loss of Jane and the loss of the happiness she used to feel in Ryan's presence.

"I was being polite," she said. "And shouldn't we be alone for our wedding tour? Why should we search out parties and socials when we've got plenty of that here?"

"Catra," he protested, "you *like* parties and socials."

"Ordinarily, yes. But couldn't we make this tour a time for us alone?" She could hardly believe she was arguing for time alone with a man she didn't even want to marry.

"We'll have plenty of time alone," he said dismissively. "The whole trip to New York and then home. I want to go to Boston."

Catra's ire was raised at this statement. "Don't I have a say too? This is my wedding also, you know."

"Honey," Mrs. Chester broke in with a soft hand on Catra's arm, "you should want to do what your husband wants.'' She chastised Catra with gentle doe eyes.

Catra glared at her. ''My husband should be thinking a little of his wife.'' She turned to Ferris. ''I have absolutely no desire to go to Boston. Your friend is an insolent boar with a scandalous reputation. Do you have any idea what they're saying about him in Richmond? I can't believe you expected me to want to go.''

Mrs. Chester whimpered softly at the aggressive tone of Catra's voice.

Ferris's face went white, then suffused with red. ''You are speaking of one of my closest friends—''

''Closest friends!'' she scoffed. ''You barely know the man. Why, in ten years of doing business with your uncle, have we never met him before just recently? And how in the world did he get back to Boston so quickly—I just saw him in Richmond last week.''

''He only decided to move south a few months ago. And you have not been involved in Uncle's business dealings, so why should you have met him? Or me, for that matter. As for being back in Boston, his plan was always to move here in the spring.''

Catra could not argue with this but was reluctant to let him off the hook. ''In any case, he is a rogue, from what I've heard. I have no desire to be in the same house with him.''

''What have you heard?'' Ferris demanded, looking angrier than she thought she'd ever seen him. But she did not care; she was defending something far more important.

''He's a womanizer! He has an affair in every town he goes to. There are other things, as well, which I decline to mention in front of your aunt,'' Catra evaded. For some reason she had no desire to tell Ferris of the Candace Fairchild incident. Perhaps he would confront Ryan with it, divulging his source, and incite Ryan into revealing *their* affair.

"Aunt Joan, please leave the room," Ferris commanded. "I would like to hear what Catra has to say about Ryan."

Mrs. Chester rose obediently to leave.

"Sit down, please," Catra ordered. "I have no desire to justify my position any longer, particularly when it involves unpleasant issues about which I would rather not speak."

Mrs. Chester hovered hesitantly over the couch. Ferris waved her impatiently away and she scurried off. She closed the door behind her with fastidious care.

Catra stood and paced to the bookshelves.

"Tell me what you've heard," Ferris demanded. Catra turned furious eyes upon him.

"You think you can order me about the way you do your aunt?" she exploded. "Do you think that with a wave of your hand you can have me do what you want? Think again, Ferris Chester. I'll do as I please."

He reached her in two strides. "You haven't told me about Ryan yet. Is it that you know nothing? Why won't you visit him?"

"I told you!" She jerked away from him. Why was he being so insistent? "He's a womanizer. I've heard tell of dozens of affairs he's had."

"What makes you think it's not just idle gossip? Are you afraid of being one of them yourself?" he accused with narrowed eyes.

Catra felt her face freeze. Did he know something? Why did he say that? "No, of course not," she said. "What a ridiculous thing to say."

Ferris turned and walked back to the tea tray. "I've heard that many women have fallen victim to Ryan's charms, but is that his fault or theirs? The only reason I can see for your fearing such gossip is that you're afraid of becoming part of it.'' His tone was almost conversational now. And though she was relieved that his question about her involvement with Ryan's reputation was just rhetorical, his regained composure infuriated her.

''That makes no sense, Ferris. I can certainly exercise my desire to avoid immoral people.''

''If you have nothing to substantiate the claim that Ryan is immoral, I would appreciate it if you did not further such gossip.'' He sat and poured himself a cup of tea.

Catra felt the ground loosening under her argument. The only evidence she had was evidence she could not possibly share. Catra seethed but said nothing.

''We shall go to Boston,'' Ferris said. ''And that's final. Now, have some tea.''

Chapter Ten

Two days later Bethia fixed Catra's bath as Catra sat in bed with her breakfast tray on her lap.

"You eat some of that, missy, or I'll have your hide for sure," Bethia warned. "I'm glad to see you getting your figure back. You were getting thin as a stick. Wasting away to nothing over some no 'count man."

"What are you talking about?" Catra frowned, holding a piece of sausage between two delicate fingers.

"Oh, don't you think I don't know, missy. I've been watching you like a hawk these last few weeks and I can tell when someone is pining away over a man." Bethia watched her as she hung the new gowns just in from Madame Jeanville.

"Who in the world would I be pining away for, Bethia?" Catra asked, looking away. "If not for poor Jane."

"You were peculiar long before Jane Atherton's unhappy end and don't I know it. I had to sit, day after day,

watching you waste away in love for that Mr. St. James,"
Bethia said and was rewarded with confirmation of her sus-
picions on Catra's red face.

"I am *not* in love with Mr. St. James, of all the men in
the world." Catra's voice held a note of desperate absur-
dity. "I don't know where you got such a wild notion. And
if you don't hush your mouth about it, you're sure to get
me in trouble with Ferris, my *betrothed,* remember?"

"Oh, I remember, all right. But you were sure acting
like you were pining away. Look at your face, thin and
pale. Why if I ever saw anybody in love with the wrong
man, it's you." Bethia snorted. "Look at the way you pick
at your food. These dresses won't barely fit, with you looking like that."

"I am *not* in love with the wrong man, Bethia," Catra
said and stuffed a piece of ham into her mouth. "I am not
in love with *any* man. I am perfectly reconciled to my marriage with Ferris. And if anyone thinks differently, they can
go to the devil."

"If you say so, Miss Catra." Bethia turned back to the
dresses.

After eating and taking her bath, Catra dressed and descended to the parlor. Ferris was to visit that afternoon and
she wanted to collect herself before he came. She had not
seen him since their argument and could put him off no
longer. The wedding was only two days away.

If she was to have to see Ryan on their wedding tour,
Catra thought morosely, then she would have to reconcile
herself more thoroughly to her marriage with Ferris. She
was determined to make peace with him.

Besides, if Bethia could see her broken heart, then Ryan
would also. She was not going to have herself pining away
before Ryan's very eyes; he would be looking for it. No,
she was going to look as beautiful and as in love with her

husband as she possibly could. Ryan's heart was going to break into tiny pieces when he saw what he could have had and threw away.

She rang the bell and waited for the parlor maid to appear. "Fetch me some cakes, Bella," Catra said, "and warm chocolate."

"Yes'm," the girl said, curtsied and left.

She would go out of her way to be kind to Ferris, Catra decided. He would never know what treachery she had planned for him. She would be a faithful, loving wife. If that was her only option, she would make it her choice.

Ferris arrived precisely at the appointed hour and was ushered into the parlor.

"Darling!" He rushed to her side where she sat on the love seat. "I've been beside myself since our tiff. Please accept my apology for my loss of temper the other day." He took her hand and kissed it.

Catra smiled at him. "It's all right, Ferris. I'm sorry also. I didn't mean to upset you."

Ferris looked earnestly at her. "Catra, will you really forgive me for being such a pompous husband-to-be? I didn't mean to accuse you of anything improper. You'll see, everything will be fine when we get to Boston. Then the whole argument will be forgotten."

Catra looked into his eyes, wide and innocent as a child's. His blond hair was combed perfectly into place, and his milk-white face flushed slightly as he bent and kissed her hand again. He really saw nothing wrong in ordering her to go to Boston, she thought.

"I'm so relieved. I was so worried. I hated for us to quarrel so close to the wedding." He smiled, bringing out two dimples. "The wedding!" He laughed. "Sometimes I think it will never get here. It feels like an eternity since I asked you; and now our wedding is only two days away."

Thrill to the most sensual, adventure-filled Historical Romances on the market today…

FROM  LEISURE BOOKS

As a home subscriber to the Leisure Historical Romance Book Club, you'll enjoy the best in today's BRAND-NEW Historical Romance fiction. For over twenty-five years, Leisure Books has brought you the award-winning, high-quality authors you know and love to read. Each Leisure Historical Romance will sweep you away to a world of high adventure…and intimate romance. Discover for yourself all the passion and excitement millions of readers thrill to each and every month.

SAVE AT LEAST *$5.00* EACH TIME YOU BUY!

Each month, the Leisure Historical Romance Book Club brings you four brand-new titles from Leisure Books, America's foremost publisher of Historical Romances. EACH PACKAGE WILL SAVE YOU AT LEAST $5.00 FROM THE BOOKSTORE PRICE! And you'll never miss a new title with our convenient home delivery service.

Here's how we do it. Each package will carry a 10-DAY EXAMINATION privilege. At the end of that time, if you decide to keep your books, simply pay the low invoice price of $16.96 ($17.75 US in Canada), no shipping or handling charges added*. HOME DELIVERY IS ALWAYS FREE*. With today's top Historical Romance novels selling for $5.99 and higher, our price SAVES YOU AT LEAST $5.00 with each shipment.

AND YOUR FIRST FOUR-BOOK SHIPMENT IS TOTALLY FREE!

IT'S A BARGAIN YOU CAN'T BEAT! A Super $21.96 Value!

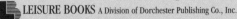 **LEISURE BOOKS** A Division of Dorchester Publishing Co., Inc.

GET YOUR 4 FREE* BOOKS NOW—
A $21.96 VALUE!

Mail the Free* Book
Certificate
Today!

4 FREE* BOOKS ❧ A $21.96 VALUE

Free Books Certificate

YES! I want to subscribe to the Leisure Historical Romance Book Club. Please send me my 4 FREE* BOOKS. Then each month I'll receive the four newest Leisure Historical Romance selections to Preview for 10 days. If I decide to keep them, I will pay the Special Member's Only discounted price of just $4.24 each, a total of $16.96 ($17.75 US in Canada). This is a SAVINGS OF AT LEAST $5.00 off the bookstore price. There are no shipping, handling, or other charges*. There is no minimum number of books I must buy and I may cancel the program at any time. In any case, the 4 FREE* BOOKS are mine to keep—A BIG $21.96 Value!

*In Canada, add $5.00 shipping and handling per order for first shipment. For all subsequent shipments to Canada, the cost of membership is $17.75 US, which includes $7.75 shipping and handling per month.[All payments must be made in US dollars]

Name _____

Address _____

City _____

State _____ *Country* _____ *Zip* _____

Telephone _____

Signature _____

If under 18, Parent or Guardian must sign. Terms, prices and conditions subject to change. Subscription subject to acceptance. Leisure Books reserves the right to reject any order or cancel any subscription.

(Tear Here and Mail Your FREE* Book Card Today!)

Get Four Books Totally
FREE* —
A $21.96 Value!

(Tear Here and Mail Your FREE* Book Card Today!)

PLEASE RUSH
MY FOUR FREE*
BOOKS TO ME
RIGHT AWAY!

Leisure Historical Romance Book Club
P.O. Box 6613
Edison, NJ 08818-6613

He smiled happily, and as Catra looked at him her heart warmed—as it would to a puppy clamoring for attention, she thought.

"Kiss me, Ferris," she said suddenly, wanting to wipe out the pathetic image. "Kiss me now, as you will when we are married."

Surprised, Ferris leaned forward and tentatively touched her lips with his. Her hands came up to his shoulders and pulled him close to her, her eyes closed tightly. Her heart willed him to respond ardently, commandingly—as Ryan had.

But Ferris pulled back, flustered. "Catra, I—" He laughed nervously and flushed to the roots of his hair.

She sighed. "I'm sorry, Ferris." She lowered her eyes to mask her disappointment. "I don't know what came over me." She thought of the kiss in the garden, the first time Ryan had held her. Her hands clenched in her lap. "Oh, I just wish we were getting married tomorrow," she said impulsively.

Ferris straightened with a self-important air and took her hand. "We'll be married soon enough, Catra." He smiled again. "It seems like a long time to me, as well, but you'll see. Before we know it we'll be sailing for New York, just you and I, in the bridal chamber."

Absolutely sure of Catra's forgiveness, he could hardly contain his good humor as he left. He laughed and inquired how everyone was from the parlor maid to the butler, as his heels clicked spiritedly across the marble hall to the door. He departed with a flourish, bubbling with confidence and anticipation.

After witnessing Ferris's exit, Catra's father joined her in the parlor. She was sitting by the window staring out, unfinished needlework in her hands.

"Ferris seems in the best of spirits and ready to make

you a doting husband,'' he said with amusement as he seated himself in the chair across from her. He regarded her in silence for a moment, then added quietly, ''Have you done with your regrets? And have you forgiven me for having to cause them?''

''I have no regrets, Father,'' Catra said. ''And I've found that I have nothing to forgive you for. I know you were protecting me. I'm sorry I made it so hard for you.''

''I imagine it was harder for you,'' he said and looked at her contemplatively. ''You're putting on weight. You look much better.''

She inclined her head to acknowledge the compliment.

Her father stretched his legs in front of him and leaned back in his chair. Taking a cigar from his pocket, he perused the room idly. He rolled the cigar between his thumb and forefinger but made no move to light it. Catra thought he looked as though there was something he wanted to say but didn't know how to begin, which was strange for her father. He was the type of man who always knew what he was about, and nothing could deter him from his purpose. To see him acting anything less than sure of himself was a rarity of a kind to make Catra doubt her perception.

She bent her head to her needlework.

''You know, Catra,'' her father said, ''running a plantation is hard work. Hard work requiring both brains and experience. Add to that a business and you have to have a good man to handle it. Ferris is such a man. He may be young yet, but he's intelligent and capable.''

''Yes, I know, Father.''

He watched her as she lowered her eyes to her work. What was he trying to say? she wondered. She had presented a perfectly agreeable attitude to the marriage these past few weeks. Perhaps he was still worried about her other attachment.

Compulsion

He continued to roll the cigar back and forth between his fingers. "I hope you realize that I did not refuse St. James simply because of my plans with the Chesters. I made the decision with your best interests in mind. I want you to know that. Ferris will be able to care for you and keep you in the style in which you were brought up. He will also strive to make you happy, which I doubt St. James would know how to do." He sat for a moment more, then harrumphed decisively and put the cigar back in his pocket unlit. "I think someday you will see this arrangement as the suitable and propitious one that it is. In the meantime, you must trust me to know what is best for you."

"Of course. I do now, Father," Catra said. She looked up at him, slow realization beginning to dawn on her. He was feeling *guilty*. But for what? Everything he had said had been proven correct. Of course he couldn't let her marry a scoundrel like Ryan. Perhaps he was feeling badly because it was the first time he had been unable to give her what he thought she truly wanted. He couldn't know she'd been as much as jilted at the same time he was denying her request.

"Well, good, then," he said gruffly, rising. "I'm glad." He looked at her and seemed about to say something more, then changed his mind and turned to the door. He moved erectly, shaking off his misgivings as he walked. When he turned back again at the door, Catra looked for the familiar, confident look on his face and saw a close replica. Only his eyes remained regretful. "I will see you at supper," he said and left.

Catra looked back down at her needlework, her fingers still. How strange that her father should suddenly feel a need to assure her on this topic. Her fate had been sealed for weeks now, with her own consent and submission. Why would he try to justify it to her now? She shook her head

179

and admitted to herself that perhaps she did not know her father quite as well as she believed.

Catra woke from a half sleep the morning of her wedding in a cold sweat. Her stomach swam sickeningly and her taut nerves jumped when she heard Bethia's soft humming enter the dressing room next door. She knew from whence came the sick feeling, for she'd had it on and off all night. She had slept poorly and then only to wake with a start and the fear that the sun had risen. But instead of feeling exhaustion from the sleepless night, she felt perversely alert, agonizingly aware of each morning noise. It was panic. It was every nerve in her body telling her to flee.

Instead she lay still, rigid. Because she was unable to escape the dreaded day, she felt herself unable to move at all.

Bethia moved softly around the other room, and Catra heard the rustle of the wedding gown, then the petticoats that were to be worn under it, as it was taken away, most likely to straighten and press. After a moment she heard someone else enter, then the sound of water as it hit the dry bottom of the tub.

She heard the quiet click of the armoire door, then the dressing room door to the hall opened and closed. All was silent. The humming was gone.

She willed herself to move, her limbs stiff and unyielding. She sat up and swung her legs over the side of the mattress, toes habitually searching out the step stool next to the high bed. She pulled her heavy hair back from her face and pushed it to fall down her back.

It was here Bethia found her, stoop-shouldered at the edge of the bed and staring at the floor in a trance.

"There's the bride," Bethia cooed in her rich, mellow voice, a broad smile on her face.

Catra did not look up. She clutched her arms before her and shuddered violently.

"What are you doing?" Bethia asked, a crease between her eyebrows. She came around the bed to study Catra. "Staring at your cold feet?"

Catra smiled grimly and raised her eyes. "They're not just cold, Bethia. They're frostbitten."

Bethia gave her a knowing look. "There hasn't been a bride yet who walked down that aisle with anything less. Come on now, get up." She took Catra by the arm and urged her up. "Tub's awaiting."

Catra undressed mechanically. "What sort of day is it?"

"It's a cold one," Bethia stated. "Gray. But makes for a nice cozy time inside. We're gonna have both hearths lit tonight and hot toddies for everyone. It'll be just perfect, don't you worry."

Catra lowered herself into the steaming water. She picked up the lilac-scented soap and smoothed it between her hands underwater. The water's warmth seeped into her bones, warming her deep inside like a sip of strong brandy. She felt her muscles relax under its spell. The smell of lilac drifted up with the steam, evoking bittersweet memories of warm spring days spent freely playing barefooted in the grass. Those days were long ago, before the reality of life was discovered.

She leaned her head back in the water. Her hair sank slowly around her and the water filled her ears to blot out all sound. It was a peaceful underwater world. She sank lower, the water covering her face. She could feel her hair drifting like seaweed about her, along her arms, across her face. Suddenly she thought of Jane, of her long tresses drifting with the current and her skirts pulling at her legs. She thought how much simpler it would have been to sink into a bathtub . . .

181

She had held her breath for maybe thirty seconds when her head began to ache. She willed herself to stay under. Presently the ache dissolved and she began to feel light-headed, almost as if she could open her mouth and safely breathe the water. She let her arms drift to the surface. The world behind her eyelids went red. She felt her lungs burn.

She opened her mouth to let the water in, not yet trying to breathe but knowing she could if she wanted to. Just when she was sure she could stay there forever, she felt her lungs burst. Her stomach twisted and she bolted upward out of the water. Water splashed recklessly onto the floor as she heaved herself out of the tub. She threw her hair back from her face, it slapped loudly on her back and she skidded across the wet floor to the basin near the mirror. Stomach roiling, she retched into the bowl.

The water still danced crazily in the tub when Bethia entered to see her, naked and dripping, braced over the basin.

"I can't do it, Bethia," she cried. Her hair clung like snakes to her wet back and arms. "I can't face it. How am I going to go through with it when the very thought . . ." She coughed again and sputtered. Her shoulders shook as Bethia wrapped her in a warm robe.

"I'll grow to hate him. I know it," Catra continued. "My life is going to be miserable. I'll turn into a shrew and make him miserable as well. And there's no way out. There's no way out . . ." A sob pushed its way out. "I know just how Jane felt. I am almost just like her. How can I stand it when she couldn't? She was so calm and accepting, and I—I'm not, ever. I'll never survive it if she couldn't."

"You hush up now," Bethia snapped. "That's exactly why you will survive it. You're a fighter. You are. You aren't going to lie down before the lions and let them eat you. You are strong-willed. Strong enough to survive a little hardship in your life.'' She started to rub Catra's wet hair roughly with a towel. Then she stopped. "So you aren't getting your way. What of it? There's more to life than picking the right boy, for goodness sakes. You aren't like Jane a bit. You've got wealth and opportunities. You're marrying up to your station and you'll be living the life you were born to. Now you quit this caterwauling like a child that hasn't got any candy and you pull yourself together.''

Catra's tears stopped as she looked in amazement at Bethia's completely uncharacteristic display of anger.

"Only one's going to turn into a shrew's the one who lets herself," Bethia muttered, still angry. "You and Ferris are friends. That's a lot more'n most people get.''

Shamed, Catra took the towel from Bethia and started to dry her own hair. She took a deep breath and rubbed the towel across her face. Bethia was right, of course. How pompous to imagine her life was anything like poor Jane's. She was not staring into a future of scrubbing coal-blackened laundry and struggling to feed and clothe whatever babies her unwanted husband would bestow upon her. She was marrying a friend, a wealthy one, and mourning only the loss of a feeling she'd never even known until a month ago.

Catra stood and dried the rest of her body. Bethia had gone back to the dressing room and returned now with the gown. She hung it on the door to the sitting room. Then she retrieved the specially embroidered bridal underthings and laid them on the bed.

"You're right, Bethia," Catra said quietly from her seat at the dressing table. "I'm sorry I was carrying on so.''

Bethia stopped what she was doing. Then she nodded and left the room.

*   *   *

Holding on to her father's arm, Catra walked with as much confidence and grace as she could muster. At the altar Ferris, with a bewitched smile, took her hand. She barely felt the floor as they knelt before the minister.

Ferris's hand on hers was warm and dry, his grip tight, as if he feared she might try to run away. The minister's voice droned on as Catra studied the finely polished wood of the altar, noting the darkened grain, the presence of a knothole.

At long last she felt Ferris begin to rise and she allowed him to help her stand. Mayliza flurried discreetly behind her as she straightened the train of the gown and veil.

"Do you, Catherine Anne Meredyth, take Ferris Noel Chester to be your husband?" Catra came out of her trance in time to hear the minister's solemn question. A sudden panic shot through her and she felt her breath lodge in her throat. Her stomach floated somewhere up near her heart, which beat like a frightened rabbit's.

Instinctively Ferris's hold on her hand tightened.

"Do you promise to love, honor and obey him, to stand by him, in sickness and in health, until death do you part?"

Catra felt the thick silence of the room. She imagined Mayliza standing faithfully beside her, knowing something of her torment. She imagined her father waiting onerously for her answer, so that he too could breathe a sigh of relief. She saw, as if from a long distance, Ferris's waiting eyes, gentle and familiar again, penitent after their last argument.

And she knew, somewhere in the church, Bethia watched Catra's every move, waiting to see if she'd really grown up.

"I do," she said. It was a strong voice but flat, devoid of emotion. It was not an answer to a question; it was a line in a play that did not involve her, had nothing to do with her soul.

Ferris spoke then, in response to the same line, in a deep voice, decisiveness ringing in the tone.

The minister motioned for them to turn and face the crowd. From behind her she heard his voice boom, "Ladies and gentlemen of the congregation, it gives me great pleasure to introduce to you Mr. and Mrs. Ferris Chester."

Chapter Eleven

A cold sun sank below a bleak Boston skyline, but Ryan St. James did not see it. Nor did he care. Inside the dark recesses of the Hawk & Dove Saloon, he sat slumped over a short glass of whiskey, a near-empty bottle at his elbow.

"Ryan, you can't keep at this," Tom implored. He stood uncomfortably in the smoky room, his clothes and manner standing out like a new penny in coal cinders. The barkeep asked him what he wanted, but the young man waved him away with an impatient hand.

Ryan, on the other hand, was completely in keeping with the surroundings, with unkempt hair, an unshaven face and wrinkled, unwashed clothes—a circumstance that seemed to bother Tom considerably.

"Leave me alone, Tom." Ryan's voice attempted authority but was at this moment laced with drunkenness.

"I'll not leave you alone. Look at you. You're destroying yourself." Tom ignored the curious stares of the men nearest them. "Think of your father, then. He depends upon you. And right now he's beside himself with worry. At his age it's not good for him to have to worry like that. Don't you care? Can't you think of what you're doing to him? You may think he's indestructible—"

"He *is* indestructible," Ryan growled, angered that the old man had been brought into the conversation. "And I doubt he's ever been worried about anything in his life. I imagine he's probably beside himself with anger instead." He grabbed at the bottle roughly, but his aim was not sure and the bottle skittered across the varnished bar to land with a crash on the floor. "*Damn.* Nate! Another one," he yelled to the barkeep, scattering a handful of cash on the bar.

Tom ignored the bottle and the bartender. "As I was saying, you may think he is indestructible, but the company is not. He can't handle all of Standard Shipping himself anymore." His voice rose slightly. "But most importantly, Ryan, I can't stand by and watch you do this to yourself. What's happened to you? You've completely taken leave of yourself. We're trying to understand, but we haven't a clue." At Ryan's blithe dismissal of this speech Tom took him by the shoulder and turned him from the bar. "Are you *listening* to me?"

Ryan slipped on the stool as Tom grabbed him, but he righted himself quickly and stood up. At the same time he grabbed Tom by the lapel and pulled him close, their faces inches apart. Even wavering, he stood a head taller than Tom, but the young man looked steadily back at him.

"Listen close, Tom," he said, his eyes surprisingly clear and narrowed to piercing slits. "You will leave this bar and you will quit harassing me or I will kick you out. I don't want to hurt you, Tom. But you're bothering me. Now get out." With that, Ryan released him and Tom, temporarily silenced, stepped back.

Tom thought for a moment, then said, undaunted, "Will you at least tell me why you're doing this? It isn't like you. Just tell me why." His eyes were all concern.

Ryan knocked back the remainder of his drink and opened the new bottle of whiskey, sitting back down on the stool. "I don't want to tell you," he said, disgusted at the way his tongue refused to work properly.

"Why not?" Tom placed his hands on the bar and looked into Ryan's face. "Look, I may be just the guy who married your kid sister, and I know you think I wouldn't understand what's eating you, but I know you well, probably better than anyone except your sister. Please tell me. It may help."

"You couldn't possibly help me." For the first time Tom seemed taken aback at the savage tone of the words. "Besides, I can't tell you," Ryan added, more gently, but did not look up.

Tom pulled up the stool next to Ryan's and sat. "You've not been yourself since you returned from Virginia," he said. "Did something happen there? We know about the incident with the Fairchilds. Is it something to do with that?"

Ryan slowly turned in his seat and rose unsteadily to his feet. "I meant what I said about throwing you out," he said evenly. "Now go home. Standard Shipping won't fall apart because I've taken some time off. Tell Father and Lydia I'll be home eventually. There's something I have to work out for myself."

"With *this?*" Tom gestured toward the bottle of whiskey. "Ryan, you've been saying the same thing for weeks. We don't believe it anymore—"

"I don't give a goddamn *what* you believe," Ryan shouted. In one smooth motion he turned, scooped up his glass and threw it against the wall. It exploded into pieces, the whiskey splattering into a large, spiderlike shape on the wood. "Go home to your *wife*," he muttered. He picked up the bottle, and the fresh glass the barkeep had instantly produced, and moved across the room, sliding into a chair at a table.

Tom stood fixed in indecision. The rest of the bar, after assessing that the commotion was not going to result in a fight, turned back to their own business. He's going to kill himself, Tom thought as he looked at Ryan, slouched in the chair, peering intently through red-rimmed eyes at the label on the bottle he had just purchased. His skin was pale in contrast to the dark stubble along his jaw, and his face was wan and tense. His thick, dark hair straggled down his neck, and several locks fell on his forehead, only to be pushed away every few minutes by an impatient, often inaccurate hand.

Tom shook his head. There was nothing for it. The man had been running himself into the ground for weeks over God only knew what, and it looked as if he were deeper into it now than ever before.

Tom ran a hand over his face. How could he go back and face Lydia? How could he tell her that, as far as he could discern, her brother was hell-bent on killing himself and there was not a damn thing he could do about it? He couldn't even find out why.

Ryan leaned back in his chair, his eyes closed, the bottle and glass clutched in his hands in front of him. For a moment Tom's heart leapt. If he had passed out, he could be carried to the brougham and taken home. Home, where his father could get the truth out of him and pull him out of this sloth. But the hope was squelched when Ryan's eyes opened again and he poured himself another drink, splashing some on the sleeve of his jacket only to brush it off on his pants. Tom sighed and turned to the door. He would have to think of something to tell Lydia, something more hopeful than the truth.

Ryan viewed Tom's departure with relief, then swung the bottle back and drank; the full glass sat on the table in front of him. Soon thereafter, a man who had sat down the bar from Ryan all afternoon rose and joined him at the table.

"Couldn't help overhearin' yer convershashon," the man said and looked at Ryan through watery eyes. "Stan's my name. But everone calls me Walter."

Ryan looked at him dispassionately for a long moment. The man returned his stare with an unfocused look. "That's a strange nickname—Walter," Ryan said finally, making a conscious decision to speak with the man. He took another pull at the bottle.

"Yep," the man said. "Don't know where it come from, neither." He spoke with such a look of despair and confusion on his face that after a moment Ryan laughed. It was a harsh sound in the gloomy room. The man turned red-rimmed eyes to him.

"Lemme buy you a drink," Ryan said and filled the man's near-empty glass from his own full bottle. Suddenly the idea of a companion appealed to him. Anything to get his mind off himself. "To you, Walter," he said and raised the bottle, drinking again. Walter smiled and drank with him.

Walter said, "Look, I know you gots troubles. I heard you talkin' to that boy. I got troubles too. We wouldn't be here lessen we did, right? Am I right?" He looked as straight as he could into Ryan's eyes.

"Damn right," Ryan said, and they both raised their glasses and drank.

"Mine's woman troubles. Goddamn woman troubles.

They're a sorry lot, women," Walter said as Ryan filled his glass again.

"Damn right," Ryan repeated.

"You got woman troubles too," Walter said. "I can tell a man with woman troubles a mile off. An' you got woman troubles."

"Damn right," Ryan said yet again, but with considerably less energy than the first two times. "Damn woman got married." He looked at his drink, as if the voice that had spoken had come from inside the glass, then drank the whiskey down.

"Ooooh." Walter flinched dramatically. "That happened to me too. Yep, up and married shome other guy. Leff me high and dry. Stupid gal. No regrets."

Ryan wasn't sure if the man meant he had no regrets or the woman had none but decided not to pursue it.

As he sat staring into his drink, an image of Catra formed in his mind. Catra, as she had looked that last day by the river, slender as a willow in her closely tailored riding habit, her hair catching the light and reflecting it back with a rich, honeyed glow. He pictured her as she'd turned toward him, her calm eyes transparent as glass and saying everything he wanted, and needed, to know. Those same eyes that had turned on him with such fierceness at the ball in Richmond.

"I thought she was so honest," Ryan said bitterly. "So beautiful and true. Like no other woman I'd ever met. But there she was at that goddamned ball, throwing everything back in my face. Ridiculing me for falling in love with her. Or what I thought she was."

"Oh, yeah, they'll do that to ya too." Walter slapped the table in outrage. He shook his head. "Shly beasts. Goddamn, and they'll do anything to get what they want, and never even know why they want it. Damn women."

191

"My God, but she was beautiful," Ryan continued, not listening to Walter. His mind was consumed by his vision of Catra. "Like nothing you've ever seen. And full of fire." He closed his eyes against the image that would not leave him.

Walter was silent for a moment. Then he leaned toward Ryan and said conspiratorially, "I know what you need. I know 'zactly what you need. I bet you ain't had any since it happened. Have you? You ain't had *any,* right?" Walter nodded knowingly, though Ryan had not answered. "Damn right. Yer problem is just that. You let that little thing tek away yer goddamn manhood, that's it. You need to git back yer manhood, that's all. Ain't ganna let no little piece git to you so bad you ain't a man anymore." Walter looked at Ryan.

But Ryan was concentrating, looking at Walter and concentrating on getting rid of the image in his mind by trying to focus his eyes on the man. He found he could not do it. So when Walter took his arm and pulled him to his feet, he offered little resistance.

"Where're we going?" he asked and grabbed the bottle just before Walter pulled him away from the table.

"I'm gonna fix yer problem," Walter said with assurance.

A moment later they were in the street. As night fell the sidewalks had become an icy mess and the roads a mire of mud and slush. Ryan's elegant topcoat was buttoned improperly and hung askew, his gloves were forgotten in his pocket and his hat had been missing for days.

Walter slipped along the sidewalk, clutching anything within reach, from hitching posts to people, until Ryan took him by the shoulders and dragged him into the street. With Ryan supporting him, Walter began to hum a sea ditty that made Ryan laugh. A few people snickered as they passed, watching the two drunks making their feeble way down the street in the growing gloom of twilight.

Their destination was a brothel not three blocks from the bar. In a section of town that did not normally see gentlemen, Ryan and Walter entered the house and were greeted like royalty. The madam had an eye for fine clothing, and despite the mud and dishevelment she spotted in Ryan the opportunity for making a healthy sum of money. They were escorted into the sitting room and relieved of their wet coats. The madam gave them each a heavy snifter of brandy and had one of her girls remove their shoes and provide them with slippers.

Ryan's head was spinning so badly it was all he could do to remain upright on the sofa. He drank the cheap brandy down, however, and tried to listen to what the madam was saying.

"My name is Madam Rose. You fine gentlemen have come to the right place." Her voice was a husky purr and she concentrated on Ryan, who was obviously the one with money. "We have just procured a fine number of new girls to add to our already impressive selection. What type of girl are you interested in Mr.—ah—?"

"Smith," Ryan said as clearly as he could, realizing even through the haze that, in his condition, it would be best to remain anonymous.

"Smith, yeah," Walter added. "I like redheads, m'self. Got more life, redheads, goddamn."

"Mr. Smith?" the madam inquired, peering at Ryan. She motioned to the attending girl, who left the room and returned a moment later with two coffees. Couldn't have all that money just passing out on the sofa.

"Blonde," Ryan said then, decisively. "Golden blonde with eyes of ice," he intoned, his eyes half shut.

"Well, Mr. Smith," the madam exclaimed, "we have

got just the girl for you. She is lovely. Just one thing, though. She's a virgin, and that's a bit more money. But worth every penny.''

"Virgin!'' Walter snorted. "He's here to forget a virgin. He needs someone can make him forget.''

The madam looked at Walter with irritation and snapped her finger at the girl, who again disappeared. When she returned she was accompanied by a short, buxom girl with bright red hair that looked to Ryan suspiciously like a wig. Walter did not seem to mind, however, and was led off grinning and fondling the girl's buttocks.

"Now then,'' the madam said after Walter had gone, "let me take you to her. Would you like to follow me?'' She rose and took Ryan's hand.

Ryan tried to rise, but his legs felt like rubber and the room began to spin so violently that he clutched at the couch. The brandy snifter tumbled unheeded to the floor. He blinked his eyes hard but was unable to still the room even for a moment.

"Come on, darlin','' Madam Rose was saying, evidently using every ounce of her strength to pull him up by the arm.

But Ryan felt as if a ton of bricks had landed on his head. He was unable to help the madam's efforts, and the way the rotund woman huffed and puffed, her face becoming a mottled red as she yanked futilely at his arm, made him start to laugh. He watched with growing hilarity as her face grew angry, and thought briefly about the strangeness of the situation, before he passed out, there on her ruby red sofa, with a smile on his face.

"Get up, you mangy cur.'' Ryan heard the gruff voice of his father as if from a great distance, then felt a sharp poke in his ribs. The old man's cane. "Get up and tell me what's the meaning of this."

Ryan groaned and rolled onto his side, his back to his father.

"Your friends' ship has landed," the voice continued. "They'll be here before long. I thought maybe you'd want to wash the stench off you before they arrive."

Ryan's pounding brain slowly translated the old man's words. With great effort he rolled onto his back.

"They're not my friends," he muttered thickly. He ran a hand across his face and stopped when it reached his nose. He opened squinting eyes and glared at the offending limb, sniffing it again. Whiskey. He rubbed his fingers together. His hand was sticky with it.

The old man regarded his son critically. "They won't be if they see you like this," he agreed. "I imagine you left your real friends, along with your coat and your wallet, in that bastion of friendliness in which we found you last night. Passed out and snoring like a camel."

"Do camels snore?"

Benjamin St. James glared at his son with steel gray eyes beneath bushy white eyebrows. "You know, I'd hoped you had finally lost your wild ways, but then you had to go to Richmond and get embroiled in that whole unpleasant business with the Fairchilds. Is that what's got you determined to saturate yourself in alcohol?"

"That," Ryan said, pushing himself up to a sitting position and wincing with the effort, "was a gross exaggeration of a very small incident."

"Then I don't know what the hell your problem is. You're a damn fine businessman when you put your mind to it," Benjamin conceded, "but you're a goddamn hellion. Is there no place you can go without getting yourself involved in some kind of scandal? For God's sake, boy, it's been that way ever since you were old enough to be looked at by a woman."

"Just too fine-looking," Ryan said with a wry twist of his lips. His mother had always said that in his defense, and while Ryan didn't believe it, he'd chuckled many times over the way that response infuriated his father.

"So the women can't resist you and you don't know how to say no, is that it?" Benjamin scoffed. "No, I think you're nothing but a spoiled peacock. You know exactly how to say no, you just don't want to."

Ryan sighed. "I want to now, you can be sure of that."

"Good. Now get your sorry ass out of bed," his father commanded, with a last savage poke at Ryan's ribs with the cane. "And come down looking presentable for your friends."

Lydia Stewart sat in the parlor knitting while waiting for her parents to join her. She had heard them loudly discussing Ryan's condition in the library when she'd come downstairs and knew they were arguing about the cause of it all again. Her father believed Ryan was simply indulging a mood, while her mother contended that something was seriously wrong this time. After all, for all his faults and all his scandals, he'd never reduced himself to a drunken sot before. Which was a good point, Lydia thought. She had never even seen him drunk until she'd seen Tom and the footman dragging Ryan's big, limp body upstairs last night.

Lydia had her own theories about Ryan's digression. She wondered that no one else saw what she could see so clearly: that the cause of his problem was love. Nothing else could bring a man down so fast. Did they not think Ryan susceptible to that emotion? Or had it perhaps never occurred to them that if Ryan ever did fall in love, the object of his emotion might not feel the same?

But Lydia was sure love was the problem. She could not imagine the woman who would turn down her handsome, indomitable brother, for she doted on him; but she could think of nothing else that would cause him to so abandon himself.

When he had first arrived home from Virginia she had seen him only once, at the dinner she and her parents had arranged for his homecoming. It was a small affair; the only guests were Tom's parents and his two sisters, Mary and Roberta.

Ryan had shown up inebriated. Apparently he had stepped off the boat that way, and he proceeded to denigrate everything from the weather to the liquor. He looked almost demonic in his thinly controlled anger, and Lydia, at the time, thought only that business must have gone quite badly in Richmond for him to be so incensed at everyone and everything.

He was rude and boorish, and everyone except young Roberta Stewart, who'd had a crush on him since they had met two years before, had avoided even looking in his direction for fear his bad temper would fall on them.

Roberta, on the other hand, had seemed titillated by his roguish behavior and had flirted shamelessly, even while he patronized her and joked about the nefariousness of women at her expense. Just as it was becoming clear that Ryan was not himself and was perhaps warming up to Roberta's flirtations for no honorable reason, the Stewarts left.

Lydia and Tom had already gone to bed that night when her father and Ryan had locked themselves in the library. Lydia had assumed they were to discuss how business had gone in Richmond and she had hoped her father would chastise Ryan for his treatment of their guests. They had, after all, been invited to welcome him home. But Lydia had not fallen asleep immediately, so she was awake to hear when the door to the library slammed open and Ryan shouted.

"I don't give a goddamn *what* people think of me and I'm *not* glad to be back."

Lydia heard his heavy footsteps on the hall floor, then the familiar creak of the front door and a bang as it hit the inside wall. She heard her father's wheelchair enter the hall.

"And I'm *damned* sick of watching out for the virtue of silly girls who give no thought to it themselves," Ryan had continued. "From now on they can watch out for me, because I no longer have any intention of sparing them. If they want it, they're damn well going to get it."

Lydia heard her father say something, but his low, rasping voice did not carry as well as Ryan's. Then Ryan said something she couldn't quite hear and the front door slammed. After that all was quiet, and Lydia had not seen her brother since.

Not, that is, until he'd arrived home unconscious last night.

Lydia heard her parents in the hall, and a moment later they entered the room. Her father's face was taut, angry; but her mother's was as calm as ever. She knew how to handle the difficult men in her family without losing her temper. It was something Lydia had always admired about her.

"Your father thinks Ryan's lost his mind," her mother stated. Lydia could just make out the humor in her tone. "He's planning to ship him off to the West Indies to learn a lesson."

"That's what I should do, dammit," the old man growled, moving slowly on his cane to one of the wing-backed chairs. He tried not to use his wheelchair, but it was increasingly rare these days that he felt well enough to use the cane.

198

"He'll come around," Lydia said, rising to help him into the seat. "I think something must have happened down there. Ryan's done a lot of things we don't approve of in his life, but indulging in drunkenness has never been one of them."

"He's probably just bored with all the usual ones," her father spat.

Lydia smiled and returned to her knitting. "In any case, he'll have to clean himself up for the Chesters' arrival," she said confidently.

"I wouldn't be too sure about that," the old man said. "He seemed less than enthused just now when I told him that the ship had docked."

Lydia frowned at her knitting. "I wonder if he's had some sort of argument with Ferris Chester?" she mused, half to herself.

"I don't know how that youngster could get his goat so thoroughly," Cora St. James said. "And he would never react this way to a business transaction. I think it's a woman."

Lydia turned to her mother in surprise. "I think so too!"

Benjamin St. James scoffed. "*Bah*. Romantic female nonsense." He thumped his cane on the ground beside him for emphasis. "That boy's got no more romance in his soul than any two-bit libertine. He's spoiled, that's all. He didn't get his way in something. He's got to learn to act like a man, and that's all there is to it."

At that point the door knocker sounded. All turned expectantly to the door of the room when Simmons, the butler, entered. But he only announced the arrival of a man from the shipyard, with whom Benjamin then left to convene in the study. Lydia and her mother looked at each other.

"Well, I imagine we'll find out one day what's caused

all this silliness,'' Cora said, situating herself by the fire with her needlework.

Lydia nodded. She absolutely hated seeing Ryan in this state. "I hope we do soon." A thump sounded from an upstairs room, followed by a curse, and she murmured, "Very soon."

Chapter Twelve

Ryan whipped the muslin cravat from his collar, shook the knot out of it and once again tried to tie it. It was his third attempt, the first two having ended in fumbled fingers, uneven ends and a pounding frustration behind his eyes.

He focused intently on his neck in the mirror and worked at the material again. His forehead glistened with a light sheen of perspiration as the alcohol in his system tried to sweat its way out. He ran his fingers along his brow, holding the half-tied knot in his left hand, then continued with the task that had never before seemed so arduous.

Finally it was done; not to his exacting standards, but well enough for today, he decided. He pictured Catra's icy eyes raking him, noting the pallor, the bloodshot eyes, the uneven cravat . . . He jerked the thing off and began anew.

Finished again, he stood before the mirror and critically examined his appearance. He wore a dove gray tailcoat and off-white trousers with a double-breasted cashmere waistcoat. If nothing else, he wanted Catra to be aware that she hadn't jilted a clod. He supposed this would have to do. If it weren't for his hangover-ravaged eyes, he would look like a respectable gentleman, he supposed.

He fished a handkerchief from his pocket and wiped his brow again. Damn, who would've thought the blasted ship would arrive early? They never arrived early when you wanted them to. But bad news traveled fastest, and Ryan could only think of Catra's arrival with her new husband as bad news.

He half wished his brother-in-law, Tom, hadn't found him last night, so he could have missed the awkwardness of their arrival. Then again, the idea of being carried in, unconscious and smelling like a brewery, before Catra's very eyes was even more distasteful than having to welcome her to his family home.

He turned from the mirror and drank from the cold water that stood in a crystal glass on the table. A large, full pitcher sat next to it. God, how he hated hangovers. Not to mention the self-recriminations that went along with them. There was nothing worse than feeling like hell and having no one to blame for it but yourself. Ordinarily he avoided alcohol in large quantities. He'd always disliked the way otherwise rational, likeable people became idiotic bores when they imbibed. But what he did ordinarily had had nothing to do with what he'd done since he'd met Catherine Meredyth. Catherine Chester, he corrected, disgusted.

He tried to stroll quietly to the hall and down the stairs, because the pounding in his head increased as he moved, but the stairs nearly did him in. As he approached the drawing room, he heard his mother and sister speaking, so he straightened his shoulders and did his best to assume a casual air for his entrance. Both were impeccably dressed for the reception of his guests, Lydia in a wine-colored dress with her dark curls in sausage-shaped ringlets that just touched her shoulders. His mother wore one of her better day gowns of fine blue broadcloth, over which a cashmere mantelette with black and blue paisleys draped gracefully.

"So the cock rises and greets the day," his mother said wryly. "How lovely to have you home again."

Ryan gave her a sideways look as he entered the room. "You're looking lovely, both of you," he said.

"You certainly don't," Lydia pronounced. "You look like you've been beaten from the inside out."

"Yes, you do look rather a mess," his mother agreed. "Straighten your cravat."

Ryan reached for the offending article. "I'm so happy I joined you." He frowned as he grabbed the blasted tie and undid the knot. "Is there anything else you'd like to point out?"

Lydia rose, brushed Ryan's hands away from his throat and proceeded to re-tie his cravat with quick, nimble fingers.

"Quite a bit," his mother said with lightly pursed lips. "But we probably haven't the time now. Your guests are to arrive any minute."

Ryan scowled as his stomach dropped. When Lydia had finished with his attire, he moved to the sideboard and poured himself some water from the decanter there.

Lydia and her mother exchanged interested glances.

"I thought you enjoyed young Chester's company," his mother said. "You act as though you didn't want him to come."

Ryan rubbed his forehead again, his eyes closed. "Where's Father?" He was not about to be drawn into a conversation about his feelings for Ferris Chester. Not in his present state of mind. He just might be tempted to spill the truth and horrify them all.

"He's in the study with Charles. Apparently something dreadful happened at the yard that needed to be dealt with right away," his mother said. Her tone was nonchalant. She was used to crises popping up at odd hours. It seemed to be the nature of the business.

Ryan felt a pang of remorse at the thought of his father having to deal with all the business headaches because of his descent into self-pity.

"But don't you worry about that," his mother added. "I'm sure you've more important things on your mind, as you have these last several weeks."

Ryan gave her a steady look that she returned. He was not angry. Bluntness had always been his mother's way, though he could have done without it today. Between the hangover, the guilt of abandoning his business and the dread he felt at the imminent arrival of the lover who'd jilted him, he felt barely able to cope with general conversational pleasantries, let alone his mother's challenging brand of banter.

"I care when I need to," he said shortly.

"Hmph. Yes. When *you* need to," she said. "In any case, I'd like to hear more about this sudden dislike you have for Ferris Chester."

"I don't suddenly dislike him." Ryan drank from the water glass in his hand.

"You're certainly acting like it."

"As you might have guessed," Ryan said dryly, "I'm not feeling myself today."

Cora St. James laughed and looked at her son with amusement.

"And what of his new wife? Do you dislike her?" Lydia ventured from the couch.

Ryan immediately turned his back to her to reach for the water decanter.

"Her, I could do without," he said as casually as he could manage. "But she'll make him happy, I imagine."

Lydia and her mother shared a significant look. "What's she like?" she persisted. Ryan's shoulders stiffened. "Is she pretty?"

He turned on her so quickly that water from his glass sloshed onto his hand. "What the devil are you asking me for?" he snapped. "You'll meet her yourself any minute."

Lydia and his mother gazed at him with identically stunned expressions.

"What in the world has gotten into you?" his mother demanded.

But Ryan was saved from answering this question by the sound of the front door knocker. The three turned their eyes to the hall as the butler passed to answer the door. They heard a suppressed murmuring in the hall, and then the butler reappeared, announcing, "Mr. and Mrs. Chester have arrived."

Ryan's insides twisted as he placed his glass on the sideboard. He heard his mother and Lydia rise, their petticoats rustling, then he turned on suddenly wooden legs to await their entrance.

"Mrs. St. James, Mrs. Stewart, how wonderful to finally meet you both." Ferris entered with a bustling aura of cold from the chilly outside air and a breezy smile. He bent first over Lydia's hand, then her mother's. Ryan was careful not to look for Catra as he watched Lydia and Ferris meet, but he felt her presence. "Forgive me if I seem overly familiar, but after hearing so much about all of you I feel as if I know you already."

"As we do you," Lydia replied. "It's lovely to meet you. How was your journey?"

"Wonderful, wonderful so far. We made fantastic time coming up," Ferris said. "But allow me to introduce my bride." He turned a beaming look behind him and pulled Catra forward by the elbow. "Catherine Mere—oh my! I'm still doing that!" He laughed. "Catherine *Chester*. This is Lydia Stewart, Ryan's sister. And Mrs. St. James, his mother."

"How do you do?" Catra curtsied to each of them with a polite smile. At the sound of her voice, the soft southern accent distinctly noticeable in this northern drawing room, Ryan's eyes finally moved to her. Her face was partially hidden by her bonnet and the set of her head as she faced his mother. Dark blond curls peeked out from the brim of the hat and her slim form was still blanketed by a heavy woolen cloak with fur trim at the collar and cuffs.

"And Ryan!" Ferris exclaimed, spying him behind Cora and Lydia, where he leaned against the sideboard. Ryan caught only a glimpse of Catra's face and sky blue eyes as they shifted to him, before he turned to Ferris. But it was enough of a glance to set his heart to pounding an even more insistent beat than the one already in his head.

"Good to see you, Ferris." He strode across the room to take his hand.

Ferris clapped Ryan on the shoulder with his free hand and smiled into his face. "It's good to see you too. You remember Catra, of course."

When Catra raised her eyes to his Ryan felt the breath catch in his throat. She was more beautiful than he remembered.

Her cheeks were pink from the cold and her eyes shone like twin tourmalines in contrast. Her expression was carefully blank, but her eyes were decidedly cool.

"Mrs. Chester." Ryan drew the name out slowly and bowed. "How tiresome for you to have to visit the humble St. James home on your wedding tour. I'm surprised you wished to."

Ryan was acutely aware of Lydia's interest as Catra's cheeks became even redder than the wind had left them. She placed her hand almost reluctantly into Ryan's, leaving it only a second before snatching it back, as if he'd bitten her.

"Actually, it was *Ferris's* idea," Catra stated with a firmness that Ryan was sure no one in the room missed. Well, except Ferris.

"To tell you the truth," Ferris added, "I think it was *Ryan's* idea." Ryan's head jerked to look at Ferris. "He invited us up months ago, even before he'd come to visit Virginia."

Ryan frowned as the memory of the long-ago invitation returned to him. Hell, he *had* invited them. What folly that had turned out to be.

"Let's get you out of those coats," Mrs. St. James said into the silence that followed Ferris's last statement. "What were we thinking of, letting you stand here like that for so long? And where is Simmons? He'll show you to your room. You two must be exhausted."

"Yes, we are a little—" Catra began.

"Nonsense, we feel great," Ferris interrupted. "The trip up was a breeze. Can't beat Standard Shipping."

There was polite laughter as hats, coats and gloves were shed.

Ryan took the opportunity to take in Catra's appearance. She was thinner and decidedly less lively than she had been in Virginia. Perhaps sea travel did not agree with her. He could tell she felt his eyes on her, for her movements were self-conscious and her mouth was pinched at the corners. Could she be unhappy with her choice of husband? he mused.

He remembered the way she had looked that day she'd run down to the river to meet him, the day he'd asked her to marry him. Vibrancy had radiated from her every pore. Her lips had parted with breathlessness and her honey hair had loosened from its plait to frame her face. But it was the eyes he remembered best. Those compelling eyes had radiated a thousand emotions that could never be put into words. At least he had thought they had.

His own eyes refocused after his reverie to find her gaze upon him. There was confusion in her expression, doubt in her eyes instead of the hostility of a moment ago. And something else lurked there that he did not recognize. Was it sadness?

His mind rejected the idea. Too late for regrets, sweet, he thought, his own expression hardening. You've got your husband now.

He saw her eyes drop and her mouth tense again. She looked wilted, a shadow of the spitfire she had been just two months ago.

Ferris was conversing about something with Ryan's mother when Catra abruptly asked to be excused. The two stopped short and Ryan's mother immediately complied with her wish to retire before dinner. Lydia led her from the room.

Ryan was consumed by an urge to follow and see that she was all right, but he squelched it. No doubt it was newlywed nerves that had her so pale, he thought, punishing himself. She probably hadn't gotten much sleep since the wedding.

Ryan pushed the hair back from his forehead impatiently and looked around for his water.

Catra felt as though she would burst into tears the second she walked from the room, but Ryan's sister was beside her. Lydia Stewart was disconcertingly similar to Ryan. Catra had noted it the moment they'd met. So much so that

Catra believed she would have known Lydia to be Ryan's sister no matter where she'd encountered her.

Lydia had the same translucent gray eyes, shrewd and perceptive, and the rich dark hair of her brother. But the most marked resemblance was the subtly intimidating mannerism they shared of looking directly, almost scrutinizingly, into one's eyes as one spoke. Catra had previously believed it was something Ryan did to unnerve people, but she could see now that it was a family trait.

"Perhaps after dinner you'd like me to show you around the house. We want you and Mr. Chester to be perfectly at home here, so any time you wish to choose a book from the library or to knit by a fire you must know exactly where to go," Lydia chirped as they ascended the stairs.

"That sounds lovely," Catra managed in a reasonably steady voice.

"The one thing you must remember," Lydia continued, "is not to be afraid of letting us know if there's anything you need, anything at all. It can become quite cold in the house if the fires are not properly tended or some other such thing, so be sure to call Simmons or Katy, the housemaid." Catra was grateful for Lydia's chattering; it gave her a much-needed moment to collect herself. "I heard your husband call you Catra. Is that a nickname?"

"Yes, it is. Since I was a child. My full name is Catherine, as you know," Catra finished inanely.

"Well, it's a charming nickname. For a time my parents called me Liddy, but you know it's not so much shorter than Lydia, and after a while . . ."

Though she tried to concentrate on Lydia, Catra could not get the picture of Ryan's brooding countenance from her mind. He had looked so forbidding at first, only to fall into—what?—what had that strange expression meant?

How could this have happened? Catra asked herself for

the millionth time. How, after that disastrous affair, could she have ended up in the very home of the man who had thrown her over?

And how was it that he could still look so good to her? He stood both taller and stronger than Ferris. Like the difference between a pony and a stallion. His eyes still held that demanding energy she remembered so well, that knowing look that unnerved her. Even hearing the sound of his voice again had sent barely containable shivers up her spine.

"Well," Lydia breathed, "here we are."

She opened the door to a large room with a well-stoked fire blazing in the hearth. A canopied bed stood along the left wall with a thick comforter across it. Two tapestried chairs rested near the window. Catra thought the moment Lydia left she would drop into that bed and never awaken.

"If there's anything you need . . ." Lydia let the sentence drop, no doubt aware of having covered that subject more than adequately already.

"Thank you," Catra murmured. "It's a lovely room."

After Lydia murmured something polite and disappeared, Catra walked slowly about the room, running her fingers along the furniture and peering into picture frames. Ryan's house, she thought. These were things that Ryan was familiar with. She felt a tightening under her ribs.

Well, at least he'd been courteous, she told herself, and turned away from the personal touches on the dresser. She proceeded to remove her shoes and lay back on the bed.

The next thing she knew, Ryan was gently shaking her awake. No—not Ryan—Ferris. She'd been dreaming about Ryan when Ferris woke her. Lord, had she spoken his name?

Ferris's expression was benign, she noted with relief.

"Cat, honey, wake up. Dinner will be ready soon," he said softly.

She stretched in the plush featherbed, reluctant to rise. "Oh." She yawned. "I feel like I could sleep for ten hours more."

Ferris used a finger to brush the strands of hair from the sides of her face, then leaned over and kissed her.

Catra sat up, unwilling to lead him on to anything more than that brief peck. His eyes held the same uncertain expression they had for the last couple of weeks, ever since the wedding night, when she'd pleaded with him to have pity on her nervous state. She was afraid of the marital act, she'd cried, and needed time and understanding before she would be able to carry it out. Ferris had understood. In fact, he had acquiesced almost immediately, making her wonder if he was as reluctant to consummate as she was. But now it had gone on a long time and Catra was beginning to think that putting off the inevitable was making her feel even more unsettled about the marriage. But how could she consummate the union now, in the house of Ryan St. James?

Ferris rose and moved to the mirror. He pulled his vest straight and flicked some lint off his sleeve.

"I've just had a talk with Ryan," he said. "Seems he's got something of a hangover today, but don't let on I told you." He chuckled. "He apologized if he seemed rude. Said he wasn't feeling one hundred percent."

Catra mulled that over. Hungover? Perhaps that was what had caused that queer expression on his face earlier. Odd, though, she thought. He didn't seem the type to get drunk.

"Anyway, they've got a special dinner prepared for us, so you'd best get ready." He turned back to her. "Shall I have Lydia send a maid up for you?"

"Yes, please," Catra said, wondering how she would sit

across the table from Ryan every day for the next three weeks. ''I'll be ready for her soon.''

Catra entered the drawing room on Ferris's arm. Ryan was not yet there, but another, younger man, with straight brown hair and a round, pleasing face, rose upon her entrance. Lydia's husband, Tom Stewart, it turned out. Lydia and Mrs. St. James greeted them warmly.

The room was made cozy by a crackling fire in the marble fireplace and lit by refined brass wall sconces. She felt more at liberty to survey the room this time, now that it was without Ryan's overwhelming presence. She marveled at the understated elegance of it and slowly took in the thick Oriental rugs over dark, polished hardwood floors. Lydia sat upon a black walnut sofa upholstered in brocaded satin, and along the side wall stood a pianoforte. Over the fireplace hung a full-length portrait of Cora St. James in younger days, a striking woman with feather-soft brown hair, high cheekbones and richly lashed, penetrating eyes.

They just had time to exchange good evenings and be introduced to Tom Stewart before Ryan entered, pushing a wheelchair in which a broad man with a shock of thick white hair sat. Catra had been told that Benjamin St. James was nearly unable to walk. He had been captaining a small sloop several years back when, caught in a sudden squall, the mast had broken free and pinned him to the deck. It had broken both his legs and shattered one hip.

But even had she not known of his handicap, the gray, hawklike eyes and the manifestly powerful frame, unmistakable even though he was sitting, would have betrayed his relationship to Ryan.

''Father, you remember Ferris Chester,'' Ryan said, his voice once again sending ripples of excitement down Catra's spine. "This is his wife"—here just the barest of pauses—"Catherine Chester."

Catra extended her hand, conscious of Ryan's eyes upon her, and curtsied.

"Pleasure to meet you," Mr. St. James said in a gruff voice. "I trust your trip up was not too taxing."

"Not at all," Catra replied. "I believe I've regained all my strength in one two-hour nap."

Ryan had to believe she was right. She looked considerably more rested and lacked the wilted air she'd had this afternoon.

He allowed his eyes to rest on her for a moment, noting the healthy glow in her cheeks brought out by the soft rose-colored dress she wore. Her silken mass of hair was held in a loose topknot with ringlets framing her face.

Ryan tore his gaze from her face and directed his next statement to the air. "I gather you both have met my brother-in-law, Tom." He moved toward the brandy decanter. Tom bowed his head again in their direction as Ryan asked, "Ferris? Brandy? Tom, a refill?"

Tom shook his head. Ryan felt the other man's frown as he poured himself a glass.

"Absolutely, thank you," Ferris answered and settled himself in the chair next to his bride.

Ryan turned a questioning gaze on Catra. "Ca—" He stopped himself short and glanced quickly at his mother. If she hadn't noticed the near slip, no one else would have. She did not look up from her needlework. "What about you, Mrs. Chester? Some sherry, perhaps?"

"Thank you, no." Her tone was firm, even if her voice was quiet. She was having a hard time keeping her eyes from the way his dark curls bent over the edge of his collar. She remembered so well the feel of them.

"Water? Cider?" he could not help pressing.

"Have some cider, Mrs. Chester," Lydia urged. "It's from our own presses. We serve it hot with cinnamon. Have you had it that way before?"

"No, I haven't."

"Then you must try it. Ryan, pour her some."

Ryan did as he was bid and crossed the room to hand it to her. When she took it, their fingers brushed, sending a current of excitement up her arm and into the deepest reaches of her body. When his fingers did not let go immediately, her eyes flew to his face. Her uncertain gaze fused with his unreadable one for an instant before he released his hold.

"Thank you," she murmured, her breath lodged somewhere in the middle of her chest.

Small talk went on all around her as Catra allowed herself to covertly follow Ryan's movements. He stood for a while near the sideboard, swirling the liquor in his glass, pensively studying a spot on the carpet. She studied his lean, strong-knuckled fingers against the delicate crystal, blue veins standing up beneath the bronzed skin, testifying to the strength of his hands.

She remembered those hands cupping her face, resting against the nape of her neck, tracing the outline of her bodice. Her face warmed at the memory and she raised her eyes to find his upon her. She swallowed hard.

"Isn't that right, Catra?" Ferris turned to her and asked. She spun her head to him, her eyes wide, her heart thrumming. "Except for that cold snap a few weeks ago, we've had quite balmy weather."

"Yes, oh, yes," Catra agreed. "Warm, it's been. Warm weather." She felt herself nodding like an unmanned marionette in a stiff wind.

"Mrs. Stewart was just saying she believed we might see

some snow while we're here. I told her that would be just fine with me," Ferris continued.

"Yes," Catra agreed. "I would love to have snow while we're here. It's so rare that we get anything more than a dusting at home."

"Tell me, Chester," Benjamin's gruff voice intervened, "I understand you breed horses. Ryan tells me you've some fine stock. Are they racing stock?"

The conversation took off from there. Once they'd gotten past the weather, Ferris was on firm footing with the subject of his prized horses, and Catra had the feeling that that was the sole reason Benjamin St. James had brought it up. She wondered if everyone in the room could feel the tension stretched taut between herself and Ryan.

Dinner was announced and they removed themselves to the dining room. Deep red wine and a thick juicy roast served to loosen everyone up even more, and Catra found herself drawn into the laughter of the family that was obviously close in spirit as well as blood. Even Ryan showed flashes of the heart-stopping smile Catra remembered so well, as Tom regaled them with stories of his courtship of Lydia and his intimidation by the ominous St. James men.

Apparently Lydia would not submit to his courting without the expressed consent of her esteemed father and protective brother. The two of them, in defense of the youngest child and only daughter of the St. James household, had banded together to interrogate the poor, but determined, suitor. In their zeal for the task, they persisted until Tom had had nothing left to say but that he was in love with the girl and would they please at least let him *tell* her that.

The whole family exploded with laughter at the end of the story, each character adding what they believed to be the one pertinent detail he'd left out. Then they expressed how glad they were that he had persevered. Lydia leaned over to squeeze Tom's hand, and Catra watched with envy the private look they exchanged. She stole a glance at Ryan and found him also watching the two with an expression halfway between amusement and antagonism.

Once the meal was finished, the diners moved into the drawing room, the men opting to stay with the ladies rather than sit over their brandies and cigars. Tom and Lydia walked arm in arm, reliving the details of that not-so-long-past courtship, and Benjamin was wheeled smoothly behind them by his wife. Catra found herself left with only Ryan and Ferris and quickly turned her back on Ryan to take Ferris's arm.

Lydia seated herself at the pianoforte with Tom standing beside her, one hand on her shoulder. "Play the Haydn piece," Catra heard him whisper as she passed.

"Do you play?" Cora St. James asked as Catra sat next to her on the sofa.

Catra grimaced. "I was given lessons, of course, but I'm afraid I hadn't the natural talent necessary for a true love of playing. There's nothing I enjoy more than listening, however."

"So you developed an appreciation, if not the actual means of expressing it." Mrs. St. James nodded.

"Yes." Catra was acutely conscious of the fact that Ryan had seated himself on the other side of his mother.

Ferris and Benjamin St. James were engaged in conversation near the windows, where someone had pulled the curtains closed to keep the room toasty warm. Lydia was involved in her playing, a lively, lilting tune to which Tom moved slightly next to her, as if dancing in his head.

Ryan watched the two at the piano until his mother turned to him. "Why is it that you never play anymore, Ryan?"

The revelation that Ryan had musical talent surprised Catra, and Ryan himself looked a little embarrassed by the mention of it.

"Too busy," he said. "The piano requires a lot of discipline. I suppose I'd rather make no music at all than bad music."

"I can think of one or two things you could clear from your schedule to allow you more time." His mother smirked. She turned back to Catra. "Ryan was a gifted student, though I guess every mother thinks such things of her children. He has a strong voice, as well."

He crossed his arms over his chest. "Which I now employ to berate lazy employees and over-talkative parents."

Catra could not help smiling at that and wondered at her ability to be party to so normal a conversation with the man who had broken her heart.

"Yes, as well as using unseemly language and all sorts of manly things," his mother added. "Some day you'll come back to music, though. When you're happy."

Ryan shot his mother a hard look, then let his glance flit to Catra. She looked away.

"How is your father?" he asked her.

She forced herself to look at him. "He's fine. I imagine he's not very busy now. Most of the crop has sold by now, of course."

"Hmm. Yes." Ryan gazed at her thoughtfully.

"Your father is a planter as well, then?" Mrs. St. James asked.

"Yes. Braithwood, our plantation, is just next to Waverly, which belongs to Ferris."

"And you too, dear. Now," Mrs. St. James reminded her with a smile.

"Yes, I suppose so. I hadn't thought." Catra reached for her coffee. She wished Ryan's eyes would stop plaguing her.

"You'll have them both, then, eventually," Ryan said. "Since your brother can't inherit and you have no sisters."

"Yes, I guess I will." She sipped the coffee, which burned her tongue and threatened to make tears come to her eyes. She blinked them away.

"Your brother can't inherit? That's unusual," Mrs. St. James said.

"Yes. My mother died in childbirth with him and he has never developed normally. He's very sweet, but not quite . . . normal."

"And your father—why did he never remarry after your mother died? He should have found you and your brother a stepmother," Mrs. St. James continued in her knowing voice.

"I don't suppose he fell in love with anyone after my mother died. Though there were many women who tried to catch his eye, and still do."

"He needn't have fallen in love with someone," Mrs. St. James proclaimed. "It was his obligation as a father to find a suitable woman who could raise his children. Goodness, if every man who lost a wife in childbirth waited to fall in love again, we'd have a country full of motherless sons and daughters. As it is, most sensible men find women they can trust to raise their children."

Unbidden thoughts arose in Catra's mind with that idea. "These days love has very little to do with marriage, it's true," she said, finally looking at Ryan, who regarded her warily. Then she turned to his mother. "But I can't help thinking that I would have been sorry to see him marry for the sake of practicality. I had a nanny who raised me and I could not have loved her more if she had been my own mother."

"Very worthy of you, dear. But you don't know how it

could have been, had your father remarried and given you more sisters and brothers to play with.''

"I know how it was, though. I was always a happy child. And marriages of convenience, I believe, frequently create a sadness so subtle in those involved that it can be hard to detect overtly. But children feel it. And I'm glad I didn't have to grow up wondering why Mother and Father never spoke, or why married people never laugh together.''

"Perhaps there is some lack of vitality in a marriage of practicality, but I don't think they create any sadness. Not if the partners are well-matched. While not everyone is fortunate enough to marry for love, people can be quite happy together if they respect one another.''

Ryan spoke then, his fingers templed before him, his eyes narrowed. "You're very adamant on this point, Mrs. Chester. Did you, then, marry for love?''

Catra's eyes flew to his. How had she let herself be trapped in this corner? "I—I—That was my—desire, yes.''

"Your desire, perhaps, but did you realize it?''

"Ryan!'' Mrs. St. James intervened. "What sort of question is that for a newly married woman? Of course she married for love. One should always assume so.''

Ryan leaned back, a smug expression on his face. "My apologies, Mrs. Chester. It was an inappropriate question.''

But Catra's ire had been raised. How dare he put her on the spot with such a question, when he knew perfectly well what the answer was?

"What about you, Mr. St. James? Why have you never married? Certainly you're old enough.'' Catra's eyes held his.

"I'm not a very practical person, I'm afraid,'' he answered, his eyes narrowed.

"We've already established that practicality is not the only reason for marriage. Have you never fallen in love, then?'' Had she stopped to consider, the question would never have left her lips; but she was so incensed by his thoughtless probing that she sought only to embarrass him before her.

Ryan looked at her for a long moment before answering. "On occasion. But it always passes."

Catra scoffed. "How like a man. To confuse love with something that passes. What you were feeling, if you were able to let it go so easily, was doubtless some lesser emotion, if not something completely dishonorable and inappropriate to mention in polite conversation."

Mrs. St. James glanced at her in surprise. She had never heard a woman so challenge her son and she turned her gaze to him to see how he took it. He was fiercely attentive, his entire posture concentrated on the woman across from him.

"I defer to your superior knowledge of emotions, then," Ryan answered the attack. "I could easily have mistaken the feeling I had. I've made so many mistakes."

"No doubt you have," Catra replied. "How fortunate that you never inflicted them on anyone else by marrying on a flimsy emotion that passes so quickly."

"I don't recall saying that it passes quickly," Ryan corrected.

"It matters not if it passes quickly or slowly. Anything temporary is a misfortune and frequently the sign of a weak character."

Mrs. St. James looked on the two with misgiving. It was obvious that they had forgotten her presence altogether. She had the distinct impression that they were not speaking in generalities. Catra's color was heightened and Ryan's gaze had not left the woman's face. This was not his typically good-natured bantering. And he was definitely not flirting.

They were having an argument right here in front of her about something she was afraid to discern.

Fortunately Ferris came to the rescue, rejoining the conversation soon after a particularly biting salvo that left the two glaring at each other.

After several minutes of Ryan and Catra trying to compose their tempers to participate in a significantly lighter discussion, Mrs. St. James rose to adjourn the party. She watched with trepidation as Catra and Ryan made their strained good nights, and Mr. and Mrs. Chester went up to bed.

Chapter Thirteen

Several days later Ferris paced nervously about the library, waiting for Ryan to join him. The women were upstairs, readying themselves for a ball to be given that evening by friends of the St. Jameses, and Ferris had decided that now was the time to ask his friend a few questions.

He'd asked Ryan to meet him for a brandy beforehand and, though he was a few minutes early, he was impatient for Ryan to arrive before he lost his nerve. He glanced again at his watch. The hall outside the library was quiet. Finally, he helped himself to the brandy.

At long last Ryan's firm step was heard in the hall and the door, which had been standing ajar, sprung to life as he opened it and entered the room. Ferris had not known this man long but never had his friend seemed as intimidating as he did now, when Ferris needed to speak with him about something considerably more personal than shipping crops. Ryan was dressed in a formal, dark broadcloth tailcoat with a crisp, ruffled shirt. His hair was burnished back, accentuating the powerful set of his jaw and strong cheekbones. He looked larger than life and completely at home in the dark, polished splendor of the library.

"Good, you've helped yourself to the brandy. I could use a draught myself. These infernal balls benefit from a fuzzy point of view, I've found." Ryan's presence seemed to eat up the room, and Ferris felt less sure than ever about approaching him on such a subject as he had in mind. "Care for a cigar?" Ryan extended the box to him.

"Might as well," Ferris said. "You know it'll be an age before the women are ready to go. You know how women are." He laughed, counting on the fact that Ryan did, indeed, know how women were.

Ryan smiled. "We've got some time. What can I do for you? You said you needed some advice?"

Ferris fidgeted with his glass, then turned to look for a match for his cigar. "A match?" he asked then, seeing none.

Ryan took a box from the mantel and tossed it across the room to Ferris. Ferris made a production out of clipping off the end of the cigar, finding an ashtray, then taking the match to the tip of it.

"Yes, um . . ." He puffed with great exaggeration. "It's, uh, it's rather a personal matter."

Ryan leaned a shoulder against the mantel, legs crossed, one arm folded to support the arm holding the cigar. His expression was intrigued.

"I really wasn't sure who else to go to. For advice of this sort, you know," Ferris continued without looking at him, pacing in front of the bookshelves.

Ryan straightened and moved to the chairs in front of the fire. "Should we sit down? Perhaps we would feel less formal that way."

Ferris took a seat but did not lean back; instead he propped his elbows on his knees and stared into the fire. Ryan relaxed back into the cushions.

"Well, it's about marriage," Ferris started.

Into the silence that followed this weak beginning, Ryan said, "I'm afraid I don't know much about that."

"No, no, I know you don't. But, well, I know you know about some of the things involved in marriage. Things I don't know a lot about. Never had the opportunity to learn, you understand." Here he met Ryan's eyes briefly, then drew them back to the fire. "Things like, well, like the things that happen, after the wedding—"

Ryan suddenly got a sick feeling in the pit of his stomach. "Are you talking—about lovemaking?" he asked reluctantly. He was hardly able to believe he was going to have to talk about sex with the man who had married the woman he had wanted. He hoped to God Ferris answered negatively.

Ferris sat up straight and gazed at him with eager, childlike eyes that had, for the moment, cleared into relief. "*Yes*. Yes, I am," he breathed, obviously happy he didn't have to say the words himself.

It was all Ryan could do to keep from groaning aloud.

"You see, I know you have experience in that respect," Ferris said. "So you were the logical one to ask. There was no one else I could think of. What I'd like to know is, well, have you ever, I mean, what do you do when you're supposed to make love to a girl, but she doesn't—well, she's afraid and—to tell you the truth, ah, I haven't—that is, we just haven't done it."

If Ryan thought he'd sustained all the shock he was going to at the mention of sex from Ferris, he was drastically mistaken. He gaped at Ferris, brandy and cigar forgotten in his hands. His face became warm. He leaned forward. "Are

you telling me you haven't had sex with your *wife* yet?''
He held his breath while Ferris struggled with an answer.

"It is rather embarrassing, but, well, I guess you could
say it that way, yes.'' He drained the brandy from the snifter, then began talking faster. "You see, she's afraid. At—
at least she was that first night. She said it wouldn't be
enjoyable for either of us if she were so nervous. She said
she needed time to adjust to the marriage, to rest after the
wedding. And I allowed it, of course. I don't want to hurt
her. But the truth is, I'm not exactly sure—that is to say,
I'm not confident enough, to be able to do it without her
willing participation.''

Ferris's face was red to the roots of his pale blond hair.
Even his ears were red.

Ryan's breath escaped him with a gush and he dared not
analyze the sudden weightlessness in his chest. They hadn't
consummated. The only thing they'd done was speak a few
words in a church and take off on holiday. Ryan could
barely contain the rush of emotions he felt.

"I can see I've shocked you.'' Ferris's voice was loud
beside him. "Is it that unusual?'' His voice held such de-
spondency that Ryan felt guilt creeping in on the heels of
relief.

"I don't,'' Ryan started, then cleared his throat, "I don't
know that it's so unusual.''

"Then why do you look so stunned?'' Ferris asked.

What a time for him to become perceptive, Ryan thought
lamely.

"I suppose it's just that I, I didn't take Catra to be the,
ah, timid type,'' he said truthfully. Catra was about as far
from fearing sex as he himself was, he thought, remembering the way she'd kissed, pressing her firm young body
hard against his in such an artlessly seductive way. "Are

you sure it's not your own—underconfidence hindering you?''

Ferris flushed an even deeper red, which Ryan had not thought possible. ''Perhaps it is. That's another odd thing, because in the beginning I thought I was ready. But then came the night of the wedding, and . . . well, I just didn't feel I could, you know, do it. You know what I mean, don't you? I just don't seem to feel that kind of—of attraction to her. Not that I feel it for anyone else, mind you.''

Ryan gazed at Ferris's boyish face and wondered what type of woman it would take for him to feel attracted, if Catra didn't do it. She was the most sensual creature he'd ever seen, and for a moment he fell into imagining her as she'd stood on the beach by the river, her hair loosened from his hands as he'd kissed her and she'd clung to him, wanting more. The contradiction between that and her apparent fear on the night of her wedding sent a myriad of questions catapulting through his mind. What sort of game was she playing? Egging on her lover and denying her husband? Could it be that she was still in love with him? Could she not stomach the idea of Ferris?

The hope that shot through him at the thought disgusted him. She'd made her choice, and she'd made it perfectly clear at that ball in Richmond that it *was* her choice. Now here he was in the ridiculous position of having to instruct the senseless puppy she'd chosen how to seduce her, even though the senseless puppy claimed not to even want to.

Anger welled up inside him. ''If there's a God, she'll rue the day she played the tease, mark my words,'' he announced angrily. Beside him, Ferris jumped with the sudden words and gawked at him in surprise. But Ryan continued, oblivious to Ferris's reaction. ''She wants it all, or she wants none of it. Someday she'll learn she can't have her own way all the time.'' He took a deep breath to try to calm himself. "So she's suddenly afraid. Of course she's afraid. She's a virgin." Then he was struck by the unwelcome thought that perhaps she was no virgin at all, and the fear of discovery was what kept her from making love to her new husband. The idea burned in him.

"She knows just what she's doing," Ryan growled, his eyes glittering and ominous. "You tiptoe around a woman like that and she'll keep you on a string forever. Don't let her get away with this game she's playing. She'll test the limits of your strength, and take pains to exceed it. It doesn't matter if you're inexperienced. She doesn't know what to expect any more than you do. Tell her what she wants, Ferris. That's my advice."

Ferris looked at him with something akin to awe. "I wish I had your way of seeing things," he said. "I think you're absolutely right. I just don't know if I can. Like I said, I feel . . . that is, I'm just not sure if I . . . *can.*"

Ryan was bitterly thinking that his way of seeing things hadn't gotten him anywhere. In fact, his way of seeing things had lost him what Ferris had a right to seek. But he said only, "You can if you want it badly enough. She'll go on like this indefinitely if you let her. Just remember, you're her husband." *And I am not.*

Ferris assumed a look of determination. "Of course. I have an obligation. There need to be children, after all. I—I'll just have to." He stood with the energy of his new conviction. "I can't continue to mollycoddle her. I'll tell her just what has to happen and we'll . . . we'll do it."

Ryan's mind held an image of Catra on the beach with him, her lips parted, her eyes sultry. He'd had the feeling then that she'd wanted him as much as he'd wanted her. There was no fear in her eyes, no resisting the passion they shared.

Well, she'll get what she asked for now, he thought bitterly. But it won't be me who gives it to her.

They rode to the ball in two separate carriages, the ladies' skirts being so wide that one could not accommodate them all comfortably. Catra found herself alone in a carriage with Ryan and Ferris while Lydia, Tom, and Mr. and Mrs. St. James rode in the other.

Ryan's face was forbidding, and, unlike the relaxed posture he'd held the last few nights at supper, he sat stiffly in the seat, talking to Ferris in businesslike tones.

One or two times in the past several days, she'd caught him looking at her with an expression that was not as angry as when she'd first arrived. Indeed, it was more studious than anything else. But tonight it was Ferris who was loose and relaxed, while Ryan sat straight as a ramrod against the plush green interior. In fact, Ferris seemed a bit more than relaxed, and she wondered if he was not a touch drunk since she smelled brandy on his breath. He was also being much freer in his affectionate gestures with her. His arm was propped on the seat behind her, and his fingers played with a ringlet of hair, then dropped to caress her skin.

She'd worn one of her more daring gowns without admitting to herself that it was Ryan's eyes she hoped to capture, not her husband's. But now it seemed imprudent to have worn it, considering the way Ferris had been looking at her, and the way he now ran his fingers along her collarbone.

On the other hand, she thought, it was time she put an end to this limbo she and Ferris had created and made this a real marriage. But thinking about making love to Ferris was impossible when Ryan sat just across from her, so she pushed the thoughts from her head.

When they arrived at the ball Ryan exited the carriage

first, then Ferris handed her out to him. As she stood on the step from the carriage, Ryan's large warm hand clasped hers, and when she bent to go through the doorway she watched as his eyes drifted to the low bodice of her gown through the open cape, then back to her face. His expression was impassive and she felt herself color at the display the gown made.

The ball was tremendous in size, like nothing she'd ever attended before. It was the annual Christmas season ball and it seemed to Catra that the whole city must be in attendance. Ferris danced the first dance with her and held her closer than he ever had before. She pushed at him lightly with a soft, "Ferris, how unseemly."

Ferris immediately loosened his hold, seeming more comfortable himself once he did so. He acted quite peculiar throughout the evening, and Catra, who was having enough trouble keeping her eyes from following Ryan, noticed Ferris partaking of every champagne tray that passed.

Catra danced with Tom, a courteous, engaging partner, who then introduced her to Cliff, a friend of his, whose appreciative gaze, instead of filling her with satisfaction, made her feel ashamed of the amount of skin she was showing. She was so far from feeling any gaiety or confidence that she decided to sit out several of the next dances. She was just sinking into a chair beside Lydia when Lydia, sensing something amiss in her mood, did precisely the wrong thing. She snagged Ryan from a group heading toward the punch bowl and urged him to dance with her.

"Mrs. Chester is here all alone, Ryan; why don't you dance with her? I just love to see that gorgeous gown pirouetting to the music. She does dance beautifully, doesn't she?" Lydia said, smiling.

The situation was so awkward, with Ryan looking as if

he'd been pinched and Catra blushing, that she had to believe even Lydia noticed.

Ryan extended his hand to Catra. "Mrs. Chester? Would you do me the honor?" His face was closed, his eyes flat, and Catra was powerless to refuse. Every excuse was there on the tip of her tongue: she was tired, thirsty, needed some air, but not one would budge from her lips.

She took his hand, conscious of the eyes of the women in the room following Ryan's every movement. All night she had seen them casting covetous glances his way, plotting to be near him when a dance ended, smiling engagingly at him as he passed. And while she felt some pride in being on his arm, she shook with nervousness inside.

"Don't they look fine together?" Lydia mused to her mother.

Mrs. St. James looked on and shook her head. "It would be just his way to fall in love with another married woman."

Lydia waved the statement away with her hand. "He wasn't in love with Therese. But, you know, I could swear something is going on between these two. Ryan said he didn't like her, but rather than goad her unmercifully, the way he does, say, Georgia Talbot, he freezes up around her. It's very strange. Not like him at all."

Mrs. St. James eyed them critically. "There goes your fanciful imagination again, Lydia. Don't go starting gossip where there isn't any."

"Mother, you know I wouldn't say these things to anyone but you." She patted her mother's hand.

Eventually Lydia tired of watching and theorizing about Ryan, and she accepted Tom's invitation to join the dance.

But Mrs. St. James's attention was not so easily swayed from the sight of her son, tight-lipped and obviously uncomfortable, dancing with the beautiful southern matron.

Catra and Ryan danced in silence for a long while. Catra relished the feeling of weightlessness in his arms and the touch of his hand on her waist. It was a light hold, but it felt as though it seared her skin through the satin of her gown.

"Are you enjoying yourself?" he asked finally. His low voice was just barely audible over the orchestra.

She glanced up to find his eyes on her, looking down as if from a great distance, lids half closed. Her heartbeat accelerated. "No. I'm too nervous," she heard herself admit. She was tired of having to act like there was nothing between them when they both knew that there was. Or had been.

He looked surprised at the admission. "Does my family make you uncomfortable?"

Catra gazed at him steadily. "No. Your family is wonderful. *You* make me uncomfortable."

He nodded slowly and concentrated for a moment on the dance. She felt his hand tighten slightly. She looked away from him to the room filled with people, many watching the dancers, and the softly lit walls beneath the high, molded ceiling.

"You have nothing to fear from me," he said quietly, as if coming to a decision. "You're too young to suffer forever for your mistakes."

Catra was left to puzzle over this strange statement as the dance ended and she was claimed by another partner. She watched Ryan's retreating back and wished she could call him back. As awkward and uncomfortable as the whole ridiculous situation was, she still preferred his company to any other.

The evening progressed and Ferris seemed to partake of every drink that was offered him. The last time they danced together he'd fumbled the steps and trod firmly on her instep, so that they decided to give it up altogether.

They rode home the way they'd come, except that Ryan had decided to stay a bit longer. Catra and Ferris were alone in their coach. Catra was consumed with thoughts of who Ryan might be dancing with and whether it was possible that he'd stayed because of that gorgeous dark-haired woman in the clinging cream gown. It was obvious he hadn't enjoyed dancing with her; he'd been too stiff and his odd comment hinted at dark thoughts. But they were the first civil words he'd spoken to her when they were not within earshot of someone else. For that, at least, she was thankful. If she had to live in the house and endure the presence of the man who had used her, the least he could do was be civil.

Alone in the coach Ferris, in his befuddled state, apparently believed the time was ripe for action. His arm was draped around Catra's shoulder and he pulled her close to him, her shoulder in the hollow of his.

"Ah, Catra, did you have a good time tonight?" He brushed her temple with a kiss.

She stiffened at the touch. "Yes. It was very nice."

"You look beautiful." His hand awkwardly reached for the opening of her cape, but his finger caught in one of the button loops and it took him a moment to extricate it, at which point he put the hand decisively back in his own lap.

She could smell the alcohol on his breath and wished she'd had more than two glasses herself. Though Ferris had been completely respectful of her wedding night jitters, Catra continued to feel guilty that theirs was not a real marriage. She ought to just do it, she told herself firmly. She would have to eventually, and the sooner she did so, perhaps the sooner she would stop thinking about Ryan.

How bad could it be? Besides, perhaps she would get

pregnant, and then there would be a baby to care for. She'd always loved babies.

Ferris's mouth descended to her ear and he kissed it wetly. She jumped and wiped her ear with her palm. "Ferris, I think this should wait until we're in our room at the house."

"Yes," he said, and she was not sure, but the word sounded slurred. "I think, you know, we should do this tonight. I mean, don't you?"

As awkward as it felt to have Ferris—her lifelong friend—touching her in this way, it was much more uncomfortable to have to talk about it. Catra murmured something she thought sounded affirmative and hoped he would say no more.

His lips met her cheek and worked their way around to her mouth. It was a sloppy, wet kiss that she did her best to submit to. Her hands rested lightly on his jacket front, denying the urge to push him back. But he stopped after a moment and rested his forehead against her temple.

"I mean, we kind of have to, don't you think?" he asked, and this time she was sure his speech was slurred.

"Have to what?" she asked mildly.

"You know, do what—what married people do."

"Yes, I suppose we do." Her cheeks felt hot despite the dark carriage.

"But you don't want to much either, do you?"

Thankfully they arrived at the St. James house before Catra had to answer, because she feared if they both admitted to their platonic feelings, they would live in this strange limbo for the rest of their lives. As much as she resisted making love with Ferris, she didn't want to live her whole life without family, without children. They could never have a normal home without them.

Everyone was tired from the long night. It was past midnight. So it was with fatigued good nights that they all retired to their rooms.

Once in the privacy of their chamber, Ferris nearly fell onto the bed. She gazed at him, wondering if she should say something. Part of her desperately wanted to get the act over with, while another part wanted to put it off for as long as humanly possible.

"Ferris, are you feeling all right? Perhaps we should wait until you're sober," she said.

Ferris straightened and looked at her with great indignation. "I *am* sober."

"No you're not. I can smell the brandy on your breath and I watched you drink every glass of champagne within reach tonight. And just look at you. Look." She led him to the dressing table mirror, which reflected back a man in a rumpled jacket with sweat-soaked hair that did not even remotely resemble the style in which he'd had it combed at the beginning of the evening.

Catra couldn't help smiling at the pitiful sight. He was like a young boy who'd been playing with his hoop for too long in the sunshine.

"I've been dancing all night," he said lamely. "I was really thirsty."

Catra could not get mad at him. After all, she felt the same reluctance he did about making love. "Listen, Ferris," she began, carefully, "I think we both feel the same way about this, but I want you to know that I do want children. I mean, we don't have to do this tonight but someday, you know . . ."

"What?" Ferris said, his tone a trifle belligerent and his eyes more than a little unfocused. "You don't think I can do it? Well, I can. I bet. I bet I can."

Catra regarded him sadly. What a pitiful marriage she had picked for herself. "Of course you can. I can too. And

we should, for the sake of children, and the future. Despite
what we may feel ourselves, we owe it to—''

''Oh, blah, blah, blah,'' Ferris slurred, waving his hands
over his head. ''Talk, talk, talk. Sure, we can do it. I mean,
I don't always have to have things the way I want them.
I'm a man, after all, I can do it. How are we to have heirs
if I don't?'' He pronounced the *h* in the word, causing
another smile to come to Catra's lips.

''Of course you can, Ferris. Don't let's argue. This discussion can wait until tomorrow.''

''Tomorrow?'' he questioned. ''Well, of course there's
always tomorrow.''

Catra sighed. ''Yes. Tomorrow.''

Ferris nodded and made his way unsteadily to the bed.
He plopped down on the edge. ''Oh, tomorrow, tomorrow,
tomorrow.'' He sighed, flinging himself back on the covers.
And before Catra could ask him to untie her laces he'd
fallen into a deep, fast, snoring sleep.

She stood above him and looked down. His face was
clear and unlined, the eyebrows somehow achingly innocent above closed eyes. His mouth was open, his lips pale
pink and soft as a baby's. She sat on the edge of the bed
and brushed the hair back from his forehead. She didn't
mind touching him this way, like a sister and without his
knowledge. It was so noncommittal, this light, friendly
touch.

She rose then and went to the door. She had to find Katy
or another of the housemaids to help with her laces. But
when she entered the hall it was so dark that she despaired
of finding anyone. She crept down the hall to the stairs and
paused momentarily to gaze into the foyer below. Her eyes
adjusted to the dark and she thought she saw a faint glow
in the direction of the library.

She practically glided down the stairs and along the hall

on silent slippers until she was even with the partially open door. Suppose it was Mr. St. James? she pondered. How awkward to have to ask him for a maid to unlace her dress. Surely he'd wonder why her husband was unable to do it. Or maybe he wouldn't. No doubt everyone had seen Ferris drinking himself silly tonight.

Just as she was steeling herself to peer into the light, someone inside the room moved toward the door. She only had time to take one step backward before she was face to face with Ryan.

Chapter Fourteen

Ryan stood before her with a loosened cravat, his jacket off and his sleeves rolled up. His large eyes held the same look of startled surprise that Catra was sure hers held, before he masked it with the flat expression with which he'd regarded her most of the evening. How had he gotten home so quickly? she wondered. Had he pretended to stay just so he wouldn't have to ride back with her?

His left hand held a brandy snifter while his right raked through the thick waves of his hair.

"Mrs. Chester," he said finally, after moments of the two of them standing mutely in the lighted doorway. "I thought I heard something."

"Ryan, I—" She stopped at the sardonic rise of his eyebrow. "Mr. St. James," she began again, "I was in search of a maid. I didn't realize you'd—that it would be you—that you were home."

"Yes. Your expression said as much." His lips curved

faintly. He moved back into the library, as if expecting her to follow, but she hovered uneasily at the door.

"I was just in search of a maid. Do you know if they've all gone to bed?" she asked stiffly.

"I'd imagine so." He reached the desk and turned back to her.

Catra fidgeted with the pleats of her gown, wondering how in the world she would get the stupid thing off, not to mention the stiff whalebone corset beneath it. Even standing, the corset bit into her skin and made breathing an almost conscious effort.

In any case, it was obvious he wasn't going to offer to wake any of the servants, so she started to turn away. "Well, then, I'll not disturb you further."

"Is there something I can help you with?" he asked solicitously. "We hate for our guests to be lacking something they need."

Catra glanced around the room. "No, I—I'll—I really need a maid. I, you see, my laces—" She broke off, flushing.

His eyes narrowed. "I'm sure your husband"—he drew the word out pointedly—"would be more than willing to help you."

"No, ah, he's asleep. He would help me, of course, but he was just so tired," she explained.

"Yes. Hmm." He regarded her steadily.

"Well," she said, glancing around the room, then out into the hall. "I'll just wake him, then. No need to disturb the maids at this hour."

"Why don't you join me for a drink, Mrs. Chester?" he asked. He walked toward her, making her heart leap to her throat. He stopped by the bookshelves, where on one shelf were lined a small arsenal of bottles. "Can I offer you a sherry?"

"No, no. I really must get to bed. I—it's so late." She backed away from the doorway.

"Mrs. Chester." His voice stopped her. "Why don't you come in? I think we should talk. If we are to be thrown together as we have been this week, we should probably come to some sort of understanding."

The last thing in the world she wanted was to have Ryan St. James tell her to grow up and out of the obvious infatuation she'd had for him. If he thought that after dumping her so cruelly he could now patch things up with a why-don't-we-just-forget-it conversation, he had another thing coming.

Her eyes hardened. "No. Thank you. I really must be getting back to my husband. He only sleeps well when I'm there."

Ryan's eyes narrowed. "Actually, I was under the impression that he sleeps all too well with you there." He caressed the brandy snifter in his hand and watched her. "Yes, your husband came to me for advice this evening." He let that statement hang in the room for a moment before asking, "You sure I can't get you a sherry?"

Catra stood rooted to the spot. What had Ferris done? What had he said? Could this situation possibly get more humiliating?

"What sort of advice?" Her voice emerged a near whisper.

He set down his drink and moved toward her. Her heart hammered in her temples and she could not take her eyes from his face. He looked like the devil, dark and ominous. And tempting. He continued forward until he was very close to her.

"That's the funny part," he purred. "He asked me the best way to get you into bed with him. Isn't that just"—he stepped closer—"too"—he raised an arm to lean

239

against the door jamb by her head—"funny?"

He grabbed her wrist the exact moment she turned to flee.

"Let go of me," she whispered, not trusting her voice. She glared at his hand around her wrist. She couldn't raise her tear-filled eyes to his mocking glare.

"I think we'd best have a talk." He pulled her forcibly into the room. He shut the door and pulled her toward him, turning as she avoided coming close by passing him. He let go of her arm. "I didn't think I wanted one, but since you're here and the circumstances are so perfect, I think I'll take an explanation."

She whirled to face him. "An explanation? I hardly think Ferris's and my marital problems are any business of yours."

Ryan watched her chest rise and fall in breathless fear beneath the clinging green satin of her gown. "I just wanted to hear you admit, through those precious, lying lips of yours, that the reason you won't sleep with your husband is that he'll discover you are no virgin."

Catra stood stock-still for a moment in shock. Then she stalked forward, fury governing every muscle, until she stood just before him. "You, of all people, should know how untrue that is," she stated before raising her hand and flinging it toward his face. He grabbed it and pulled her to him, almost nose to nose.

"I, of all people, know what a good chance there is of it being absolutely true." His breath was warm along her cheek. "I don't flatter myself that I was the only one you took to your private spot by the river. That beach was tailor-made for a string of little trysts. But I can't imagine they all acted as gentlemanly as I did. I'm sorry if I was a disappointment to you, but you see, I was inexplicably fooled by your outrage at my suggestion of an affair."

Catra's breath came in rough, gasping waves the more he spoke. "Stop it!" she cried. "Oh, stop it! Stop it!" For some reason she could get no more out than this, no explanation, no heated retort, nothing but the pain-induced pleading for this torment to stop. Tears spilled over her eyelids and she bowed her head, one free hand rising to cover her face. She tried to stop them, but the sobs overwhelmed her, shaking her entire body as his grip loosened on her wrist.

"You were the only one," she choked. She swallowed convulsively in an attempt to regain control. "I took no one else there."

"Prove it to me," he said. When she did not move the hand on her wrist jerked her forward. She braced her hand on his chest to keep from stumbling. His other hand grabbed her upper arm. "Look at me, Catra."

She turned burning eyes to his. Her face was wet with tears, her jaw clenched.

"I don't believe you," he said quietly. Then his mouth swooped down upon hers. His lips were rough, demanding, his grip relentless. Her senses awakened with a rush of tingling sensations, up her spine, all the way to her fingertips and down to her most private regions. She gave in to them immediately, with a willingness she had never felt for the childlike kisses Ferris gave her.

Her hands, that had lain on his chest in protest, rose now to his neck. Her fingers touched the dark curls she'd longed to feel again and her arms pulled him tightly to her.

Ryan's hands loosened their viselike grip on her arms and raised to cup her head, his fingers plunged deep in the silken mass of her hair. With a moan his head dropped to her shoulder, trailing hot kisses along the base of her neck. His hands ran down from her head, along her sides, then up along her ribs to push her barely covered breasts toward his mouth.

Catra's head fell back as a delicious excitement ripped through her. Her fingers moved to Ryan's hair, to tangle themselves in the soft, rich locks, as his hands pushed up and his mouth sought and found a pink nipple that emerged over the edge of her bodice. A low sound emanated from her throat as his tongue played with the hard bud of her breast. Her hips moved forward as she pulled his head close against her.

His fingers found her laces and loosened them. Her bodice dropped and he pushed the sleeves impatiently past her elbows. Drawing back, he turned her by her shoulders and swiftly unlaced her corset. Then he pulled the stiff garment off, leaving only her chemise. The bodice of her gown dropped over the broad skirt.

Catra did not question his moves, did not even allow herself to think beyond, *yes, this is the way it should be.* She turned back and their lips joined again in frenzied passion. He pushed her back against the door.

Her hair was loose and streaming down her shoulders when he stopped, pinning her where she stood with his gaze. His eyes searched hers, their expression one of torment and wonder.

"Don't speak," she said softly. She did not want to talk, she did not want to think. She pulled his head down to hers and her lips met his, searching, probing, demanding.

He pulled up the skirt of her gown, the many layers of petticoats jamming between their bodies, until he found her bare legs. With an urgency born of waiting, he ran his hands along her thighs to their juncture. Her hips moved to meet his fingers as he rubbed them rhythmically along the hot fabric between her legs. Then he stopped and grasped the waist of the pantelettes. He pushed them from her hips and plunged his fingers inside the hot, throbbing moisture.

Catra gasped with both shock and pleasure. Their kisses escalated to new heights of passion when suddenly he pulled back.

His breath was rapid as he looked at her. "Are you sure?" His voice was deathly quiet.

"Yes," she breathed. "Oh, yes."

He needed no more. He loosed his pants and parted her legs with a knee. Lifting her effortlessly with his arms, his long, stiff manhood touched her silken heat. Her hips pressed forward to meet it.

He guided himself to the soft, wet opening and eased himself inside. Then, with one sudden motion he thrust. She gasped and clutched his back. Alarmed, he stared down at her in horror. "What is it?" he asked pointlessly, realization dawning.

He slowly pulled back, releasing himself from inside her. Her heavy skirts fell between them. Tears glistened on her lashes as she looked down and away. His breathing slowed. Eyes closed, he leaned his head against the door beside her head. His breath caressed her shoulder, his arms held her lightly, unsure.

"Why did you let me do this?" His voice was low, thick. "Why not Ferris?"

"I don't love Ferris," she stated, the implication clear.

He raised his head and studied her face, confused. Her words hung in the air.

"Then why didn't you speak with your father? Why didn't you send word?"

Catra stared at him.

"Never mind," he said, misinterpreting her dumbfounded expression. He backed up, straightening his clothing. He could have continued—part of him wanted desperately to continue—but he knew it was wrong.

"No," she said, turning his face back to her with her hand. Her eyes searched his. "I spoke with my father. You know that. I sent you a note—which you destroyed." Her eyes clung to him now, unsure if she actually wanted to hear that it was all a mistake, that her life was now all a mistake.

Ryan's mind worked furiously over all that she'd said. Could it be? He scrutinized her expression. "Catra," he insisted, "you asked your father for permission to marry me?"

"Yes. And I sent you a note. I asked you to come for me. I waited—" Her voice broke, but her eyes did not leave his.

"I never received it," he said quietly, as if in wonder. "I never received anything. *Dammit.*" He closed his eyes with the curse and threw his head back. "How could I have been so stupid?"

Catra could only stare, her breath coming rapidly, her eyes raking his face.

"Oh, God, Catra," he moaned. His hands ran up her arms and pulled her tightly against his chest. "He won. Your father won. Damn it."

Catra's hands rested lightly on Ryan's ribs. She, in disbelief at what was being revealed, stared dumbly at nothing. "My father? What do you mean?"

Ryan stroked her hair.

"I spoke to your father, Catra. After two days of not hearing from you, I went to him." Ryan held her tightly as he related the story of his visit. "It was after that encounter that I ran into you in Richmond."

"A misunderstanding," Catra murmured. "My whole life is based upon a misunderstanding." Panic rose in the back of her mind, but another, more important idea overtook it. "But you went to my father. You wanted to marry me.'' She gazed at him as the realization hit home. ''Is that right?''

He took a deep breath and exhaled the words, *''God, yes.''* He took her face in his hands. ''Catra, I love you. I've never stopped. I've been a bastard to you all this time because I thought you'd jilted me.'' He sighed and closed his eyes. ''I wouldn't blame you if you never forgave me for what's happened here tonight.''

Catra's eyes softened. ''Forgive you? Ryan, this is my only opportunity for happiness. You *love* me.'' She couldn't contain her smile. ''That's all that matters. If this hadn't happened tonight, I might never have found out the truth. And the truth is so important, Ryan. You love me. I can hardly believe it.''

''I hope you feel that way tomorrow,'' Ryan said, doubt filling his voice.

''Ryan, I love you. I want no one but you. And I'll live the rest of my life happy that this happened tonight.''

He smiled sadly into her eyes. ''Do you know, that's the first time you've ever said you loved me? That was one of the arguments I used against you when I learned from your father that you'd left Braithwood.''

''I never said it?'' She was shocked. ''I must have thought it a thousand times. And it was so obvious.''

He sighed and stood back, holding her hands. ''A lot of good the truth does us now. Perhaps we'd have been better off hating each other.'' He turned her around, leaned over and picked up her corset and began lacing it up her back. ''What are you going to do about Ferris?''

''What do you mean?''

''I mean,'' he took a deep breath, ''that eventually he'll find out you are no longer a virgin. Won't he?'' he asked quietly.

Catra's head bent. He had finished lacing her—loosely

so she could undo it herself later—but she did not turn.

"I suppose," she whispered. If she had hoped he'd beg her to leave her husband she was disappointed. But she didn't allow herself the luxury of divining what she had hoped he would do. "I'll think of something."

He moved away from her. There was a long silence between them, neither of them sure what to do next. Catra's heart pounded furiously in her ears.

"I suppose I'm an adulteress now," she said into the void that was her heart, the stillness of the room and his silence.

"Catra, don't."

"But I don't care." She turned to face him. "Does that make me a horrible person? I love you, Ryan. I don't care what the rest of the world thinks of me. I don't care what Ferris thinks of me. I just want you. I can't—I don't want to go on, knowing—" Her voice broke and she buried her face in her hands. He reached her quickly and took her in his arms.

He raised her face to his and kissed her wet cheeks, her eyelids, her lips. He was just about to say something when they both heard a door close upstairs. They froze, listening as quiet footsteps descended the staircase. Then, of one accord, they split and searched for a place to stand that would not be immediately incriminating. Catra spied her pantalettes on the floor by the door jamb and sprinted to pick them up. Just as she reached the doorway, the footsteps turned in their direction. She ducked behind the door just as it swung inward, opening wide enough to conceal her in its corner.

"What are you doing still up?" It was Tom's voice, groggy with sleep.

Catra had the sudden horror-struck feeling that what

they'd done would be obvious, that there'd be more clothing on the floor, a rug turned askew.

"Couldn't sleep," was Ryan's brief reply. "What are
you doing up?"

"I don't know. Something woke me. Then I couldn't get
back to sleep."

Catra heard him move farther into the room, and she held
her breath lest he move far enough to see her.

"Come on, then." Ryan's voice. "Let's go get something to eat. I'm famished."

"Eat?" Tom's voice was dangerously close.

"Yes, come on. Cook's got some scones in the kitchen,
I think. Let's ruin her morning and eat them now." Ryan's
steps moved toward Tom's voice.

"All right," Tom conceded as, Catra presumed, Ryan
led him from the room.

She waited a long time before emerging from behind the
door. They'd left one candle standing, and in the dim light
she studied the room. Nothing amiss. No one would ever
know what had taken place here.

She sighed and tiptoed to the door. Her legs were stiff
and there was an uncomfortable burning between them that
she tried to ignore in her haste to be gone. After looking
in both directions down the hall she crept out. She moved
with unaccustomed stealth up the long stairway, careful not
to place too much weight on any stair without first determining if it would creak. At the top step she turned toward
her room—the room she shared with Ferris.

She stopped at the door. Her hands rose to her hair, futilely pushing strands into place. When yet another lock
came loose she gave up and rested her head against the
unopened door, her hand on the knob. She swallowed her
tears and turned it. Just another harlot, she condemned her-

self, returning to her husband's bed with disheveled hair and the scent of another man on her body.

She entered the darkened room to find Ferris in the same position on the bed as when she'd left him. He'd only moved to throw an arm across his forehead. He snored heavily. She sighed.

Ryan had left her laces loose so that all she needed to do was pull at the material to free herself from them. She moved to the bedside table and picked up the oil lamp. From there she went to the far side of the room and lit it, immediately lowering the wick until the flame just barely lit the corner where she stood.

She started to pull the gown from her shoulders. The silk was wrinkled, probably beyond repair, and her chemise had ripped slightly at the shoulder. She hung her head.

What a mess her life was. She glanced over at Ferris. He slept peacefully, if not soundlessly. He was all innocence lying there, completely clothed. The dim lamp cast shadows across his young features. She could never leave him. She was legally bound to him. The only option would be divorce, an enormous step that almost never took place. She'd heard stories about divorced women—mean, filthy stories. She herself had always thought of divorced women as little more than whores. But even if she dared brave divorce, she could not claim that they'd never consummated the marriage without admitting herself to be an adulteress. She'd heard of women who, in an attempt to divorce without the dirty scandal, claimed that their marriage had never been consummated. They had been subjected to a physical exam to prove it.

If she said, on the other hand, that the marriage had been consummated, Ferris would know it was a lie. And who knew what he would do with that information if she attempted to scorn him with divorce? He could use it against her, of course.

But it would never come to that. She couldn't divorce him and he would never let her. What it *would* come to was Ferris bedding her, as was his right as her husband, and discovering her stolen virginity. How would she explain it? And what would he do if she couldn't?

She ran her hands over her face. Either way he would discover that he was not her first. She looked over at him again, passed out.

Not only would she have to sleep with him, she realized, but she'd have to figure out a way to fool him into thinking it was her first time. But how? Good God, how?

She felt something on her thigh. She turned her back on Ferris and lifted her skirts. The blood that had trickled along the inside of her thigh had stained the petticoats behind it. There was the proof that would undo her. There was the evidence that would put her to shame before the whole world.

She could tell him it was her monthly course, but that had ended over a week ago, and since he now slept with her and shared her room he knew it.

She dropped her skirts and lowered herself onto the dressing table chair. Elbows on the table, she buried her face in her hands. She was doomed. Her life was one huge mess. And now even Ferris would know of her folly. She felt tears come to her eyes and let them fall where they would.

Why couldn't it have been Ryan whom she'd married? She imagined a wedding night filled with the glory of passion they'd just briefly shared. Imagine feeling completely right and justified in the consummation of passionate desires, instead of having to feel consumed with guilt afterward. If only he'd gotten her note, if only her father hadn't interfered, if only . . .

She sat up. It was useless to feel sorry for herself. She'd been doing that for months. The only thing left to do was to figure out how to make this situation bearable.

She looked over at Ferris again. His mouth had dropped open; his snoring grew louder. She could smell the alcohol on his breath from where she sat across the room. Tomorrow he probably wouldn't even remember the argument they'd had before she'd gone downstairs. He'd passed out.

Her teeth caught at her bottom lip. He'd passed out, she thought again. Her heart's pace quickened. He probably wouldn't remember.

The seed of an idea took root in her mind.

She rejected it, appalled at the level of deception she was capable of conceiving.

But her thoughts returned to it. There would never be a better opportunity. She would not have to explain the ruined gown, the petticoat . . . She rose slowly and went to the bedside, gazing down at him thoughtfully.

She was desperate. He was out cold.

She poked his leg. Nothing.

She pushed his arm from his forehead. It flopped limply to his side.

She took a deep breath and heaved his legs over the edge of the bed until he lay lengthwise along it. He never flinched.

With blind, unthinking determination, her fingers flew to his pants, swiftly unbuttoning them. With some effort, she yanked them over his knees to his ankles. After struggling to remove his jacket, she unbuttoned his vest and shirt, leaving them open. Finally she was finished; he was naked from chest to ankles.

She looked at his face. Dead asleep. She turned away

and pulled her bodice down. She removed her corset and dropped it beside the bed. Retrieving her pantelettes from the place she'd dropped them near the dressing table, she placed them next to the corset. She examined the place where her chemise had begun to tear, and in one impulsive movement she tore it through. The shoulder strap split in two and fell to expose her breast.

She moved quickly across the room to extinguish the lamp, feeling her way back along the unfamiliar furniture. Ferris's snoring had stopped, but she heard the steady breathing and knew he had not woken. She climbed over him to her side of the bed and lay gingerly atop the covers. She imagined what he'd find upon waking. Himself half-undressed, her corset and pantelettes by the bed, her chemise torn, her dress half off.

She looked at his naked body, pale in the dark. With trembling fingers she lifted her skirts and left them in carefully orchestrated disarray. The bloodied petticoat would be obvious to him when he awoke.

She felt a lump of self-loathing grow in her throat. She would tell him someday, she thought. She would confess it all. But for now, she had to do this. It was the only way to buy herself some time.

She did not look at him again. Instead she turned her back and stared at the wall. At long last, after grappling unceasingly with panic and horror at her own actions, she dropped into a fitful sleep.

Chapter Fifteen

Ferris believed her. She had not even had to put voice to the lie. He had looked at the evidence, at her and at himself. Then he had apologized. Profusely.

Catra felt no satisfaction in the success. She tried to convince herself that she should at least feel some relief, but even that small compensation was not to be granted her. She was simply disgusted with herself. To have sunk so low, in so short a time. She found herself descending into confused reveries of passion and guilt. And all the while fear lurked in the back of her mind that Ferris would discover the lie and expose her.

Still, she could not bring herself to regret what had happened. Ryan loved her and she wanted him now more than ever. As wrong as she knew it was, Catra felt she would do anything within her power to be with him again. To prove once more that their love was alive and real, even if destined to be denied.

Ryan sought her out in the afternoon. She wasn't sure how he'd contrived it, but Ferris was getting a tour of the shipyard without him.

He arrived at the house in the early afternoon to find Catra and Lydia engaged in needlework in the drawing room. A plate of cookies lay partially consumed on the table between them and a healthy fire wafted a welcome heat into the room.

Catra was startled when she saw him in the doorway of the drawing room. Her heart leapt in her chest and her breath felt suddenly thick. She had wondered what they would say to each other, now that they'd shared such an intimacy, and now that they both knew the truth. But she hadn't gotten past her guilt over Ferris far enough to formulate any idea of what she wanted said.

She tore her gaze from him, glanced at Lydia, then looked back at her needlework. She paused, then stopped the pointless sewing and looked up at him again.

He wore a contemplative expression and moved toward a chair with a slow grace that belied his uncertainty.

"Oh! Hello, Ryan," his sister greeted. "I thought you were to spend the day at the yard. Is everything all right?"

"Everything is fine, Lydia." His voice was solemn.

Catra watched him as if he were an actor and she, the audience. What would he say? What would he do? How would he fix this ghastly situation?

But he couldn't fix the situation. She could tell by the expression on his face. It was not the expression of a man who had answers.

"Lydia," he said slowly, "I wonder if you'd mind giving Mrs. Chester and me a moment alone."

Lydia looked surprised. A dozen questions danced in her eyes, not the least of which was probably what in the world these two people, who had barely spoken to each other since they'd been together, could possibly have to speak privately about.

"Well, of course. Certainly." Lydia rose and folded her needlework. She stuffed the fabric and threads into her arms and eyed the two of them again. Catra did not look at her. Ryan simply raised his eyebrows at her questioning expression. Lydia moved to the door and, once there, turned as if she would say something more.

"Thank you, Lydia," Ryan said.

Lydia nodded once and left, closing the door discreetly behind her.

Ryan sat motionless, and for a moment after Lydia's departure neither said anything. It was as if, upon leaving, Lydia had abandoned each of them to an empty room. Then Ryan turned his face to her, elbows on knees, hands clasped before him.

Catra had the sudden frightening thought strike her that Ferris, after confiding in Ryan about his lack of success in bedding her, might have told him that he'd finally accomplished the task. Would Ryan think she'd gone straight from his arms to her husband's? Or would he realize the deception she'd employed and despise her for it?

Ryan picked up a cookie from the plate and turned it in his hands.

"I need to apologize for last night," he said at last, staring at his hands.

"No you don't."

Her hands folded on top of her needlework as she watched his long, elegant fingers manipulate the cookie.

He sighed. "I made a grave error in not trusting you."

She was sure her heart was in her eyes as their gazes met. "That's all behind us," she said softly. "I made mistakes too. But I don't consider last night one of them."

His reply was swift, decided. "But it *was* a mistake. One we cannot repair, nor repeat."

She stared at him and felt her face heat. "What do you mean?"

"I mean that what happened last night cannot happen again." He was unable to maintain his steady gaze and glanced toward the bookshelves. "I was angry, unjustifiably so, but angry nonetheless. My anger prompted my actions and I regret them now. I promise you, they will not be repeated."

Catra continued to stare at him, feeling a void in her chest as if her heart had left along with her breath. "Suppose I want you to repeat them? If I don't regret what happened, why should you?"

He crumbled the cookie in his hand. The crumbs fell to the table in a haphazard pile. "This is my family home. You and your husband are guests here. How can you ask me that?"

"So it's the location that bothers you." Her voice was flat. An unreasoning anger began to build within her.

He snapped his eyes to hers. Anger burned in his, as well. Or perhaps it was frustration. His voice emerged hard. "I do not want to compromise you again. I also do not want the guilt, and the shame, of cuckolding your husband in my own house. Is that what you want?"

He was incensed, but his eyes were questioning. The cookie was a forlorn bunch of crumbs before him.

Guilt tripped in her chest for the irreverent feelings she had about her marriage. And Ryan's sudden morality made her feel even more corrupt.

"I remember," Catra said steadily, "after our first meeting, all those months ago, you dared to assume I would engage in an affair much like the one you claim not to want now. I refused you then. But how can you be shocked by my change of heart when all hope of happiness for me is lost? And what has changed within you to make you reluctant to be with me?''

"I'll tell you what has changed. *I* have. I don't feel triumph in deceiving others. I do not feel pride in taking surreptitious advantage of people I regard as friends. And I do not, particularly, want to be party to your downfall.''

"My downfall!'' She could not have been more surprised. "It's a little too late for that, don't you think? I've gone further than I ever thought I would have, done and felt things I could not even have guessed at six months ago. So perhaps now I am simply admitting the type of woman I am. Perhaps now I am ready to give in to it, be a harlot for love, for I've already soiled my soul beyond redemption.'' Tears sprang to her eyes, but she fought them back. She did not deserve the luxury of sadness.

Ryan stood and moved to the sofa next to Catra. He took her hands in his and looked at them. Her heart thrummed at the contact and she wanted nothing more than to throw herself into his arms, to be lost in the oblivion of passion as she was last night. Instead she gripped his strong hands tightly.

"You're not soiled, Catra,'' he said finally. "You've made a mistake. We both have. But we cannot repeat it. If we did, the risk would be all yours. There is no such thing as privacy here, as you well know. Whatever we engaged in would be discovered. Whether by Ferris, or my family, or simply the servants, it would be discovered. And *you* would be the one to suffer. Your reputation, your marriage, perhaps your whole way of life could be destroyed.''

Catra laughed, a hard, harsh sound. "What of it? My reputation, like all good southern women's, was built for one purpose only: to get a husband. Well,'' she scoffed, "I've got a husband.''

Ryan's eyes looked on her steadily. Catra saw the beating of his heart in a vein at his temple.

"Don't be bitter, Catra. Please. I couldn't stand that." His voice was quiet, sure. "Whatever you may think of my reasons, I'll not allow a dishonorable passion to be the cause of your destruction."

A dishonorable passion, is *that* what he thought of her? Stung, Catra spoke the first words to come to her. "You had no such similar qualms with Candace Fairchild. Were her charms so much harder to resist?"

Ryan's eyes narrowed. "So you've heard that story, have you?"

"Oh, yes. My father was kind enough to enlighten me when I asked permission to marry you. Imagine my surprise." Her anger—or was it fear?—was barely controlled now, coupled as it was with shame and rejection. Her hands, still clasped in his, had balled themselves into fists within his warm palms.

"The situations are not comparable," he stated.

"Apparently not." She struggled to keep the emotion in her chest from rising and choking her.

"I love you, Catra," he said softly. His eyes reached out to hers, but in them she saw only concern, not the driving passion she felt for him, needed from him.

The lump in her throat nearly succeeded in blocking her words. "Then—*love* me," she choked over a sob. "Don't you see how empty my life will be without you?"

Ryan dropped his head, his grip on her hands as tight as the fists she held there. His eyes were closed. She could see the fine lashes, dark against his cheeks, so vulnerable in such a hard face.

"Your life is not empty." He let go of her fists and stood, looking down upon her upturned face. "You just don't know it yet."

He started toward the door when she stood and stopped him with quiet, hard words. "You have no idea what my life has become. When I am gone you will go back to your life as you've always known it. You may be sad. You may think wistfully of that girl you thought you loved once. But I will be forced to live with someone else, someone I do not love. A man who will kiss me and share my bed and—" She strangled a sob. "I will not be able to confess to a lost love, nor even to think upon it sadly, without making my life a living hell." She buried her face in her hands.

Ryan stood silently for a long moment. "Candace Fairchild seduced me with the intention of forcing me into marriage," he said quietly. "I had no idea who she was at the time. I"—he gave a short, disbelieving laugh—"won her in a poker game. The gentleman she was with—well, suffice it to say he decided against telling me who she was. I thought she was a courtesan."

Catra dried her eyes, not looking at him.

"Her family," he continued, "made it known that they thought the honorable thing would be for me to marry her. My family concurred. I declined, as you know."

He turned, moved back into the room and sat on the armchair across from her. Catra sat as well. There was a beat of silence before he continued.

"Candace Fairchild is a pitied soul. At least by those open-minded enough to feel something other than disapproval. I was decried by all who were considered paragons of society as an immoral rogue." A slight smile played on his lips at the harmless title. Then he sobered. "But Candace Fairchild is shunned from society as a ruined woman. She is spoken of with scorn by otherwise polite people. She is an object of ridicule for pious adults and a grisly lesson in morality for impressionable young girls. But *I* am still admitted into the finest homes in Richmond. I, who committed the same sin she did. No, it isn't fair, Catra. But that's how it is. And you'd fare no better than she. Perhaps at one time I was able to ignore that, or disbelieve it, but I can't do that now. Now I *know* it's true.''

Catra studied her own hands. She knew what he said was true. When she was in Richmond she'd heard all the stories. She'd even looked upon Candace as the soiled woman Ryan spoke of, though she had felt some sympathy for her.

''To let the story die down,'' he continued, ''I took myself off to the country. To Waverly. I'd been asked to come many times, but there never seemed so opportune a moment. The Westbrook wedding seemed as good an excuse as any. I arrived there feeling—somewhat jaded. I was angry at society for trying to pigeonhole me. I was angry at young girls who would do anything for the man they set their sights on. And I was more than a little in the mood for some sort of revenge. That was my mood when I met you.''

A carriage passed beyond the windows of the drawing room. Catra dimly registered the soft clop of the horses' hooves and the squeak and rattle of coach springs and leather.

''I had no intention of falling in love with you. But when I did, something happened to me. I began to see the things I did through someone else's eyes, *your* eyes, Catra. And as I saw myself from your young, unscarred perspective, I saw someone I wanted to be. I knew you didn't know about Candace, but for some reason I couldn't tell you. It would have destroyed something—something *you'd* created. And that might have changed the way you felt about me. I wasn't willing to risk that.'' He gazed at her thoughtfully. ''But it did change things, didn't it? It came back to haunt me, just as surely as Candace had shrieked that it would. Maybe you wouldn't have believed your father, maybe he wouldn't have been so against our union if I hadn't provided such a sterling example of my character. So I missed my chance, Catra. Through my own errors, I missed my chance at having something fine and pure and good.'' He stopped and drew a deep breath. ''Don't ruin what you have with Ferris. Don't do something you'll surely regret.''

But Ryan had no idea what she'd already done, Catra thought. She was so far from having anything fine or pure or good in her marriage or herself that it shamed her all over again to think of what she'd done.

''How can you speak to me of ruining what I have with Ferris, when we both know what transpired last night?'' she whispered futilely. ''It's too late.''

''Last night was *my* fault,'' Ryan said.

Catra looked him dead in the eye. ''No. It wasn't.''

Ryan's eyes softened as he held her gaze, the unfinished act of the night before practically a living thing between them.

''Oh, yes, it was,'' Ryan said so quietly she barely heard him. ''You didn't stand a chance last night.''

Benjamin St. James sat in the study, silently brooding over the situation at hand. Namely, his son Ryan and his cursed propensity for scandal. Cora had confided in him her concerns about Ryan and the Chester woman after the ball last night. And, upon thinking about it, Benjamin had concluded that it would be just the sort of thing Ryan would do after emerging from a drunken binge, to have an affair with a married woman beneath his parents' very roof.

He had watched the two of them at dinner, and the pointed way they had of not looking at each other had made him suspicious. The husband, Ferris, had been oblivious to their overly polite conversation, thankfully. Benjamin had no desire to see his son called out over the stuffed pork roast. But the way the girl had jumped when Ryan had handed her the winter squash and their fingers had inadvertently touched, made Benjamin wonder if the Chester boy was simply ignoring the obvious. Of course, he himself had not noticed until Cora had pointed it out; but then, he was not one of the principal players.

Benjamin wished, as he had on dozens of other occasions, that his son would just meet someone and get married. He had seen Ryan go through years of philandering and had watched countless eligible women try to win him over, only to be cast aside when their schemes became too obvious or the outcome of their courtship too predicted by the local gossips. Each time Benjamin had wished that Ryan would find what he was looking for in one of them.

And then there'd been Therese. Thank God that was over. It wasn't just that she was married, but that they had flaunted their affair all over town. Ryan had actually seemed to relish the gossip generated by that one. Of course he'd been lucky that the husband was a notoriously dreadful shot and frightened to death of Ryan.

Benjamin chuckled reluctantly. There were quite a few mothers after that incident who would have forbidden their daughters to aspire to be the rake's wife if the rake had been anybody but Ryan St. James. For the name St. James was practically synonymous with *position* in their insular Boston society. Ryan was rich, he was smart, he was heir to one of the nation's most powerful shipyards and he was handsome. This last was what most of the young ladies admired, Benjamin knew. But a significant number were attracted by the idea of being the one to tame the savage beast.

So along comes a woman who can tame the beast, or so Cora claimed, in the form of Catherine Chester. Who, according to Cora's theory, after taming the wretched animal decides she does not want the damn thing after all. The beast goes and gets drunk for weeks on end only to show up all spit-shined and spiffy when the tamer happens to appear. But when she goes, what does one then do with the beast?

Benjamin snorted with disgust and opened the book on his lap. What the devil was he doing, thinking about all this nonsense anyway? Perhaps the stupid beast should be shot. Or castrated. No woman should be able to do that to a man, he thought angrily. The boy just needed to be kept busy, and out of the way of trouble, he decided. Tomorrow he would make sure Ryan had not a moment to spare for useless, troublemaking thoughts of a married woman.

While the men talked in the study and the women worked their needlepoint in the parlor, Catra excused herself to go up to her bedchamber. Her heart was heavy from her conversation with Ryan, but even as she wondered at her own inability to deny her desires the way he could, she admired him for his principles.

She had no doubt that he was right, that being together now was a wrong of immense proportions. But abandoning her desire for Ryan was a feat made even harder by the knowledge that they had lost their chance at happiness because of her father. Just thinking about her father's duplicitous behavior nearly incapacitated her with fury, so she turned her thoughts to the more immediate problem.

She was married. To a man she wouldn't hurt for all the world, though she had already done more damage than he would ever know. For weeks she'd been delaying the realization that she had well and truly committed herself to Ferris. Now it was time to resign herself to it.

She opened the wardrobe and removed the sheer white silk and lace nightrail she had received for her wedding night. It was a beautiful gown, with a matching white silk robe and slippers, that showed her figure to advantage while leaving little to the imagination.

Once the maid had helped unlace her gown, Catra dismissed the girl and donned the negligee. Then she sat on the edge of the bed to wait for Ferris.

Foolish as it was, Catra had the feeling that if she could have relations with Ferris now, the night after her disastrous meeting with Ryan, she could somehow repair the fact that he was not the one who'd taken her virginity.

It took a long while, but it was still sooner than she would have liked when Ferris's step sounded in the hall. As he turned the knob and opened the door she rose, the silk robe drifting open, and faced him.

"You're still up." His face held surprise, and it took a moment for him to notice the garment she wore. "That's pretty."

He averted his eyes as entered the room, heading straight for the bureau. One pale hand took the watch from his vest and set it, along with the contents of his pockets, on the immaculately polished top.

"Thank you. It was a wedding gift from Mayliza. Do you like it?"

Ferris glanced up and Catra dropped the robe down her back, turning to give him full view of the clinging material's sheer elegance. Rounding back to face him, she noted that he had turned away from her and was blushing from his neck to the tips of his ears.

She laced her fingers together in front of her while he doffed his jacket and fumbled with the buttons of his waistcoat.

"Let me help you with that." She came toward him.

He turned to face her but did not meet her eyes. Instead he dropped his hands to his sides and looked at the floor.

Catra unbuttoned his vest, then untied his cravat and removed the studs on his shirt. Parting the layers of material, she gingerly touched the skin of his chest, then lay her palm flat against it. His skin was warm and smooth, hairless, and she slid her other hand to his shoulder.

Ferris's gaze remained steady on the floor, shifting to look beside her as she moved closer.

"Ferris, look at me," she said softly.

He glanced at her, but his eyes skittered away as she pushed his shirt over his shoulders and stood closer. He shuffled back a step or two until his back hit the armoire.

"Cat . . . I . . . I don't know—"

"Shhh . . ." She pressed a finger to his lips, then moved it to to take his hand. She tilted her head to look into his face, pulling his hand tentatively toward the bed. "Do you . . . ?"

She hated having to do this, having to lure him to her, because pretending that she wanted him felt more like a lie than anything she'd done yet. But since their wedding day he'd made no move to touch her, or treated her as anything but the friend she'd been since they were children, so she was at a loss for what to do. She had to force the issue.

Still, he did not move. He gripped her hand tightly, his back against the armoire.

Tears welled up behind her eyes and she blinked them away. If he would only kiss her, hold her like, like Ryan, she might be able to forget what she had lost. If he would take what was rightfully his, there was a chance she could feel differently about him, feel more as she should for a husband instead of a childhood friend.

But Ferris's response was nervous and reluctant, threatening to snuff out Catra's tiny flame of ambition to make her marriage to Ferris a real one.

Finally he looked up at her. Pulling the hand she held,

he drew her toward him, shrugging his shirt back up onto his shoulders. He took her by the arms. "Catra, I don't . . . I don't know how it happened last night, but I—I feel I have to be honest with you."

For a second Catra feared he knew about her and Ryan, but Ferris's expression was so pained and self-conscious that her fear evaporated. In its place grew concern, and pity. He looked so unnerved, so . . . *embarrassed*.

"What is it?" she asked gently.

He laughed once, without humor, dropping his hands from her arms. His eyes sought the ceiling. "I don't know how to say it, how to put it, into words. I'm—afraid . . . I just don't know."

"Ferris, you know you can tell me anything. We've been friends too long for you to be afraid to speak plainly to me."

Maybe *he'd* had an affair. Maybe *he* was in love with someone else too. A small billowing of hope blossomed in her chest. That would, at least, alleviate some of her guilt.

He smiled at her sadly. "I know. We've been friends for a long, long time. That's why I thought this would work. But Cat, I . . . I didn't know . . . I guess I didn't think. That is, that you—you'd want to make this marriage include . . . you know."

"What do you mean?" Catra held her breath.

He exhaled and folded his arms, tucking his hands under his arms. "I don't know how what happened last night—happened. You see, I've never . . . never done that before."

Catra sighed and smiled slightly. "Neither had I." Only this time it was she who could not meet his eyes.

"But you don't understand. I've never even *wanted* to. Not . . . not with a woman." His last words emerged a whisper, and after a long minute Catra raised her eyes to his.

"What do you mean?"

Ferris's flush, if it was possible, grew deeper. Catra gazed at him with a sudden feeling of foreboding. He took her by the shoulders and pulled her to him, hugging her tightly, an embrace that was simultaneously desperate and chaste.

"You're so innocent," he said in a strangled voice. "I hate to be the one to damage that."

Funny, Catra thought, she felt the same way about him.

"You see, I can't. I just can't," Ferris began, still holding her tight, mainly, Catra believed, so she would not move to where he would have to look at her as he spoke. "I can't make love to you. Some men, you know, they can, and some . . . have trouble making love."

Here he hesitated so long that Catra felt the need to say something. "Well, we all have to start somewhere. We're both beginners, Ferris. We'll help each other through it. I'm nervous too." And she was. She was scared to death.

He took a deep breath and let it out slowly. "No, that's not what I mean. I mean . . ."

Catra could feel the tension in his back through her fingers. He practically quivered with it.

"God, I feel horrible," he whispered.

She swallowed and the sound was loud in the silent room. "What are you saying, Ferris? You don't even want to try? You *never* want to . . . to make love to me?"

He sighed. "I thought it would be all right. Because I thought we had that deal, that we'd get married to preserve our independence. You remember that, don't you, Cat? I thought because we'd said that it would be all right, that you wouldn't want . . . you wouldn't expect . . ."

"But what about *children?*" she asked, pushing back so she could look into his face. Her voice emerged pleading more than angry. "I don't expect you to love me, Ferris. I know—we both know how we feel about each other. But did you think I wouldn't want children? And don't *you?*"

He looked at his hands. "Honestly . . . I didn't think about it." He shrugged and looked up at her, looking as if he were ready to cry himself. "It never occurred to me."

Catra swallowed hard again, and then again, feeling as if she were going to choke.

"Cat, I'm *sorry.* God, I'm so, so sorry. I wish I could, but . . . I really can't."

She held his arms in her hands, her grip tight. "But, Ferris—"

He made a fist and brought it back hard against the armoire. Catra jumped at the sudden, hollow sound. *"No,"* he said, his voice hard with desperation. "No, I *don't* want to try."

This time she tried to back away, but he grabbed her by the shoulders.

"Please forgive me," he said, his voice breaking. "You can't know . . . I'm so sorry. I suppose I—I deceived you. I didn't mean to. Honestly, I didn't."

His face contorted and she looked up at him, at the tears streaming down his cheeks, and felt her own spill over.

"Oh, Ferris, there's nothing to *forgive.* It's just . . . I just . . ." She felt emotion threaten to overwhelm her and put her hands over her face. Her whole life had twisted into some warped, bizarre arrangement. She had, she suddenly felt, somewhere along the line sold her soul. And for what?

"Cat, don't." Ferris took her in his arms again, his voice thick. "I'm so ashamed. I'm so sorry." He held her too tightly, but she said nothing, feeling numb. "I *hate* myself for this, you have no idea. I'm a failure to you, and to my family. I know it, and they'll know it too before long. I'm sorry, Cat, so, so sorry."

His voice trailed off and she could feel him trembling

with sobs. His tears dampened her shoulder where he'd laid his head.

"Don't keep saying that, Ferris. Please." She stroked his back automatically. "Don't be sorry."

She should be glad he did not want her. She would not be expected to share his bed. She would not have him touching her, looking at her, wanting her, wondering how she felt. She would not have to look into his face, touch his body, lie next to him night after night after night, and wish he were Ryan.

But another voice told her that instead she would lie alone and virginal for the rest of her life. She would never be kissed or held, caressed or truly loved. And all the while friends and neighbors would speculate as to why Catherine Chester could not conceive and muse that it looked like Baker Mansfield would inherit everything after all.

"Maybe," Ferris said into her hair, a hopeful note in his breaking voice, "maybe we could adopt a child from somewhere. Or . . . or . . ."

Catra buried her head in his shoulder. "Oh, Ferris."

Part of her wanted to confess now to what she and Ryan had done last night, but she couldn't even think of the words she would use. And the scene was so odd already, she decided her confession should wait for another time, a time when she could make sense of everything that had happened. For she *would* tell him, she knew now. There was no reason to keep it from him.

"Can you . . ." she began hoarsely, then stopped to clear her throat. "Can you tell me *why,* Ferris? Is it just that you don't desire me? Is there someone else?"

Ferris ducked his head into her shoulder again.

"You can tell me," she said. "I won't be angry. I'll understand, truly I will. I just need to know, Ferris. Because if there's not, maybe we could, someday, you know, just for children . . . ?''

A muscle jumped in his jaw as he clenched his teeth. "No. There is someone else.''

Catra's stomach lifted, surprise and relief buoyant within her. "There is? Who is it? Why didn't you marry her?''

Ferris cleared his throat and turned halfway away from her. She grabbed his shoulder and moved to look into his face.

"You can tell me, Ferris. I won't be angry. *Believe* me. Who is she?''

"He," he said quietly.

She'd heard him wrong, she was sure. "He?''

Ferris nodded.

"I don't understand.''

He threw his hands down and his head back at the same moment, expelling a breath. "I *know* you don't. That is precisely why I don't want to explain.''

Then something occurred to her. "Ferris, you don't . . .'' But she shook her head. She'd heard rumors, once, about her cousin Baker, but she thought it was just vile talk about a man who was generally disliked. Even then she couldn't credit that such things happened.

She looked up to find Ferris gazing at her, his blue eyes uncharacteristically intense.

"Yes," he said then, forcefully. "I do. I do mean just what you're thinking.''

She flushed. "No, you don't know—''

"Yes I do. It's just as you think, Cat. I am one of those men.''

She stared at him. Ferris? Like the men she'd heard were . . . that way? No, it was impossible. And yet, of course he would not lie. Kind, gentle Ferris . . . her best friend . . . Suddenly she felt such a wave of feeling for him, of worry and care, along with shock and disbelief, that she was momentarily breathless with it. For as difficult and complicated as her life was seeming at this moment, if this were true, his was and would continue to be even more difficult.

"Why didn't you tell me?" Her words were barely a whisper.

He stepped around her and moved toward the door.

"Wait—where are you going?" She stepped after him, hands clasped white-knuckled in front of her, then stopped. What could she say? Lord, what a mess. What was going to *become* of them both?

At the threshold he turned. "I wouldn't blame you for hating me now. Trust me, I often hate myself." He stepped out the door and slammed it behind him.

"Ferris, no!" Catra raced to the door and grabbed the knob. Whipping it open, she followed him out. *"Ferris,"* she called discreetly, trying to keep her voice from rousing the whole house. But he would not stop and she was forced to follow him. She ran down the hall.

He turned on her at the top of the stairs, holding a hand out to ward her off, as if she would grab him. *"No,* Catra. There's nothing more to be said."

"But I *don't* hate you. Please, let's talk some more. I want to understand." She reached out for him.

"No. It doesn't matter." His voice was hard. She could see tears still wet on his cheeks. "None of it matters." He took the stairs two at a time and ran across the foyer, his coattails flying behind him as his dress shoes slipped on the polished entryway floor. He looked for all the world like a young boy fleeing his nanny.

An hour later Catra heard the carriage pull up from where she sat in the middle of the staircase. She hadn't moved since Ferris left except to sit down, waiting for him to return so they could talk. The house was dark, silent. She imagined all the occupants in their beds, sleeping the unencumbered sleep of innocence.

She tried not to think of Ryan, asleep or otherwise.

She would not push Ferris, she'd decided as she'd sat there. He was her friend and had been true to her for almost her entire life. He was obviously suffering untold guilt over what he'd told her this night, and if there was one thing she knew about, it was guilt. Never would she inflict on him what she had been feeling herself. It was corrosive, paralyzing, and there was no reason *he* should be feeling it. She would tell him, when he entered, that everything was all right.

She waited to hear his footfalls on the path outside. They came, crunching slowly on the broken ice, and with them her heart beat a slow tattoo of dread.

She knew what she wanted to do. She wanted to tell him the truth about her and Ryan and her father and everything. But that would be too much on top of what he'd told her tonight. Why burden him further, when doing so would only cleanse her soul and perhaps make him even more unhappy? No, she could wait for a time when he was stronger, when the news would be something they could understand together, not something more to deal with on the heels of this revelation.

As if she deserved forgiveness in light of what he'd said. No, her guilt was independent of his proclivities. Her guilt was her own doing.

The door opened and she stood, but instead of Ferris's thin frame being the one silhouetted in the doorway, she found herself looking at Ryan's agile physique.

He lit the candle by the door and turned, starting when he caught sight of her in the dim light. She watched as his posture shifted from alarm to slow wariness.

271

"Mrs. Chester," he said, his voice low and butter smooth in the darkness.

Despite herself, her breath quivered with the sound of it.

"What are you doing up?" he asked, glancing around as if expecting the others to be somewhere nearby.

Tears pricked the back of her eyes. He looked so strong standing there. So safe and capable. At that moment she wanted nothing more than to run to him, to lay her head on his chest and have his arms encircle her, and then tell him all her troubles. God, she wanted it so much, she could almost taste it.

"Catra?" he said then, taking a step toward her. "Is everything all right?"

She swallowed and felt emotion threatening to overtake her again. She shook her head.

"What is it?" he asked. He was close enough now that she could see the concern in his eyes.

She took a deep breath. "I'm all right. I don't mean to alarm you."

He raised himself onto the first step and took her forearm in his hand. She shivered at the contact.

"Come here," he said. "We can talk in the library."

The door was ajar, and as they moved through the opening she could see that a fire burned in the hearth. She looked around to be sure no one else occupied the room, then closed the door.

Noting her look as he walked toward the liquor cabinet, Ryan said, "They keep the fire lit for me when I'm out. I frequently come here before going to bed." He smiled wryly as he poured himself a brandy. "Especially lately. Would you like something?" He gestured with the decanter.

She shook her head.

"Would you care to sit down?" He motioned her to a

chair in front of the fire and sat next to her in another one.

"You're sure you're all right?"

Catra nodded, watching the firelight play across his features. "You've been gone a lot," she said, drawing her robe more tightly around her.

Ryan leaned his elbows on his knees, hands cradling the brandy snifter, and looked into the flames. The firelight made his eyes glitter.

"Yes." He nodded once.

Catra's breath caught. "You're avoiding me," she half whispered, drowning in the sight of him.

He sat up, raised the snifter to his lips and drank, his eyes not leaving her face. Then he set the glass carefully back on the table, his gaze dropping to watch his own hand deposit it there. "Yes."

The house was silent around them, giving Catra the dizzy feeling that they were alone in the universe. She looked past him to the darkness of the room beyond them, then let her gaze slowly refocus on him. They were alone. It was a luxury she never thought she'd have again.

His eyes studied her. Shrewd, unyielding. Wherever he'd been, he had not been drinking.

"I'll not ask why," she said.

He tilted his head. "I don't imagine you need to."

She shook her head. "No."

Silence stretched taut.

"You know, I would have thought," he began, stretching his legs out in front of him, "a few months ago, that having you in my house would be a dream come true. You would be my wife. You would belong here." He leaned back in the chair and looked at her enigmatically, his face thrown into shadow by the wing of the chair. "But now it tortures me. *You* torture me. Like a spirit long dead you haunt me, only so much the worse because I can reach out

273

and touch you. Warm blood and soft flesh.'' He laughed to himself and turned to look at the fire. ''Yes. I *am* avoiding you.''

''I hate that,'' Catra whispered. ''I hate that you have to do it. But if I know you're near, I can't avoid you. I want to, but I can't. Am I selfish or are you? I don't know. I only know I can't be here and not see you. Not want to touch you.''

''We're both selfish, Cat. We both want what we want. We've always had what we wanted, haven't we?'' His eyes bored into hers. She nodded. ''Not this time, Catherine . . . Meredyth . . . Chester,'' he drew the words out carefully, a dry smile on his lips. ''I do believe we're supposed to be learning some sort of lesson.''

Catra bent her head and her loose hair fell forward. Wishing things were different was such a small, impotent thing to do, but it seemed the only thing she was capable of. She looked at her hands in her lap, hands that shook with the desire to reach out and touch him. What harm would it do? What *more* harm could possibly be done?

She looked up, sure her longing was naked in her eyes.

He shook his head. ''We can't have it, Catra, what we want. We can never have each other.''

''No, not forever. But for a time, a short time, maybe . . . maybe we can.'' She wet her suddenly dry lips. ''We're here, together. Alone. We can have each other, Ryan, just for tonight. God, I want to be with you so badly I ache with it. Don't you? Don't you feel that pain? Ryan, don't you see? After last night there is nothing left to lose.''

He leaned toward her, his eyes intense. ''Nothing left to lose? This is what we're settling for now? Are we going to take something more precious than anything I've ever known and turn it into that?''

''But it's *not* just that. We both know it.'' She pushed

274

herself from the chair and knelt on the floor in front of him, her hands on his knees. "I want *you,* Ryan. I want you to hold me, to treasure me, to take me in your arms and act on the love you feel, let me act on the love I feel. I want you inside of me, all of you ... I'll never have that, not from anyone else. And I can't go to my grave without knowing what it's like to be with you, even if it's just one time."

Her hands ran up his thighs and he grabbed them with his.

"You don't know what you're doing," he growled. "You don't even realize what you're proposing."

"I know *exactly* what I'm proposing, Ryan." She stood and closed her hands around his, pulling him to his feet. "I'll do anything to have you. Please. Just this once."

As he stood, she moved closer, running her hands up his chest and around his neck until her body touched his. She stared up at him with calm, purposeful eyes.

Ryan grasped her by the shoulders, but he did not push her away. Instead he glared down at her for a long moment before moving one hand to the back of her head and plunging his fingers into the loose profusion of her hair. He pulled her mouth to his.

She opened to him immediately, her hands clutching his shirt and her body molding to his. Then she pulled back, keeping her gaze steadily on his, and pulled him gently toward the door.

"Come," she said, opening it. "Give me this one night."

He followed her from the room to the darkness of the hall. She turned toward the foyer, head tilted to look up the stairs as they rounded the balustrade.

"Catra," he whispered, but she turned a fierce look on him, one finger on her lips.

She held his hand tightly and started up the stairs. Ryan stopped her, pulling his hand from hers. "You go," he said quietly. His expression was dark. "Go, and I'll come to you."

Chapter Sixteen

He entered his room to find her sitting on the bed, leaning back against the pillows. Her hair cascaded around her shoulders, a sheath of burnished gold in the candlelight. The sheer robe fell away from her body to pool on the coverlet. It was a dream, he thought. She was here, in his bed, looking up at him with eyes that spoke of every emotion contained in his heart; it had to be a dream. He sat alongside her and stroked the side of her face, gently moving strands of pale hair from her cheek. Her skin was soft and so supple, the feel of it caused his gut to clench.

His fingers traced the line of her jaw, then dipped down the column of her throat to the edge of the silk nightgown.

Tonight, when he'd arrived, she'd looked like an angel standing on the stairs. For one foolish second he'd wondered if she was a spirit sent to torment him, or soothe the desire that raged in him every night as he imagined her sleeping.

Indulging himself, awed by the temporary ability to touch her as he pleased, he cupped her breast, his palm grazing the erect nipple. She shuddered beneath his hand.

His eyes met hers.

"Catra, you're sure?"

She laughed, and the low sound sent pleasure spiraling up his spine.

"I've never been so sure of anything in my life."

His lips curved and he leaned forward to touch them to hers. A soft, chaste kiss that sent desire rocketing through him. His hand stroked her breast between them. He rose and with his other hand pushed the nightgown from her shoulder, down along her arm, the pert breast below the thin silk standing at attention.

God, she was beautiful. All shadow gold and moon white.

She sat up, her hair falling over her shoulders, and let the material slide off her arm. He pushed the other side down and both the robe and nightgown dropped to her waist, exposing two pale, perfect breasts, their nipples high and tight.

He touched one with his fingers and bent to kiss the other. Catra lay back against the pillows, her hands twining in his hair as his lips closed over her nipple. He heard her gasp, felt her quiver, and pulled the nipple sharply into his mouth. She arched her back.

Her skin was warm, more silky than the silk nightgown, and tasted sweet and salty at once. He clasped his hands round her waist as he moved from one breast to the other.

She exhaled slowly, her hips rising with the rhythm of his mouth, and he took as much of her into him as he could. Catra pulled herself more tightly to him, her breathing rapid and coarse.

His lips trailed down to her stomach, his hands pulling

the nightgown down over her hips, along her legs and off. She was naked before him, lying on his bed in all her silken perfection like any one of the torturous dreams he'd had about her for months. But this time she was real. This time when he laid his hands upon her thighs they opened to him, warm and soft and suppliant.

"Let me," she said softly, reaching out to him. "I want to touch you."

He felt himself stand rock hard at the words and he shifted toward her on the bed. She hastily untied his cravat and pushed the shirt from his chest. He shrugged it off. Then she started on the buttons of his pants. Helping her, he shed them in moments. Then he lay beside her on the bed, guiding her hand to his manhood and watching her face as she touched a man for the first time.

He let out a long shuddering breath as she closed her fingers around him. She looked up at him, her eyes wide with wonder at the effect she was able to provoke. He closed his hand around hers and gently moved it, showing her, teaching her, how to pleasure a man. He tried not to think about who would benefit most from his instruction.

To block the thought, he kissed her hard, tasting again her sweet mouth and reveling in the willingness of her.

"I love you," she whispered against his lips.

"I love you," he whispered back, their breath mingling, their mouths never parting.

He rolled over onto her, taking her hand and kissing it as he did so. Then he pushed her knees open with his and touched himself to her core. With his fingers he found the spot and was gratified to feel it slick with desire. He pushed himself against her and felt her tense.

"Don't worry," he said, looking down into her trusting face. "It won't be like the last time. I promise."

He kissed her again, long and hard, his fingers touching

her most private area, sliding over, across and inside until he felt her relax again. Then more, moving farther and harder as she began to thrust her hips toward him, wanting more, moving, cresting, nearly toppling over that sexual peak as he slipped inside her.

She was so sleek and tight, he nearly came the moment he entered her. But no, he would have to be careful.

She exhaled and pushed her head back into the pillow, her back arching. "Oh," she breathed.

He began to move, slowly at first, but as her hands gripped him and her breathing quickened, so did her movements beneath him. She clutched his hips and pulled him toward her, faster and faster. Sounds came from deep and low in her throat as he pumped into her. Her body grabbed and released him, grabbed and released as she arched with every motion, met every thrust and angled for more. Then she was calling his name and her whole body shuddered, then stilled, held in thrall with sensations.

He silenced her with a kiss but could not stop himself as he thrust deeper and deeper into that hot well of desire, harder and stronger until he felt himself burst within her. The release was a shattering summit, a spilling forth of a cauldron of emotions, the climax of craving he felt seeing her beneath him, her skin slick with sweat from the fire of their union.

The weather was bitterly cold. Wind howled around the eaves of the house and whistled through the bare tree limbs. It wasn't snowing yet, but the sky was darkening and the snow already on the ground swirled violently with the gale's force, piling drifts against houses, fences and trees. The short brick wall enclosing the front yard was already buried and the stately homes just across the broad street were lost in a blinding white wind. Everything normally seen from the large bay window was obliterated by the frozen melee.

Inside, a crackling fire burned in the great brick fireplace, radiating warmth and comfort into the cheerfully lit drawing room. A steaming mug of cider waited on the table by the sofa—the iron kettle in the fire was full of the fragrant mulled brew—and an open book lay face down on the cushions. The scent of cinnamon and cloves filled the room.

Catra entered somberly and strolled to the couch to determine whose book and cider lay waiting for them. Though she hoped, as she had for days, that she would once again stumble upon Ryan, the belongings were obviously Lydia's. Days after they'd made love, Ryan was making quite sure they didn't run into each other again.

Ferris had arrived home the morning after his confession, contrite over his abrupt departure, but determined not to speak about it. They understood each other, he'd said firmly, and that was all that was necessary. Respecting his wishes, Catra said nothing further but made it clear by her words and actions that their friendship was intact, even if their marriage was a disaster.

Catra moved toward the bookshelves, thinking to divert herself from thoughts of her night with Ryan, but was captivated instead by the icy maelstrom outside the window.

Not a soul moved on the street. Catra found it interesting that an entire city could become paralyzed by something as light and beautiful as snow. It was deadly, they said, a killing softness. Frostbite, chilblains, suffocation. Looking at the angry icicles clutching the trees, she believed it. Several downy flakes settled softly on the windowpane, protected from the wind by the window.

"There you are," Lydia said, entering, "I was just checking the upstairs windows. One of the shutters was banging. And between that and the wind, screaming the way it does around this house, I thought I'd lose my mind.''

"Yes, it's quite dramatic." Catra half turned toward her. "Strange how something so beautiful can also be so deadly."

"I suppose it is." Lydia settled herself by the fire and picked up her book. "It must be new to you, this type of storm. Do you get snow, where you live?"

"Not much. A few inches, perhaps. But nothing to rival this."

Lydia smiled. "I love it. There's nothing I love more than sitting warm and cozy inside during a blizzard. Only, of course, if everyone I know is safe and warm, as well."

"Yes, everyone is home," Catra murmured, wondering if Ryan might possibly join them or continue to avoid her even when she was with others. He had made it quite clear, after that night, that they could not indulge their desires in such a way again. It only made it all more difficult for him, he'd said.

The night she had found him after Ferris's dreadful confession had been intense and, considering their feelings and proximity, unavoidable. She had wanted him so badly she hurt with it. She would never regret what they'd done. But she could see how, if they continued, instead of something beautiful the act could come to feel like something sinful, something with more power to destroy than comfort. She frowned and turned from the window.

Lydia watched her pensively. "It's hard for you, being here, isn't it," she said quietly.

Catra turned her head toward the soft voice. Lydia's look was compassionate, unjudgmental. Catra was afraid to ask what she meant. What did she know? How much did she know?

Without Catra having to ask, Lydia provided the answer. Speaking hesitantly, she said, "I've seen the way you and

Ryan look at each other. Everyone else in this house may be dumb as a post, but I know. You're in love with each other.''

Catra's limbs went cold. Hearing it out loud was shocking and somehow frightening. Her life was so swathed in secrets that the emergence of even one to the light of day made her worry about the others. She wondered if Lydia would be so understanding if she knew everything that had happened between herself and Ryan right under her family's very roof. For that's what made it so much more iniquitous, she realized suddenly. And that must be what Ryan meant.

If Lydia knew the whole truth, would she still be sympathetic? Perhaps the idea of unrequited love was romantic to her. But to be engaged in an illicit affair—that had to be something else entirely. If she knew, would Lydia go to Ryan's parents and tell them? Would they ask her to leave? Would they make public her shameless actions, as Ryan seemed to fear?

''I've embarrassed you. I'm sorry,'' Lydia said. ''I just wanted you to know that I know. And that I understand.''

Catra left the window to sit across from Lydia. ''It's not the way it seems,'' she said, feeling a sudden need to assure Ryan's sister that he had done nothing wrong. That he had tried to do the right thing, that circumstances had conspired against them. ''We knew each other before—before Ferris and I wed. And my father didn't want me to marry Ryan. But I didn't know—there was this misunderstanding—''

Lydia leaned forward and laid a hand on her arm, effectively halting the tumble of words. ''You don't need to explain if it's painful for you.''

Catra leaned back, embarrassed. It was horribly painful for her, but there was no reason Lydia should know the whole sordid story. Her knowing would change nothing.

The entire family could know and it would change nothing. In fact, it would probably be best for all concerned if everyone ignored or forgot all about the awful situation.

It wasn't fair. They had started out properly, not dishonorably. They were simply two people who had fallen in love.

But even that was not entirely true, she thought. For even in the beginning she had been betraying Ferris. Perhaps Ryan really was right, and the liaison had been wrong from the start. Perhaps it had always been too late for them.

At that moment the front bell rang. Catra was relieved at the distraction, for Lydia had looked ready to say something more. She was not sure she could handle hearing Lydia speak of it when her own feelings were in such turmoil.

They both watched the butler pass on his way to the door. A moment later he emerged with the mail.

"The post, madame." He bowed and handed the letters to Lydia.

Lydia took the letters from him. "Imagine sending someone to traipse about in this weather, just to retrieve our mail. Here's something for Ferris. And look, one for you too." She flipped through the small stack and extended an envelope to Catra.

Catra rose and took the missive from her. Across the front her name was scrawled in her father's hard, masculine script. *Mrs. Catherine Chester, In care of Benjamin St. James, Beacon Street, Boston, Massachusetts.*

Mrs. Catherine Chester. She hated the name, the sound of it, even the way it looked on the page. She tore open the envelope and scanned the note. It was not long—her father was not an avid writer—but the news it contained was enough to jolt Catra's self-absorbed worries from her head.

"My father's getting *married,*" she burst, shocked.

Lydia's eyebrows rose. "Congratulations," she said uncertainly. "Do you know his betrothed?"

Catra read the letter again, more carefully. "He doesn't say who she is! Can you imagine? He only says that it is someone I know and that he hopes I can find it in my heart to wish them well." She paused, then continued, reading, " ' . . . for it is not often that a man like myself finds such happiness so late in life, and from so unexpected, nay, undeserved, a source. We shall wait for your return to celebrate our nuptials, for we both consider your opinion and happiness to be of the utmost importance. Your devoted father.' "

"He sounds happy," Lydia said.

Catra lifted her head to glare at her for a moment. "He was happy before," was all she could think to say. Her father, the man who had willfully destroyed her chance at happiness by tricking both she and Ryan, had then gone merrily along and fallen in love with someone in the short month she'd been gone. It hadn't even *been* a month. And now he was going to marry.

Was he getting so on in years that he needed a companion? Was that his reasoning? Did he think that he needed someone to take care of him? But no, he said in the opening paragraph that he had fallen in love with this creature. And it was someone she knew.

Catra searched her mind for possibilities. What single, elderly women did she know? Mrs. Williams was a widow, but she was an insufferable bore whom her father had often said had talked her husband into an early grave. Miss Trellis, who owned the millinery shop, was an unmarried woman, but Catra was not even sure her father knew her. And besides, she was such a . . . such a . . . *spinster.* Mrs. Grant was too old. Miss Sylvester, too prudish. Miss Trundlow, a weak possibility. Catra thought she would explode with angry curiosity.

She remembered back to her recent conversation with Mrs. St. James about her father's responsibility to remarry. A fine time for him to find a mother for me *now,* she nearly scoffed aloud. She could have used one a month ago, before her father's treachery and her own travesty of a marriage had taken place.

But could this really be love? Her father had courted no one before she left. What woman that she knew would give her heart so quickly?

That was an absurd question. Her father was one of the richest men in the state; any unmarried woman he turned his attention to would fall at his feet in an instant, she knew. Especially at *their* age. Not to mention the fact that he was handsome, generous, kind and still quite vigorous despite his age.

"I must tell Ferris," Catra said suddenly. Ferris might have some idea who the woman could be.

She excused herself from Lydia and went in search of him. She found him in the study, reading. He sat alone before the fire. She shuddered slightly as she crossed the threshold into the room where Ryan and she had consummated her marriage to Ferris.

"Ferris," she said urgently into the silence, causing him to jump at the unexpected sound, "I have the most dreadful news. My father is getting *married.*"

Ferris turned toward her. He closed his book and placed it on the table beside him.

"Married?" He looked as stunned as she must have. Then his face broke into a smile. "But that's *wonderful.* Who's he marrying?"

From behind her, Catra heard the sound of another body

placing a book on a shelf. She whirled and caught sight of Ryan. Her heart clamored to her throat.

Catra turned back to Ferris, clutching the letter in an instantly sweaty palm. "Heaven knows! Here, read it for yourself." She thrust the wrinkled paper at him.

"Congratulations," Ryan's low voice said from behind her. The sound of it sent shivers up her spine.

She half turned, not looking at him. "Thank you." Her voice betrayed her agitation. "But I cannot consider it good news."

She saw him from the corner of her eye as she gazed at the floor but could not make out his expression.

"Perhaps he was worried he'd be lonely without you in the house," Ryan said.

"He said he's fallen in love," Catra said disdainfully, meeting his eyes. "I would not even have thought him aware of the emotion."

Ryan plucked another book from the shelf, then moved slightly toward her, flipping through its pages as Ferris read the letter. "I don't doubt you have little sympathy for his romantic notions," he said quietly. They looked at each other, each knowing the other's thoughts.

"He says here that you know her," Ferris mused. "If he wasn't going to tell you her name, I wonder that he wrote you at all."

"I'll leave you two to discuss this privately," Ryan said.

"That's not necessary," Catra said quickly. She had barely seen him in the last few days and, though this meeting was uncomfortable and hardly of the sort she would have liked, she did not want to lose his company.

Ferris added his voice to the sentiment. "This is not a private matter. I imagine everyone at home knew of it before now. I only wish we knew who she was. Strange that he'd be so mysterious about it."

Ryan leaned back against the bookcases.

"I've thought of every widow or spinster I know and can think of no reasonable possibilities," Catra said.

"What make you so sure it's a widow or spinster?" Ryan offered. "Perhaps he's found some young woman to warm his bed," he added with just a trace of bitterness.

Catra stared at him, aghast. It hadn't occurred to her that he might marry someone young, even though wealthy older men did so all the time.

Ferris looked up and frowned. "That's rather a cold way of putting it, don't you think? Perhaps he's trying for an heir."

Catra's heart hit her stomach and she turned a now stricken expression on Ferris. "What do you mean?"

"I mean, perhaps he wants an heir—a male heir. He's not so old that he can't father more children. Is he?"

"But *I'm* his heir," Catra objected. The new thought cast an even more threatening light on the situation. Not only would her father have stolen from her the only man she'd ever love, now he was going to give Braithwood to some—some *stranger's* child. Would they care about Jimmy? Of course not!

"Yes, but now you're married. You don't need Braithwood, not with Waverly as your home," Ferris said. Then he turned a significant look on her, his cheeks turning pink. "Catra, this could be a good thing. This could keep Braithwood out of Baker's hands."

Catra felt a wave of nausea wash over her. She knew what Ferris meant. That because *she* would never have children, it would be up to her father to provide an heir for Braithwood when she passed on. "But what about Jimmy?"

"He can come to Waverly, of course."

"No. Impossible. You *know* he cannot stand change. He

would never understand a move like that. Braithwood is his home. Where he grew up. He would live out the rest of his life in confusion if he were turned out of Braithwood."

Ryan came forward. "We are supposing an eventuality that may never take place. And Braithwood is an enormous place. Even if he were to have more children, there's nothing to say that you would not still get a good part of it. You are, after all, the firstborn."

"But suppose he has another son," Ferris said reasonably. "Of course any normal son would get all, as is only right. He'll have to marry, have heirs of his own to keep it in the family and all that, but the woman goes unto the husband, or however that proverb goes."

"And loses everything in the bargain," she whispered, near tears.

Ryan looked at her with concern.

"I think you might be absolutely right, Ryan," Ferris continued, oblivious to his wife's distress. "I feel certain he's chosen a young woman. It makes perfect sense. Now that Catra is taken care of, he can provide Braithwood with an heir."

Catra felt a pool of tears spill over her lashes. She was shunted off in marriage to a neighbor to make room for the *real* heir? It crossed her mind that her father might even have *known* about Ferris's . . . problem. Perhaps he *wanted* her to remain childless so he could leave his estate to someone else.

"Catra," Ryan said quietly.

She almost didn't hear it, so engrossed was she in the dire scenario, but when she turned he was gazing at her intently.

"And the reason he wouldn't tell you who it is, is obvious," Ferris crowed with discovery. "It must be someone you don't like! Who don't you like?" He turned to her.

His expression registered shock at her tearstained face and he rose instantly. "Whatever is the matter?"

Catra covered her face with her hands. "Catra," Ferris pleaded. He reached her and tried to take her hands from her face.

But she could take no more. Faced with the option of either publicly condemning Ferris for his celibacy or leaving, she turned and ran from the room.

Ferris stared after her. Into the silence, he said, "Well, I guess I made of muddle of that."

Ryan looked at him inscrutably. Then he walked to one of the chairs before the fire and sat down.

"What do you think got her all upset like that?" Ferris ventured.

Ryan sighed. "I imagine she was upset over the idea of being replaced. And I'm not sure the idea of it being by someone she dislikes was any great help."

Ferris sighed as well and sat in the chair opposite him. "Well, dash it, what does she care?" he said in exasperation. "She's got Waverly now and she'll have it for as long as she lives. What does she need Braithwood for?"

Ryan tried to read the opening paragraph of the book he had randomly snagged from the shelf and was discouraged to note that it was written in Latin.

"And Jimmy would learn to live at Waverly. It's not as if he's never seen the place. She should be happy for her father. Besides," he said, casting a shy glance at Ryan, "she could have an heir of her own on the way right now."

Ryan turned his eyes to Ferris, questions on the tip of his tongue that he dared not utter.

Ferris held his gaze. "Oh, we've finally consummated," he said. "Once. Not that I can remember it." He slumped in his chair.

"You can't remember?" The question forced its way out. Ryan knew he shouldn't ask, knew he wouldn't want to hear the answer. Still, the words would not be stopped.

"Drunk. I was dead drunk. It was after that blasted ball we went to. After you and I had that conversation. I'd had quite a bit of champagne that night, and, well, I guess I overdid it a little. But I went to bed and the next thing I knew I woke up to—well—the evidence was indisputable."

Ryan gaped at him. "After the *Rutherfords'* ball?"

"Yes, yes. You remember. That night I spoke to you about the whole blessed problem. I guess I took your advice, though I'll be damned if I can remember a minute of it."

Ryan could not think of even one thing to say to the man. His mind raced with thoughts of Catra's obvious deception. How sly. How smart. She'd done what she'd had to, he thought, stunned. She'd landed on her feet. If he was hoping that the fact of her stolen virginity would cause the marriage to fail, he was bitterly disappointed. But he had never allowed himself to acknowledge the hope, and so would not acknowledge the pain.

It was time to let go of her. Time to admit defeat.

"You should go to her," Ryan said. He clasped his hands around the book and stared at them. "She's afraid of being replaced in her father's affections," he continued. "And she's probably afraid of too many changes, too fast. You should try to help her, even if by simply listening to her."

Ferris turned to him. "Too many changes, yes. You're probably right. You know, I've known her a long time but I guess never in these kinds of circumstances. Lately she's been behaving in ways I barely recognize. You think listening will be enough to get the old Cat back?"

Ryan gazed down at the incomprehensible book. "I don't know, Ferris. Sometimes people change. Just be kind to her."

"Of course," Ferris said and stood. "I'll go get her to talk. Shouldn't be too hard. We never had trouble talking in the past." He moved toward the door.

"And Ferris?" Ryan stopped him. "Try not to say much, all right? Not even if you think it'll help. Just listen."

"Not say much?" Ferris puzzled. "Well, all right. You know more about women than I do. If you think it best."

"I do think it best."

"All right, then. I'll just take her in my arms and comfort her and all that. I guess that'll make her feel better. I'll tell her that I love her anyway. I should say that at least, shouldn't I?"

Ryan closed his eyes. "I wouldn't say anything."

Ferris paused. "Nothing? She usually likes me to say *some*thing, but if you think it best . . ." His voice trailed off as he left the room.

Ryan opened the book in his hands, but his eyes glazed over the printed pages.

"It is best," he said to the empty room. He expelled a long breath and leaned his head against the back of the chair. "It is best."

Chapter Seventeen

Catra emerged from the privy feeling even more shaken than she had for the past anxious week. Her stomach coiled in dread and her hands trembled. For days she'd rationalized away the fear, telling herself that the pressures of travel and the unaccustomed activity her body had undergone had most likely affected its normal functions. But it was no use.

She'd gone to the privy almost every hour now for days, hoping, praying, fearing the worst. But there was nothing. Her monthly courses were never late. Yet here she was, a week beyond their due. Panic gripped her.

What would she do if the improbable—the *unimaginable*—proved true? She didn't know what to think about it. Of course it would be Ryan's. She took that comfort. And she had planned to tell Ferris about her deception, so this only confirmed that she would. But upon the heels of those thoughts came the unpleasant one that Ferris and Ryan could not look less alike. She and Ferris were both blond.

How could she possibly give birth to a dark-haired child without someone someday posing an awkward question?

Ryan was broad and muscular, where Ferris was thin and slight. Ryan's face was hard, strong-boned; Ferris's rounder, less defined. Of course, these things would not be obvious until later, much later, in the child's life. But suppose the child turned out to be "the spitting image of his father" as so many people's children did?

She hugged her stomach tightly. But it was a baby, her baby, *Ryan's* baby. Half of her exulted over the possibility of Ryan's child growing within her, the piece of him and his love that she would have to take back to the bleak life that awaited her in Virginia. It would probably be the only child she'd have, and that, beyond everything else, was the gift.

But the other half of her stood back in horror over the lies upon lies that would need to be told, and the shameful truth that could someday break free.

In addition, she wasn't sure what Ferris's reaction would be, though there was no doubt that she would tell him. As awful and desperate as she had been, she couldn't possibly pass off one man's child as another's. But suppose he wouldn't back her? Suppose he threw her out as the adulteress she was?

She felt nauseous and wondered if it was the beginning of the sickness she'd heard accompanied pregnancy, or just the reaction of a body unprepared for so much emotional turmoil.

She entered her room, her hands still unconsciously holding her stomach through the wool gown. Ryan's child, she thought, Ryan's baby. She imagined a little gray-eyed boy gazing up at her with love and innocence in his eyes. Ryan, before life had hardened him. She imagined the moment when the child would be first handed into her arms, and she pictured Ryan at her bedside instead of Ferris.

But no, it would be Ferris. She imagined Ferris looking into her baby's face and thinking about what she'd done with his friend. She imagined him trying to act the father, fielding well-wishers' comments that its little fingers were like his own, its little face just as his was at that age. She imagined his family holding the child to feast their eyes on the heir, Ferris's progeny, only to have him watch them with bitter irony. She imagined watching Ferris with the child, all the while resenting the dead wish in her heart that another man was in his place.

The prospect was too awful. She was not sure she could bear it.

But there was still time, her rationalizing mind told her. A week late was not unheard of for many people, even if it was for her. And she had been under unfamiliar pressures lately.

Someone knocked on the door.

"Yes?" she called. Her voiced sounded strangely normal.

"Supper's on," the housemaid called.

"I'll be right down." Catra rose and went to her dressing table. She sat before it and picked up her brush. Lightly, she straightened the waves of her swept-back hair and gazed into her own eyes.

They were the same eyes they'd always been. Large, blue, steady and forthright. But what duplicity they were capable of. She had looked right into Ferris's eyes that morning after Ryan had taken her virginity, and these same eyes had given nothing away. He had apologized, she had accepted it, these eyes gracefully modest. He had asked her if it was bad for her; she had said no, her eyes gentle and forgiving.

She was a fallen woman. She could not hit a lower depth,

she believed. She'd cuckolded her husband, deceived him into believing he had taken her virginity, and now she might be carrying another man's child. How much further could she fall?

If she were to have a child, how good a mother could she be with such self-serving morals? How could she possibly teach another living creature what was right and what was wrong when her whole life would be based upon a lie that she herself would be bound to perpetuate?

Catra stood and straightened her gown, gazing dispassionately at herself in the mirror. She had to leave Boston. She had to go home and build a life, a secure, moral home in which her child could be raised. She had to tell Ferris and, if he didn't renounce her, they had to decide how they would handle this.

It might be a sham, and it might be hypocritical, but it would at least be an effort to do the right thing. She might have told the lie, but she would not let that stop her from living by the truth from this day forward. The lie would stand now only to benefit the innocent.

For the first time in her life, Catra would give up what she wanted most for the good of someone else. She would give up her only love for the good of her child.

Her resolve weakened only slightly that night at dinner, when Ryan entered the room. There was something about him that made every room he entered reverberate with his presence. She was invariably drawn to him in a way that was not simply physical. When their eyes met she felt complete understanding, when she watched him move she felt she could see into his thoughts and when he spoke, she felt his words, his voice, to the core of her being. What she felt for Ryan was almost frightening in its scope, yet profoundly comforting in its depth.

"I've some news," Ferris announced during a lull in the mealtime conversation. "I received a letter today too and it seems my spinster cousin is to marry at last."

Catra glanced at him in surprise. "Dahlia is getting married? Who's going to marry her?"

She felt a brief, horrified fear that Dahlia would turn out to be her father's mystery woman, but then recalled that her father disliked her almost as much as Catra did.

Ferris had taken rather a large bite of his roast beef and held one finger up to her while he chewed. He swallowed and pointed his fork at her. "You'll appreciate this, Cat. *Your cousin*, Mansfield! Seems he met her in Richmond and fell for her. Who would've thought?"

"Dahlia is marrying *Baker Mansfield?*" Catra repeated with such abhorrence that Lydia and Tom turned curious faces toward her. She noticed Ryan's head snap to attention when she said the name.

"Yes, can you believe it? Our family trees are growing quite tangled," Ferris said.

"But—what—he's . . ." She stared at him, astonished. "He's a *beast*. What could she possibly see in him?"

"A husband, I suppose," Ferris replied, unconcerned. He cut his meat and fed himself.

Catra glanced at Ryan. He looked away and concentrated on his food as well.

"What is it that's so awful about him?" Lydia asked.

Catra searched for words. "I—he's—Forgive me. It's perhaps indelicate of me to say. It's just that . . . despite manners that are, if one were to analyze them, basically correct, he is a rude . . ." She remembered his conversation with her at Wendy Thompkins's ball, when she'd been watching Ryan and he had seen right through her. But what had he said that wasn't true? "Well, at the very least he engages in inappropriate conversation. I think he seeks to shock people.''

The St. Jameses were looking at her, clearly expecting a more despicable revelation. She could think of no specifics from that meeting that would adequately convey the distaste she felt for the man. And she certainly wasn't about to pass on the topic of their conversation.

"Perhaps I judge him too harshly," Catra said, "but he does quite a bit of gambling and is rumored to have been involved in several duels."

"I've met the man," Ryan offered. "He has acceptable manners and a respectable family name that gains him entrance to most of society's events. But if it were left up to sheer personal amiability, he would never go anywhere."

"Do you know him well, Ryan?" Lydia asked.

Ryan looked thoughtful for a moment and gazed at his plate. Whatever memory he was experiencing was not a pleasant one, Catra could tell.

"Better than I'd like to, but no, not well," he answered.

"Well, that's a shame," Ferris said, soaking up the beef juice on his plate with a crust of bread. "Uncle said in his letter that the two'll be married before we return and staying on at Waverly for a month or two. Apparently Mansfield's having a house built somewhere or other."

"I'd look into that if I were you," Ryan said.

"Into what? The house?" Ferris queried.

Ryan sipped his wine. "I don't mean to belittle your cousin"—he inclined his head in Catra's direction—"perhaps for no reason, but I believe the man worthy of some mistrust. You'd be wise to check his status with his immediate family—his parents are in Charleston. The last I'd heard, they were on the verge of disowning him."

"Well, thank you, Ryan. I'll most certainly do that."

"What is their rush, Ferris?" Catra asked. "Does your

uncle say anything about why they're to be married so quickly?'' Then, realizing the implication of her question, she colored deeply. ''I only mean, do you suppose he wants to evade any such investigation you might conduct?''

She glanced up at Ryan and caught him watching her with an amused expression. She looked quickly away, sure that if he were to look into her eyes, he would discern her secret. That, she was sure, would wipe the amusement from his face.

Ferris sighed. ''Lord knows. Perhaps they're simply swept up in love with each other. Although Uncle did say something about the unsuitability of a large wedding for a bride of such advanced years.''

''Goodness, she's not that old,'' Catra said, thinking that was probably the nicest thing she'd ever said about Ferris's cousin.

''Between your father and your cousins, you're going to be quite busy when you get home, Mrs. Chester,'' Mrs. St. James said. ''Two weddings and Christmas just around the corner. Did your father say anything about when he planned to wed his chosen lady?''

''No, he didn't. I suppose he thought we'd all discuss it when we arrived home,'' Catra said.

''You're not planning on leaving us early, are you?'' Lydia asked. ''We've such grand plans for Christmas.''

Catra glanced at Ferris and spoke before her resolve could waver. ''I'm afraid we will have to leave before Christmas.''

Ferris looked at her. ''Do you really think so?''

She could have kicked him.

''Ferris, it's just as Mrs. St. James has said. There'll be Father's wedding. I couldn't live with myself if I vacationed while there was so much to be done at home. Besides, who are we to make them wait when they must be so eager to be wed?"

"But there's plenty of people—"

"We should discuss this later." Catra stole a glance at Ryan. He regarded her thoughtfully.

"Yes, of course," Ferris acceded, confusion still on his face.

"And much as we would like to, we can't impose on the St. Jameses forever," she added.

But the disappointment she found on Lydia's face was clear. She glanced at Mrs. St. James and met there a look of understanding.

"Of course you have things to do. Your father's probably beside himself wondering what you will think of this new development in his life. You must go to him. Don't you think so, Ryan?" she asked pointedly.

Catra's stomach went weightless at the question. Had she, as Lydia had, guessed Catra's feelings for Ryan? Could she know about the affair?

No. No, of course not, she told herself. And even if she had guessed Catra's feelings, she would understand them far better than Lydia did. Catra suspected that Lydia had a charming, romanticized notion in her head about their unrequited love. But Mrs. St. James appeared to know it for the dangerous and painful situation it was. Catra needed either to escape it or surrender to its destruction of her character. Yes, Mrs. St. James knew the decision Catra was making. Looking in her eyes, Catra knew it as surely as she knew her own thoughts.

"I believe Mrs. Chester should go if she so desires," Ryan answered his mother.

Catra glanced around the faces gathered at the table and felt cornered, possessed by a need to justify her position. "It's not that I desire to go," she began, looking from one face to the next. "It's just that so much has happened—at home, I mean, and—and—" She'd reached Ryan's face and could go no farther. His clear eyes were steady, yet she read in them regret, and hurt. It was the hurt that caused her to lose her train of thought. "I'm sorry," she said then, to him.

Then she started, remembering that they were in a room full of people. Her gaze skidded from Ryan to his father, seated at the head of the table.

"Of course, we understand, dear," Mrs. St. James said easily. "Don't think another thing about it. You must do what you think is right. And I've no doubt you are right."

But Catra's eyes did not leave Ryan's father. What was he thinking? The elder Mr. St. James regarded her thoughtfully through steel gray eyes that were very like Ryan's. She smiled faintly and looked down at her plate. Would Ryan look like his father as he aged, she wondered, with impeccably white hair, a weathered face and hard, knowing eyes? Would the years make Ryan harder? For though he had a temper and could be intimidating, he was not the callous man that his father appeared to be.

She would never know, she thought. She would be a stranger to the worn lines that would grace Ryan's face, a stranger unable to trace the life that was lived there. He would become as unfamiliar as his father was to her now. And there would be nothing she could do about it. Not now, not ever.

The evening before they were to leave, Tom's family, the Stewarts, had invited them all to dine at their home. The party, as it turned out, was larger than Catra had expected. Both daughters, Roberta and Mary, were there, as well as the Parks, an older couple, and a friend of Tom's named Sidney Johnson, whose sole purpose in life, it seemed, was to take advantage of every dinner party to which he could secure an invitation.

The company was quite enjoyable, Catra discovered, and she found herself laughing easily at Sidney Johnson's outspoken humor. She was glad of his silliness, as it kept at bay the lurking sadness of leaving, and caused her to forget for moments at a time the issue of her missing monthly course.

The weather had calmed considerably from the blizzard of a week ago and had even warmed somewhat, making the prospect of travel not quite so dangerous or frightful. All the same, they had been able to bring the sleigh tonight, which Catra had greatly enjoyed. The cozy warmth of the furs against the chill night air had filled her with a sense of security, and the smooth movement of the sleigh, as compared to a coach, was hypnotizing.

As it happened, Ryan had sat across from her, and because of the way they were all squeezed into the sleigh, her calf had rested against his beneath the cover of the fur blankets. A calm contentment suffused her at the contact, though Ryan, in an effort to avoid her, had shifted uncomfortably more than once. He hadn't been able to avoid helping her down from the sleigh upon their arrival, however, giving her cause to place her hand in his.

Stray snowflakes had dusted his dark hair and the shoulders of his coat. His cheeks had become ruddy from the cold, and the glow made his eyes stand out like twin icicles. The penetrating way he had gazed down at her as she alit, and the split second they had touched before Ryan had dropped her hand, as if the contact had burned him, was enough to fuel Catra's now constant reveries of if only it were Ryan. *If only it were Ryan whose arm lay around my shoulders, if only it were Ryan who lay beside me in bed, if only it were Ryan who was my husband . . .*

Compulsion

Throughout the evening Ryan was close enough to her that she could always have him in sight, sometimes directly, sometimes from the corner of her eye. It was a comfort, an illusion that she was with him, though they could not engage in any conversation that did not consist of innocent banalities. But all the while the scenario of her telling him of the child that might be growing within her ran repeatedly through her mind. In this mental scenario she envisioned him taking her in his arms in joyous abandon at the news and demanding that she go away with him. They could go to Europe, he would say, or South America, anywhere that they could be together without shame.

But she was still unsure of the pregnancy. And Ryan had made it more than clear to her that he would not break up her marriage. Whether or not that would change if he knew she were with child, she could not be sure. And so the thought of telling him lingered like an unasked question in her mind.

It was after dessert had been served, after the men had lingered over their brandy and cigars, after the company had been reunited, that the subject of poetry had arisen. Sidney Johnson was regaling them with jokes about various poets, when he brought up a line from a John Donne poem that caused some controversy. It seemed no one could agree upon the exact wording of a particular line. Ryan volunteered to fetch the volume from the library, and as he was a stranger to the Stewarts' collection, Roberta offered to direct him.

Catra watched them go with misgiving. Roberta was a pretty girl with a round, laughing face, a pert nose and no earthly cares with which to burden a man. Surely Ryan was tired of the problems with which they had wrestled for so long. Perhaps a girl with such youth in her eyes and such a light heart would seem appealing.

303

She shook herself from her reverie. If she were to punish herself like this simply because he'd left the room with a nice-looking girl of marriageable age, she would be paralyzed with agony once she left him to a whole city full of women. She concentrated on Sidney Johnson's diverting conversation.

Ryan left the room and heaved a silent sigh upon entering the hallway. He couldn't stand watching that Johnson fellow cozying up to Catra in that insidious way of his. And she could have looked less alluring as she laughed at all his stupid amusements. He recalled bitterly how she'd once complained of such idiotic conversations. She seems to have resigned herself pretty well, he thought. She positively glowed tonight. Her hair shone coppery-gold in the lamplight and her cheeks were a becoming pink. Her tender lips had been curved into a contented smile whenever she'd looked at him, and he'd longed all evening to cross the room, take her into his arms and damn the whole assembly to hell.

"What are you thinking of with such a scowl, Mr. St. James?" Roberta Stewart asked.

He'd nearly forgotten she was there. He straightened his expression. "I was just remembering some work I've left undone. Please excuse me for letting my mind wander." He forced a smile.

She smiled back at him, her cheeks blushing as they always did when he looked at her. She looked precariously young, he thought then, mentally calculating her proximity to Catra's age. Only months apart, he surmised, but years apart in maturity. Catra's perception and intelligence put her in a class by herself, particularly when compared to a piece of fluff like Roberta Stewart.

They arrived at the doorway, and Ryan stepped aside for

304

Roberta to enter. She brushed closely by him and he caught a whiff of rosewater.

"Now, Dryden, was it?" she asked, tilting her head and placing a finger along her cheek.

Ryan watched her coquettish display dispassionately. "Donne," he corrected.

"Oh, yes." She floated toward the bookcases and perused them idly. "Do you read much poetry?" she asked, turning back to him. "You seem so well-read."

"I haven't much time for poetry. Not lately," he answered. "I read quite a bit in school. But that was many years ago." He emphasized *many*.

She glanced down at her feet, where one slipper emerged from beneath her gown to trace a pattern on the floor. "I thought you quoted it beautifully. I should love to hear you recite an entire poem someday. You have such a strong, romantic voice." She looked up at him from beneath her lashes.

Ryan smiled, amused. "I didn't know voices could be considered romantic."

"Oh, they definitely can. And yours is so—so rich, and low. You would have made a wonderful clergyman. You could project so impressively from a pulpit, I'd imagine."

"Is this a gentle way of telling me I've a loud mouth?" he teased. But Roberta colored sharply and looked horrified.

"No, I didn't mean that *at all*," she cried and crossed the room toward him. "Please, don't be offended." She placed a hand on his arm. "I meant it as a most sincere compliment."

Ryan patted her hand and started to pick it up from where it had landed with some threat of permanence on his arm. "I'm not offended, Miss Stewart," he said with a smile. "I was making a poor joke."

As he took her hand from his sleeve, Roberta quickly turned her palm upward so their hands clasped. "Mr. St. James," she whispered urgently, "I do so want you to know—that is, I've wanted to tell you for some time—"

"Please, Miss Stewart," Ryan interrupted. He had a sinking feeling he knew just what was coming. He could not extricate his hand from hers. She moved closer. He placed his other hand on her upper arm to move her away, but just at that second the door, which had stood ajar, swung inward.

"*There* you two are!" Sidney Johnson's voice boomed.

Ryan saw only Catra's stricken face. She stood beside an amused Sidney Johnson, and Ryan knew with a plunging heart just what the scene they'd entered into looked like. Ryan and Roberta, in the center of the room, hands clasped, stood incriminatingly close. With his hand on her arm that way, it had looked like an embrace.

Roberta backed slowly away from him, but not far enough for Ryan's taste.

"We wondered what had become of you two." Johnson smirked. "I guess our poetic argument slipped your minds." His eyebrows rose.

"Please, don't let us interrupt," Catra's voice said quietly, and she disappeared from the doorway.

Ryan made two steps in her direction before realizing the wholly inappropriate sight he would make charging after her. He could not very well call after her, and he'd no doubt that she would not respond to the distantly polite manner he would have to employ to try to explain anything.

He turned back to Johnson. "We hadn't forgotten," he said in too hard a voice. He turned to Roberta. "Where is the book?"

She went wordlessly to the bookcase and pulled it from

the shelf. She handed it to Ryan. Ryan handed it to Johnson.

"There. Look it up," he said.

"Thank you," Sidney Johnson said with a broad smile. "I'll just take this back to the other guests." He waved the book in the direction of the party.

"I'll join you." Ryan followed him to the door. Roberta's voice stopped him.

"Mr. St. James!" she called.

Reluctantly, he turned.

"I'm terribly sorry," she said, obviously distressed. "I've embarrassed you and I've shocked Mrs. Chester. Do you think she'll say anything?"

"I've no doubt she won't," he said. His stomach twisted at the knowledge of Catra's thoughts, for he knew them as surely as if she had spoken them to him. Candace Fairchild's ghost rose again, he thought with clenched teeth.

Roberta wrung her hands. "I hope not. My intent was certainly not to embarrass you. I just—I get so—"

"It's all right," Ryan interrupted, anxious to be gone, to join the party, to dispel the anguished thoughts he knew coursed through Catra's mind. "It's all right," he repeated more calmly. "But we should join the others before they conclude more than they have already."

"But don't you wish to know my intent?" she asked.

"I know your intent," Ryan said, as gently as he could while wishing she would simply vanish. Every minute he delayed in returning to the party was proof positive in Catra's mind that what she'd seen was true. "And it's impossible." She looked hurt and about to say something more. He continued quickly, "I am far too old for you, Miss Stewart. And I'm not at all the right sort of man. You're very sweet and attractive, but you need someone who is more—suited to you." He was making a mess of a delicate situation and he knew it. But when her tears began to fall he nearly cried out in desperation.

Catra would not understand his failure to return to the party quickly and she was to leave on the morrow. He could not have her returning to Virginia, for God knew how long until he saw her again, believing that he had seduced his sister-in-law while she had sat in the very next room.

But Roberta would not be ignored. "I'm sorry to be such a nuisance," she choked, dabbing at her eyes with a handkerchief.

She had no idea, Ryan thought, what a nuisance she truly was at this moment. "Please pull yourself together," he said. "We really must get back to the company. Do you want them all to suspect something's happening in here?" Ryan took a step toward the door.

"Oh, Mr. St. James!" Roberta cried. She put her hand on his arm while her tears continued to flow. "Who *cares* what they think is happening? I've had these feelings for you for so long. I care not who suspects them."

"Miss Stewart," he said firmly, "with my reputation, they won't be speculating on your feelings. They'll be speculating on your virtue after you leave this room. Surely you can see how ill-suited I am to a girl of your tender years."

She colored. "I don't care," she repeated. "I'm not ashamed of what I feel for you. And I don't mind your reputation. I understand that a man like you is bound to have one, whether through your own fault or not."

"Oh, it's through my own fault, all right," Ryan said. "There's not much doubt about that."

"I don't care," Roberta insisted. "That's my point. I know you're a libertine and a gallant, just as Father says . . ."

In another situation Ryan could almost have smiled at that.

". . . but I can see past all that. I can see the quality of the man you are. All you really need is love, true love. And I can give you that."

Ryan closed his eyes with an exasperated sigh. "Please stop. Someday you'll hate me for all you've said tonight. Your father is right about me. He would throw me out on my ear if I were to show up on his doorstep as your suitor. And he'd be right to."

"He'd never do that," Roberta claimed. "You're Lydia's brother! And he adores her."

"I'm sure he does," Ryan agreed. "But not half so much as he adores you. Now, let's join the others before your reputation is in tatters." He gently pulled her toward the door. To his relief she came.

Just before they entered the parlor, Roberta whispered, "But I'll not give up on you." And with a wink of her eye, she entered the party.

Ryan scanned the room for Catra and could find her nowhere. A second perusal of the room turned up Ferris missing. He felt a gnawing pain in his stomach.

"I'm afraid you've missed the Chesters," Ryan's mother informed them. "They said to tell you good night. Mrs. Chester was not feeling well and they have to leave so early. They asked us to convey their apologies."

Ryan stood as if struck. "They've left?" he asked dumbly.

His mother gave him a hard look. "They've left."

Chapter Eighteen

Virginia lay in the damp torpor of winter when Catra and Ferris arrived home. Christmas was just days away, and a light rain misted from a gunmetal gray sky. A determined wind drove needlelike drops into every nook and fiber exposed, chilling to the bone all who braved the inclement weather. The coach that met them at the docks was warmed by a coal brazier and braced with blankets, but nothing could dispel the cold cloud around Catra's heart.

For Catra, the route home was even worse than the weather. It was no different from all the other trips home from Richmond she'd embarked on, except for one thing: when they came to the road to Braithwood, they did not turn. They did not even slow down. Her heart constricted as the coach rattled past, like any stranger's would have on its careless way to Waverly.

Her stomach lurched. She placed a nervous hand over her mouth, reluctant to stop the coach yet again. There was no doubt in her mind now. She was either pregnant or dying of consumption. She could keep no food down, though she could not stop trying to eat, and motion sickness, to which she'd never been susceptible before, was now common during any sort of transportation. Each morning she'd awakened to the dreadful queasy slosh of her stomach and each morning she'd fought it, only to discover, when she had a moment to get away unobserved, that if she just went ahead and got sick she felt fine for the rest of the day.

They were almost to Waverly. She saw the Chesters' white roadside fence and stand of skeletal oak trees; then the tree line broke and Waverly's brick facade came into view. The fields around the house were bleak and muddy. The stables, with their crisp white trim and orderly paddocks, were hidden from view by the house, and Catra realized that they had always been her favorite spot at Waverly.

"I wonder what we'll have for dinner," Ferris said. "I'm simply famished."

The thought of food did nothing to settle Catra's stomach. "I could use a hot bath," she murmured.

They waited in silence for the coach to pull to a stop before the house, and heard the coachman descend clumsily from his perch to open the door. Catra was handed from the coach and ran through the rain to the front door. She'd always mourned the absence of a porch on this house, but now she did so for practical reasons. The rain pelted her head as she waited for Ferris.

He followed her to the door and threw it open. No one appeared.

"Hello!" Ferris called into the cavernous hall. The slate floor was cold and the rain from their coats dripped into slick puddles on its hard surface.

A clatter arose from a back hallway. Catra unbuttoned

her coat and pulled it off. She looked around the hall as if seeing it for the first time. She'd been here more times than she could count; but now, as its mistress, she saw it with new eyes.

The decorations were appropriate but impersonal. The paintings of hunting scenes, always at home in a Virginia parlor, now seemed to her unoriginal and dull. The furniture was not tasteless but was not unusual or even particularly inviting. She thought of the gay yellow sitting room at Braithwood, with its tapestried chairs and graceful, cherrywood furniture. Then she thought of the great warm hearth and afghan-covered sofas in the St. Jameses' drawing room. The aroma of spiced cider and Lydia's gentle touch on the pianoforte were as vivid to her in this instant as if she stood in the lace-curtained room again.

Then, as vivid as that image, there rose another. A darkened library in which Ryan and Roberta stood, locked in an embrace. She pushed the memory from her. Ryan had tried to explain about Roberta the morning that they'd left, but she had not listened. She had wanted only to be gone. Nothing could have made it clearer to her that Ryan would have no further relations with a married woman, and she suspected that was why he'd done it. She did not blame him, but she could not hear him speak of it. Nor would she let herself think on it now.

She was awakened from this reverie by the brisk clip of heels on the slate down the hall. Joan Chester emerged from the darkness.

"My dears!" she exclaimed. "We didn't expect you until tomorrow."

"I sent word we'd most likely arrive on Wednesday," Ferris said, looking about him. "Where's Uncle Bernard? Dahlia? The servants?"

Joan shuffled nervously. "Bernard and Dahlia have gone

out.'' She wrung her hands. Then, as if poked from behind, she sprang forward to take the coats from Catra and Ferris.

"Have the servants gone out as well?" Ferris asked.

"Oh, no, of course not. But it was just me here, all alone, so I told them to go on about their own business." She fluttered about uncertainly until finally she laid their wet garments across a hall chair.

"I wish you hadn't done that." Ferris sighed expansively. Joan looked guiltily at the coats. "You see if you give the servants time off, they expect it every time it appears slow to them."

"Oh, well. You're right, of course," she said.

"No matter," he said, running a hand through his damp hair and gazing blankly around the room. "I suppose we can make do without them for the moment."

Despite herself, Catra thought of the reception they would likely have gotten at Braithwood. "Please don't worry about it," she said to the distressed woman. "Have my things been brought from Braithwood?"

"Oh, yes! Yes!" Joan's relief at being able to respond affirmatively to any question was obvious.

"Wonderful, then I won't be needing my trunk anytime soon."

"Yes, your things are all here and set up, just waiting for you, in Ferris's chambers. Do go wash up and rest, if you please. Oh, I only wish we'd known it would be today that you were arriving. We have such a party planned for tomorrow night."

Catra was intensely glad the party was not to be that evening, as her stomach had not stopped moving even though the carriage had. It angered her to be plagued with sickness now, when she needed all her strength. She made a supreme effort to ignore the queasiness that threatened. She would simply not indulge it any longer.

Ferris cleared his throat. "Where did you say Uncle Bernard and Dahlia are?"

"They're over at the Wilsons'. They've been so busy introducing Mr. Mansfield around. Everyone is so delighted at Dahlia's find, just when we were all ready to give up hoping for her." She beamed. "And such a gentleman your cousin is, Catherine. I'm surprised we've never met him before."

Ferris scoffed.

A powerful wave of nausea gripped Catra. Ignoring it was out of the question. "I'm afraid," Catra began, and ran a clammy hand across her forehead, "that I must retire. I'm not feeling very well."

Ferris took her elbow. "I'm sorry, Cat, I wasn't thinking. Poor thing had to stop to be sick at least five times on the way home," Ferris added to his aunt.

Catra was embarrassed at his casual revelation of her weakness. "I'm sure it's nothing," she asserted, cursing her traitorous stomach. "I'm not used to so much travel. I'll be fine."

"And you did so well on the way up," Ferris said as they made their way toward the stairs.

Joan scurried to the base of the stairs behind them. "Let me bring you some tea," she called. "Cook's just made some cookies."

"No, thank you," Catra said firmly. Anything she put in her stomach now, she was sure, would come vaulting back up.

They reached the top of the stairs. "I'll call you when dinner is ready!" Joan called as they passed down the hall and out of sight.

Catra readied herself for their welcome-home dinner. She had stayed in her room all day, ostensibly to get over the unfortunate illness she'd had yesterday, but mostly because she was reluctant for Dahlia Chester and Baker Mansfield to see her in such a weakened state, dashing to the nearest chamber pot at embarrassingly unpredictable moments.

She was surprised that she could spend the entire day napping, as naps had never been something she could abide in the past. Afterwards she felt so much better, she had the brief thought that perhaps her illness was in fact due to the traveling and not the other reason she'd feared. Though nothing could alter the fact that her monthly courses had never arrived.

Catra's maid was just brushing her hair when Ferris entered the room. Catra was still not used to him barging in on her whenever he pleased. She wished Bethia was with her to cast that steely eye on Ferris she used whenever someone did something against her wishes. But here Catra had to make a conscious effort to remember that not only was it his room, it was his right.

He sat down on the bed. One leg dangled over the edge as he propped himself up on straight arms behind him. "I've found out who your father's mystery woman is," he announced.

Catra turned sharply, sweeping her hair behind her, and sending the maid's brush flying toward the wall. "Who is it?"

The maid moved to retrieve the brush.

He shook his head. "You won't believe it. I shouldn't tell you. Your father wanted to tell you himself, but I think you need to know. He's coming to dinner tonight, you know."

"Ferris," she said in a low voice, one she barely recognized as her own. *"Tell me."*

Ferris gave her a steady look. "Mayliza Thayer."

Catra's mouth dropped open and her breath left her.

"May—" She could not even form the word. Her limbs stiffened. "That's impossible."

"I told you you wouldn't believe it," he said, shaking his head. "Incredible, isn't it?"

She squelched an almost overpowering urge to throw something, then wondered at her short temper. She had to get herself under control. So much anger and sadness and worry was turning her into someone she truly disliked.

But *Mayliza Thayer.* Catra could scarcely credit it; the idea was absurd. Mayliza wasn't even nineteen years old yet. And her father was—well, old enough to be *her* father. God in heaven, just the thought of them courting was enough to flabbergast her. Were they in love with each other? How could he possibly be in love with someone so young? The thought was preposterous.

"Cat, are you all right? They'll both be here tonight," Ferris continued, watching her with concern. "Aunt Joan told me they were quite anxious for your approval."

"With a plan to just show up and spring it on me, they were hoping for my approval?" Catra asked, incredulous.

He straightened, massaging his hands, which must have fallen asleep. "No, I think your father is coming early to talk to you about it. But I wanted to tell you now because I knew you'd need more time to adjust to the idea."

"Thank you," she said, truly grateful to know in advance. How she would be civil to her father at all after discovering his treachery had been a mystery to her for weeks. But to have had to face him moments after finding out he was marrying Mayliza would have been dreadful.

Imagine! Mayliza, her stepmother. She hardly knew what to do with the thought.

"I know, it's hard to believe," Ferris said. "He's so much older than she is. I keep trying to remember times I've seen them together, to see if I could've told what was coming. But I can't remember even seeing them speak.''

Catra remembered seeing the two of them dancing at her wedding party. She had been watching them with interest, and with just the seed of a thought, when she had been interrupted and her attention diverted. It had been such a fleeting thought, though, not even complete enough for her to have been able to say that it was romance she saw or just an odd conversation. Now, however, she remembered that they had been dancing closely, and talking in an intimate way.

If Mayliza had known even then, how could she not have told her? Catra's heart hammered in her chest with an intense emotion she dared not acknowledge as anger lest she explode with it. Besides, these days she did not trust her emotions. She was as likely to be in tears over getting boiled potatoes instead of mashed as she was prone to a worrisome preoccupation if the weather threatened to turn cloudy. She simply couldn't expect herself to react rationally to anything.

Catra noticed Lucy standing near the corner where the brush had fallen. The maid held it uncertainly. ''Did you know about my father, Lucy?'' she asked her.

''About him'n Miz Mayliza, you mean?'' she asked.

''Yes.''

Lucy looked down at her feet, then glanced at Ferris. ''Well, Miz Mayliza was over at the house a bit, just after you left. There was people who suspected, but we weren't sure 'til they announced it.''

Catra gazed at her sadly. ''I imagine they seemed pretty happy about it.''

''Oh yes, they did,'' she replied with a smile. ''Bethia says that's the most happy she's ever seen your daddy.''

Catra nodded. How easy it was for *him* to be happy.

317

"That'll be all for now, Lucy. I'll call you to finish my hair later."

"Yes'm." The girl curtsied and left.

Catra turned back to the dressing table and rested her head in her hands. The depth of her anger was staggering, almost crippling. For her father to have the gall to intercept her letter to Ryan, to lie to her in such a way, then to stand back and watch her sentence herself to life with a man he knew she did not love, all the while knowing that Ryan had loved her enough to come after her—and then to turn around and make himself happy with the woman of *his* choice, no matter how inappropriate—well, it was all too much for her. Bile burned in her stomach and her breath come in deep, angry gusts.

Ferris laid a hand on her shoulder. "Catra, your father loves you still," he said. "He's just found someone else to love after all these years without your mother. You should be happy for him."

Her head snapped up and her eyes flashed fire at him in the mirror before her. "I hate him," she said venomously. "At this moment I don't care if I never see him again." And then, at the sound of her own words, at the idea of having come so far from the home that lay in her heart, she burst into tears.

Ferris stepped back, aghast. "Good Lord, Catra," he said. He stroked her hair tentatively. "Don't upset yourself so. They'll be here soon for dinner."

"I'm not going to dinner," she spat. "I'll not entertain him. Tell him I refuse to see him."

"Isn't this a little extreme?" Ferris asked. "I know it's a shock and all, about Mayliza. But this is going a bit far."

"*He'll* understand it," she said. "And if he doesn't—" She broke off. "Well, if he doesn't, it's not something I'll explain to him."

318

Ferris backed away from her, straightening his creaseless vest and adjusting his cuffs. "Well," he said. He looked around the room and rubbed his hands together. "Well," he said again.

She turned to him then, thinking he must believe her to be losing her senses. From the evening in Boston when she'd begged him to take her home early to this evening's tirade against her father, she'd been acting unpredictably— and uncharacteristically—volatile. She'd been alternately sick or upset for so many days that he'd been tiptoeing around her, obviously unsure what her reactions would be from one moment to the next.

He looked at her now with what was becoming a familiar expression of misgiving.

She tried to smile and ended up sighing. "Oh, Ferris, you must wonder what has become of me."

Ferris looked down, his features sagging with relief. "No, no . . . Though, yes, it had occurred to me that you've been acting a little . . ." He circled his hand out in front of him as if to reel in the word.

"Unstable?" she offered.

He dropped his hand and glanced back up at her, red-faced. "I assumed it was my fault. Because of, you know, what I told you, about me." He crossed his arms over his chest and walked toward the window.

"Because you cannot consummate our marriage." She turned on her seat to watch him.

He laughed nervously, looking out the window. "Well, I guess we've already done that, at least."

Catra took a deep breath. It's now or never, she thought, and leapt into the void. "No, Ferris, we haven't."

He turned, his brow furrowed. "Sure we have. You know, that night I can't, ah, remember." He laughed again, feebly. "And you know I am so sorry about that."

"Ferris, there's a reason you can't remember it," she said quietly.

He tilted his head and looked at her, a reserved, protected look that seemed to understand that what she was saying would not be easy to hear. He jerked his face away and started for the door.

"I know, I was drunk. But I won't do that again, as I told you, and anyway it matters not what happened because we've already discussed all of this and, I believe, yes, you remember, we've come to an agreement." He reached for the doorknob as if for a lifeline in a churning sea. "So there's really no point in talking further, is there? No. So I'll just run along and see if your father has—"

"Ferris, wait." Catra's voice was firm enough to stop him, the door ajar in his right hand. "Close the door. Please," she said in a gentler tone.

He pushed the door shut, keeping his eyes upon it and his back to her.

Folding her hands in her lap and steeling herself for anything, she said, "Ferris, there's something I have to tell you."

"Whatever it is, Cat, I don't want to know," he said to the door. "Truly, I don't want to know."

Catra rose and approached him, laying a hand on his back. "But you must. It concerns you. And me. And our future."

He turned, taking her hand that had been on his back in his. His palms were damp, she noted, and clutched hers tightly.

"Catra, I know you're going to tell me something you think you must, but I want you to know that I trust you. I mean, I trust you to—to do what you have to and not—not—"

"Ferris, I've lied to you," she said, jerking his hands so

320

he would look at her. "You're practically my best friend and I deceived you in a way that is so totally reprehensible, I cannot believe you will ever forgive me. But I must try, Ferris. Please let me try."

"I forgive you!" he cried, looking truly distraught. "Whatever it is, you're forgiven."

"No. If this marriage, or this deal we have, is going to work at all and not make us both miserable for the rest of our lives, then we have to be honest with each other. And I haven't been. I've been selfish and conniving—"

"Cat, no. You couldn't—"

"I'm pregnant."

Ferris stopped, as if the air had been sucked out of him. Shock made his hand tremble in hers.

"And it's not yours. It couldn't be yours because you and I never made love."

He closed his eyes, expelling air. "You see," he said calmly, "this is what I don't want to hear."

"I lied to you about that night you got so drunk. And I'm so ashamed of it. I'm so sorry to have done that to you. It's inexcusable. I was confused and upset, but that justifies nothing. The baby . . . it's Ryan's, Ferris." She finished softly, and they stood in paralyzed stillness for a long moment.

Then Ferris ripped his hand from hers. *"Ryan's,"* he repeated, his voice harsh. "You lay with Ryan St. James. You—you had sex with him. You."

Catra took a step back as he brushed past her, pacing to the other side of the room. But when he turned, instead of the fury she expected on his face she saw tears.

"Yes," she said, quietly. "I did. And I regret it for your sake, but for my own I cannot. Because I love him. I don't tell you this to punish you, but to make sure you understand everything. We won't touch each other again, Ryan and I, but we had wanted to marry—we fell in love while he was here. Then my father intervened." Briefly, she told him of her father's actions, her reactions that led to the marriage to Ferris, and her discovery of the truth when she saw Ryan again in Boston. "That's why I am so angry with Father. And that's why what happened, happened. I don't mean to give you excuses, Ferris, just reasons."

"Ryan loves you?" Ferris said at the end of it, his mouth contorted with an effort not to cry. "You and Ryan love each other?"

She nodded, slowly. "But Ferris, you knew I was not in love with you. That was part of the reason we made the deal to get married. Just as you're not in love with me."

"I know I know. It's not *you* . . ." He turned aggressively away, and with one arm swept a chess set from a table along the wall, for all the world like an enraged toddler pushing his dinner to the floor. The pieces hit the wood like marbles, pawns bouncing off the toe molding and rolling along the floor toward the rug.

"No," he repeated, then, more calmly, "I'm not in love with you. You and I are friends. It's just . . ."

Catra swallowed hard, blood rushing to her face. "Ryan?" she whispered.

He stood quietly, head bowed, the fingers of his hand still resting on the now empty tabletop.

"Ferris—"

"It doesn't matter!" He spun, clutching his arms before him again, his face conflicted and angry now. "I mean, I knew . . . I knew he would never . . . It's just, I thought he was *my* friend. Close to *me*. When I thought you didn't like him . . . well, I was glad about that. Perfect, I thought. But now I find that you—that both of you . . ."

"We were loathe to hurt you, Ferris."

Ferris waved a hand dismissively and paced over to sit

on the edge of the bed. He exhaled. "Let's not even talk about it. I know what I thought was absurd. Let's forget this whole conversation. I mean, you know, the parts that don't matter."

Catra lowered her brows, unsure what to say next, and sat next to him on the bed.

After a minute, Ferris shrugged. "This could work out to our advantage."

Catra slanted her eyes toward him.

He laughed once, without humor, and ran a hand over his face, wiping away tears and anger at the same time. "You wanted children."

Catra looked down at her hands, fidgeting with the material of her gown.

"I mean it." She felt his face turn toward her, his eyes look at her. "I'm glad you're going to have a child because, honestly, I could never have given you one. And I'll need an heir. When you told me that we had consummated the marriage that night, I guess I wanted to believe you. But something inside me doubted it, though I didn't try to figure it out. I'd never—I told you—I'd never done that with a woman. Never been able to, because I did try a couple of times. So, I guess what you're telling me now doesn't really surprise me."

"I hated to lie to you," she said. "I hate that I had that kind of deception in me."

"Well, you come by it honestly, judging by your father's actions."

Catra looked up at him, surprised, and was even more surprised to see the hint of humor on his face. She smiled, a profound relief coursing through her.

"Yes, I guess I do." She sobered. "But I promise you now, Ferris, that I will never lie to you like that again. Never."

"I know you won't. Cat, if you think about it, I've been lying to you too. I spent years before our engagement pretending to be in love with you, hoping that our engagement could take place and I wouldn't be forced to find another woman willing to make the deal that we did. I mean, I knew I wasn't husband material."

She shook her head. "That's different."

He sighed. "I don't know if it is or not. But in any case, we're in this together now. And if we stand together, no one can discover the secrets we have."

"Yes," she murmured, with a sinking feeling. "Our secrets can remain ours for the rest of our lives."

The dinner hour approached. Catra was not surprised when there came a knock at her bedroom door. It was her father, she knew. She let him knock twice, three times. Finally, she rose and opened the door.

Her father stood before her, tall, elegantly dressed and wearing an expression of wary joy upon seeing her.

Her first impulse was to go to him, to be welcomed home by his warm, strong embrace. She wanted to hear him call her Catherine. She wanted him to know all the answers to her problems, as he always had until the fateful day he'd meddled so destructively in her life. She wanted everything to be the way it was.

But now he was just a man, a foolish man marrying a woman twenty-five years younger than himself. He was helplessly human in his passion, and arrogantly wrong in his maneuver to protect her from hers. He was no longer the demigod he'd been to Catra all her life.

She regarded him coolly. "There is no explanation you can make to me that will repair what I feel for you."

His formerly beloved face looked disconcerted, and despite herself she felt her heart reach out to him.

"Now, Catherine, be reasonable. Can't we talk about this? Don't you want your old father to be happy?"

She stepped back from the door. "You may say what you will, but there is no adequate excuse you can make for the lies you've told me."

He looked puzzled as he entered. She closed the door and stood, facing him.

"Sit down, Catherine," he said, "We need to talk about this."

She raised her chin. "I have no desire to sit. I don't expect this interview to last long enough to warrant it."

He raised his brows. "Do you not? Is your mind so irrevocably closed, then?"

She shook her head. "Not so closed as yours has been. If I cannot show the happiness at your betrothal that you showed at mine, perhaps it is because I was not so instrumental in ensuring yours as you were mine."

Comprehension dawned. His voice was resigned. "You've spoken to St. James."

She did not reply. Her gaze did not waver from his face.

He folded his arms across his chest. "No doubt he acquitted himself admirably."

"And damned you." She folded her hands in front of her.

He could not hold her look and turned away. "I did what I felt was best for you, Catherine. What I still believe is best. I presume there is doubt, now, of his guilty role in the Fairchild scandal?"

"There is no doubt of his role in the matter. As for his guilt, there is considerable question, yes."

He cleared his throat. "I see no difference between his role and the guilt attached to it."

"I suppose you wouldn't. You tried and sentenced him on your own." Her eyes burned with the intensity of her

Elaine Fox

glare. "But you've sentenced me, as well. And Ferris. Did you know that? Did you do that on purpose?"

"I did what I thought best for you. As I said, I still believe marriage to Ferris is the better choice for you. In time you will see that."

She blinked back tears. "What do you know," she paused to emphasize the word, "of marriage? You were married once, to my mother, during which I can barely remember seeing the two of you speak. Apparently this was so successful, you decided to spend the next eighteen years alone rather than risk marrying again. But now—now you've changed your mind. I imagine, because of what you've found with Mayliza, you now see the place for love in marriage. I'm happy you learned that lesson in time to save *yourself*."

Her father looked at her thoughtfully, the uncertain air gone from him, replaced by one of sadness. "I had no idea that my decision would create such bitterness in you. I did not foresee that this is the way you would become."

His comment cut her to the quick. For surely she had become far worse than he could see. "You know nothing of what I've become." Her voice was deep with emotion, her eyes clouded by tears.

Her father moved toward her, but she straightened and glared at him. He halted.

"Tell Mayliza," she said, "that I harbor no ill feelings toward her. But I do not wish to see you, the two of you, together. Ever." She felt her throat constrict. "I do not know how you could think it fair that I should witness your happiness after being robbed of my own."

His eyes held deepening concern. "There will be no happiness for either of us if you do not accept us," he said. "I see where your reasoning lies, Catra. You think I've stolen the only man you'll ever love, but it isn't so. I told

326

you before that I loved your mother, and it is true that I did. But we did not marry for love. In fact I barely knew her when we wed. But I grew to love her, as I know you will grow to love Ferris.''

''Father, if I have not grown to love Ferris in the years I've known him, why would I grow to love him now?''

''You will know him in a different way,'' he said knowingly. ''You must already have experienced some of that.''

Her father would mistake the burn in her cheeks, she knew. But she would not tell him of Ferris's preference. She had agreed to that secret beforehand, and she would honor her promise until the day she died.

He continued, ''You are right in one thing, Catherine. I am marrying Mayliza for love. But surely you cannot find fault with her. You, who have loved her as your friend for so long. Imagine my dilemma upon being presented with Ryan St. James as a choice for my only daughter. A man with a black reputation and an eye for young heiresses. Surely you must see my reasoning.''

''You take much at face value,'' Catra commented, thinking mostly of Ferris. ''But your reasoning is not what concerns me. That you told me at the time. What I want to know is how you could do what you did to me. How could you perpetuate the lie that Ryan didn't love me, never loved me, even though he came to you himself and asked you for my hand? How could you let me walk down the aisle with Ferris knowing that what Ryan and I had was real? How, Father, how could you do that to me?''

She inhaled deeply, the air quivering over the emotion in her chest.

''Because he was not good enough for you!'' he nearly shouted. ''He still isn't. He's a rake and a rogue, and he would have used you just as he used that Fairchild woman. I don't care what sort of story he came up with. Women in love are the easiest beings in the world to fool.'' His face was red as he rubbed a hand across his forehead.

A million protests rose to her throat, but she choked them back. He would rationalize away all of them, she knew, and she was in no mood to bicker. ''Be that as it may,'' she said, turning to sit on the straight-backed chair at her dressing table. ''I believed him then and I believe him now. It is you who have dropped in my estimation. You see, there is no evidence that he has ever lied. And yet there is ample proof that you have.''

''If I lied, it was only to protect you, to ensure that you got the life you were meant to have.''

She smiled wryly. ''Things don't always work out the way you plan them, Father.''

He shook his head. ''I don't understand this. I do what any father would do to keep his daughter from the arms of a philanderer and this is what I get. Well, I don't have to stand here and be beaten over the head with ingratitude.'' He moved toward the door.

''What any father would do?'' Catra flared. ''You denigrated my feelings, stole a letter I had written from its messenger, spread falsehoods about me to the man asking for my hand, coached Seth to lie to me about Ryan, and you think I should be *grateful* to you?''

Her father turned, his expression haughty. ''I expected you to respect my edicts. Writing that letter in the first place was disobedient. Now, come down to dinner. Your friend Mayliza is waiting and anxious for your appearance.''

''No,'' she said, shaking her head and rising to her feet. ''Your edicts are beneath me now. I know what sort of man you are, and I cannot respect you or your wishes. I will not go down to dinner. Not tonight—not ever. Give my apologies to Mayliza. But you are no longer kin to me.''

''Catherine—''

"Get out." She pointed to the door.

"You're being foolish."

"Get out." Catra took one step forward, fixing her father with a steely gaze.

After a tense moment of looking into her eyes, her father turned and left the room.

Chapter Nineteen

Christmas was thankfully over and Catra was just beginning to feel the difference in her body from the pregnancy. Her dresses were becoming snug, and each day she could hardly wait until evening to remove her painful corset. She retired earlier and earlier at night, just to be able to take off her clothes and sit in comfort.

Despite the understanding she and Ferris had come to, he appeared to be avoiding her, which seemed to suit both of them perfectly. For her part, every time she looked at him she could not help but think how her life would be different if Ryan were her husband.

As for his, she suspected that he was spending time with someone who satisfied his intimate needs, but she did not want to know who and did not question him about his whereabouts. He was adept at discretion—even knowing him her whole life, she'd had no idea that his romantic inclinations lay anywhere other than herself—so she was unconcerned that his activities would be discovered.

They had not announced the news of the baby yet, but they would have to soon. Though Ferris knew the truth, the enormity of the lie upon which they would be embarking when they announced her pregnancy was hard to bear. Certainly when she'd first lied to Ferris about the night with Ryan it had been awful, but even then she'd had the sense that she would tell him the truth someday, and she had. To initiate a lie that would last a lifetime was another matter entirely. She could come up with no other alternative, however, and before long her condition would be embarrassingly obvious. The house was quite full, not just with Chesters but with Dahlia and Baker Mansfield. People might even wonder why she hadn't shared the joyous news earlier.

Catra breathed a sigh of relief as the laces of her corset expanded and Lucy pulled it from her body. Catra peeled the wrinkled chemise from her skin and rubbed the indentations the corset had left beneath its viselike grip. She had just stepped out of her petticoats when she heard a knock.

"Someone to see you, Mrs. Chester," one of the housemaids called through the closed door.

Lucy held the nightdress up for Catra to slip it over her head.

"Who is it?" Catra asked, looking at the clock. Just six o'clock. She hoped it was someone she could put off, as she had no desire to wedge herself back into her corset.

"It's Miss Thayer, ma'am. She said she'll understand if you don't want to see her."

Catra had spoken to Mayliza after the confrontation with her father, but the meeting had been strained and unsatisfying. Catra had left Braithwood feeling lonelier than she'd ever felt in her life.

It was not that Mayliza had been particularly cool, but

between them stood the suspicion that each had betrayed and been betrayed by the other. For Catra, the guilt over her own behavior was the stronger of the two, but she could not help feeling that Mayliza might have said something to her about wanting to marry her father. Still, Catra knew Mayliza should not be blamed for following her feelings. Hadn't Catra done the very same thing, with far greater impact?

So it was with anxiety and trepidation that she told the housemaid to have Mayliza wait in whichever parlor was not being used by other members of the household. Instead of donning her nightgown, Catra had Lucy help her into an old gown that used to be too large for her, but now was a trifle tight, that she could wear without her corset.

She dismissed Lucy and looked at herself in the mirror. She looked pale and somewhat malnourished, she thought, yet she felt bloated at the same time. She turned sideways, trying to see whether she looked pregnant, but though she believed she could fool most people, she was afraid Mayliza's sharp eyes—eyes that had known her so long—would be able to tell.

She ran her gaze down the aging gown she wore. Ugly, she thought. She should have tried to look better despite the discomfort, but it was too late to change. She threw on a shawl to cover it and descended the stairs.

Mayliza was standing by the window in the back parlor, removing her gloves as Catra came through the door. Catra had forgotten how lovely her friend was—or had she grown prettier somehow?—with her soft strawberry-blond curls and doe-brown eyes. Her complexion glowed, presumably from the chill wind outside, and was beautifully complemented by the dark green gown she wore. She seemed distant and beautiful to Catra.

"Hello, Mayliza." Catra stood in the doorway, feeling

ridiculously awkward. "Thank you for stopping by." She moved toward her friend on legs that felt as if they were made of lead.

Mayliza approached her hastily. "Catra, how are you?" she asked, concern tingeing her voice. Her hand took Catra's.

Catra took a step backward at the warm assault but did not remove her hand from Mayliza's. "I'm fine," she responded, surprised. "How are you?"

"I've been just sick with worry," she pronounced. "And now I see I was right. I thought you looked unwell at our last meeting. Of course, those were such—well, such odd circumstances. But now you're so pale. Tell me my thoughtless behavior hasn't driven you to this."

Mayliza's eyes were so full of concern and remorse that Catra's conscience stung. "Oh, May, I'm fine, truly I am. And I told you that I'm not angry with you. I've finished acting like a spoiled child. That was all it was. I just hope you're not angry with me."

Mayliza sighed, not taking her eyes from Catra's face. "Of course I'm not angry. I admit I was surprised at your reaction, but the more I thought about it, the more I understood what you must be feeling. I should have told you what was happening between me and your father. But it was just so awkward. You understand, don't you?"

Catra nodded and squeezed Mayliza's hands. "I do."

"But you look so ill, Cat. You even have dark circles under your eyes. Are you sure you're all right? I've never seen you this way."

Catra's throat closed with emotion at the heartfelt concern in her friend's voice. "How can you be so kind to me," she asked, forcing the words out over the sadness in her chest, "after the awful way I've behaved?"

Mayliza pulled her toward the chairs by the fire and sat

333

them both down. "After all we've been through together in our lives, you can ask me that question? Come now, I've just told you. I know you were shocked. As you should have been. How could I hold that against you? Now, will you tell me what's really wrong? Because I won't believe it's nothing."

Catra looked down at her hand clasped in Mayliza's. Part of her wanted to warn her friend about her father, that he was capable of great deception. But then, so was she.

Besides, even as much as she resisted the idea, deep in her heart she knew her father had believed he was acting in her best interest when he'd plotted to keep her from Ryan. Granted, he facilitated an end he had wanted all along, but looking at the situation through his eyes, she could perhaps see how Ryan might not look like the best suitor. Perhaps.

In any case, if she'd learned one thing from her father's duplicity, it was that doing anything to separate two people who wanted to be together was wrong. And often didn't work.

"May, I hope you and Father will be very happy together," she said impulsively. "Truly. I want for you the best, most fulfilling marriage possible. Just . . . just promise me one thing. Promise me you're marrying for love."

Mayliza's beatific smile eliminated any worry Catra might have had that she might have been coerced or felt pressured to agree to marry Thurber Meredyth because of his wealth or status in the community.

"It's a promise I can make, and gladly, Catra. I *am* marrying for love. You may be sure of it."

Catra nodded, looking down. Truly, she was glad her friend would have the happiness she would not. She was. But if she was a tiny bit jealous, surely that was all right too, because it only meant that she believed Mayliza and thought her likely to have the sort of life Catra had lost.

"But tell me what has you so down. Is it Ferris?" Mayliza asked gently. "Is the marriage difficult?"

Catra started to shake her head no but stopped herself. She was so tired of lying.

She had an irresistible urge to confess all to her friend, to release from the close confines of her bruised heart the terrible burden she carried. But she couldn't, could she? Could she risk Mayliza—kind, generous Mayliza of all people—despising her for her sins?

Mayliza stroked her hand with soft fingers. "Are you not getting along?"

"We get along. I believe we'll always get along. It's just, well, the marriage is not—typical," Catra admitted. She pulled her shawl more tightly around her.

"What do you mean, not typical?"

"Oh, I don't know. Perhaps it is typical—what do I know of marriage? It's just . . . it's very hard." She bit her bottom lip. "I mean, you know the circumstances under which I went through with the marriage. Now Ferris knows them too, and that has made things . . . awkward."

Mayliza gaped at her. "Ferris knows the circumstances? Cat, what are you saying? Ferris knows you were in love with Ryan?"

Catra nodded. "I had to tell him. It wasn't fair not to."

"Was he angry?" she asked incredulously.

Catra smiled sadly and squeezed her hand. "No. Well, maybe a little. But we went into this marriage knowing we weren't in love with each other. I believe the hardest thing for him was reconciling that I'd fallen in love with his friend."

Mayliza was silent for a moment.

"Let me get some tea," Catra offered, rising. "Would you like some tea?"

She did not wait for an answer but rang for the house-maid and ordered tea and cakes.

"Catra," Mayliza began slowly, once the maid had left, "do you mind if I ask you a question?"

"Of course not."

"I know it's none of my business, but . . . how did you come to tell Ferris of your feelings for Ryan? Did it have anything to do with your staying with the St. Jameses in Boston?"

Catra took a deep breath. "In a way."

"Did anything—happen there?" Mayliza studied her.

Catra felt herself go crimson under Mayliza's scrutiny. "I'm not sure what you mean by 'happen,' " she said carefully.

"Catra, you really don't look well," she said. "I'm so worried about you, I don't even care if I'm being insufferably rude. Did something happen between you and Ryan, and is that how Ferris found out?"

Catra made a decision and acted on it before she could change her mind. "I told Ferris about Ryan, so he did not . . . he did not catch us acting inappropriately, if that's what you mean."

Mayliza nodded, blushing, and looked at her hands in her lap.

"But he could have, May," she continued. "He could have."

Mayliza looked up at her. "Could have . . . caught you acting inappropriately?"

Catra nodded.

"Oh, Cat . . ." she breathed. "So you are still in love with him?"

"As he is with me." Catra felt emotion well in her chest. She dropped her head and took several deep breaths. But instead of calming her, they intensified her feelings. "And

336

sometimes I feel like it's a crime we are not together. Honestly. That's why . . . that's why I allowed some things to happen that probably should not have.''

Mayliza's eyes scanned her face.

"But you don't need to know all of this. Goodness, it was not my intention to burden you with my problems," she said over the lump in her throat, trying to sound gay. She couldn't tell Mayliza everything. She simply couldn't. And the closer she came to confessing all, the more afraid she felt of losing the closest friend she had.

Desperate to change the subject, Catra blurted, "But I haven't told you the good news yet! You'll be the first to learn that I am pregnant!''

As the words came out, Dahlia swept into the room. Upon seeing the two women and hearing Catra's last words, she stopped dead in her tracks. The three women gaped at each other.

"You're pregnant?" Dahlia gasped, in a tone that left no question as to her feelings about it.

Catra's face went white and Mayliza quickly hugged her. "Congratulations," she said, squeezing her tightly.

"Pregnant?" Dahlia nearly shrieked this time. "Is it true?''

Catra rose hastily and held her hands out in a gesture of defense against the loud words. "Please, Dahlia," she said. "I did not mean for the whole family to know yet. I haven't discussed announcing it with Ferris yet.''

"So it is true," Dahlia continued. "That was quick work. I suppose you think you've got Waverly all sewn up now for your little brat.''

Catra raised her eyebrows in alarmed bewilderment. "What in the world are you talking about?''

"You know perfectly well," Dahlia said acidly. She gestured toward Mayliza. "We all know Miss Thayer is going to claim Braithwood. So I guess you thought you'd get yourself with child and usurp my claim here.''

Catra turned amazed eyes to Mayliza, who colored deeply. She turned back to Dahlia. ''Just what claim did you think you had here?''

''Why, after Ferris, I was next in line to get Waverly. Now I suppose you think I'll get nothing.''

Catra laughed incredulously. Nothing was indeed what she would get, Catra thought. For Ferris had taken Ryan's advice and checked into Baker Mansfield's financial status and prospects. If he did not inherit Braithwood—which he certainly would not—the man was penniless. He'd been disinherited from his immediate family and was not, as was previously believed, building a home for his new bride. It had become painfully clear to all involved, with the merciful exception of Dahlia, that the reason this man had come out of nowhere and swept Dahlia off her feet was for her quite substantial dowry.

''I cannot believe you're saying these things,'' Catra continued reasonably. ''Surely you must have thought that when Ferris married he'd have children. No matter whom he married.''

At that moment, footsteps sounded in the hall. Catra heard them with anxiety, but Dahlia ignored them.

''Well, I'll not be so easily robbed of my rightful inheritance. I've lived here most of my life and it's my home. I'll not be put out on the street for any sniveling child of yours.''

''Dahlia, nobody said anything—''

''And my husband feels the same way. We'll fight for our due,'' she said. ''So you can forget about any offspring of yours getting everything.''

Ferris appeared in the doorway. When she perceived the eyes of the other two women focused on something behind her, Dahlia wheeled around. Seeing Ferris, her expression hardened.

"Congratulations, cousin," she sneered. "Your wife may be pregnant with your child, but don't think it changes anything." With that she stalked from the room.

The silence was deafening. Catra heard Mayliza rise behind her and turned toward the sound.

"I'd best be going," she said quietly. "Catra, I'll come see you another time. I'm sorry it turned out like this." She hugged her again. "Congratulations."

Catra hugged her feebly in return. Then she and Ferris were alone in the room. His eyes were unnaturally large in his face. "You told them?" he asked. His voice was small, boyish, and his eyes held a look of concern.

"I told Mayliza. Dahlia just happened to overhear. I'm sorry, Ferris. I know I should have discussed it with you first. I just felt like telling May, and then Dahlia . . ."

Ferris silenced her with a wave of his hand. "I don't care. It had to come out sometime." He sighed and moved toward the fire, warming his hands against its heat. "So I guess this is it. I'm to be the proud papa. You, ah . . ." He turned around and looked at her timidly. "You're not going to tell Ryan?"

Catra's head began to spin. Perhaps the day's excitement had been too much for her. She sat down. "No. I don't think it would be wise."

"When is the baby due?" he asked.

"About six months, I think," she answered breathlessly. What was wrong with her? She felt so odd, so dizzy and sick.

"Six months."

Catra began to panic. She gasped for air. For some reason she could not take a normal breath. She inhaled again and again.

"Catra, are you all right?" she heard Ferris ask from a great distance. "Catra?"

The room began to go dark. She saw Ferris run to catch her as she fell into unconsciousness.

Chapter Twenty

Catra awoke in a cold sweat again. For the last week she had woken at least once a night gripped by an unreasoning panic. Sometimes it was a feeling that descended upon her the moment she awoke, causing her to come to consciousness with a jolt and a blind, groundless fear that something awful had occurred. But usually it was brought on by a dream, as it was this time.

The dream she'd had this night was not significantly different from the others she'd had over the past few weeks. In it, she'd given birth to a child with black hair and a face so like Ryan's that it looked like a miniature, grotesquely painted over a child's face. She was then hauled from the birthing bed onto a city street and stoned by the citizens. She would look slowly from one face to the next, alternately recognizing them as her neighbors and then wondering who on earth all these people were.

She'd been confined to her bed since she'd fainted in

Ferris's company, but it was just as well. Since the dreams had become so prevalent during the day she walked about half asleep because of the restless nights, only to become anxious and afraid again the moment it was time to go to bed.

Catra raised herself up in bed and looked at the window. The gray dawn was rising. She heaved a sigh of relief. She especially hated it when the dream woke her in the small hours of the morning, forcing her to try to conquer her fears and return to sleep.

She pushed herself to a sitting position and slid her legs to the side of the bed. She would simply rise at this ungodly hour and ready herself for the day. Mayliza was coming again this morning, as she had each morning for several days now. She had taken it upon herself to make Catra some maternity clothes and today was going to take some measurements. Their friendship had healed itself, it seemed, and Catra did not know what she would have done without her.

Mayliza's concern grew visibly with each visit. Catra could see it in her eyes when Mayliza looked at her. She could see the intense study in her expression, but she knew not what to do to dispel her friend's fear. Catra knew she looked awful. She was pale and drawn, her eyes ringed with dark smudges, and she lacked energy for anything but the most modulated conversations.

She felt that if she could only get one good night's sleep all would be well, but the moment darkness fell her paranoia returned. One night she was simply too tired to give in to her fears and so she dropped off quickly. But that night she'd awakened from the dream with renewed anguish.

Catra awaited Mayliza in the parlor, knitting an afghan. She felt hot doing the work, but she needed something to do with her hands. She was on edge this morning. Earlier she had met up with Baker in the dining room, eating breakfast. The man was truly insufferable. Since she'd arrived, she had tried to be kind to him and ignore his offensive manners. She had even tried not to hold against him the awful circumstances of his marrying Dahlia, before Catra and Ferris had returned to Virginia, but he had acted as though it were through his good graces that her presence was suffered. He was superior and condescending in his manner, going so far one time as to ask Catra to leave the dining room, as he wished to dine alone with his bride. She'd refused, incensed, and they'd spent a tense twenty minutes while Catra wolfed down her breakfast out of principle but with a strong desire to be gone from his obnoxious presence.

Mayliza was ushered in, looking airy and cool in a pale gray dress. Catra thought she herself might spontaneously burst into flames at any moment, so hot did she feel.

"I wish I felt as cool as you look," she said, wiping her brow with her handkerchief.

"Step outside a moment," Mayliza said. She plopped onto the sofa. "You'll cool off in no time. They say there might be snow tonight."

"Snow." Catra sighed. She brushed a damp strand of hair from her face with the back of her hand and remembered looking out the window at the St. Jameses' as a blizzard swallowed the house.

Mayliza turned critical eyes on Catra and laid a hand on her damp brow. "You *are* hot."

"No, just warm. Perhaps I should move away from the fire."

"Catra, why won't you see a doctor? You look like the living dead. Perhaps he could give you something to help you sleep."

343

Catra sighed. "I don't need a doctor. Not yet, anyway. And you know how I hate having to summon doctors. They're always so serious. Besides, the last time I saw him, he told me to drink warm milk before bedtime. As if I hadn't already tried everything like that."

Mayliza nodded. "I'm surprised they wouldn't give you something stronger. Perhaps Ferris should speak to him. Surely he's seen you suffering. Isn't he worried about the child?"

"I don't know whether he is or not," Catra said truthfully. "He doesn't have much enthusiasm for becoming a father."

"Yes," Mayliza said slowly, unsure of how much to tell her of the rumors she'd heard about Ferris lately. "I'd noticed that a little."

Catra pressed her handkerchief to her forehead again. "He seems to spend a great deal of time in town lately. I don't even see him every day anymore."

"Yes, I'd heard he was in town quite a bit," Mayliza admitted. "Mrs. Wilson was over yesterday, and she mentioned she often sees him there."

"I wonder what he does?" Catra asked without much interest. She closed her eyes briefly and wiped her eyelids. "One of the worst things about pregnancy," she said, "is that every movement I make is so much more work than it used to be. I can't wait until I get my energy back. I can't even remember how it was to simply saddle Jupiter and go for a ride. What heaven that will be!" She rested her head on the back of the chair.

Mayliza bit her lip thoughtfully. "I'm not sure if I should mention it . . ." Mayliza started. Catra's eyes opened and focused on her. "But Ferris has been seen quite a bit at the pub in town."

Catra laughed slightly. "That makes sense," she said wryly, not lifting her head.

"It seems he's drinking quite a lot. And some say he's got a favorite there." Mayliza was puzzled by Catra's reaction and so said a bit more than she'd planned.

"A favorite?" Catra asked mildly.

Mayliza played with the skirt ruffles in her lap. "One of the girls."

Catra closed her eyes again and laughed. "I doubt that."

Mayliza glanced at her. "You do? Why?"

"He's not interested in sex," Catra replied matter-of-factly.

Mayliza saw the sheen of perspiration across Catra's white forehead and moved to the arm of her chair to wipe her brow.

"Are you feeling all right, Cat?"

Catra did not answer right away. She simply smiled at the contact and sighed.

"Catra, open your eyes," Mayliza demanded, alarmed.

Catra's lids lifted slowly, but her gaze was unfocused. "I'm sorry; I suddenly feel so—so light. My head feels like it's floating. I must really be tired."

"Come on," Mayliza ordered, standing. "Get up." She pulled Catra to a standing position. Catra swayed against her.

"I don't know what's wrong with me," Catra murmured. "I feel weak as a kitten. My knees . . ."

She began to crumble. Mayliza clutched her arm and backed toward the chair. But it was too much for her. Catra folded to the floor like a newborn foal.

Mayliza raced for the door. "Zack! Pru! Come quickly!" The housemaid rushed from the back hall toward her. "Run get Dr. Collins, quickly! Mrs. Chester has become ill. And find Zack! I need someone to help me get Mrs. Chester to her bed.''

The servant scurried off while Mayliza rushed back to Catra's side. Gently, she turned her onto her back, straightened her clothing and fanned her frantically. Her eyes searched the door for Zack's strong body.

"May?" Catra's eyes were slitted and focused intently on Mayliza. Catra's hand gripped her forearm.

"What is it, Cat?" she whispered.

"I have to tell you. I have to tell someone." She swallowed convulsively. "I'm afraid. If something happens to me"—her grip tightened—"if something happens, tell Ryan . . ." She closed her eyes again.

"Yes? Tell Ryan what?" Mayliza asked. Catra didn't answer. "Catra? I'll tell him anything you want. Talk to me!" Mayliza demanded desperately.

"Tell him—tell him I'm sorry," she whispered, her voice little more than a rasp. "You see, the baby—it's his, May."

Without a shred of doubt or a moment's hesitation, Mayliza wrote to Ryan. The situation was too unbearable to watch.

The doctor had said Catra suffered from exhaustion and malnutrition. He had given her a sleeping draught and said that childbirth was very hard on a woman, so it was important that she regain her strength well before the ordeal.

The potion he gave her appeared to help, and for several days Catra slept more than sixteen hours a night. Some color even returned to her cheeks, though she still could not keep much food down.

The evening that she had collapsed, Ferris had been nowhere to be found. It was several hours after the doctor had come and gone that someone had spotted him lurching down the street in a drunken fog, apparently from the direction of a small cabin that belonged to a man known to frequent the pub where Ferris was seen earlier.

It was obvious to Mayliza that Ferris either knew Catra's secret or at least suspected enough to warrant a great deal of self-pity. In any case, Catra's health problems were not the only ones she had, and Mayliza was determined to try to rectify the situation.

She wrote to Ryan to request his immediate dispatch to Waverly. She told him of Catra's illness, though not of her confession, and of the fact that Ferris was somewhat indisposed and in need of assistance. She was not sure what she expected to happen when he arrived, but she was enough of a romantic to hope that the truth would win out and somehow order would be restored to the lives of these three people.

Catra could not possibly stay with Ferris and raise the child of the man she really loved. It was an absurd idea. She couldn't even manage the pregnancy without destroying herself over it. Wouldn't it be better to feel guilty only for leaving Ferris? Instead of feeling guilty for the multiple sins of lying about the baby, robbing Ryan of his own progeny and denying the child his rightful parentage?

This was the course of her rationale and she acted on it. They could go away, she thought reasonably; they could move to Europe or something. Mayliza was sure Thurber would give them whatever they needed to start a new life together. It was true he did not think much of Ryan St. James, but as the father of his grandson he would have to view him differently.

As well, Thurber had confessed to Mayliza his interference in the affair of Catra and Ryan. When Mayliza reacted with shock and anger at his role in their separation, he had been genuinely confused. He had clung doggedly to his reasons for meddling, but doubt shadowed his eyes when she told him of the depth of Catra's hurt. Her intention had not been to make Thurber feel bad, only to make clear to him the true emotions he had thwarted. It would be important for him to see that he had not ended the love between them by denying them marriage, but only complicated its natural expression. And that would be important for him to see if he were to help them now.

Mayliza temporarily moved to Waverly to help Catra. Dahlia had raised a fuss, claiming that she and her mother were perfectly capable of taking care of a pregnant woman. But Mayliza was determined that Catra would have at least one person she could trust and feel close to near her. She also enjoyed being closer to Thurber, who came to call every day to check on Catra, though Catra would not see him.

She did not admit to having invited Ryan, however. She did not even tell him that Ryan was expected, preferring to cross that bridge when she came to it. She was hopeful that Ryan and Catra could talk and come to some understanding to present to Thurber before he even had to know of Ryan's presence.

Ryan arrived a week and a half after she'd sent her letter to him. He hadn't even bothered to reply; he had simply come. She was pleased with this response. It told her all she needed to know of his feelings for Catra.

She met him at the door, after watching him approach the house, and led him to the library where they could talk privately. The library was the last place any of the Chesters were ever found, the lot of them being less than avid readers. And she had only informed the housemaid that there was to be another guest in the house so she could make up a room. She planned to track Ferris down after she'd had the opportunity to talk to Ryan.

''Thank you for coming so quickly,'' she said upon entering the library with him. She closed the door behind him.

He strode to the center of the room and turned questioning eyes to her. "How is Catra?" he asked without preamble.

"She's better. She's regained a great deal of strength."

He took a deep, satisfied breath. "Do they know what caused her collapse? You mentioned exhaustion in your letter. Isn't it unusual for a young woman to be beset by such an illness?"

Mayliza hesitated. "Do know that she's with child?"

Ryan's face went slack and he looked as if he'd had the breath knocked out of him.

"So that's it, then," he said, mostly to himself, and raked a hand through his hair. He turned away from her and placed a hand on the back of a nearby chair. "I'm sorry," he said after a moment, turning back to her with a shake of his head. "I didn't know that. I'm sorry for looking so inappropriately—"

"It's all right." Mayliza stopped him. He met her eyes. She looked at him steadily and shook her head slightly. "You don't need to stand on formality with me."

He assessed her from across the room. "I kept hoping," he said, seeming to come to a decision about her, "for something to happen. Something to help us. I don't know what." He laughed shortly, without humor, and rubbed his hand over his eyes. "Not this." He gazed about the room thoughtfully. "I imagine Ferris is pretty proud of himself."

Mayliza neared him and placed a hand on his arm. "Mr. St. James," she said, "Catra is nearly three months along."

He looked at her hand on his sleeve and absorbed the gentle tone of her voice. And then the words sank in. Slowly Ryan's face turned to hers. His expression had turned intense, alive, his eyes compelling.

"Miss Thayer," he said in a low voice, "are you saying—that that child is—was conceived in my house?"

Mayliza smiled and nodded. "Yes, Mr. St. James."

She watched as he drank in the meaning of her words. It seemed he breathed the knowledge in with every pore; she could almost see the thoughts race through the translucent depths of his eyes.

"I must speak with her," he stated.

"Yes," Mayliza agreed.

"Is she well enough to receive me?"

"I'll need to consult the doctor, but she should be able to receive you. He'll be coming this afternoon. First we need to announce you to the rest of the household, however. I'm afraid I told no one that I invited you. There would have been many questions."

Ryan nodded. "Of course. Where is Ferris?"

"He's here somewhere. Perhaps on the back terrace. But I must warn you, Mr. St. James, he's taken to drinking of late."

"Ferris?" Ryan turned a surprised expression on her. "Why, he's got the tolerance of a kitten."

"I'm afraid he's been working to change that. His uncle, Bernard, has been running the plantation. Ferris has been absent a great deal lately."

Ryan made for the door. "I'll find him," he said. "And you"—he turned to her with a conspiratorial half smile—"knew nothing of my plans to visit. Understand?"

"Thank you." She smiled, reassured once again that she'd done the right thing in summoning him.

Ryan strode down the hall feeling as close to exultation as he could in the current situation. His child! It was his child that Catra carried! Though she had not said so in as many words, he was sure of Miss Thayer's meaning; and the knowledge renewed his faith that he and Catra would be together in the end.

He was rounding the doorway to pass through the sun-room to the porch, when a short, portly man emerged and nearly bowled him over. The two stepped back abruptly, voicing automatic apologies before their eyes met and recognition sparked between them.

Baker's eyes narrowed and took on a feral glint. "Mr. St. James, how distasteful to find you here."

Ryan's mood descended a notch. "I'd forgotten this was the most recent rock you'd slithered under, Mansfield. I'd have thought the Chesters would have discovered your money-grubbing nature by now and turned you out on your greasy ear."

Baker gave him a pointed smile. "Actually, they did discover it—too late. I'm a member of the family now."

"Dahlia?"

Baker bowed slightly. "My wife."

Ryan regarded him, a half smile on his lips. "A fitting end, I would say."

Baker shifted uncomfortably. "I'm curious why you're here," he purred. "There are no virgins to ruin. Unless you consider my poor cousin Ferris to your taste. He's the closest thing to a virgin you'll find around here. Closer by far than his wife, I'd wager."

Ryan stared at him coldly. "I'll not ask why you'd say something like that."

"I'm no spy," Baker protested mildly. "People just seem to confide in me, for some reason. Take Candace Fairchild, for instance. She was so anxious to have you."

Ryan folded his arms over his chest. "Do you think it wise to bring up that incident now?"

"Whyever not? It amused me greatly to see you so taken. And by my own cunning hand, at that."

"Because it will remind me of the retribution I have yet to inflict on you. Although perhaps your recent wedding has superceded my ambition to ruin the rest of your life."

"My wife has hardly ruined my life," Baker sneered, patting his vest pocket, wherein lay an imaginary sum of money.

Ryan smiled at the man's smugness. "Give her time," he said with confidence. "Don't forget, you've squandered far greater sums than that gained by a mere dowry. How long do you think it will sustain you? A month? A year? Don't forget, you'll have Dahlia for the rest of your life."

"Dahlia is a bigger ticket than you imagine," Baker offered with a mysterious smile. "But then, you never did go in for actually marrying the wealthy heiresses you defiled. Perhaps if you did, you'd find yourself less likely to become, shall we say, embroiled in something ugly." His piercing brown eyes looked knowingly at Ryan.

"Where is Ferris?" Ryan asked.

Baker grimaced. "By his lovely wife's bedside. Where would you be if you were him? I've no doubt you've pondered the question."

Ryan forced a laugh. "That's always been the problem with you, Baker. You think you know so much more than you actually do." He turned on his heel and headed for the stairs.

He had just reached the bottom step when Ferris careened out of the hallway to the top of the stairs, just avoiding a long tumble down them by holding tightly to the rail and dangling for a moment with one foot over the drop.

"Ryan!" he blurted in surprise. His face was a deep crimson and he continued to clutch the railing even after regaining his balance. "Where's Mayliza? Where's the doctor?"

"The doctor?" Ryan asked, alarmed.

"Catra's bleeding!" Ferris shouted.

Chapter Twenty-one

Ryan entered the darkened room with Mayliza by his side. She dismissed Lucy and held the door while the woman left. A single candle burned by the bedside where Catra lay with her eyes closed.

The room was warm, but as the evening's storm brewed a cold chill penetrated the edges of the room.

Ryan approached her cautiously as Mayliza retreated to the attached dressing room, her presence only required to give respectability to his entrance. He folded his frame into the chair by the bedside with the brief, unwanted thought that this was where Ferris had probably just sat, hoping against hope he would not lose "his" child.

Catra was in danger of losing the child, and the news had shaken him badly. For the first time in his life, he felt unsure of what to do next.

Catra stirred, raised a pale arm in the dimness and pushed the blankets away from her. Then, in half-consciousness, she brushed her arm against her forehead and opened her eyes.

"How are you feeling?" Ryan asked quietly.

Catra's eyes widened, and for a moment she just drank in the sight of him. "Ryan," she breathed. "Is it really you?"

He smiled sadly. "Can't keep me away for long."

She smiled in return, relaxing back into the cushions. She stared at him for a long moment, as if to assure herself that he really was there, and tears clouded her eyes.

"Don't cry, Catra," Ryan said. "You're not going to lose this child. I promise."

Catra tore her eyes from his and looked at the ceiling. "You can't promise that," she whispered. She looked pale, tired, but never more beautiful.

Ryan didn't know what to say. He could take her from here, he thought. Spirit her away to some distant continent where they could live as man and wife with their child. But she could never make the trip now, not in her condition.

An odd, distant roll of thunder sounded outside the window and a gust of wind rattled the window in its frame. Ryan tried not to think about the portent of a midwinter thunderstorm. No doubt it meant nothing more sinister than colder weather tomorrow, he told himself.

He looked down at her tired face, eyes closed again, and moved the hair from her damp forehead with his index finger. Something about the soft skin awakened a strong protective instinct within him. "I'm not going to let you do this, Catra," he said.

Her eyes opened. "Do what?"

"Carry this whole burden yourself. Live this way. Live this charade."

"I . . ." Her throat moved as she swallowed. "I'm only doing what's best for my child."

"Your child, Catra?" he asked, the words heavy in the solemn room. "Yours and who else's? Tell me, Catra. I want to hear it from your lips."

Catra's face betrayed an inner battle, and he took her hand in his. "I can do the math, Catra," he said. "There's no point in keeping this all to yourself. Just tell me, please . . ."

"Ferris is the father of this baby," she said. Then added, quietly, "Legally."

He shook his head. "That's not good enough. Don't you think lying has gotten us into enough of a mess?"

She folded her hands on her stomach. "Yes. But I am telling the only truth I am able to tell."

He tried to look into her eyes, but she kept them downcast. Instead, she stared at her pale hands as they gripped each other, white-knuckled, on top of the blankets.

He brushed the backs of his fingers along her cheek. When she did not look up, he took her chin firmly in his fingers and turned her face to him.

"Listen to me, Catra. I've made many mistakes in my life. But this will not be one of them." His soft voice was tinged with a hardness that expected no argument. "Even if this deception is not making you ill, it's not helping you get well. We can go somewhere where people don't know us. The decision we made in Boston was wrong, and this baby proves it. You and I are meant to be together. I'll not have it any other way."

Catra's heart seemed to throb in her temples. She was having trouble keeping her mind on what had to be done. Ryan, seated so close, was seductive in his reasoning. But she knew she had to cling to her resolve; for the good of the child, she had to forsake the father. She couldn't leave now and claim the child was Ryan's. It would be branded a bastard.

355

She swallowed hard. "The child's father is Ferris," she repeated. He released her chin. She glanced at him with pleading eyes. "Surely you see the way it has to be."

Ryan's gaze was relentless. "I won't let you do this," he said, with a barely perceptible shake of his head. "It's too much for you, to live this lie day in and day out. And I know it's too much for me."

Catra met his eyes squarely. "It is the price we must pay for what we've done. Surely you don't mean to punish the child for our sins, do you? Because it is he who would suffer most."

"Would he? I don't know about that. And what about Ferris? Does he deserve this lie?"

"He knows, Ryan. I told him. I owed him that. He's agreed to claim the child as his." She closed her eyes briefly. "It was the best we could hope for. You know that, don't you?"

Lightning flashed, momentarily illuminating the room with a ghostly light. A second later thunder rolled, and the door to the bedroom creaked open. Ryan glanced up and saw no one. Another sign, he thought, then shook his head. Foolishness; he was getting downright superstitious in his old age.

Ryan bent to place his lips on hers. A soft kiss, pure. "I won't pressure you while you're ill. The doctor said you're to have complete rest for a while. We'll discuss this when you're better." He stood, preparing to leave.

She looked up at him with weary eyes. "No, Ryan. There's nothing to discuss." Outside the window the rain began to fall in sheets, slapping loudly against the flagstone patio beneath her window.

"Nothing to discuss? You're pregnant with my child and there's nothing to discuss?"

A sound at the door made him turn. There, agape in the

doorway, stood Ferris and Thurber Meredyth. In front of them, holding the door, was a grinning Baker Mansfield.

"I don't suppose we could hope for you to repeat that." Baker's tone was pleasant.

Ryan glanced from Baker to Thurber to Ferris and back again. "You should have made your presence known," he said cautiously. Thurber Meredyth's gaze lay upon him as hotly as burning coals.

Baker shrugged. "No matter. We heard well enough. Well, Ferris?" He turned to his companion. "What do you mean to do about this? Your friend has just claimed to be the father of *your* child. What do you intend to do about it?"

Ryan glanced back at Catra, who was struggling to sit up.

"No," she said, her weak voice shaming them all.

"This is no place for this discussion," Ryan said. "This is a sick room. Let us take this to a more appropriate location."

Ferris stood struggling for composure, looking from Baker to Ryan, avoiding Thurber's glare.

"It isn't so," Catra said. "Ferris . . . please."

Mayliza stepped from the sitting room and stopped at the sight of the men in the doorway.

"What's going on here?" she said.

"We were just leaving." Ryan moved toward the door.

"Good. This is too much," Mayliza said. "Catra needs her rest."

"She's right," Thurber said. "St. James, come with us."

Ryan looked back once more at Catra, giving her a slight smile of confidence, then grasped the door handle and closed the door behind him.

The four stood solemnly in the narrow hallway; then Ryan took the lead and led the group to the library. He was through the door and turning when Thurber threw the first punch. Ryan dodged a second too late and the blow glanced against his temple, sending him slamming into the book-shelves.

Ryan put a hand to his head and slowly pushed off the shelves, facing Thurber. "Strike me again, Meredyth, when I'm prepared, and the outcome will be vastly different."

"You bastard," Thurber growled. "When she told me about your affair she swore to me that you had not violated her. Her virtue was intact, ready to give to Ferris, she said. And though Candace Fairchild had not been so lucky, I believed her. God knows why, but I did."

Baker chuckled behind them.

"She didn't lie to you," Ryan said. "But we cannot say the same for you, can we? Your conversation with her was riddled with falsehoods." He lowered his hand and glanced at the blood congealing on his palm.

"Gentleman, gentleman," Baker intervened, spreading his arms wide as he walked between them. "This is not between you. This is Ferris's fight, is it not, Ferris? Tell us, Ferris. Tell me and your father-in-law what you intend to do with this man who defiled your wife. You heard it from his very lips. He believes the child is his. Why would that be?"

Ferris looked at Ryan, his eyes wide. Then he glanced at Thurber, and the look he received from that man made him visibly wilt.

"Mansfield," Ferris said tentatively, turning to him, "surely this doesn't need to be so ugly—"

"So ugly?" Thurber exploded. "St. James has obviously cuckolded you, and all you can say is that it doesn't need to be ugly? What's the matter with you, boy? Where's your pride?"

Ferris's face burned red.

"Ferris, you know what the truth is," Thurber added. "Now do something about it."

"We all know what the truth is now," Baker said with a pointed smile. He turned to Ferris with a short bow. "I would be happy to act as your second. Which would you prefer, pistols? Or swords?"

"I—I—" Ferris's face went from red to white in the space of a heartbeat.

"Oh, you're quite right." Baker waved his hands, as if erasing what he'd just said. "That's for the challenged party to decide. Very well. Mr. St. James, Mr. Chester gives you the choice. Pistols or swords?"

Ryan did not spare him a glance. "I'll not duel with you, Ferris. You know it doesn't have to be this way—"

"Don't listen to that snake," Thurber demanded. "He has sullied my daughter's good name, her reputation, her honor. It's up to you to defend her, Ferris. You're her husband, are you not?"

Ferris's shoulders straightened and he brought himself up to look Ryan in the eyes. His expression was sad, resigned.

"Pistols," he said quietly. "In the morning. S-six o'clock." Then he turned and left the room.

Thurber followed closely behind Ferris, vowing to have the truth from his daughter, leaving Baker to eye Ryan with beady, shark eyes. "A little injudicious, wasn't it? Talking so openly with the lady, alone?"

"Miss Thayer was within," Ryan replied evenly. He studied Baker for a moment, noting the look of triumph and anticipation on the man's face. "Don't think you've fooled me, Baker. I know that forcing this duel was your intention."

Baker shrugged. "I may have taken advantage of the

circumstances, but I was as surprised as anyone to find you alone in the lady's boudoir.''

"I'll bet."

Baker turned and moved to the desk at the end of the room. "I was. Not that I wasn't delighted to find you so unsuitably engaged. The kiss you gave her might have been enough for my purposes, and I almost broke in then. But then you provided me with so much more. I do appreciate it.''

"There is but one flaw in your plan, however," Ryan said. "I have no intention of killing Ferris Chester."

Baker sighed and sat down, crossing his feet on the desk. "I was afraid of that. Which is why I wanted to talk to you about young Mrs. Chester's future. I think perhaps we could do each other a favor." Baker's tongue, small and ferretlike, emerged to wet his thin lips.

"Her future is none of your concern."

Baker grinned, exposing brown, pointed teeth. "Let's not beat around the proverbial bush, shall we? You are in love with Catherine Chester; she stands in the way of Dahlia's inheritance; and Ferris is a useless sot who deserves whatever he gets.''

Ryan laughed at the audacity of the man. "So, you have a plan."

Baker laughed with him, a short, wheezing sound. "No, of course not. Nothing so wicked as that. I've merely put these three elements together and wondered if circumstances might further conspire to give us all what we want. It's a possibility worth pondering, don't you think?''

Ryan folded his arms across his chest. "No."

Baker pulled his legs off the desk and opened a bottom drawer. Ryan heard the clink of glass and saw a bottle emerge, followed by two glasses.

"Care for a snort?" Baker asked solicitously.

"No." He watched the man pour a generous helping into the short glass and return the second to the drawer.

Baker studied him over the rim of his glass. Then he lowered it and smacked his lips with satisfaction.

"You know"—he gestured toward Ryan with the glass—"I don't understand why you don't simply take Mrs. Chester and your soon-to-be junior away from here." He raised his eyebrows. "You don't particularly need her inheritance, and then you'd have the woman and the child."

"Typically shoddy planning, Baker." Ryan seated himself in the chair across from Baker and stretched his legs long, crossing them at the ankle. "You forget, the lady is married."

Baker scowled and shook his head. "My dear man," he said expansively, "how woefully uncreative. Do you think the entire country—the entire world—knows she is married?"

"Ah, I see," Ryan stated. "So you'd have me leave my home, as well. Avoid everyone who's ever known or heard of her."

Baker shrugged. "If you really wanted her, it could be arranged."

"I appreciate your giving my situation so much thought." He steepled his hands in front of him. "Is there a reason I warrant so much attention?"

"It's been a slow winter. And there's very little in the way of entertainment in this part of the world."

Ryan chuckled, amused by the man's slithery smoothness.

"It's very like a play," Baker continued. "And to have all of this happening right here, in one's own home—well, it's as convenient as recreation gets. Imagine, if you will, if at this duel tomorrow you were to actually kill poor Ferris. Well! A tragedy, certainly, but ultimately a gift for you and the young woman, wouldn't you say?''

Ryan raised his brows.

''But you're right,'' Baker carried on. ''That's no doubt how the authorities would see it, as well. So instead of spending the rest of your days blissfully in the arms of your paramour, you would sit rotting in some tasteless prison. No, best to miss him tomorrow, I suppose.''

''I thought you were through toying with me, after conspiring with Candace Fairchild to trap me into marriage, arranging for you to lose her in that poker game and assuring me that she was nothing more than a common harlot. In a way, you won that round, you know. I suffered for that scandal.''

Baker sighed and shook his head. ''I don't know, my friend. I suppose I'm just bored.''

Ryan pondered what Baker could be plotting, for plotting he certainly was. For Dahlia to inherit—or rather, for Baker to inherit—would require Ferris and all of his heirs to be gone, out of the way, dead. Hence, Baker's suggestion that Ryan kill Ferris tomorrow morning and leave with Catra. But surely he didn't truly believe he could talk Ryan into some sort of illegal arrangement, did he? The man would have to be even more of a fool than he seemed.

Ryan rose. ''While there's nothing I'd like better than to sit here and alleviate your boredom, I have traveled a great distance today and need to get up early in the morning. Thanks to you.''

''As I said,'' Baker smirked, ''I do apologize.''

''Yes . . . as you said.'' He turned away from Baker and strode from the room.

The early morning was cold and ice covered everything from the trees to the grass. Sleet crackled against the ground as Ferris stared out the window, mouth dry, palms sweating, nerves quivering.

"Ferris?" Catra's voice was tentative in the dark room behind him. She shifted under the covers. "What time is it?"

He turned from the window. "Not yet six."

"Are you all right?" She pushed herself up slightly and leaned back against the pillows.

He came toward her. "Everything's fine. Just fine." He hoped she didn't notice the way his voice wavered.

She studied him for a moment. "Were you able to calm my father last night? I told him it was all a lie, that Baker hated you for standing in the way of Dahlia's inheritance, but I'm not sure he believed me."

"Oh, yes. He did," Ferris said, kneading his hands together. "He certainly did. There's nothing to worry about." He tried to swallow, but his mouth was dry. He sat on the chair by the bed, reached for the water glass next to Catra's bed, and downed half the contents. "Cat—" He cleared his throat. "I wanted to come to tell you . . . I just wanted to tell you that I'm going to make you happy."

He placed the glass back on the table and leaned forward until his elbows rested on the coverlet and he knelt beside her bed. "I want you to know that I never meant to hurt you, getting you into this sham of a marriage and making things so awful for you."

Catra took his hand from where it lay on the coverlet. "You didn't hurt me, Ferris. You've done nothing to make things awful for me. I've done that myself. But you, you're all goodness."

"But I'm going to make it all up to you," he continued, as if she hadn't spoken. "You'll see. Everything will be fine. I've got a plan, and you'll be happy, Catra. I want you to be happy."

"Of course. I know that. And we will be happy." She held his hand in both of hers. "Don't worry, Ferris."

He leaned back on his heels, took up the water glass again and drank, leaving but a swallow in the bottom of the glass. "I'm sorry," he said, noting it. "I'll have the maid bring you some more."

"It matters not. I haven't been able to eat or drink anything lately anyway. Even the water smells odd to me." She smiled at him.

"But you must try, Cat. You must eat something. Then the doctor said you'd be fine." He pulled his handkerchief from his pocket and dabbed at his forehead.

"Ferris, what's the matter? Why are you so nervous?"

He stood and pushed the handkerchief deep into his pocket. "Nothing! I'm not!" He swept around the foot of the bed and moved toward the door. He stopped, clutching the bedpost.

"Ferris?" Her voice held concern now, and he could hear her shifting the covers, as if she might be getting up.

"No, no! I'm fine." He stumbled forward and reached for the door. He turned back to her.

She sat on the edge of the bed, her feet on the floor, and reached for her robe on the chair.

"No." He held out a hand to stay her, then moved it back to clutch his throat. Nervousness was making it hard for him to breath. "Don't get up. I'm fine. I just wanted to tell you . . ." His eyes scanned the room, alighting finally on the mantel clock. Five minutes before six. "I must go."

"Ferris, wait."

"Good-bye, Catra."

He turned and fled.

Catra pushed herself out of bed and quickly donned her robe and slippers. She paused, a thought hitting her, and returned to the bed. Her heart suddenly pounded a frantic rhythm in her chest. She picked up the glass and brought it to her nose, sniffing deeply.

She jerked her head back. She'd been sensitive to smells of all kinds lately, but when she smelled the glass, the odor was bitter enough to make her stomach roil. Almonds, she thought.

Cyanide.

Catra raced from the room and ran down the hallway. At the bottom of the stairs she stopped, panting for breath and feeling dizziness wash over her. Had she drunk any of the water? No, she thought. It had smelled too awful to her.

She glimpsed a servant entering the dining room and ran down to catch her.

"Sarah," she said to the stout cook's helper, breathing heavily and leaning against the door jamb. "Have you seen Mr. Ferris?"

"Why, yes, ma'am. He just left out the back door. And a mighty odd time it is to be taking a walk, I'd say. But then, Mr. Mansfield went too." She shook her head. "Ain't no accounting for it."

"Mr. Mansfield?" Catra repeated, dread dropping in her chest like a cannonball.

"Yes, ma'am. They went back that way." She gestured vaguely toward the back of the house. "Out by the trees over to the culvert."

"Sarah, send for the doctor immediately. Tell him Mr. Chester is sick—poisoned! Now go!"

"Poisoned?" Sarah gasped.

"And get the constable!"

Catra didn't stop to explain. She ran to the back door and out into the driving sleet. Her slippers were instantly soaked and she slipped on the flagstone patio, just catching herself before she fell. She fled across the lawn behind it, past the stables to the thick stand of trees beyond.

There, she saw the doctor was already present. As was her father, Baker and Dahlia Mansfield and Ryan. She stopped in the underbrush, clinging to a tree and trying to catch her breath.

Baker held two pistols and handed Ferris the one from his right hand. Ryan was walking toward Ferris, empty-handed.

"I won't do it," Ryan was saying. "And if I can't talk you out of it, you can shoot me where I stand. But I'll not duel with you, Ferris."

Ferris inhaled sharply and backed away, lifting the gun. "Don't come any closer." His voice was high and reedy, his face red. He seemed to be having trouble breathing.

Ryan stopped. Baker extended a pistol toward him, but he batted it away. The gun slid across the icy grass, coming to rest against the base of a tree.

"Ferris, I won't shoot you. Put down the gun and talk to me."

Ferris lifted the gun higher. He was gasping for air, one hand at his throat. "I know you won't. But you should, Ryan, because I don't want to live." With that he turned the gun on himself.

Catra's scream caught everyone's attention, freezing Ferris where he stood. But as she broke from the forest, Ferris took one step back, then another; then his legs bent like broken matchsticks and he crumpled to his knees.

He fell backward, his head hitting the ground, and the arm that held the pistol dropped ramrod-straight back over his head. The moment the gun hit the ground it went off, but instead of firing harmlessly into the trees it blew up in Ferris's hand like a bomb.

"Ferris!" Catra screamed, running toward him.

Ryan caught her in his arms as she tried to pass and wrapped his cloak around her. She didn't struggle but

366

looked back over her shoulder to where Ferris lay.

The ensuing silence was deafening. The shot seemed to echo endlessly through the glassy, ice-covered trees.

They all stood paralyzed, staring at the dismembered body on the ground before them. The explosion had blown off Ferris's arm and blackened his face. After one stunned moment the doctor moved swiftly to Ferris's side.

As they watched, the doctor felt Ferris's neck, then his wrist; then he laid his head to Ferris's chest. He straightened slowly, looking at the stunned group.

"He's dead," he said gravely.

Catra turned her face into Ryan's chest and clutched at his coat with frozen fingers.

Baker broke the silence. "Very clever, St. James." A smile pierced his face. "I know you said you wouldn't shoot him, but jamming the gun like that was brilliant. Good thing I warned the constable that a duel was going to take place this morning. He ought to be here any minute."

Catra twisted in Ryan's arms to look up at him. He looked down at her, his hair wet and rain running down his face.

"Catra—" he began, shaking his head.

She turned back to Baker. "That's a lie," she hissed. "Ryan would never do that."

Dahlia's voice emerged from the gloom. "You said no one would get hurt."

Everyone's eyes turned to her.

"You said it wouldn't kill him," Dahlia continued, her voice rising to shrillness. She glared venomously at Baker.

"Shut up," Baker said, making a grab for her and missing. He turned an apologetic look on the group. "She's distraught."

Dahlia backed up and Thurber stepped forward to take her by the shoulders.

"Let her speak," Thurber said, his tone ominous.

Dahlia was visibly shaking and her face twisted with the words. "You promised he would only be wounded and they would leave together. That's what you said, Baker. That's what you promised. I didn't want him to be murdered."

Catra trembled in Ryan's arms.

Thurber looked at Ryan, who nodded once. Then they descended on Baker.

Baker tried to run. He turned swiftly but tripped on his own feet. Ryan and Thurber grabbed him just as the constable and his men broke through the trees.

"Captain," Thurber called, "arrest this man. He has killed my daughter's husband."

Chapter Twenty-two

Catra sat in the secluded garden at Braithwood. The day was a glorious one. Trees rustled softly in the breeze and the heat, which had been stifling, had broken for the day, so that it felt more like an afternoon in May than one in August.

She sat on the wrought-iron bench beneath the oak tree, where she had first conversed with Ryan that evening so long ago. It felt strange to remember how innocent she'd been then. That kiss in the garden had seemed important at the time, but little had she known what changes that meeting would engender.

She pictured Ferris as he'd been that evening. Light and happy, so proud to be her betrothed. She could hardly believe that he was gone, he, who had always been present, whose mild, easy temperament had endeared him to her all her life. She had loved him, she thought. But she should never have married him. If she hadn't, he would be alive today.

Baker might have been convicted of his murder—and attempting hers as well, with the poisoned water—but at times she felt as guilty as an accomplice. Oh, her father and Mayliza told her that was ridiculous, that Baker would have killed Ferris whether he'd been married or not to get Dahlia's inheritance, but Catra couldn't help the feeling. What she could do, however, she had done. And that was turn over the inheritance that Ferris's child would have gotten to Dahlia. Though she never liked the woman, it was still the right thing to do.

She had also decided that should Braithwood fall to her, she would divide it with whatever children Mayliza might have. Since May was in the house, Jimmy would be well cared for, she knew. And any children of Mayliza's would be doubly loved, as they were her best friend's progeny as well as her father's.

Catra rose and walked up the garden path to the terrace, then around the house to the front porch. From here she could see the fields across which the Richmond road was visible.

Catra scanned the lush summer landscape for the sight of a carriage. There was nothing for as far as she could see. Barely visible through the leafy tree limbs, the hard-packed road stretched out in the summer sun, away from Braithwood in both directions with not a soul upon it.

"You have hours to wait, missy, even if he docked on time," Bethia chided from the doorway. "You'll be drenched in sweat before long, and how pretty'll that be, hmm?"

Catra felt the old nurse take her elbow and urge her from the verandah.

"Why isn't he here yet? He said he'd be here today if

he had to swim the last leg.'' She looked anxiously at the pocket watch she held for the fifth time in fifteen minutes.

"He's coming," Bethia said with a smile in her voice. "It's only four o'clock now. Don't you worry. He's coming."

It had been seven long months since she'd seen Ryan. Seven anxious, excited, painful months. After Ferris's death, her father had insisted that they separate for a time, and they had agreed. Indeed, because of their respect for Ferris they felt they had no other choice.

But now he was coming. Ryan had sent word that he would wait no longer. Her father had glowered and cursed the impatient rogue when he had read the letter, but Catra had smiled. It was so like Ryan. And she was sure that while writing it he had not been unaware of what her father's reaction would be to the aggressive tone. The two would never be friends, but they had agreed to a truce, and Catra believed it would hold.

"Come on now, missy," Bethia said. She walked Catra upstairs and sat her on the bed, turning away to get a knitted afghan. "You rest while you've got the chance. Little Marse Gregory will be waking up soon, and you've got to nap just as bad as he does. You don't want Mr. St. James thinking you're all wore out like old Bethia, now, do you?"

Catra eyed her wryly. "Sounds to me like you'd be better off napping."

Bethia chuckled and swung Catra's legs up onto the bed, removing her slippers while she was at it.

Catra glanced toward the windows again. "Bethia, I'm just too excited. He'll be here tonight, I'm sure of it. I can't believe this day has finally come."

"I'm going to send you up some chamomile tea, send you off to dreamland. And when you wake up, you'll be all pretty and rested, and Mr. St. James will be sitting in the parlor waiting for you.''

Catra's eyes grew dreamy at the mental image. Ryan, sitting in her parlor, his gray eyes dancing with the heat of his desire. She felt her cheeks grow warm with the thought and shook herself out of the reverie.

Bethia regarded her with a raised eyebrow. ''Hmph,'' she snorted. ''You're too far gone on that man.'' She shook her head. ''I've seen it before. You aren't going to see anybody else 'round you once he gets here; you're going to be so wrapped up in him. If you have something to say to me, you'd best say it now, 'cause I'm going to be invisible as far as you're concerned, next few months.''

Catra laughed and lay back on the pillows. ''All right. If you're going to get all ornery, I'll take a nap.''

Bethia nodded her approval.

''But you wake me as soon as he arrives,'' Catra ordered.

Bethia smiled and headed for the door. ''Oh, don't you know I will. I will.'' She was still laughing as she closed the door behind her.

Catra propped her arms behind her head. Yes, he would be here any time now. She felt the butterflies rise again in her stomach and reveled in them for a moment. This time next week they'd be married. At long, long last they'd be together, bound in marriage forever, so that nothing could ever part them again.

She glanced at the clock. Four-twenty. She squelched the urge to dash to the window again. A watched pot never boils, she heard Bethia's voice in her head. She flopped onto her side and punched the pillow into a comfortable shape beneath her head. She'd never fall asleep. Her stomach was floating with excitement, and every time she pictured Ryan's face her heart nearly burst from her breast with anxious drumming.

But suppose he didn't come? What if something happened to him? What if, after all this time, he'd changed his mind? It was possible, an evil voice in the back of her mind prompted. He's been a bachelor a long time. And he's just spent seven long months in a city full of beautiful women who would not be nearly so plagued with troubles as she had been.

She turned onto her back in irritation. This was ridiculous. She would not talk herself into bad news, she determined. But still the voice in her mind continued, until finally she dropped off into a fitful sleep.

It was nearly dark when she awoke. She could see from the bed that the sky was streaked with red in a spectacular sunset. She crept from the bed, feeling disoriented upon waking, fully dressed, to such an odd dawn. Then she remembered. In a rush, her excitement and fears tumbled down upon her and she rushed to the window.

It took a moment for her eyes to adjust to the odd light, with that low, bright sun burning just above the trees. She squinted her eyes into the light and just made out through the silhouetted trees a lone man on horseback.

She did not wait for the figure to become clearer. She felt in her heart the surety of plain sight. She knew it was Ryan.

She ran to the wardrobe and threw it open. In one whirlwind motion, she slipped into her shoes and blew from the room. Down the stairs she flew, past the parlor doors on silent feet, then through the front door and into the warm, smoke-scented air outside.

She never felt the verandah beneath her feet, nor the steps down to the lawn. But the grass felt like clouds as she saw the man on horseback catch sight of her. In a fluid, long-legged motion she remembered well from their rides by the river, he dismounted, dropped the reins of his mount and ran toward her.

Her dress flew out behind her and she almost felt as if she could lift her feet from the carpet of grass and glide the rest of the way to him. But before she had the chance, he was there.

She threw herself into his arms. He caught her deftly, his hands strong and sure about her waist. He lifted her to his chest and her arms wrapped immediately, instinctively, around his neck. It was him. He was in her arms. She could smell the soap on his skin and the soft woodsy, outdoor smell in his clothes and hair. And she could hear his laughter.

"Thank God you've come!" She laughed with him. She pulled back to view his handsome face. White teeth and intensely burning eyes blazed in the smiling face. "I can hardly believe you're here."

He squeezed her so tightly, she thought her lungs would burst, but the feeling was sheer pleasure.

"You sound as though you doubted I'd come," he said, his voice tinged with humor. "Did you think I'd leave you at the altar?" He placed her back on her feet but kept his arms encircling her waist.

"I may have been anxious, Mr. St. James, but I was not waiting at the altar just yet. A week is a bit much, even for me." She gave him an irrepressible smile.

Ryan pulled her to him again. "I'd wait for you forever."

She closed her eyes with the joy of his words, squeezing him tightly. "Now you're the one acting as if you doubted I'd be here," she said softly. She twined her fingers in the thick silk of his hair, gently holding his head against hers.

He held her close. "I just need to be sure you're real," he murmured, "and not just another dream to torture me."

Catra pulled back and met his eyes. "I love you, Ryan. And that is very real."

Ryan smiled slowly into her eyes. Strong arms pulled her against him, but he did not relinquish her gaze. Desire kindled in his eyes and she felt her pulse quicken. With slow deliberation, he lowered his lips to hers. Her arms around his neck pulled him close.

"You two get in here." Bethia's voice rose from the doorway. "There's someone here hungry, and I expect he's got a thing or two to say to the both of you!"

Catra and Ryan broke away from each other; then laughter caught them both as the reedy wail of a small boy floated to them on the soft summer air.

"Come," Catra said, taking him by the hand. "Come meet your son."

Lair of the Wolf

CHAPTER ONE

Constance O'Banyon

On January 1, 1997, *Romance Communications*, the Romance Magazine for the 21st century, made its Internet debut. One year later, it was named a Lycos Top 5% site on the Web in terms of both content and graphics!

One of *Romance Communications'* most popular features is The Romantic Relay, an original romance novel divided into twelve monthly installments, with each chapter written by a different author. Our first offering was *Lair of the Wolf*, a tale of medieval Wales, created by, in alphabetical order, celebrated authors Emily Carmichael, Debra Dier, Madeline George, Martha Hix, Deana James, Elizabeth Mayne, Constance O'Banyon, Evelyn Rogers, Sharon Schulze, June Lund Shiplett, and Bobbi Smith.

We put no restrictions on the authors, letting each pick up the tale where the previous author had left off and going forward as she wished. The authors tell us they had a lot of fun, each trying to write her successor into a corner!

Now, preserving the fun and suspense of our month-by-month installments, Leisure Books will present, in print, one chapter a month of *Lair of the Wolf*. In addition to the entire online story, the authors have added some brand-new material to their existing chapters. So if you think you've read *Lair of the Wolf* already, you may find a few surprises. Please enjoy this unique offering, watch for each new monthly installment in the back of your Leisure Books, and make sure you visit our Web site, where another romantic relay is already in progress.

Romance Communications
http://www.romcom.com

Pamela Monck, Editor-in-Chief
Mary D. Pinto, Senior Editor
S. Lee Meyer, Web Mistress

Chapter One

by Constance O'Banyon

Wales—1296

Edward I of England—also known as Longshanks—was a warrior king intent on uniting England with the conquered nations of Wales and Scotland. To keep control over the rebellious Welsh people, King Edward required his most trusted lords to marry into their noble houses.

It was ghostly quiet throughout the halls of Glendire Castle. For more than three centuries, the gray rock fortress atop a limestone hill had been a formidable sentinel and guardian for the nearby villages. But no more—all was lost.

The old Duke of Llewellyn and his two strong sons had perished in battle heading an army that had valiantly, but futilely, tried to keep the English from conquering their homeland. Now, only the old, the young, the ill, and the women remained within the castle walls.

The servants, who would normally be going about their appointed tasks, were assembled in the Great Hall in fearful expectation of what would happen when their new English overlord reached the castle. A courier had managed to slip through the English lines, bringing word that the enemy was less than an hour's march away.

Lady Meredyth, the only surviving member of the Llewellyn family, hurriedly climbed the narrow steps to the watchtower, clutching her cape about her as protection against the chilling spring wind. Her sad gaze swept past the neglected barley fields, beyond the blackened ruins of the village of Glendire, to the dark forest that bordered her lands. Alas, nothing remained to stop the English conquerors now.

As she focused on the distant treetops, she saw a flock of blackbirds suddenly take flight, as though something had startled them. Meredyth felt her breath catch in her throat when, only moments later, a column of armed soldiers astride their great warhorses entered the clearing. She did not need to see the coat of arms emblazoned on the blue banners that fluttered in the breeze to know it was the English warrior, Sir Garon Saunders, who rode at their head. He was one of King Edward's most trusted men, a warrior so loyal and so fierce that he was known as Longshanks' Wolf.

The very name struck terror in Meredyth's heart, and she resisted the urge to flee, to hide. Straightening her spine, she called on all her courage as she spoke to the woman who had just come up beside her.

"So, Sir Garon comes at last to claim what he has won. What the English invaders cannot pilfer, they endeavor to gain by marriage into our noble houses. They have sacked our villages, raped our women, and slain our men. Think you that I would link my honorable name to one of them?"

Dame Allison glanced at the advancing cavalcade with growing fear, then turned to the young girl she had tended since birth and loved better than her own life. "There's none to stand your champion—those nobles who would have come to your aid are either dead or have long ago fled to safety. You should have taken flight when you had the chance, my lady."

Meredyth shook her head. "I could never abandon my home and those who depend on me. My father would have expected me to remain to give courage to our people. As for Sir Garon, I will defy him with my last breath."

Concern etched Dame Allison's wrinkled face, and dark circles sagged beneath her eyes, as if she had slept but little of late. "Your people would not ask you to place yourself in danger for their sakes. You cannot help them, my lady— you cannot even help yourself."

"Can I not? We shall see about that!" Meredyth's chin rose to a stubborn tilt, and her eyes sparkled with defiance.

The old woman wondered if the battle-hardened Sir Garon would see her lady's worth and treasure her as she deserved. The girl was slender of form, and her face was lovely, from her finely arched brows to the bound tresses of her golden hair. Her skin was creamy, her cheeks rosy with health. She was intelligent, kind, and brave, a prize her father had protected while he lived. And now she was to be at the mercy of a barbarian. "The English Wolf means to have you as his wife, my lady."

The young girl's brow furrowed. "I will not take any Englishman to husband, and certainly not the Wolf, even though the English king has ordered me to do so. I am not Edward's subject, and I shall never submit to his demands nor pledge him my fidelity."

"You'll have no say in the matter. Sir Garon will demand that you comply with King Edward's commands . . . and with his."

Meredyth felt the cold wind sting her cheeks, and she pulled her cape more tightly about her, her pride the only weapon she had left. "It is an insult to my person and to my ancestors that I should be ordered to marry so far beneath me. Sir Garon is nothing but a lowly knight, while I am descended from kings. I shall fight him if I must, die if God wills it, but I shall never marry him!"

"Sir Garon will not allow a prize such as you to escape. He knows you are connected by blood to the royal house of Wales. And even if that were not so, he would never allow one of the richest fiefdoms in the country to elude his grasp." Dame Allison reached out a comforting hand. "Sadly, my lady, it's always been the fate of gentlewomen to accept arranged marriages. Now that the Englishman is at your door, it'll cause you less grief if you accept him without resistance."

By now, the column of soldiers had reached the winding road that led to the castle, and Meredyth could clearly see the outline of a black wolf on the shimmering banners. For all her brave words, her fear was strong.

Dame Allison shook her head in resignation. "I have heard much of the Wolf, and none of it good. How can any woman withstand such a man?"

Meredyth was asking herself the same question as she wrestled with her fear. Slowly, a plan began to take form, and she knew what she must do. "Come with me, Dame Allison. I need your help," she said, urgently grabbing the woman's hand and half-dragging her toward the tower door. "I know how to elude the Wolf and still remain here for my people."

Once in the privacy of her bedchamber, Meredyth found a pair of heavy shears and stared at them for a long moment in indecision. At last she gave a nod and handed the shears to Dame Allison. "Cut my hair. And do it quickly, before I change my mind!"

A look of horror came over Dame Allison's face as she watched Lady Meredyth loosen her long braids, releasing a golden curtain of hair that cascaded down to her waist. "I certainly will do no such thing! Your hair is so like your dead mother's, and it was your father's pride. What can you be thinking, my lady?"

Time was against her, so Meredyth spoke more harshly than was her custom. "Cut it short, and do it now. Then fetch me the clothing that my father's squire left behind. Hurry, the enemy will soon be upon us!"

Flanked by five of his most trusted men and several yeomen, Sir Garon entered the Great Hall, his silver spurs jingling with each step he took. His gaze moved quickly past the simply garbed servants cowering near the door and leveled on the woman in the white wimple at the far end of the room. As he approached her, a quick assessment of her aged face made him hope that she was merely an upper servant and not the Lady Meredyth.

Garon stopped before the woman, and she bobbed a quick curtsy.

"What is your name?" he asked in the voice of one accustomed to commanding.

"I am Dame Allison, lord."

He felt momentary relief that she was not the woman he was expected to wed. Then his eyes narrowed. "Where is your mistress? Why is she not here to greet me?"

Dame Allison lowered her eyes. "Lady Meredyth is away, and I do not expect her to return for a fortnight. In the meantime, it falls to me to attend to your comfort and that of your men."

Sir Garon hadn't expected to be welcomed warmly by Lady Meredyth, but she should have been there to receive him; she had been ordered to do so by King Edward. He was weary of the Welsh nobles and their damned arrogance. Didn't they know they were a conquered people? Removing his wolf-head helm, he tossed it onto a wooden bench, then proceeded to work his hands out of his gauntlets. He slapped them impatiently against one long, muscular leg.

"Where has your lady gone?" His voice sounded calm, but there was a dangerous glint in his cold black eyes.

Dame Allison's eyes widened when she looked upon his face, for she had not expected such a handsome knight, nor one so young. The thin scar across his cheek—likely from one of his many battles—did little to mar his comeliness. Surely this could not be Longshanks' Wolf. Although, on closer inspection, he did somewhat resemble a wolf. His shaggy hair curled around the nape of his neck, his face was finely chiseled, and his dark eyes were watchful, suspicious, and cunning.

Belatedly she realized that he was awaiting her reply. "My lady has traveled to A . . . Aberconwy, a shire requiring many days' travel, Sir Garon."

Anger flared within Garon's breast. He was a warrior, and he had no desire to woo and wed a reluctant bride. He knew naught of the Lady Meredyth, nor did he care to. But he had been ordered to take her to wife, and he would obey Longshanks in this, as he did in all else.

"Who are you, old woman, that you speak for your mistress?" Garon asked.

"I am lady-in-waiting to the Lady Meredyth." Pride laced her voice. "I also served her mother."

Garon's eyes bored into hers. "You think me gullible enough to believe that a lady of your mistress's rank would go abroad without her attendant?" His voice was hard and cold. "Can it be that Lady Meredyth has not left the castle but instead hides herself from me?"

"My, lord, I—"

Garon held up a hand to silence her. "Tell Lady Mer-edyth that it is my command—" His jaw clenched tightly as he remembered the king's instructions to treat the lady gently. "No, inform her that I would . . . very much like her . . . to receive me."

Dame Allison felt no guilt for deceiving this man, but she did feel trepidation lest he learn of the deception and punish her lady. "Lady Meredyth is not here, lord," she said stubbornly. "Therefore, I cannot relay your message to her."

Garon dropped down into a high-backed chair, stretching his long legs before him while one of his yeomen rushed forward to unfasten his armor. "Fool," Garon said with a snarl, pushing the man away. "Know you so little of armor that you think to remove it while I sit?"

"Your pardon, Sir Garon," the man said, quickly taking a step back. "I was ordered to assist you, though I have no knowledge of such fine trappings."

"Away with you," Garon commanded, sending the man scampering out of the Great Hall. Wearily, he pressed his hands over his eyes. He had been on the march since day-break and had not slept the previous night. He wanted nothing more than to see his bed.

He turned his attention back to Dame Allison, who had been hovering nearby. "Set the servants about their tasks, and have someone fetch food, woman," he ordered. "I assume someone has prepared quarters for me and my men?"

"They have, Sir Garon."

"Leave me then. We will talk more of your lady after I have dined and rested. Tomorrow will be soon enough. However," he said as she turned away, "should you happen upon your mistress, be so kind as to inform her that she will be far safer with me than alone when that rowdy lot that follows me arrives."

Garon was watching Dame Allison carefully as he dismissed his men, and he noticed her eyes dart nervously to a curtained window, as if she feared that the men without might suddenly, barbarously invade the castle. Even after she gave orders to the servants, she seemed reluctant to depart the Great Hall.

"Why do you hesitate, woman? he asked in irritation. "Go to it. None will harm you."

When he was alone, Garon moved to a window that overlooked a vast lake and a rolling meadow now choked with weeds. Little he knew about the ways of a nobleman, and surely these lands that were to come to him through marriage would require a man's full attention. Glancing about the Great Hall, he noticed the fine furniture and magnificent tapestries that bespoke great wealth. He had never courted wealth or the tedium of the existence of a landed lord. Being the younger son of an impoverished knight, he'd had no recourse but to take to soldiering. On the Scottish campaign, however, Garon had saved the life of his king by blocking with his own flesh an arrow that had been meant for Edward. After that, the King had looked on him with favor, immediately raising him to knighthood. This marriage arrangement had been meant to further honor Garon, but he would sooner have refused the privilege, had he been asked.

Suddenly, hearing a noise, Garon moved silently across the floor, his sword unsheathed. His weapon poised to strike, he approached the curtained window, his senses alert to danger. With a mighty swing of his blade, he cut down the heavy drapery, sending it crashing to the floor in a blanket of dust. And there, perched on the window seat, seemingly unafraid, was a young boy.

With a frown, Garon shoved his sword back into the scabbard. "Why do you hide there, lad? Were you sent to spy on me?"

Meredyth stood slowly. When she had watched Sir Garon's actions through a crack in the curtains, her fear of him had intensified, though she tried not to show it. "No, lord," she said hurriedly. "I merely fell asleep and only awoke when I heard voices."

Garon's eyes swept over the boy with little interest. "So, you know who I am."

"Of course. You are the Wolf," Meredyth replied, lowering her head so he could not see the hatred in her eyes.

"Have you ever had cause to remove armor, lad?"

His question took her by surprise. She had many times observed her father and brothers being attended by their squires. "Yes, I know the workings of the hinges and straps."

"Then, in God's name, get me out of this contraption."

Meredyth came forward and with nimble fingers soon loosened the heavy breastplate, stripping him down to his chain mail.

With a contented murmur, Garon dropped into a chair and leaned his head back. "Now the spurs, lad."

She deftly unhooked the spurs and placed them with the armor. When she would have risen, a muscular hand settled on her shoulder, and she was held fast.

"You did that well. How would you like to become my squire?"

Meredyth blinked. She had not anticipated this. She had only meant to see what the Wolf looked like—she had not intended even to speak to him. "But, lord, I serve this castle. Therefore, I cannot serve you."

She felt the heat of his fierce gaze. "Surely you do not quibble about being raised in rank. What are you now, a kitchen boy? A stable hand?"

Meredyth tried to think clearly, but Sir Garon's presence was so dominant that he seemed to control even the air she breathed. "T'would be no rise in rank to serve you, since I was squire to my late lord. He was, of course, a duke, while you are only a knight, and an Englishman at that."

Of late Garon was surrounded by people who satisfied his every want and agreed with every word he spoke, so, instead of being offended, he found the boy's candor refreshing. "Have you not heard that I am to be your lord?" he asked, suppressing a weary smile.

"Aye, I heard that. But you have not reckoned with my lady."

Garon shrugged indifferently. "She will come to submit to me in time, lad. Meanwhile, I will have you serve me as you did your late master."

A cry of defiance escaped Meredyth's lips as she stood, backing away from him. "I will never serve you!"

Garon's voice was deceptively soft but a challenge nonetheless. "No?"

"I . . . Lady Meredyth wouldn't . . . approve."

Garon's eyes gleamed with a dangerous light. "You shall minister to me, and your lady be damned."

Meredyth's anger flared. "Think you to win my lady with such honeyed words? You cannot know women if you speak of them so," she said with contempt.

Garon looked reflective. "You may be right, lad. Give me a battle to fight, and I can map out a strategy and win, but as to the workings of a woman's mind, I have no knowledge. Tell me about your lady."

"You would not like her," Meredyth blurted out. "She has a fierce temper."

Garon smiled. "I have no objection to a strong-willed woman. In fact, I favor a bit of spirit."

"She . . . is exceedingly ugly," Meredyth continued. "Her teeth are blackened, her breath is foul, and she is . . . she is . . . taller than you. Surely you would be reluctant to wed a woman who towers above you. She is old and would have been married long ago were it not for her unbecoming manners.''

She was surprised by his laughter.

''What is your name, lad?''

Her oldest brother's name came readily to her lips. ''I am known as John. And shall I call you Lord Wolf?'' she asked boldly.

''No. That is not a title of my liking, although it will be associated with me to the death, I fear.''

''A wolf is a dangerous animal, lord.''

He arched a dark eyebrow. ''Your mistress would do well to remember that.'' He smiled slightly. ''Go now, John, and see to my armor before it rusts. Look for Hanes, the captain of my guards, and he will instruct you in your duties.''

''You . . . are not leaving, even after I have told you how undesirable Lady Meredyth is?''

Garon had just stood and turned his back to the boy, but something in the lad's voice made him swing around, his eyes taking in every detail. How could he have been so blind?

The Wolf stared at her so long and with such intensity that Meredyth was forced to drop her gaze.

''No, John,'' Garon answered at last. ''I believe that I shall delight in becoming acquainted with your lady.''

The bold way he looked at her, the tone of his voice, made Meredyth inch away, intent on fleeing as soon as she reached the door. There was something ominous about him, something that an enemy might perceive just before being struck down in battle.

''John, attend me,'' Garon called out, his voice like a whiplash, echoing against the high-vaulted ceilings of the Great Hall.

Constance O'Banyon

Slowly, Meredyth retraced her steps, approaching him with caution, wishing she dared defy him.

"My armor," he reminded her.

She quickly scooped up the heavy armor, struggling with the weight of it. As she tottered to the door, she called over her shoulder, "I shall give it the attention it deserves, lord."

"And, John?"

"Yes, lord?"

"After you have seen to my armor, await me in my chambers. You shall assist me with my bath."

Watch for Chapter Two of Lair of the Wolf *by Bobbi Smith, appearing in January 2000 in* Cinnamon and Roses, *by Heidi Betts.*

Lair of the Wolf

Constance O'Banyon, Bobbi Smith, Evelyn Rogers, Emily Carmichael, Martha Hix, Deana James, Sharon Schulze, June Lund Shiplett, Elizabeth Mayne, Debra Dier, and Madeline George

Be sure not to miss a single installment of Leisure Books's star-studded new serialized romance, *Lair of the Wolf*! A tale of medieval Wales, *Lair of the Wolf* was originally featured in *Romance Communications*, the popular romance magazine on the Internet. Each author picked up the tale where the previous chapter had left it and moved forward with the story as she wished. Preserving the fun and suspense of the month-by-month installments, Leisure presents one chapter a month of the entire on-line story, including some brand new material the authors have added to their existing chapters. Watch for a new installment of *Lair of the Wolf* every month in the back of select Leisure books!

NEXT MONTH: Chapter Two by Bobbi Smith can be found in:
___4668-7 *Cinnamon and Roses* by Heidi Betts $4.99 US/$5.99 CAN

**To order call our special toll-free number 1-800-481-9191
or VISIT OUR WEB SITE AT: www.dorchesterpub.com**

WESTON'S BOBBI
Lady SMITH

There are Cowboys and Indians, trick riding, thrills and excitement for everyone. And if Liberty Jones has anything to say about it, she will be a part of the Wild West show, too. She has demonstrated her expertise with a gun by shooting a card out of Reed Weston's hand at thirty paces, but the arrogant owner of the Stampede won't even give her a chance. Disguising herself as a boy, Libby wangles herself a job with the show, and before she knows it Reed is firing at her—in front of an audience. It seems an emotional showdown is inevitable whenever they come together, but Libby has set her sights on Reed's heart and she vows she will prove her love is every bit as true as her aim.

___4512-5 $5.99 US/$6.99 CAN

Elaine Fox
Untamed Angel

Bestselling Author of *Hand & Heart of a Soldier*

With a name that belies his true nature, Joshua Angell was born for deception. So when sophisticated and proper Ava Moreland first sees the sexy drifter in a desolate Missouri jail, she knows he is the one to save her sister from a ruined reputation and a fatherless child. But she will need Angell to fool New York society into thinking he is the ideal husband—and only Ava can teach him how. But what start as simple lessons in etiquette and speech soon become smoldering lessons in love. And as the beautiful socialite's feelings for Angell deepen, so does her passion—and finally she knows she will never be satisfied until she, and no other, claims him as her very own...untamed angel.

___4274-6 $4.99 US/$5.99 CAN

The Brightest Flame
Sonya Birmingham

Molly Kilmartin leaves Ireland on a ship bound for New York City, determined to stand on her own two feet—to find her piece of the American dream and never ask a soul for anything. She certainly doesn't need a man like the dashing Burke Lassiter. So what if he is publisher of the *New York Telegram* and she wants to make her living as a writer? Though he seduces her with champagne and kind words onboard ship, he turns out to be a chauvinistic womanizer like all the rest. It is her fiery spirit and sharp wit that first draw Lassiter to the auburn-haired beauty. Molly Kilmartin isn't afraid to stand up to him, and she makes him laugh. It is just that spunk that might save his paper, he reasons. But he doesn't realize she has the power to save something else: his soul. And if he trusts his heart, she will show him a love more precious than gold.

___4564-8 $5.99 US/$6.99 CAN
Dorchester Publishing Co., Inc.
P.O. Box 6640
Wayne, PA 19087-8640

Please add $1.75 for shipping and handling for the first book and $.50 for each book thereafter. NY, NYC, and PA residents, please add appropriate sales tax. No cash, stamps, or C.O.D.s. All orders shipped within 6 weeks via postal service book rate. Canadian orders require $2.00 extra postage and must be paid in U.S. dollars through a U.S. banking facility.

Name_____
Address_____
City_____State_____Zip_____
I have enclosed $_____ in payment for the checked book(s).
Payment <u>must</u> accompany all orders. ❑ Please send a free catalog.
CHECK OUT OUR WEBSITE! www.dorchesterpub.com

DECEPTIONS & DREAMS

DEBRA DIER

Sarah Van Horne can outwit any scoundrel who tries to cheat her in business. But she is no match for the dangerously handsome burglar she catches in her New York City town house. Although she knows she ought to send the suave rogue to the rock pile for life, she can't help being disappointed that his is after a golden trinket—and not her virtue. Confident, crafty, and devilishly charming, Lord Austin Sinclair always gets what he wants. He won't let a locked door prevent him from obtaining the medallion he has long sought, nor the pistol Sarah aims at his head. But the master seducer never expects to be tempted by an untouched beauty. If he isn't careful, he'll lose a lot more than his heart before Sarah is done with him.

___4582-6 $5.99 US/$6.99 CAN

WHITE WOLF

SUSAN EDWARDS

Jessica Jones knows that the trip to Oregon will be hard, but she will not let her brothers leave her behind. Dressed as a boy to carry on a ruse that fools no one, Jessie cannot disguise her attraction to the handsome half-breed wagon master. For when she looks into Wolf's eyes and entwines her fingers in his hair, Jessie glimpses the very depths of passion.

___4471-4 $5.50 US/$6.50 CAN